PRIVATE
MOSCOW

'Great action sequences . . . breathtaking twists and turns.'
Anthony Horowitz, bestselling author of *Magpie Murders*

'An unmissable, breakneck ride into Moscow's
dark underworld.'
James Swallow, bestselling author of *Nomad*

'Exhilarating, high-stakes action set in sub-zero temperatures,
but so fast-paced you won't have time to feel the chill!'
Lesley Kara, bestselling author of *The Rumour*

THE PRIVATE NOVELS

Private (*with Maxine Paetro*)
Private London (*with Mark Pearson*)
Private Games (*with Mark Sullivan*)
Private: No. 1 Suspect (*with Maxine Paetro*)
Private Berlin (*with Mark Sullivan*)
Private Down Under (*with Michael White*)
Private L.A. (*with Mark Sullivan*)
Private India (*with Ashwin Sanghi*)
Private Vegas (*with Maxine Paetro*)
Private Sydney (*with Kathryn Fox*)
Private Paris (*with Mark Sullivan*)
The Games (*with Mark Sullivan*)
Private Delhi (*with Ashwin Sanghi*)
Private Princess (*with Rees Jones*)

A list of more titles by James Patterson
appears at the back of this book

PRIVATE MOSCOW

JAMES PATTERSON

& ADAM HAMDY

CENTURY

1 3 5 7 9 10 8 6 4 2

Century
20 Vauxhall Bridge Road
London SW1V 2SA

Century is part of the Penguin Random House group of companies whose
addresses can be found at global.penguinrandomhouse.com

Penguin
Random House
UK

Copyright © James Patterson 2020

First published in Great Britain by Century in 2020

www.penguin.co.uk

A CIP catalogue record for this book is available from the British Library

ISBN 9781529124446
ISBN 9781529124453 (trade paperback edition)

Typeset in 12.25/18.25 pt ITC Berkeley Oldstyle Std
by Integra Software Services Pvt. Ltd, Pondicherry

Printed and bound in India by Thomson Press India Ltd.

Penguin Random House is committed to a sustainable future for
our business, our readers and our planet. This book is made from
Forest Stewardship Council® paper.

For the brave men and women of our intelligence services

CHAPTER 1

"REMEMBER DUNKER TRAINING at Pendleton?"

There was a smile pinned to Karl Parker's face, but his eyes made a liar of his mouth. Something was wrong and, as we waited for our breakfast to arrive, I wondered when he was going to share the real reason he'd contacted me after so many years.

"Yeah, Hudson almost drowned," I replied, recalling the helo underwater egress training we'd undertaken at Camp Pendleton, just outside San Diego. The Marine Corps had a chopper fuselage in a deepwater pool at Pendleton that was designed to be almost impossible to escape. It was intended to train Marines how to survive a crash at sea, but with an escape rate of less than 10 percent, it just hammered home the very real prospect of dying if your bird dunked.

"You looked like you were crying, but you were so wet, it was hard to tell," Karl said.

"I swallowed half the pool, so a little water might have leaked out of my eyes."

"Leaked!" Karl's laugh was genuine, but it only served to accentuate the shift of mood that followed. His smile fell away and he looked as though he was plucking up the courage to tell me something.

Karl Parker had been my Marine flight instructor and was one of the straightest shooters I'd ever known. The kind of guy who'd not only confess to chopping down the tree, but who'd also tell you exactly how many cherries he'd eaten from it first. Whatever he had to say was clearly troubling him. The towering, strong, jovial African American I'd looked up to as a newly minted leatherneck had been replaced by a jaded man with haunted eyes and hunched shoulders. The smile returned, but it was a politician's grin, the kind worn by a senator when he's been caught cheating on his wife, flickering, hesitant, as though it might shatter at the slightest touch of truth.

I tried to make it easier on him. "It's great seeing you again, but you didn't invite me to New York to reminisce about old times. What's up?"

The vulnerability I'd sensed vanished and his smile broadened. "Up? Nothing's up. I wanted one of my oldest friends here to celebrate. Remind me just how far I've come."

Karl's business, Silverlink International, was one of America's most successful telecoms companies, and today it would be listed on the New York Stock Exchange. Karl had been invited to ring the opening bell to mark the occasion. It seemed strange that he'd chosen to start this momentous day with me rather than his wife Victoria, his son Kevin or any of the thousands of people who worked for him. We were old friends, but I'd lost count of the number of years that had passed since we'd last seen each other.

"Come on, Karl," I said. "I know up from down."

"You didn't in that helo training tank," he tried, but the attempted joke fell flat. His smile vanished and he looked away, troubled. "Jack Morgan, war hero, superstar detective, patriot." Was there a hint of sarcasm in his voice? "You always were a smart one. I should've known I couldn't put anything past you." He fixed me with sad eyes. "I've run into some trouble, Jack. I need someone to watch my back."

I was puzzled. Karl had a four-man security detail stationed in the lobby of Augustine, the upmarket brasserie in the Beekman Hotel where we'd met for breakfast. His back was well watched.

"Someone I can trust."

"You want to tell me what's going on?" I asked.

He bit his lip and opened and closed his mouth a couple of times, but before he could respond, a member of his security detail approached and discreetly interrupted us.

"Mr. Parker, it's time, sir."

CHAPTER 2

WE WALKED THE short distance along a snow-covered Nassau Street to the intersection with Wall Street, where we were searched by Exchange security in a large heated tent before being allowing into the building. Once inside, Karl was greeted by Rachel Glennie, the President of the New York Stock Exchange. She gave me a cursory hello—I wasn't the billionaire—and led us onto the Exchange floor, where dozens of financial movers and shakers milled around the trading stations.

"We can have a maximum of sixteen on the podium," Rachel said, indicating Karl's security detail.

The men waited at the foot of a stone staircase, while Karl and I followed Rachel. We climbed the steps to a podium where Karl's wife, Victoria, a beautiful, accomplished woman, ten years his junior, waited with their bored-looking seventeen-year-old son, Kevin, and a dozen Silverlink executives, lawyers and bankers who'd advised on the deal. I was introduced to everyone, but I didn't absorb their names. I was still puzzling over why, on this, one of the biggest days of his life, Karl had invited me for breakfast rather than spend it with his family and friends. I couldn't shake the feeling he'd planned to tell me something, but had balked at the last moment.

Standing on a rostrum high above the booths and clusters of screens that cluttered the trading floor, I could sense the anticipation of those around me. The lawyers, bankers and executives stood to make millions, but Karl, Silverlink's majority stockholder, stood to pocket more than twenty-five billion from the listing, making him one of the richest men in America. Maybe there was some truth in his having invited me to remind himself just how far he'd come. Karl was from humble beginnings, and the busy trading floor, packed with financial movers and shakers, was about as far as it was possible to get from Clarion, Iowa, the small town where he'd grown up.

It was almost 9:30 a.m. and Karl stepped away from Rachel Glennie to take his place by the oversized gavel and sounding block. Next to them were a control panel and the large button that activated the New York Stock Exchange's famous rotary bell.

"You ready for this?" I asked.

Karl looked at me with sad eyes, and an even more forlorn smile. "Of course." But I knew he was lying.

And then, suddenly remembering the eyes of the world were on him, honest Karl was replaced by the grins-and-chuckles fake.

"You going to hit this thing?" He waved the oversized gavel at his son, and Victoria ushered the reluctant teenager forward. "Give it a good smack," Karl said as he handed the giant hammer to the boy.

The clamor in the marble hall rose a pitch as traders gathered around the podium. Rachel Glennie checked the time, and as she stepped forward, many of the traders closest to us stopped what they were doing and looked up.

"Good morning, ladies and gentleman," Rachel said. She was wearing a suit that looked as though it cost more than most family cars. She exuded refined elegance, but her voice carried like the cry of a New Jersey market trader. "We'd like to celebrate the listing of Silverlink International by inviting the founder and chief executive, Karl Parker, to ring the opening bell."

Karl placed his hand on the large button and kept his eyes on the clock. An image of the rostrum was broadcast on screens throughout the vaulted hall, and the traders applauded and cheered. Men and women in suits gathered around the J.P. Morgan and Goldman Sachs booths that were immediately to the left and right of the rostrum, clapping and yelling their congratulations. Silverlink's stock was a new product, and more product meant more money.

"Ten, nine, eight," Karl said, counting down the seconds. "Here goes." He raised his hand theatrically.

It never touched the button again. A gunshot echoed off the marble walls, silencing the cheers, and Karl tumbled back with a single smoking hole in his skull.

CHAPTER 3

VICTORIA SCREAMED AND rushed to Karl's side. Kevin dropped the gavel, which tumbled onto the trading floor twelve feet below. He froze and looked in horror at his father's lifeless body. Karl's team of bodyguards raced to the stairs that would bring them to the podium.

"Get down!" I yelled, tugging Kevin behind the marble balustrade that lined the perimeter of the rostrum.

Karl's colleagues followed my lead, while the trading floor erupted in pandemonium as millionaire financiers and their employees fought each other for the quickest route to the exits. I was numb with shock, but years of training kicked in, and part of my mind swiftly adjusted to the new reality. Someone had just shot my friend with a small caliber firearm, which meant they had to be close. I suppressed my rising grief, peered over

the balustrade and focused on pinpointing and neutralizing the danger.

I scanned the trading floor and, amidst the noisy panic of the stampede, I saw one man standing perfectly still, his cool eyes on the rostrum. He wore the navy blue uniform of an Exchange security guard, but his trousers and jacket didn't fit right, and unlike the guards who'd searched me in the tent, he wore heavy boots instead of smart shoes. He just stood there watching and waiting. And then it hit me. Karl's body had fallen behind the balustrade, which was wrapped in a New York Stock Exchange banner. An assassin couldn't be certain of a kill until a third party gave some kind of confirmation. This man was waiting to be sure his bullet had struck its intended target.

He must have sensed me watching him, because at that moment his gaze shifted and he stared directly at me. His face seemed out of proportion, as though his features had been changed by prosthetics. Only his eyes told the truth, and I'd encountered enough stone-cold killers to know when I was looking at one.

I jumped over the balustrade, and the assassin started running the moment my feet hit the marble trading floor. I pushed past panicked traders and up ahead I saw the assassin doing likewise. Men and women were knocked to the floor as the desperate killer tried to outrun me.

I followed the assassin through the crowd and saw him burst through the doors onto Broad Street. He sprinted toward the security tent and shouted something at the two guards who were on their way to deal with the growing crowd of evacuees.

"He's the shooter!" I yelled as the guards turned toward me.

I pointed at the assassin who ran south along Broad Street, but the guards weren't interested in the man. Instead they tackled me, and drove me into the drift of gray snow that was piled beside the entrance.

"We've got the suspect in custody," the older guard said into his radio as the real killer sprinted away.

CHAPTER 4

"YOU'RE LETTING HIM escape!" I yelled.

The assassin was halfway along Broad Street, about eighty feet from a roadside booth and security barrier that marked the perimeter of the New York Stock Exchange.

The younger guard made the mistake of trying to pin me by the shoulders. I shrugged him off, and smacked him on the chin. He collapsed in the snowdrift and the older guard tried to draw his sidearm, but wasn't fast enough. I tackled him, knocked him down, and was on my feet, running, before he'd even managed to catch his breath.

Pushing through the chattering crowd of evacuees, I made it to the street, and the cold air burned my lungs as I sprinted to the barricade. I glanced back to see the men I'd knocked down on their feet, running after me.

"Stop!" the older guard commanded. "Stop or I will shoot!"

I took my chances, and the old guard did me a favor when he drew his weapon. The passers-by who thronged Broad Street scattered the moment they saw the gun, and my path was cleared. I could see the assassin no more than two dozen feet from the barricade.

The sound of a high-powered motorbike echoed off the surrounding grand towers, and a motorcyclist zoomed out of Exchange Place. He made a right onto Broad Street and the engine growled as he raced toward the barricade. Two guards stepped out of the booth and yelled at the biker and signaled him to stop, but he ignored them, swerved round the wedge barricade and opened the throttle, on an intercept course with the assassin.

I was no more than fifty feet from the shooter when the bike skidded on the square cobbles and came to a stop in front of him. He jumped on the back, looked my way and fixed me with his dead eyes, before tapping the motorcyclist's helmet. The rear wheel spun on the icy cobbles before it found purchase and the bike shot forward. I heard a noise to my right and turned to see another Exchange security guard sprint from a fire exit. He got the jump on me, and the wind was knocked from my lungs when we both hit the deck.

I watched the bike swerve back past the barricade, but there was no way I was going to let it escape. As we struggled, I flipped the catch on the guard's holster and snatched his pistol. Afraid I was going to shoot him, he recoiled instantly, leaving me clear to target the speeding motorcycle. Lying on my side in the snow, I snapped off a shot and hit the motorcyclist in the shoulder.

The motorcyclist grabbed the wound with his other hand, and the bike fishtailed and skidded across the street, before colliding with a lamppost. The assassin was flung clear, but the motorcyclist was tossed into the air like a doll and hit the metal pole with a resounding crack. As the motorcyclist fell to the ground motionless, the assassin staggered to his feet, drew his pistol and opened fire on the two guards by the barricade.

The crack of gunshots scattered nearby onlookers and a number of people screamed when the two guards went down wounded. The shooter set off down Exchange Place on foot.

Realizing I wasn't a threat to him, the guard who'd tackled me grabbed his weapon and tried to restrain me.

"Get off me!" I yelled. "Help them." I indicated his fallen colleagues. "I'm going after the shooter."

CHAPTER 5

THE GUARD DIDN'T resist when I pushed him away.

"Help them!" I repeated, getting to my feet.

"Come on, Taylor," a voice said.

It was the older guard who'd first tackled me. He and his younger colleague were coming up Broad Street. The third guard, Taylor, started toward the two others who'd been shot. Passers-by had already clustered around the men and were trying to help them.

Sprinting, I soon made it to the corner of Exchange Place, a narrow cut that linked Broad Street and William Street. High buildings loomed either side, shrouding the street in almost constant shadow. Snow was heaped against the buildings and steam rose from a long vent. The assassin was about a hundred yards ahead and moving quickly. I pushed harder and my lungs burned with the effort as my legs rose and fell like pistons.

Adrenalin and training were replaced by grim determination. This man had murdered my friend.

Parking was restricted on the narrow street, and the only vehicle in sight was a solitary US Postal Service truck that idled beside giant stone columns that marked the entrance of a huge skyscraper. The assassin jumped off the sidewalk and made straight for the driver's door. As he approached the vehicle, he glanced back, saw me and opened fire. I ducked into a doorway as bullets whipped the air in front of me and buried themselves in the stonework to my rear. When I peered out, the assassin was pulling a female postal worker from the truck. He tossed her onto the street, jumped into the vehicle and drove away.

"Help!" the woman yelled as she got to her feet. "Someone help me!"

She shook her head with resignation as the stolen truck took a right onto William Street.

"Call the cops," I said breathlessly as I sprinted past her.

When I reached the corner of William Street, I saw the postal truck no more than a hundred yards away, fighting head-on traffic as it tried to drive the wrong direction down a one-way street. It was just after nine thirty, but New York is a city where it's always rush hour, and the traffic had been made worse than usual by the heavy January snowfall.

He gave up trying to clear a path through the traffic and the truck suddenly lurched up onto the curb and started tearing along the sidewalk, forcing pedestrians to jump clear.

I cast around and settled on a yellow cab waiting for a fare. The driver was watching two guys exchange farewells outside a coffee shop on the corner, and his impatient fingers tapped on the steering wheel. He didn't notice me until I pulled his door open.

"What the—" he said, but my hands were already on the collar of his sheepskin jacket, and I yanked him out.

"I need your vehicle," I told him as I pushed him away and jumped in.

His fare was finally done with his goodbyes and tried to open the rear door as I pulled a U-turn. I saw his perplexed expression in the wing mirror as he watched his ride race away with the cab driver sprinting alongside, banging on the window and cursing with every step. I swung right, mounted the sidewalk and lost the driver as I picked up speed.

Up ahead, snow sprayed everywhere as the truck smashed through the piled drifts. Pedestrians dived out of the assassin's way, which gave me a clear run. I stepped on the gas, and the cab surged forward, closing the gap between the two vehicles. The postal truck turned a bend and caught a patch of black ice, which sent it fishtailing out of control. The back end swung wildly and fell off the sidewalk, clipping a car that was waiting in traffic. The collision cost the truck its back bumper and the assassin lost valuable momentum. It gave me the chance to get within yards of him before he got going again. The driver of the car he'd hit got out of his vehicle and turned the air blue with angry shouts, but the postal truck lurched back onto the sidewalk and raced on.

When it reached the intersection with Beaver Street, the truck hopped off the curb and almost collided with an oncoming cab. The truck veered across the intersection and mounted the sidewalk on the east side of William Street. I followed, and crossed Beaver Street in front of the startled cab driver before steering my vehicle onto the west sidewalk. I stepped on the gas and drew level with the assassin, the two of us racing each other on opposite sides of the street. I kept my hand on the horn in an attempt to warn oncoming pedestrians, and they leaped into doorways or onto the street.

The assassin took more risks than me and didn't care about hitting anyone, but the truck was slower than the cab, so we were pretty evenly matched. Up ahead I saw a delivery truck double parked, blocking the northbound traffic on William Street, and realized it presented me with an opportunity. Angry drivers were honking at the delivery driver who was waving at them to be patient, but his vehicle had created a gap in the traffic. I stepped on the accelerator, swung left between two parked cars, crossed the street, and drove the cab into the assassin's stolen truck. The crash sent our vehicles smashing into a store window and we came to a shuddering halt when the postal truck collided with a structural support.

My airbag deployed, blocking my view, and the cab filled with a thick cloud of smoke and silicate powder.

CHAPTER 6

I WAS WINDED but otherwise uninjured. I gasped in a lungful of air, pushed the airbag away and jumped out of the cab. The man I was chasing staggered out of the postal truck, dazed and disorientated, but as I started toward him, his flight instinct kicked in and he started running. I followed, and within moments he'd shaken off the worst of the collision and we were both sprinting at full pelt. My chest was sore as I ran along William Street and came to Hanover Square, but adrenalin kept the worst of the pain at bay. The shooter darted between slow-moving cars, vaulted a line of low railings and raced across the tiny square, which was covered in thick snow. I followed, crunching through ice-crusted powder, matching him stride for stride. Up ahead, the building line opened out a little and I saw gray clouds hanging low in the gaps between the skyscrapers. We were near the river.

The assassin jumped the railings on the south side of the square and ran across the street, earning a horn blast from a startled driver. I followed and chased him down Old Slip, a narrow road that ran down to South Street and the river. I collided with a man and woman coming out of the New York City Police Museum, housed in the old First Precinct. I skirted past the fearful couple and sprinted on. The shooter ran across South Street, forcing an eighteen-wheeler to a halt, and sprinted beneath FDR Drive, the four-lane overpass that followed the riverfront. I raced under the busy highway. The sound of the traffic rumbling overhead was almost deafening and it masked my pounding steps, so the assassin wasn't aware how close I was until I was on him. I'd got within striking distance when the man suddenly turned and swung his pistol at me. I parried the weapon as the gun went off, and the bullet sliced the air a few inches from my ear, and the loud gunshot set my head ringing.

The assassin stood his ground, and up close I could see the seams and folds of the prosthetics that masked his true identity. He tried to bring the gun round for another shot, but I swung a punch and caught him on the chin. His gun arm flailed and I knocked it down, sending the weapon flying. It clattered across the sidewalk and skidded beneath the eighteen-wheeler. The driver was ignoring the horn blasts of the angry motorists backed up to his rear, and had his phone out filming us.

The shooter came at me with a combination of punches that made me realize I was dealing with a skilled combatant. I stepped back, ducking and blocking each blow, but one slipped my guard: a right cross that caught me on the cheek. Then came the flash of white familiar to every fighter who's ever taken a powerful head blow, and for an instant I was blind. I covered up, tucking my head into my forearms, and absorbing his assault.

My eyesight returned and I stepped back as he swung a roundhouse. His foot swiped the air in front of me, and when it landed he was turned slightly, offering me a shot at his kidneys. I went in with a left and right that made him buck with pain, and as he crouched to cover the spot, I swung a fist into his face. The prosthetic rubber flattened, and so did the man's real nose. He had no nasal bone, so there was nothing to break.

A gunshot rang out from the other side of the road and echoed beneath the overpass. I glanced in the direction of the sound and saw a man in jeans and a thick leather jacket trying to target me with a pistol. He shot again, and this time wasn't too far off hitting me. I put the assassin between us, and ran for cover behind the eighteen-wheeler. The driver ignored me and kept his phone pointed at the shooter who was trying to pick me off.

I heard the bullets hit the trailer as I took cover behind it. The driver must have thought things were getting too hot, because the truck shifted into first and an instant later it lurched forward. As I watched my cover drive away, I desperately searched for an alternative, but when the trailer cleared my line of sight, there was no sign of the assassin or his accomplice. I ran beneath the highway and reached a cycle path on the bank of the East River. I looked right and saw the two men slow to a walk as they approached a chopper at the Manhattan Heliport.

The red Bell 407 was on one of the pads on the jetty that protruded into the river, and its blades were turning. The moment the assassin and the guy in the leather jacket climbed aboard, it took to the sky.

I stopped running and caught my breath as the chopper followed the river in front of me. I saw the assassin watching me from inside the aircraft, and made myself a silent promise.

We would meet again.

CHAPTER 7

I WAS SHIVERING by the time I reached Broad Street. My coat was in the Exchange cloakroom and my Balani custom fitted suit didn't offer much protection against the bitter chill of a New York winter. My chest was sore from the car crash and, after all the exertion, each breath was like inhaling jagged shards of ice.

Two ambulances were at the intersection with Exchange Place, and teams of paramedics were administering first aid to the guards who'd been shot. The calm, measured air of the medics suggested serious, but not critical, injury. I hurried behind the gathered crowd and headed south along Broad Street before the trio of security guards who'd tackled me noticed my return. They were standing with a group of thirty or so on-lookers, many of whom had their phones out and were filming the ongoing medical treatment.

I walked toward a police cordon that been established fifty yards from the Exchange's Broad Street entrance, and flashed my credentials at one of the uniformed cops.

"Jack Morgan, Private," I said. "The victim, Karl Parker, was a friend."

The cop nodded me through and I walked toward chaos. A couple of hundred traders and support staff who'd been in the Exchange at the time of the shooting had been corralled in a space by the entrance. People were growing disgruntled, and uniformed cops were shouting instructions, telling everyone they had to wait to be interviewed by one of the detectives working the crowd. The mood was turning ugly as many of those evacuated from the building weren't dressed for the freezing cold. Coats were being brought out, and blankets provided, but not quickly enough for the most vocal members of the crowd.

A fleet of emergency vehicles was parked on Wall Street, and their flashing lights colored the surrounding buildings. News trucks were arriving and a couple of camera crews were already setting up. A growing crowd was gathering beyond the cordon on Wall Street. Passers-by who suddenly found their route through the city blocked mixed with gawkers eager to satisfy their hunger for sensation. I'd worked too many cases to kid myself about the lure of the macabre, but this incident was personal and I wanted all the phones and cameras to disappear, and the people who'd suffered such great loss to be left in peace.

I caught sight of the two people suffering most. Victoria and Kevin Parker were led through the Broad Street exit and ushered past the tent toward the line of waiting emergency vehicles.

"Victoria," I called out, jogging over.

She turned, but it was an automatic action, like a rabbit in the path of an oncoming truck. She gave no hint of recognition and seemed stunned by trauma. Kevin wore the same blank expression, and their eyes were raw with tears. They were being shepherded by a couple of uniforms and a plain-clothes detective.

"Victoria," I repeated as I reached them. "I'm so sorry."

"It's OK," she said, but her voice suggested otherwise. It was pained and cracking. I still wasn't sure she'd recognized me.

"Where are you taking them?" I asked the detective, an earnest man of Latin American extraction who looked as though he'd been prematurely aged by the job. It was a quality I'd noticed in the eyes of cops, doctors and soldiers, a depth and weariness that accompanied a life on the edge.

Before he had the chance to answer, I heard a voice behind me.

"That's him. That's the guy who assaulted us."

I turned to see the older security guard who'd tackled me, talking to a female detective with hawkish eyes and a stern, suspicious face.

"Rick," she said, "this man fled the scene right after the shooting."

The uniformed cops helped Victoria and Kevin into an unmarked car.

"What's your name?" the earnest detective, Rick, asked.

"Jack Morgan."

"I'm going to need you to come with me, Mr. Morgan," he said, looking me up and down. I could only imagine how disheveled I appeared after the chase and fight.

"Am I under arrest?"

"Not if you come willingly," he replied.

The old voluntary custody hustle. Favored by cops the world over when they were faced with a borderline collar and didn't want a paper trail that might screw their figures. I didn't object. I had a ton of eyewitness evidence to share and at least I'd be warmer in the precinct than the people being interviewed on the street.

"OK," I said.

"Wise man," Rick replied, before he walked me to a nearby patrol car.

CHAPTER 8

WITHOUT EFFORT, YOU cannot pull a fish from the pond, Yana Petrova thought as she trudged along the frozen pavement. Deep snow lay all around her, and the slabs were covered with ice crystals that sparkled in the streetlights. This was Moscow at its most beautiful, the city's sins concealed beneath cleansing powder.

The thermal leggings Yana wore beneath her jeans did little to ward off the chill, and her goose-down coat wasn't much better. She imagined how warm she'd be if she'd refused Mickey's offer of a date and had instead gone straight home after her shift. She could have caught a cab from the office to their rendezvous but travel by vehicle was fraught with danger. Cars could be booby-trapped and trains packed with knife-wielding assassins. Yana preferred to walk. At least she could see danger coming.

Her antisocial hours meant she often trudged deserted streets, which made potential threats easier to spot. If she ever saw a man coming toward her, she tightened her grip on the PSM pistol concealed in her pocket. Her uncle had given it to her many years ago, for protection, but he could have had no idea who or what she'd need protecting from.

Yana's colleagues thought her a strange loner, but she could never tell them why she preferred the late shift or why she was so paranoid about her personal safety. So she lived a lonely existence as the office weirdo and had to resort to online dating in an attempt to meet someone who might accept and love her.

Yana's breath vaporized as it traveled through her scarf and met air that was so cold she thought the tiny cloud might solidify, but as it cleared, she saw the lights of her destination, the Boston Seafood Grill, an upmarket restaurant that was one of the few late-night eateries still open in the Begovoy District. Yana hurried across Lesnaya Street and went inside.

"Good evening," the hostess said. "Bitter night."

Yana nodded. "I'm meeting someone." She scanned the faces at the bar.

"Can I take your coat?"

Yana handed it over. "There he is," she said, recognizing Mickey from his profile picture.

His dark blue suit and white shirt were evidence he'd made an effort. He had pale skin and jet-black hair, and was leaner than his photo suggested, but his brown eyes were just as warm and welcoming as the picture had led Yana to believe. He caught sight of her as she approached the bar and she saw a flash of appreciation. She'd made the effort too. Her tight jeans clung to her toned legs and her sheer black top revealed a figure-hugging bodice that didn't leave much to the imagination. She felt a number of male eyes on her as she crossed the room, and she brushed them away with a casual toss of her auburn hair. She smiled as she took the stool next to Mickey.

"Good evening, Yana Petrova," he said, making no attempt to be subtle as he looked her up and down.

She didn't mind. It was nice to feel desired after such a long dry spell. "Good evening, Mikhail Titarenko. It's nice to finally meet you. Thanks for agreeing to eat at such an antisocial hour."

"No problem," he replied, and he seemed to genuinely mean it. "I'm surprised the place is so busy."

It was a little after 11 p.m. and the restaurant was three-quarters full. Yana glanced at the young Muscovites who were full of easy confidence and flush with money. They ate, drank and filled the place with loud chatter and laughter and for a moment she longed not to be an outsider. Maybe Mickey was the one, and they'd get married and come here with friends every week like normal, happy people.

"You work for Moesk, the energy company, right?" Mickey asked.

Yana nodded. "If your electricity goes out, I'm the one you call."

"It's nice to have friends in powerful places," Mickey joked. "Do you want a drink before we eat?"

Yana picked up a bar menu. "Sure. Let's make a night of it. What have you got?"

Mickey raised his salt-rimmed glass. "Margarita."

"Another one," Yana told the barman. "And you? I still don't know what you do," she said to Mickey.

"I'm an oligarch," he replied somberly, before breaking into a broad smile. "I can't even lie well. I work in a hardware store, selling power tools. I'm no millionaire, not like some of them in here, but you know what they say, a tomtit in your hand is better than a crane in the sky."

Yana laughed. "I don't need an oligarch. I wouldn't know what to do with all that ego."

"I got you something," Mickey said, reaching for a large paper bag beneath his stool. He placed it on the bar carefully, like a museum custodian handling an exhibit. "Go ahead."

Yana stood, and when she peered inside, she gasped. "It's beautiful."

Moving very slowly and carefully, she reached into the bag and pulled out a crystal flower arrangement. Six life-size cut-glass lilies stood in a crystal vase, and each element of the fine sculpture was filled with a liquid that added realistic color. The petals of the flower contained a creamy white fluid, the stems were filled with green liquid and the vase held what looked like crimson water.

"It's magnificent," Yana said. "And far too expensive for someone as simple as me. I can't accept it. Not on our first date."

"After we're married then?" Mickey scoffed. "Don't worry. Please take it. Give it a good home. One of my customers didn't have any money to pay his bill, so he offered me this instead. He bought a screwdriver, but this is worth more than a whole toolkit."

Mickey beamed at her, proud of his prize, but Yana was suddenly on edge.

"Was this a regular?" she asked.

"I'd never seen him before," Mickey replied, and her gut tightened in a knot.

Could they have found her through her dating profile? She looked at the flowers again, and was horrified to see tiny black valves on the stamen of each lily pop open. A sudden rush of air pressure forced the green fluid in each stem down into the vase, where it mixed with the red liquid.

They've found me, Yana thought, *and I walked right into their trap.*

Mickey must have sensed her dismay, because she saw his bright, optimistic smile fall the instant before the vase exploded and a huge fireball incinerated them both.

CHAPTER 9

I WONDERED HOW many miserable stories the room had heard. Lined with soundproofing tiles that had been scored with years of graffiti, the interview room had been my home for the past two hours. As a volunteering witness, I'd been allowed to keep my possessions, and I checked my watch. It was 11:43 a.m. I read some of the messages carved in the wall tiles, my gaze lingering on those that made a particular impression.

This is no place for innocence.

Brooklyn rocks!

He had it coming, so I served it up cold.

I pushed the plastic chair back from the table that was bolted to the floor and stretched my legs. They ached after the chase and the area around my solar plexus was still sore.

The Latino detective who'd driven me to the precinct was called Rick Tana, and he was in charge of the unfolding investigation. I'd told him everything I'd witnessed and had re-counted the chase and my fight with the assassin. Like any ex-perienced cop, he'd listened with a degree of detached skepticism before probing my story for details that would either confirm or disprove the truth. After a while he'd excused himself and left the room. I knew he was checking me out, but I didn't mind the wait. It gave me a chance to chew over the shooting.

Had Karl Parker known he was a target? Is that what he'd wanted to discuss? He was a former Marine flight instructor, an extremely successful business leader and a family man, but what could have put him in an assassin's crosshairs? The guy I'd chased wasn't some random nut. The motorcycle getaway made it clear the shooting had been planned. If the guards hadn't thwarted that method of escape, we'd have never known about the helicopter, which had undoubtedly been the motorcycle's intended destination. The shooting had all the hallmarks of a professional hit, but why would anyone want to target Karl?

I was mulling over the questions when the door opened and Rick Tana entered.

"Why didn't you mention you're the head of Private?" he asked, referring to my business, the largest and most successful investigation agency in the world.

"Didn't seem relevant," I replied. The truth was I didn't want to invite scandal. Karl's death was sure to be big news and I didn't want the press drawing any conclusions from my pres-ence at the listing. I'd been there as a friend, but the nature of my work meant there was a good chance an imaginative journalist would manufacture a scandalous reason for my attendance.

"Well, it is relevant," Rick remarked. "Were you working a case?" he asked, proving I had good reason to worry about people questioning my motivation.

"Like I said, Karl Parker was an old friend."

"I'm sorry. It can't have been easy to see your friend be killed in that way," the detective replied. "Thank you for cooperating. You're free to go."

"I thought I was here voluntarily," I said.

Rick smirked. "Yeah. Of course you were."

"You get a lead on the chopper?" I asked as I headed for the door.

"Not yet. But there's a group claiming responsibility for the shooting. They call themselves the Ninety-nine. It's all over the news."

I took my phone from my pocket and checked CNN.com. Karl's murder was the lead story, and despite all my years dealing with trauma and death, seeing his picture brought a lump to my throat.

"You OK?" Rick asked.

I ignored the question and clicked on one of the headlines: "Radical Group Claims Responsibility." I scanned the story, which featured the still of a video. The image showed a masked spokesman who'd reportedly said, "Karl Parker was a legitimate target. As a member of the one percent, he had more than his fair share in life, and it's time for others to enjoy his riches. We are the Ninety-nine and we shall eliminate the one percent to once again make America the land of free and equal opportunity."

"I'm fine," I told Rick as I studied the photograph of the masked man.

I'm going to find you, I thought. *I'm going to find you and make you answer for what you've done.*

CHAPTER 10

WE PASSED A number of purposeful cops as we walked through the building. I recognized the expressions on their faces from my time in the Marines. Some joked with a colleague, others talked seriously and some walked alone, but they all had the air of people who were caught up in things greater than themselves, that sense of mission that came with civic duty.

"What did you fly?" Rick asked as we passed an empty briefing room. One wall was covered with NYPD intelligence bulletins.

"CH-46, Sea Knight," I replied.

"My brother flew Thunderbolts in Iraq."

"Tough gig," I said. "Got to get in low."

"Yeah. He had some close calls," Rick replied. "You ever hear of the Ninety-nine before?"

I shook my head.

"Were you and Mr. Parker close?"

"He was one of my flight instructors," I said. "We became friends after he left the Corps, but then we kind of lost touch."

"Any idea why he contacted you after all this time?" Rick asked as we reached the security door that led to central booking.

"None," I replied. "But my guess is he was going to tell me about whatever it was that got him killed."

Rick swiped a card reader and opened the door. "Thanks for your help, Mr. Morgan. Here's my number in case there's anything else you can think of." He handed me his card.

"Thanks," I said, and I shook his hand before stepping into the busy hall that was packed with cops, suspects and lawyers. I immediately saw two people I recognized and they hurried toward me.

Jessie Fleming was the 34-year-old former FBI agent I'd hired to run Private New York. She wore jeans and a baggy hooded top, but even her loose-fitting casual clothes couldn't hide her toned figure. Prior to joining the Bureau, she'd been a gymnast and brought the same dedication that saw her take a World Championship podium bronze in the uneven bars to everything she did. She'd been running Private's New York office for three years, ever since I'd recruited her out of the Counterintelligence Division, where she'd been on her way to becoming section chief in the New York field office. Under Jessie's deft leadership, Private New York had grown to become one of our largest operations, with a team of more than sixty investigators and support staff. Sometimes it was hard to believe I'd built this international empire, and I occasionally wondered how my life would have turned out if my dad hadn't left me the money to give Private the kick-start it needed.

Jessie's companion was Rafael Lucas, a Spaniard who worked for one of the world's largest law firms. He'd come to the US on secondment and had married a wealthy Manhattan socialite, which had come as no surprise. He was an elegant, handsome man from an old aristocratic Calabrian family. There was a hint of the 1930s in the way Rafael dressed, and even now he was in a topcoat, tailored suit and waistcoat with shirt and tie. He and Jessie were at opposite ends of the sartorial spectrum, but both wore the same expression of concern.

"You OK?" Jessie asked.

I nodded. "Thanks for coming down."

"I'm sorry about Karl Parker," Rafael said.

Rafael was Private New York's go-to lawyer and he and Jessie both knew why I was in town. We had been supposed to sit down tomorrow to run through open investigations and talk about other issues that needed to be addressed for the New York business.

"It was a professional hit," I said. "I'm not sure I buy the political motivation."

"Me neither," Jessie remarked. "Political groups usually announce themselves with something small, not a prime-time killing. It just doesn't feel like their first outing."

I nodded. Jessie's instincts were usually on the money. "I chased the shooter to the Manhattan Heliport. He had a chopper waiting. Too slick for a radical group. At least that's what my gut says. Jessie, I want you to call Justine, Sci and Mo-bot and ask them to catch the early-morning flight."

"No need," Jessie said. "They're booked on the red-eye. They called me the moment the story broke."

I was touched that their immediate instinct had been to help. I hadn't spoken much about Karl, but they all knew I wouldn't have been half the pilot I was without his help and insight. Justine was the only one who was aware of just how close Karl and I had been for a while. She knew how personally I'd take his death. I'd watched him get shot and hadn't been able to do a damned thing to stop it. All my training and years of experience and I'd been of no more use than a child. Justine and I had a complicated history, and we were going through an off patch, but there was nothing more I wanted right now than to hold her. I needed to be close to someone who mattered.

"'They'll be here first thing in the morning,'" Jessie told me.

"That's good," I replied. "We should get in contact with Victoria Parker when she's released from interview. I want to find out what Karl was into. See if you can make an appointment for us to visit the house tomorrow."

"Her attorney called me fifteen minutes ago," Rafael said. "She's already been released. She's on her way to Forty-one Madison right now."

CHAPTER 11

I SHOULD HAVE been toasting Karl's magnificent achievement on his beachfront terrace in Long Island. Instead, I was in the passenger seat of Jessie's car, watching the frozen city roll by. Even with winter at its worst, a few unfortunate souls were doomed to face the brutal chill of New York huddled in sleeping bags in the doorways of stores and churches. The city's bleak indifference to their suffering was one of many things I'd experienced over the years that had taught me justice wasn't given, it had to be fought for. And I was going to do whatever it took to ensure I got justice for my old friend.

Jessie drove us north, and after ten minutes in the midday traffic, we pulled into the parking lot beneath Forty One Madison, a thirty-six-story black glass and steel skyscraper that stood on the corner of Madison Avenue and East 26th Street, overlooking Madison Park. Private New York was headquartered on the thirty-fifth and thirty-sixth floors. I'd chosen a midtown location to put Private New York at the heart of the action. Federal Plaza, Wall Street and NYPD Headquarters were a short drive away, and Grand Central and the city's key residential neighborhoods were a brief cab ride uptown.

We took the stairs to the lobby and found a security guard and a janitor chatting by the front desk. Six elevators were all open and docked on the first floor and we went through the security barriers and took one up to Private's New York HQ. When we stepped into the lobby, I saw signs of activity all over the place.

"I tasked some of the team to get a head start on the investigation," Jessie said.

I followed her through a set of glass security doors into an open-plan office where a dozen investigators, administrators and analysts traded information on the Exchange shooting. Some of them stiffened when they saw me. It was a reaction I was used to. Even today, when I was probably at my most vulnerable, they wouldn't see a grieving human being, they'd see a boss, capable of making or breaking careers. Or so they thought. In truth, life at Private was entirely in their hands. If they cleared their cases, their rise up the ranks would be almost inevitable.

Jessie and Rafael took me up a spiral staircase that stood at the edge of the building and, as we climbed, I looked out of the huge windows at the snow-covered city. Somehow the sunshine reflecting off the surrounding skyscrapers seemed brighter than ever. Maybe it was an effect of the freezing air, or perhaps I just wanted to see warmth wherever I looked.

We made our way through the executive floor and came to Jessie's office, which was located in the northwest corner of the building. Jessie went in first and I followed.

Victoria Parker was sitting on one of two tan leather couches that faced each other. Sitting next to her was a woman in a black dress.

"Jack," Victoria said as she got to her feet.

Her eyes were raw, but there was no sign of any fresh tears. She looked furious.

"I'm so sorry," I told her as we embraced.

"Thanks," she replied. "This is Letitia Jones." She indicated the woman in the black dress. "She's our ... my attorney."

Letitia shook my hand. She was mid-forties and had a cold, suspicious demeanor.

"How's Kevin?" I asked.

"He's at home with my mother," Victoria said. "The doctor's given him some sedatives."

"I'm sorry," I repeated with a deep sigh. "I just don't know what to say."

"There isn't anything anyone can say at a time like this," Victoria replied. "You know that as well as anyone."

I nodded. She was right. My personal interest in the case was clouding my professionalism.

"Would you like a drink, Mrs. Parker?" Jessie asked.

Victoria shook her head. "No, thank you. I want us to get down to business. I'd like to hire Private. I want you to find my husband's killer."

CHAPTER 12

"WOULD YOU MIND giving us a minute alone?" I asked Jessie and Rafael.

Letitia looked at Victoria for guidance, and her client nodded. The three of them left the office, and Victoria and I were soon on our own.

I went over to the west-facing window and looked down at the footsteps in the snow-covered park. Pursuing a personal investigation was a very different matter from taking Victoria on as a client, and I wanted her to understand the risks involved. I looked up and searched the city for inspiration, but my attention was caught by my own translucent reflection, which looked like a ghost floating in the January sky. *A tired, troubled ghost,* I thought as I studied my face.

"What do you want to say, Jack?" Victoria asked. "Karl always spoke very highly of you. He never mentioned you were the type to beat around the bush."

"I'm sorry," I said, turning to face her. "I was trying to find a delicate way to say what needs to be said."

"Do I look like someone who gives a damn about delicacy? If it needs to be said, just let it out. Today of all days."

"If you hire Private, we're obliged to share the results of our investigation. Even if they're ugly."

"I know my husband, Jack. I'm not worried about what you might find."

It was the same confidence exhibited by so many clients, but I'd seen too many people break down when shown detailed evidence of treachery at the hands of a spouse, friend, family or business partner. Sometimes ignorance really was bliss.

"If I look into this myself, without taking you on as a client—" I began.

"Then you don't have to share anything unpleasant with me," Victoria finished my thought. "But then you also aren't under any obligation to take my instructions or to report back to me the things I need to know."

She hesitated, and her eyes glistened as she fought for composure.

"I don't want to be protected, Jack. I want to know the truth about why Karl was killed." She choked back a sob.

I nodded. "OK. I'm sorry. I just had to be sure you know what you're getting into."

She wiped her eyes. "I appreciate it."

"Karl seemed to have something on his mind. Something he wanted to tell me. You have any idea what it might have been?"

Victoria shook her head. "He's been … I mean, he had been really distracted these past few weeks, caught up in his own head. But that wasn't new. Whenever he had a busy time at work, he'd go into what Kevin and I called 'the Zone'. Karl would be around, but his mind would be elsewhere, crunching through whatever problems he was facing."

"He ever talk about any of those problems?" I asked.

"No. Not recently, at least. And I'm smart enough to give him the space he needs—" She caught herself again. "I'm sorry, needed, the space he needed. I just can't get used to …" She tailed off.

"It's OK," I told her. "Nothing prepares you for a shock like this."

"Not even war?" she asked, wiping away fresh tears.

"Not even war," I replied honestly. The experience of having watched friends and comrades die in combat didn't make the death of a loved one any easier.

I gave her a moment before I asked my next question.

"I'm going to apologize for this one before I even ask it," I said, and a dark smile immediately crossed Victoria's face.

"I think I know where we're going," she responded.

"I'm sorry, but we've got to rule out the mundane, and you said you didn't want to be protected," I reminded her. "Did you ever catch Karl out?"

"No, I never caught him out. Not so much as a wandering eye. And frankly, with his schedule I'd have been impressed if he'd found the time to cheat on me."

I nodded, stood and walked to the door, opening it to find Letitia and Rafael chatting nearby. Jessie was leaning against her assistant's desk, scrolling through her phone.

"Sorry for kicking you out of your own office," I said.

"No problem, boss," Jessie replied.

"You can come back in," I told the three of them. "Thanks."

They joined Victoria and me in the seating area.

"Mrs. Parker has engaged Private to identify her husband's murderer," I said. "Jessie, I'd like you to handle day-to-day contact with Mrs. Parker."

"I'll be your point of contact," Letitia interrupted.

"No problem," I went on. "I'll be leading the investigation personally."

Jessie frowned instantly and Rafael wasn't long behind her.

"Problem?" I asked.

"Your personal connection to the case—" Jessie began.

"Karl trusted Jack Morgan," Victoria cut her off, "and so do I."

Jessie nodded, but she and Rafael exchanged a skeptical glance.

"Jessie, can you issue an engagement letter setting out our terms?" I asked.

"Sure."

"Whatever you need, you've got it. You can do things the police can't, Mr. Morgan. You get results when others fail, and Karl deserves the best," Victoria said, choking back a sob. "Our family's resources are at your disposal. I want my husband's killer brought to justice. Whatever the cost."

CHAPTER 13

A CLOUD OF steam rose from the stovetop percolator, filling the tiny kitchen with the scent of freshly brewed coffee. Dinara Orlova waited until the brew bubbled and spat before turning off the gas. She split the thick black liquid between two travel cups, stirred in brown sugar and heavy cream, and screwed the lids on. She grabbed her down coat from one of the retro American-diner-style chairs that surrounded her red-topped kitchen table, and pulled on her rabbit-fur trapper hat.

"Good morning," her neighbor, Mrs. Minsky, said as Dinara left her apartment.

Mrs. Minsky had developed a strange habit of spending most of her days sitting in the corridor outside her apartment, reading a book and watching the comings and goings of her neighbors. She had a folding garden chair, matching table and had even put a couple of potted plants in the corridor, treating the tiny space outside her front door as though it was a garden.

"Good morning, Mrs. Minsky," Dinara said as she edged past the old woman.

"Off to find a husband?" Mrs. Minsky asked.

Dinara couldn't tell if the hunched old woman was joking, but she suspected not. "Off to work," she replied.

"Well, don't let me keep you."

Russia had a long history of trying to promote gender equality. It had been one of the central tenets of communism, but Dinara often wondered how much of it had been lip service, because she'd been on the receiving end of far too many critical comments about her age and the need for her to get married. Whenever she felt the social pressure of ingrained sexism, she asked herself whether a 33-year-old man would regularly be quizzed about his marital status.

Dinara admired herself in the smoked-glass mirror of the tiny elevator as it took her on a slow and steady four-story ride to the first floor. She wasn't a woman who needed the reassurances of a man's compliments. She knew she'd been blessed with great hair, beautiful features and an athletic physique, and was confident that when she set her mind to it, the right man would be found. But who had the time? Her early thirties were when she would make her mark on the world.

Dinara stepped out of the elevator and nodded a greeting at Vikto, the doorman, who spent his day in the functional but warm lobby. She hurried outside, and the moment she stepped through the front door of her apartment building, the steam rising from the tiny holes in the coffee cups thickened as it met the freezing air. Her eight-story block stood on the corner of Malaya Bronnaya Street and Yermolayevskiy Lane, opposite a small park. The children's play equipment was buried beneath huge snowdrifts, and the little lake was frozen solid. Dinara shivered as she jogged along the sidewalk.

Leonid Boykov had mounted the curb a short distance from her building, and was waving motorists past him. Dinara cradled both coffee cups with one arm, opened the passenger door, and slid onto the front seat.

"Good morning, boss," Leonid said.

His humor was dry, and rich in sarcasm. He'd greeted her as "boss" every morning for the past three months, but somehow managed to say the word so it sounded like "kid."

Leonid was fifteen years her senior and the toll of every one of his forty-eight birthdays showed on his craggy face. He'd been a Moscow police detective for twenty years, working serious crime and murder, and he had a reputation for being honest and ruthless. Dinara had yet to see his darker side, but he had the lean features and sharp eyes of a predator, and she had no doubt his reputation was well deserved. She'd hired him to be her number two at Private Moscow, but she suspected he thought he should be running the show.

"Good morning, Leonid Boykov," she replied. "I made you coffee." She handed him one of the cups.

"You're the boss. I should be making you coffee." He took a sip. "But I'm not sure I could make it this well."

Was that an insult? Was he being sarcastic? Dinara couldn't tell. "Drive," she said.

Leonid put the car in gear, waved his arm out of the window to signal his right of way, drove off the curb and headed along Malaya Bronnaya Street. Dinara loved her tree-lined neighborhood, which mixed classical architecture with elegant modern apartment buildings. It was also conveniently located, and within moments they were on the Garden Ring, an eight-lane highway that encircled the city center. After a couple of minutes, the traffic started to build, but this was more than the rush-hour grind, it looked as though there had been an accident ahead.

"Business has been slow, huh?" Leonid remarked, tapping his fingers against the steering wheel.

The man rarely spoke without purpose and Dinara knew him well enough to suspect he had an agenda. The traffic ahead of them came to a standstill. A short distance along the street, a bus had collided with a truck and the police were filtering three lanes down to one.

"It will get better," Dinara responded. "The mood toward businesses such as ours isn't favorable at the moment."

She didn't need to elaborate. She and Leonid had discussed the drawbacks of Private's foreign ownership many times. With relations between Russia and America at a low point, there weren't many establishment figures who'd engage a US-owned firm. In fact, there were none. Private Moscow's last case had been closed three weeks ago—a missing person they'd located and recovered—and they had nothing new on the books. Jack Morgan was a patient man, but if things didn't pick up soon, Dinara was certain the Moscow office would have to be shut down.

"Maybe today is the day," Leonid said, and Dinara noticed a mischievous glint in his eye. Something else caught her attention. Two men in a car four vehicles behind them. She watched the pair in the wing mirror, and noted their eyes never left Leonid's Lada Vesta. She felt a rush of adrenalin, but told herself it could be nothing. She wasn't in the espionage game anymore.

"What do you know?" she asked Leonid.

"Are you ordering me to tell you? As my boss?" He smiled.

"Stop with the boss stuff," she replied. "We both know you've got me beat on age and experience."

Leonid glanced at her with somber concern. "I'm sorry if I upset you. I was only joking ..." He hesitated. "Boss," he added with a broad smile.

Dinara punched him playfully. "You want to play that game? OK then, as your boss I command you to tell me what you know."

"I had a call from an old police contact. He wants us to meet his client first thing this morning."

"Who's his client?" Dinara asked.

"You're not playing the game," Leonid remarked dryly.

Dinara rolled her eyes. "I'm surprised none of your old partners killed you. How many of them did you drive mad with this kind of nonsense?"

"Six," Leonid replied seriously. "You'd make it seven, but of course we're not partners."

"Who are we going to see, Leonid?" Dinara asked testily.

"Maxim Yenen," he replied.

Dinara whistled. "You're kidding me," she said as they drove past the accident.

Maxim Yenen was one of the most powerful men in Moscow. An oligarch with a wide range of business interests, and high-ranking friends at the Kremlin.

"Do I look like the kind of man who jokes about such things?" Leonid asked as the car picked up speed again. "A commission from a Kremlin insider would suggest our standing with the authorities has changed."

"Perhaps," Dinara replied, looking in the wing mirror. "That might explain why we have two FSB agents on our tail."

Leonid glanced in the rear-view.

"Three cars back. I recognize the technique from my own training," Dinara said.

"Well," Leonid replied, shifting gears, "let's see if this tired old Moscow policeman can give our highly trained intelligence agents a run for their money."

CHAPTER 14

LEONID STEPPED ON the accelerator and the Lada shot forward. Ostensibly a sensible family car, the former cop had opted for the top-of-the-range model, which he'd had modified at a police garage. The improved performance didn't turn it into a Porsche, but it did give the car sufficient muscle to push Dinara into her seat as it accelerated. Leonid threaded his way past slower-moving vehicles, and when she checked the wing mirror, Dinara saw their tail was trying to keep up. *Not very subtle,* she thought.

They were heading clockwise around the Garden Ring and were near the Kalashnikov Monument.

"What's your plan, detective?" Dinara asked.

"I'm no planner," Leonid replied. "I prefer living in the moment."

He swung the wheel as he passed a truck, and the Lada jerked left and veered in front of the larger vehicle. The truck driver gave a prolonged blast of his horn and his brakes screeched as he stepped on them hard. The Lada SUV shot forward, narrowly missing a car in the other lane, and crossed the median, which was nothing more than a pair of painted white lines. Leonid pulled the wheel left again, and the car lurched onto the counterclockwise side of the busy highway. He swerved to avoid the westbound traffic, and earned more horn blasts and tire screeches from startled drivers. As they passed the Kalashnikov Monument and the sprawling gothic skyscraper that loomed behind it, suddenly all was calm. The Lada's rear end gave a final little waggle as Leonid settled into the middle lane, and when Dinara looked back, she saw the pursuing vehicle had pulled into the median and stopped. The two men got out and looked in her direction. Both seemed frustrated and one was talking on a phone.

"Nicely done," Dinara said.

"Thanks," Leonid replied, without taking his eyes off the road.

"You nearly gave me a heart attack, of course."

"Well, you can't have everything," he said flatly. "I used to do mini-moto when I was younger."

Dinara gave him a blank look.

"Racing with small motorbikes. Before I got too old and fat."

"You're not fat," Dinara told him truthfully. He was a lean, muscular man who kept himself fighting fit.

"But I am old," he said. "Divorced, old and washed up."

"I wish you'd told me all this in your job interview," Dinara joked. "Where are we going?"

"Kolomenskoye Park," Leonid replied.

"Take the long way. Go west."

"Why?" he asked.

"I want to search the car for bugs. It's unlikely given how desperate they were to keep up, but it pays to be cautious," Dinara said.

If the men following them had managed to plant a bug on Leonid's car, they wouldn't have needed to break cover, which suggested the surveillance was a new and recent thing, probably last minute and possibly connected to their meeting with Maxim Yenen.

CHAPTER 15

DINARA AND LEONID pulled off the main road near the Zhivopisniy Bridge onto a dirt track that took them into a deserted forest. The Lada left a solitary trail in the virgin snow, and when they were confident they couldn't be seen from the road, Leonid pulled over and used the EMF detection kit he kept in the boot to sweep the car for bugs. He found nothing, and Dinara's physical search didn't reveal anything either. Satisfied they weren't being monitored, they left the silent forest, returned to the Marshala Zhukova highway and headed east.

When they reached Luzhniki, they parked the Lada and took the Metro to Dubrovka. From there they took a taxi to Kolomenskoye Park, arriving fifteen minutes ahead of their scheduled 10:30 a.m. meeting with Yenen. The cab driver clearly thought they were crazy when they asked him to drop them off in the empty parking lot. The brutal cold and thick snow had turned Kolomenskoye into a hostile frozen wasteland, and there was no one else around. When the cab had headed back to the city, Leonid and Dinara found indentations in the snow that marked the edges of the curving path that led to the Church of Our Lady of Kazan. The grand white building with its blue-domed towers was one of the few imperial churches to have survived the revolution unscathed. It had become a draw for tourists and Muscovites, and Dinara recalled spending a day here with Nofel Popov, a man she'd dated six years ago. As she and Leonid traveled the same path she'd walked with her former sweetheart, Dinara wondered what Nofel might be doing now. Had he found the love and stability he'd so desperately been seeking? He'd demanded far more from Dinara than an ambitious young FSB agent could possibly have given him. She smiled at the thought of him doing pull-ups on the branch of a tree in an attempt to impress her. She searched for the spot where he'd tried to win her over with feats of strength, but the landscape had been remodeled by snow and looked very different from her summer visit all those years ago.

"Something wrong?" Leonid asked.

"Just remembering my last time here," Dinara replied.

"Stay in the moment, please," Leonid upbraided her.

Dinara frowned at him, and the two of them walked on through the snow. The path had been cleared at some point, but fresh powder had covered it, concealing any evidence that humans had ever been here. There were a few animal tracks in the deep snow either side of the path. The tracks vanished into woodland that covered much of the former imperial estate.

The courtyard that lay in front of the church had been cleared to reveal the gray stone slabs. The flowerbeds were lost to deep powder and the gray portico roof and blue domes were capped with thick crusted ice that shone in the sunlight. The sounds of Dinara and Leonid trying to stay warm, shifting from side to side, patting themselves, were deadened by the surrounding snow.

Twenty minutes later, Dinara saw flashes of black through the trees and a convoy pulled into the parking lot. A Bentley SUV positioned itself between two Range Rovers and the occupants got out. A man in a padded silver jacket was surrounded by six men in long woolen trench coats. There was no mistaking who the bodyguards' principal was. The guards' heads turned in every direction, sweeping for threats as they followed Dinara and Leonid's footsteps into the park. As they drew nearer, Dinara recognized Maxim Yenen from his newspaper photos. The deep snow made it hard to gauge his height, but Dinara guessed he was approximately 180 centimeters. He was slightly overweight, had black hair that poked from beneath a woolen hat, and watched the world with narrow, greedy eyes. He had always struck Dinara as a calculating man for whom all the riches of Russia wouldn't be enough.

Puffing clouds of steam as he walked the woodland path to the church, Yenen soon reached Leonid and Dinara.

"Mr. Yenen," she said, offering her hand. "I'm Dinara Orlova."

Yenen refused the greeting with a dismissive wave. "We live in dangerous times, Miss Orlova. Even the touch of a hand can be deadly."

Dinara recognized the paranoid glint in the man's eye. She'd seen it in her reflection when she used to work undercover. There was no such thing as too careful, she'd always told herself, and here was a man who lived by that mantra.

"How can we help you?" Dinara asked, lowering her hand.

Yenen looked at his bodyguards, but it was Leonid who picked up on his pointed expression first.

"Hey," Leonid said to one of the men, a huge bull-necked figure whose coat struggled to contain his massive frame. "You're Tisha Bobrik, aren't you?"

The man looked at Leonid in puzzlement.

"Leonid Boykov. We were on the Olympic team together in 2004." He mimed lifting weights. "You got bronze in the super heavyweight. I got silver for rapid pistol."

"I remember you," Tisha said. "You were at the team party on the last night."

Leonid nodded. "We might even have shared a toast or two." He smiled. "Listen, why don't we bore these other fellows with tales of past glory and leave these two to talk."

Tisha looked at Yenen, who nodded.

"OK," Tisha said, and he and the other guards followed Leonid to the portico a short distance away.

His work as a cop meant there were few places in Moscow where Leonid didn't know someone, and his Olympic success with a pistol had made him a minor celebrity, so he could usually find a connection. The deft way he read people and won them over was something Dinara aspired to.

"What can Private Moscow do for you, Mr. Yenen?" Dinara asked, once the others were out of earshot.

"You are to investigate the murder of a woman called Yana Petrova. She was killed in an explosion last night."

CHAPTER 16

THE BOMBING OF the Boston Seafood Grill had made the news. According to reports, police hadn't confirmed a cause and were saying it could have been a gas leak.

"Are you suggesting it was a bomb?" Dinara asked.

"Yes," Yenen replied. "And Yana Petrova was the target."

Dinara had never heard of the woman before. "How did you know her?"

"She was a friend."

Friend. A vague word that could mean anything, Dinara thought. *Was this woman a business contact? A lover? A threat?*

"What did she do?"

"She was a customer-service agent at Moesk," Yenen replied.

"The electric company?" Dinara remarked.

Yenen nodded. "You are to find out why she was killed and who did it."

"The Boston is popular with a lot of influential people," Dinara said. "How do you know she was the target?"

Yenen's eyes narrowed, but he said nothing.

"I'm going to have to consult with my superior," Dinara told him. "We have a—"

The billionaire cut her off dismissively. "You are going to take the investigation. Your business is failing because you are owned by an American. Solve this case and my patronage will change things for you."

"I need to know—" Dinara began.

Yenen interrupted her again. "I've told you everything you're going to get."

This was a man who was used to being obeyed, and his high-handedness rankled.

"What about terms?" she asked.

"Call my lawyer," Yenen replied, handing her a card. "Talk to him about the details. You will find another number on the back."

Dinara turned the card over to find some hand-scrawled digits.

"That is how you reach me. You, and nobody else."

Yenen studied Dinara for a moment, before starting toward the parking lot. "Move, Dinara Orlova. You are wasting precious time." He called to his men. "Hey!"

The guards broke off their conversation with Leonid and hurried to join their boss.

"So?" Leonid asked as he sauntered over.

"One of the richest men in Russia just hired us to investigate the murder of an office worker," Dinara replied. "How does he even know her?"

"Where did she die?"

"Last night at the Boston Grill," Dinara said.

Leonid whistled as they watched Yenen and his bodyguards walk down to the three SUVs. "Noisy death," he observed. "The mark of someone who is confident they won't be caught, or who isn't worried about the consequences if they are."

Dinara nodded. "And how does he know Yana was the target? The police haven't even confirmed the cause of the explosion, let alone identified a motive, if there is one."

Yenen and his men climbed into the three vehicles.

"Maybe we should have asked for a ride," Leonid said, looking around the deserted park.

"A little walk won't hurt," Dinara replied as she started toward the path.

Leonid grunted disapprovingly and joined her. "So are we taking the case?"

"You got anything better to do?" Dinara asked. She watched Yenen's convoy drive out of the park and speed into the distance. "Come on," she said, picking up the pace.

CHAPTER 17

WATCHING THE SURVEILLANCE footage was difficult. Up on that podium, I'd been totally oblivious to my surroundings, and had been so focused on Karl Parker that I hadn't been alert to the danger right in front of me.

I was in the security control room of the New York Stock Exchange with Seymour "Sci" Kloppenberg, the head of Private Los Angeles' science and forensic lab, and Ben Katz, the Exchange's head of security. They were standing next to Maureen "Mo-bot" Roth, Private's top computer genius, and next to them was Justine Smith, our brilliant forensic profiler, who for a while had been the woman I thought I'd spend the rest of my life with. But a combination of work, my own stupidity and a failure to communicate meant our relationship hadn't been as straightforward as either of us would have liked. The last time we'd spoken on a personal level, she'd made it clear she wanted nothing more from me than professional contact, and I suspected even that would end if someone came along with the right job offer.

She was beautiful and intelligent and even though I couldn't find comfort in her arms, I was grateful to have her with me. After everything we'd been through, the familiarity of her presence was reassuring. We watched eight screens that were broadcasting simultaneous footage shot by different cameras around the Exchange.

"He might as well have been waving a red flag," Mo-bot remarked, pointing at the monitor which showed the assassin moments before Karl walked to the front of the podium.

Why didn't you turn your head? I asked my past self.

Mo-bot was right. The assassin had come into the Exchange late and had walked around looking for a vantage point. He'd been one of only three guards in the huge chamber, but unlike the other two who stood near exits, this man had placed himself among the traders. He'd kept glancing at the genuine guards and had shone a fake smile at anyone who caught his eye. If I'd seen him, I was certain I would have sensed he was a threat.

"I'm sorry," Mo-bot said after seeing my face drop. "I didn't mean … It's a lot easier to see things after the fact. Especially when you've got a close-up of the guy."

"Any idea how he got into the building?" Sci asked Ben Katz.

Katz was a short, thin man who reminded me of a math teacher I'd once had. Dedicated and diligent by reputation, the security breach obviously pained him.

"Someone added false credentials to our system," Katz replied. "We're working on trying to find out how."

"Why wasn't he challenged by anyone?" I asked.

Katz gave a resigned shake of his head. "I don't have a good answer for that. We're going to be conducting a major review of our procedures after this."

"Should I continue?" the Exchange's security technician asked.

He'd paused the footage moments before Karl was shot. Katz sought guidance from me and my team.

"I need to see what happened," Sci replied. "Sorry, boss," he said to me.

I had no desire to see my friend die again, but I knew we had to watch it. I stood frozen as the horrific event was replayed in sharp detail, and felt suddenly overwhelmed. I needed to get out of that room and away from those screens which were showing me images I knew I'd never be able to forget.

"I've seen enough," I said to the group. "I'll meet you outside when you're done."

Justine gave me a sympathetic look as I left the room, and I nodded my appreciation.

I waited for them on Broad Street, and went over the events of the previous day. If I'd been a little faster, a little stronger, the shooter might have been in custody. But I couldn't undo the past. All I could do was use it to beat myself up.

It was another freezing day and the fresh snow being dumped by the black clouds was keeping the Saturday morning streets quiet. A few tourists braved the weather and snapped photos of the Exchange and the other grand old buildings around it. There were still a couple of news trucks on Wall Street, but no other sign that a good man had been murdered here the previous morning.

"You did what you could," Justine said when she joined me. She placed a reassuring hand on my back. "It looks like a professional hit."

"You buying this Ninety-nine story?" Mo-bot asked as she and Sci approached.

The media was running with the sensational idea that America's wealthiest were now under threat from a radical political group, and armchair pundits were chewing over my friend's murder, filling the airwaves with dangerous chatter and speculation.

"I think it stinks," Sci remarked, zipping up his vintage biker jacket so it covered his chin. "That wasn't some zealous idealist. That was a soldier."

I nodded. "I'm not buying it either. Sci, I want you to stay here. Run your own analysis on the scene. The shooter might have touched something or had contact with someone on his way in. See if you can track his arrival. Find out how he got here."

Letitia Jones, the Parkers' lawyer, had arranged for us to be accorded every professional courtesy by the Exchange. Any help they could offer to bring the killer to justice would play well in the media, and I had no doubt the executives were terrified by the prospect of being hit with a wrongful death and negligence lawsuit by the Parker family.

"What are your relationships like with NYPD?" I asked.

"Good," Sci replied.

He regularly traveled the world giving lectures on forensic science, and shared our resources with the FBI's Quantico lab and police departments around the country. He was well respected by law-enforcement agencies everywhere.

"See what they've found," I suggested.

"Will do," he replied.

"What about me?" Justine asked.

"Find out about the chopper they used to escape," I said.

She nodded.

"And Mo-bot, I want you to come with me. We're going to find out what Karl Parker wanted to tell me."

CHAPTER 18

JESSIE HAD PROVIDED us with one of Private New York's staff cars, a black Nissan Rogue. As I drove Mo-Bot out to Long Island, she talked about anything and everything other than the case. How New Yorkers were crazy to put up with this weather when California was open for business; what was happening in the world of quantum computing; the latest developments in artificial intelligence; her planned vacation to Cairo to visit the Pyramids of Giza. For ninety minutes I forgot about failing Karl Parker and almost felt like my old self again. If Mo-bot's rambling monologue was designed to take my mind off things, it worked.

Then we arrived at Karl and Victoria's beachfront home and reality came crashing in when I was confronted with the trappings of the life that had been taken. Karl had come a long way from his Marine instructing days. A double gate opened onto a long drive that led from Hilltop Avenue toward the coast. High trees heavy with snow lined the driveway, and after a quarter of a mile or so, they gave way to a paved courtyard which lay in front of a huge two-story beachfront mansion. A Mercedes G-Wagen and a Bentley were parked outside a six-car garage that stood near the house.

"Some place," Mo-bot observed as we parked beside the other cars.

We got out and crunched across the snow-covered drive to the front door, where a housekeeper waited.

"Come in," she said. "Mrs. Parker is in the library."

The housekeeper introduced herself as Ermilita. She led us through a beautifully decorated house to a large library that overlooked the beach. Bookcases lined three walls, and in the middle of the room were a couch and two armchairs that faced the floor-to-ceiling windows. Victoria Parker was standing by one of the windows, looking out at the beach. There were patches of snow here and there, but most of it had been swept away by the saltwater. Victoria turned to face us as we entered, and it was obvious she'd been crying.

"How are you holding up?" I asked.

Victoria gave a noncommittal shrug.

"Thanks for seeing us," I said. "This is Maureen Roth. Maureen's our resident technology expert."

The two women shook hands.

"Where do we start?" Victoria said.

"I'd like to ask you some questions about Karl, and Maureen will take a look at Karl's computers and files, if that's OK," I replied.

"Let me show you his office," Victoria said.

We were on our way out of the library when a buzzer sounded. Ermilita hurried ahead and we heard the front door open. Words were exchanged, but I couldn't make out what was being said.

"Ma'am," Ermilita called. "There's a package for ... well, you'd better come and see."

Mo-bot and I followed Victoria, and we found a UPS delivery driver waiting by the front door. He was holding a package about the size of a shoebox.

"What is it?" Victoria asked.

"Look at the writing, ma'am," Ermilita replied.

Victoria studied the label and her face fell. "That's Karl's handwriting," she said.

I hadn't seen anything written by him in a while, but took Victoria's assessment on trust.

"Where did this come from?" I asked.

The driver checked a handheld computer. "The package was dropped off on a forty-eight-hour service the day before yesterday at the UPS Store, North Seventh Street, Brooklyn."

Victoria took the parcel. "It's addressed to you," she told me.

"Can I get a signature?" the driver asked, and Ermilita obliged.

"Mo-bot, can you get his details?" I asked, indicating the driver.

"Sure." She nodded, and Victoria and I moved to a table in the hall.

I studied the parcel. Alongside the UPS labeling was an adhesive label with my name and the Parkers' address written in cursive. Brown paper, sticky tape, no obvious danger. I peeled back some of the tape and carefully unfolded the flap.

"Why would Karl send you a parcel here?" Victoria asked.

I couldn't shake the feeling my old friend had known his fate, but supposition and superstition were the enemies of a good detective. I removed the wrapper to reveal a plain cardboard box. No marks or distinguishing features. I lifted the top flap and peered inside.

"What is it?" Mo-bot asked when she joined us.

"A book," I replied.

I reached inside and picked up a hardback copy of Lewis Carroll's *Alice's Adventures in Wonderland*. It was a well-used, dog-eared copy and I leafed through it to find a borrowing record stuck to the first page. The book came from the Leonard branch of the Brooklyn Public Library and had been lent to Karl Parker two days ago.

"Why would Karl send you a library book?" Victoria asked.

I stared at Karl's name in the lending record, wishing I knew the answer to her question.

CHAPTER 19

A SMALL CROWD of ghoulish onlookers watched the forensic operation on Lesnaya Street. They stood behind a cordon patrolled by two Moscow Second Regiment police officers. There was one news crew still at the scene, and the reporter, a grizzled veteran Dinara recognized, was having a cigarette while his camera operator shot B-roll footage. Beyond the cordon a trio of large field lamps had been arranged around the wreckage of the Boston Seafood Grill. A diesel generator hummed nearby and steam rose from the hot lights, which illuminated a horrific scene.

The restaurant's street frontage had been torn apart and fire had blackened much of the building. Fragments of furniture, chairs, tables, light fittings, chunks of the bar had been blasted into the snow outside, and each broken item had been marked by a small numbered orange flag. There were dozens of them. There hadn't been any fresh snowfall, which meant Dinara could still see the outlines and indentations where body parts had been scattered by the explosion. She saw the shape of a leg, an arm, and the tiny shapes of fingers. The dismembered limbs had been removed from the scene but each spot was memorialized by a numbered red flag. There were thirty-five.

"What a mess," Leonid said.

Dinara nodded. Inside the restaurant a team of forensic scientists sifted through debris and wreckage. Dinara and Leonid approached the cordon, close enough to the huge lights for their heat to take the edge off the freezing night.

"See anyone you know?" Dinara asked.

Leonid scanned the faces of four senior Moscow Criminal Investigations Department police officers gathered outside a mobile command unit. Three men and a woman, all in heavy police-issue coats and uniforms.

"Hey," Leonid said to one of the officers patrolling the cordon. "Tell Rudin that Boykov wants a word."

The officer crossed the street and spoke to one of the three men, a gray-haired hawkish figure with the two-star epaulets of a lieutenant colonel.

"We worked a few cases together," Leonid told Dinara. "He's a pompous ass, but he's honest."

The gray-haired lieutenant colonel approached with the female officer who wore the three-star insignia of a full colonel. She had a chubby, chalk-white face and unfriendly black eyes.

"How's life in the private sector?" Rudin asked in what was an unmistakably mocking tone. His face was pockmarked by old acne scars. "You a billionaire yet?"

"Still working on it," Leonid replied. "You got a cause?" he asked, nodding toward the restaurant.

"I am Colonel Alena Stanika, and I am in charge of this investigation. Any questions you have will be directed through me," the woman said.

"No problem," Leonid replied insolently. "You got a cause yet?"

"What's your interest here? Who are you?" Stanika asked.

"We're from Private Moscow, the investigation agency. We think one of our clients might have been inside," Dinara replied.

"This is Leonid Boykov," Rudin told Stanika. "He used to be with MUR."

"I've heard of you," Stanika said with a frown. "And of Private. You must be Dinara Orlova. Who was your client?"

"Piotr Rykov," Leonid replied.

He was a very good liar and if Dinara hadn't known better, she would have believed they really had such a client.

"We don't have that name on the reservation system," Stanika replied.

"He could have been a walk-in or a guest," Leonid observed. "So, do you have a cause?"

"No," Stanika replied. "Could have been a gas explosion."

"The pattern is wrong," Dinara said. "Looks like a high-explosive blast." She indicated the marker flags. "Debris is scattered too far for gas."

"Really?" Stanika remarked. "And are you a forensic expert? Or an explosive specialist?"

"Just a concerned citizen trying to help," Dinara replied dryly.

Stanika eyed them both. "I know what you are, Colonel Dinara Orlova, formerly of the FSB's Counterterrorism Division."

"Then maybe you should listen to her," Leonid jibed.

"If you'll excuse us, we have an investigation to attend to," Stanika said as she walked away.

"That's the Boykov I know. Always winning new friends. Good to see you," Rudin added without a shred of sincerity before following his superior.

"What do you think?" Leonid asked as he and Dinara watched the police commanders walk away.

"They don't know anything," she replied. "Which means we can't learn anything useful from their investigation. At least not yet."

"So we're on our own?"

"Looks like it," Dinara said. "Let's see what we can find out about Yana Petrova."

She stepped away from the warmth of the bright lights, and Leonid followed her into the frozen night.

CHAPTER 20

IT WAS MID-AFTERNOON by the time we arrived at the Leonard branch of the Brooklyn Public Library. The drive from Long Island had been treacherous; for a city that was regularly hit by snow, New York was home to far too many people who didn't know how to handle the conditions. Drivers without snow chains or winter tires, driving too fast, making no allowances for the poor visibility caused by the falling snow. It wasn't quite a whiteout, but it was close, and we saw at least a dozen minor collisions and one major accident on our way to Brooklyn.

Mo-bot had spent the journey going through the library book I'd been sent, looking for markings or codes, but the well-thumbed copy of *Alice's Adventures in Wonderland* yielded nothing.

The library was a single-story redbrick building located on the corner of Leonard and Devoe in Williamsburg. It looked like an oversized water-pumping station, but there was beauty in its functional symmetry, and a sign by the door informed us of its historic landmark status. Inside, the large open-plan space was warm and peaceful. I could see half a dozen people browsing the shelves which lined the exterior walls. Others were sitting by desks or low tables, reading. The librarian was a young African American woman who was sorting books at a crescent-shaped service counter.

"Can I help?" she asked as Mo-bot and I approached.

"My name is Jack Morgan," I replied. "I'm a private investigator." I showed her my credentials. "We're looking for information on the man who borrowed this book."

Mo-bot reached into her bag and handed over the copy of *Alice's Adventures in Wonderland*. The librarian examined it and opened the front cover. "It was borrowed two days ago," she said. "I think I remember the guy. Yeah." She moved to her computer and scanned the book. "Karl Parker."

I nodded.

"Jeez, he's the one who was shot yesterday, right?" the librarian said. "I served him on Thursday. I recognized him from the television."

"He was a friend," I said.

"I'm sorry," the librarian replied sympathetically. "I'm not sure what I can tell you. He borrowed the book at three oh six p.m. I don't have any other details."

"What about the shelf it came from?" I asked.

"Classic children's literature," she replied as she emerged from behind the counter.

She led Mo-bot and me to the children's section and took us to a shelf that was packed with well-known books.

"It normally lives right here," the librarian said, pointing at a spot on the second shelf down on the five-foot-high unit.

"Thanks," I said. "Do you mind if we take a look around?"

"Sure. Let me know if there's anything else I can help you with," the librarian said before she returned to her station.

I searched the books around the space, leafing through the pages, looking for notes or messages, but there was nothing. Mo-bot did likewise, searching the books on the shelves above and below, but she too drew a blank.

"Did you find what you were looking for?" the librarian asked when we went back to the counter.

I shook my head.

"I'm sorry," she said.

I looked around, puzzling over why Karl had sent me the book. My eyes settled on something attached to the library ceiling.

"Does that work?" I asked, pointing at a surveillance camera mounted to the wall.

"It does," the librarian replied. "We don't get much trouble, but the cops recommended we had them installed a few years back."

She turned her screen so Mo-bot and I could see it, and she switched from the lending system to a camera archive.

"Could you show us footage of the time Karl Parker borrowed the book?" Mo-bot asked.

"Sure," the librarian replied. She clicked on Thursday and cycled through the footage, searching for 3:06 p.m.

"The book is meaningless on its own," Mo-bot observed. "But the borrowing record ties Karl Parker to a location and a time."

The librarian found the right moment and I watched my friend on screen. He looked perfectly normal, all smiles and friendly chatter.

"You know, now I think about it, he also asked me about the cameras. He wanted to know whether they really worked and how long they kept the footage for. Said he was in the tech industry and was interested in that kind of thing," the librarian told us.

I felt a pang of grief as I watched Karl. He seemed so real, but he was nothing more than a ghost of binary stored on a hard drive. On screen, he pushed the copy of *Alice's Adventures in Wonderland* across the counter, and when the librarian leaned toward her computer, Karl looked directly at the camera and brought his hands up to his face.

"What was that?" Mo-bot asked. "Play it again."

The librarian complied with her request, but I didn't need to see the gesture a second time.

"That was the Marine Corps hand signal for file formation," I explained. "It also means follow me."

CHAPTER 21

"YOU WERE RIGHT," I said to Mo-bot. "Karl has intentionally given us a time and place. Can you access the neighborhood traffic cameras?"

"You think he's left a trail?" she asked.

I nodded.

"I'd better get started. My machine is in the trunk," Mo-bot said. "What time do you close?" she asked the librarian.

"Five."

"Can I use your Wi-Fi?" Mo-bot asked.

"As long as you're not doing anything illegal," the librarian replied.

Mo-bot smiled, but didn't reply. "Give me the keys," she said to me.

I handed them over, and she went outside. My phone rang and when I pulled it out of my pocket, I saw Justine's name flash on the screen.

"Go ahead," I said when I answered.

"Albany Police found the wreckage of a chopper upstate. The tail number matches the aircraft you saw leaving Manhattan Heliport. Looks like a high-impact crash. Three dead, no survivors."

"They identify any of the victims?" I asked.

"Not yet. The remains have been badly burned. It's going to take some time."

I thought for a moment.

"Jack, are you there?" Justine asked.

"Yeah," I replied. "Just trying to figure out the odds of a bird crashing with an assassin on board."

"I'm not buying it either. Too neat. Someone is trying to cover their tracks," Justine said. "Albany PD are blaming it on the bad weather, pending a full NTSB investigation."

"See if you can pull any surveillance from the heliport," I said. "The shooter was disguised, but the pilot and his accomplice might not have been. If we can get a picture, we might be able to ID them."

"Will do," Justine replied. "You find anything?"

"Yeah," I said. "Karl Parker borrowed a book from a library. He gave us a time and date to pinpoint his location. I think he wants us to use the local camera network to follow him."

"Clever," Justine said. "Let me know if there's anything I can do to help."

"Will do," I assured her. "And Justine ..." I hesitated. "Thanks for coming out here. Thanks for doing this."

"It was Sci's idea," she said.

I stayed quiet.

"OK, it was my idea," she confessed. "I knew how much Karl meant to you back in the day. If it was one of my old friends, you'd do the same for me."

"I appreciate it," I told her. "Stay in touch."

As I hung up, Mo-bot entered the library with her laptop case. She kicked the snow off her boots and made for one of the vacant tables.

"Over here OK?" she asked the librarian, who nodded.

"It's bitter outside," Mo-bot said as I joined her. "Give me a moment to warm up."

She took off her gloves and blew on her hands. Once her circulation had returned, she got out her laptop, sat in front of her machine and went to work.

CHAPTER 22

IT WAS SNOWING heavily when I left the library. I was wearing the Arc'teryx jacket I'd found in the Nissan's trunk and had the hood up, but the chill still bit me. Williamsburg was eerily quiet. I could see lights in the apartment buildings that lined Leonard Street, but the road itself was empty and the snow was piling up quickly. Deep drifts formed against the wall of a dairy warehouse. Even when I reached Metropolitan Avenue, there were hardly any cars on the wide street. Snow deadened the sound of the few that passed and sidewalks were empty as people avoided the worst of the storm. The sense of otherworldliness was highlighted by the presence of a ghost on my phone. Mo-bot and I were connected via Zoom and she was simultaneously sending me pulled footage from neighborhood police and traffic cameras that showed Karl's journey from the library. I was tracing the steps he'd taken two days earlier.

"He went west along Metropolitan," Mo-bot said. "Let me pull up the next camera."

I looked at my screen and saw the footage change to show Karl walking along Metropolitan Avenue. There was snow on the ground but it was nowhere near as thick as it was now, and there were people all around him. Every so often, he'd glance in the direction of the camera. He'd deliberately chosen a location that was well monitored by cameras, but why had he gone to such lengths to conceal whatever it was he wanted me to know? His message had clearly been designed for one person. The book had been addressed to me. The Marine hand sign was something only leathernecks would recognize and there were few people in the world who would have the resources and skills to hack the neighborhood cameras. Whatever he wanted me to know, Karl Parker had gone to great pains to ensure no one else would find it.

I pressed along Metropolitan Avenue through snowfall so thick it was settling on my eyebrows and lashes. I wiped my face and pulled my hood tighter as I passed a large store that sold vaping gear. Two men were inside, puffing on their machines, indistinct shapes beyond a steamed window. A short while later, I came to the intersection with Lorimer Street and stopped outside a bagel store that was filling the cold air with the scent of warm dough.

"Which way?" I asked.

"Just checking," Mo-bot replied.

She'd spent almost an hour hacking various camera networks and setting up her system to relay to my phone. I understood the big-picture theory of what she'd done, but was in awe of people who could manipulate the digital world so effortlessly. Mo-bot and people like her were the architects of the future.

"Got him," she said. "North along Lorimer."

The image on my phone changed, and I saw Karl walking up Lorimer Street, past the medical center and subway station. I followed his route past the low-rise, traditional apartment blocks. There were no chains or fancy stores in this blue-collar neighborhood, just a bunch of local businesses struggling to survive. The weather wasn't helping. At the next corner I passed a dry cleaner that was open but empty. The man at the counter mimed shivering when he saw me and gave a sympathetic nod as I went by.

I continued along Lorimer Street, following my friend's footsteps. I couldn't stop wondering why he hadn't done more. If he'd known his life was in danger, why hadn't he done something to stop his murder? Why hadn't he spoken to me? Why leave a trail that was clearly designed only to be used after his death? I thought I knew Karl and understood how his mind worked, but this didn't fit with the straight shooter who'd trained me, a man who had never been one for manipulation or subterfuge. This trail was the product of a cunning, possibly paranoid mind, and I didn't recognize my friend in its thinking. I questioned how well I really knew him if he'd been keeping a secret that required this level of concealment. A secret big enough to get him killed.

As I continued along Lorimer Street, I started to see subtle changes in the neighborhood. Graffiti marred the walls of the apartment buildings that lined the street, and some of the store signs had been tagged. When I crossed Skillman Avenue, I noticed many of the stores had barred windows. I could see the outline of the Brooklyn–Queens Expressway cutting across Lorimer Street a block down. There were hardly any vehicles on the high overpass, but those that I could see were moving incredibly slowly.

I looked at my phone and saw we'd reached the very limit of the traffic camera's capabilities. Karl Parker came toward me, a tiny speck who'd materialized on screen somewhere near the overpass.

"You got another camera?" I asked.

"I can't find any by the Expressway," Mo-bot replied. "Can you see any from where you are?"

I squinted through the snow and searched the surrounding lights for signs of cameras. I hurried past a bike-repair store and a Catholic veterans' mission to the spot where the last camera had picked up Karl, a short way beyond the intersection with Jackson Street. I glanced around and checked the buildings. The storm made it difficult to see, and it was possible there were security cameras concealed by the snow that covered the tops of lampposts, signs and rooftops.

"I can't see any," I told Mo-bot. "Why would he go to all this trouble and then let the trail run cold?" I stamped my feet and rubbed my sides. "I'm going to keep heading in the same direction. See if I can find anything."

I was very close to the Expressway now. The abandoned store on the ground floor of the two-story apartment on the corner of

Jackson was covered in graffiti. I studied the tags, looking for some clue, but there was nothing, so I moved up the street. I could see a few cars parked beneath the overpass, and drifts of snow blown by the swirling winds had piled beside them. The building next to the apartment block was a single-story red-brick warehouse that stood on the corner of Meeker Avenue, directly below the Expressway. It was accessed by a steel roll shutter, which was closed. I walked to the corner and looked left and right. A tiny garage protruded from the side of the warehouse, covered by another shutter. I scanned for clues.

And then I saw it. Hidden in plain sight, amidst all the graffiti near the top of the roll shutter. A series of seemingly random shapes scored into the brickwork. Light pink etched dots and lines. Anyone familiar with Morse code would have recognized they formed the word "inside."

CHAPTER 23

"I THINK I'VE found it," I told Mo-bot, and I used my phone's camera to show her the message.

"I'll be there in five," she said, before hanging up.

I glanced around, and then, seeing there was no one watching, I took a running jump, kicked off the warehouse wall, grabbed the garage roof and hauled myself up. I ran across the roof and jumped into a yard that was full of high drifts. I could see lengths of scaffolding and metal protruding from the mounds of snow. It looked like some kind of junkyard. A narrow snow-free gully had been created on the leeward side of a graffiti-covered fence and I hurried down it, past the piles of metal to the back of the warehouse, where I saw a steel door that stood beside a tiny, barred window.

I grabbed a length of rusting iron rail that had a flat, razor-sharp end, and trudged through thick snow to get to the steel door. The yard was overlooked by a windowless warehouse and an apartment building that was undergoing refurbishment, and it couldn't be seen from the Expressway overpass, so I had no eyes on me when I forced the jagged end of the makeshift crowbar into the gap between the doorplate and the frame. Even through my gloves, I could feel the freezing chill of the metal, but I ignored it and applied as much pressure as I could. The plate bent, the lock snapped and the door swung open.

I stepped into a gloomy corridor that smelled of decay. An ancient toilet lay to my left and a space that might once have been an office opened up on my right. The walls were marred by damp and the floor tiles were rotten. I walked along the corridor, checking the place for tripwires and booby traps. Karl might have wanted me to find this place, but there was no guarantee it wasn't hostile, so I moved with caution.

The corridor took me to the main workshop, a thirty-by-fifty-feet space that would have suited a mechanic or body shop, but which was now empty. A steel balcony hung at the rear of the space and I climbed the rickety stairs that led up to it, but found nothing significant. Just a bare brick wall and a tiny, barred circular window that overlooked the yard. I peered down at the gloomy workshop space, wondering why Karl had brought me to a derelict, empty building. Then I noticed something on the floor below. I hurried down the steps and approached a dust-covered indentation in the concrete. I crouched and brushed away the dust to reveal a carved pair of naval aviator wings. I stood, puzzling over their significance, and as I moved around them, I felt the tone of my footsteps change. I looked down, scuffed my shoe through the thick dust and noticed a regular indentation. I bent down and traced the outline of a two-by-two-foot panel. I got my fingers beneath one of the edges and lifted the heavy square. Someone had covered a thick steel plate with concrete to conceal a manhole. A short, steep run of steps led to a basement. I pulled a flashlight from my jacket, switched it on and went down.

The steps led to a small antechamber and there was another steel door, this one controlled by a numeric keypad. There was a note stuck to the wall beside the keypad. I shone the light on it and saw it read, "Happy Birthday."

I punched the month, day and year of my birth into the keypad and a green light flashed and the lock disengaged. I pulled the door open and pointed my flashlight into the room beyond. I was shocked by what I saw.

Arranged on shelves around the room were surveillance cameras, directional microphones, location transmitters, audio and video bugs. A desk in the center of the room was covered with passports from different countries and beside them were stacks of foreign banknotes. Lying next to the passports and money was a large black diary. Lining the back wall was a gun rack that was covered by a steel mesh. The rack held assault rifles, grenades, pistols, knives and stacks of ammunition.

I approached the desk and opened one of the passports. Looking every inch an authentic document issued by the French Republic, the photo that stared up at me was Karl Parker's but the name beside the image was Claude Morel. I checked the other passports and found they all contained Karl's photo and that each was issued in a different name. These weren't the possessions of a successful CEO. This was the lair of a criminal, terrorist or spy. Who the hell was my friend?

I opened the diary and leafed through the pages. They were all blank, not a single entry anywhere. What was it for?

I pulled open the top drawer of the desk and found a laptop. There was a note stuck to the lid that read, "I did what I had to." I recognized the writing from the UPS package. It was Karl's.

I was about to open the laptop when I heard footsteps in the workshop. I kicked myself for not closing the trap door behind me, but without brushing the dust over it, the outline would still have been visible anyway. I switched off my torch, hurried to the steel door and positioned myself behind it.

I tensed as someone came down the stairs and crept toward the open doorway.

"You'd better not be hiding behind that door, Jack Morgan," Mo-bot said, and I stepped out, relieved to hear a friendly voice. "You could have given me a heart attack," she added. "I told you I'd be here in five. Took me a little longer than I expected to pick the lock on the shutter."

She shone her torch around Karl Parker's lair, and whistled loudly. "What the heck is this place?"

CHAPTER 24

"LUXURY COMMUNISM," LEONID sneered as he and Dinara climbed the chipped concrete steps that wound up the dingy staircase. The place reeked of failure and as they headed up to the fourth floor they heard the sounds of a quarrel echo off the walls.

"We don't want to know about your money problems," Leonid yelled up the stairs, and the argument stopped for a moment before resuming, except instead of fighting about their finances, the unseen couple were now rowing over who was to blame for starting disputes the neighbors could overhear.

Leonid sighed. "You're too young for communism, but I caught the end of it. Hard to believe there was a time"—he gestured at their surroundings—"when this was considered the height of luxury."

"My parents remember the Gorbachev years fondly," Dinara replied.

"Were they Party members?" Leonid asked as they reached the fourth-floor landing.

Dinara nodded. "Loyal. They truly believed in equality."

"Equality?" Leonid scoffed. "I don't remember Gorbachev or his cabal living somewhere like this."

The apartment building was one of many charmless, functional five-story blocks that had been thrown up around Moscow in the seventies and eighties. Poorly mixed concrete, terrible plumbing, shoddy electrics and a sense of neglect that was present from the day their doors opened. Buildings like these were some of the least desirable in the whole city, refuges for the poor, downtrodden and criminal. Dinara wondered why a Moesk customer-service agent would choose to live here.

They entered the central corridor on the fourth floor. The place stank of rotten fruit and most of the lights were out, casting much of the corridor in shadow. They found apartment 418 and Dinara used lock-picking tools to gain entry.

"I could have done it faster," Leonid said when she pushed the door open.

"Are you really that insecure?" Dinara replied as they crept inside.

According to the property records, Yana Petrova lived alone, but official documents didn't always tell the whole story, so Dinara and Leonid donned surgical masks and latex gloves and conducted a cautious sweep of the small two-bedroom apartment before relaxing their guard.

The police hadn't identified Yana Petrova as a victim of the Boston Seafood Grill blast, so Dinara and Leonid were a step ahead of the authorities and had free run of the place.

"I'll check the bedroom," Leonid said.

He walked down a short corridor that ran off from the living room. Taking care to leave no trace of her presence, Dinara searched the cupboards in the small kitchenette, looking for the slightest clue that might hint at why this seemingly unremarkable woman had been targeted for such an ostentatious execution. Dinara found nothing but evidence of a sad, solitary existence. There were meals for one in the fridge, and three sets of plates and cutlery. One set in the cupboard, one in the sink and the third drying on the draining board. A calendar of famous Moscow scenes listed only one appointment; the word "Mickey" was scrawled beneath yesterday and had been circled by two love hearts. Had Yana been at the Boston on a date?

Dinara found tinned food and a half-empty vodka bottle in another cupboard. There was nothing on top or underneath the kitchen units, and, satisfied the tiny room had no secrets to reveal, Dinara moved into the living room. Leonid emerged from the bedroom corridor before she'd had a chance to get started.

"I think someone has already been here," he said. "Someone who can search without leaving a mark."

"Then how do you know?" Dinara asked.

Leonid gestured at her to follow and they went along the corridor that fed into two small bedrooms and a tiny bathroom. He took her into the main bedroom, a simple space that overlooked the neighboring block. Leonid went to a chest of drawers that was covered by jewelry, makeup and skincare products.

"She wasn't house proud," he said, signaling the thick dust. "Look at the marks."

Dinara saw clear circles in the dusty surface.

"The dust build-up suggests she always put things back in the same place. Apart from today. These bottles have been placed wrong. And look at the jewelry tree," Leonid said.

Rings, necklaces, earrings and bracelets had been hung in tangled clumps. It was not the arrangement of a woman who wanted easy access to her jewelry.

Dinara noticed a laundry basket at the end of the bed, and lifted the lid to sift through Yana's dirty clothes.

"You're right," she said. "These clothes have been sorted by type. Someone's thrown in all the underwear and blouses first and put the trousers and socks on top."

Leonid looked puzzled.

"When people get undressed, they put their clothes into the laundry, so you get outfit one, then the second layer is outfit two and so on. This bin has been emptied and refilled. The underwear went in first because there's nowhere to hide anything. Then the T-shirts. Trousers and socks take longer to search, so they went in last."

Leonid nodded. "Whoever has been here would have fooled most cops. But I am not most cops."

"Will you ever stop boasting?"

"How can a statement of fact be considered boasting?" Leonid asked.

"The real question is what they were looking for," Dinara said. "And whether they found it."

CHAPTER 25

"KEEP LOOKING," DINARA said.

She left Leonid and returned to the living room. She checked the small two-seater couch that stood in front of the television, but found nothing. She searched the TV unit, but drew a blank. Her attention was caught by a flash of color across the room, and she saw a tank of tropical fish concealed behind a gilt tri-fold screen. Dinara went over to the aquarium and watched colors dart and dance through the water. Dinara felt sorry for the little creatures. With Yana gone, who knew when they would be fed again? She picked up a bottle of fish food and shook a little into the tank. The fish must have been hungry because they shimmered toward the tiny pellets and gobbled them up. The aquarium only added to Dinara's sense of Yana as a solitary person. Dinara could picture the lonely woman talking to her fish as she fed them, and there was something tragic about the image. Dinara never wanted to end up like this.

There was a small net next to the aquarium and as the light from the tank flickered with the movement of the darting fish, Dinara noticed a faint line on the net's bamboo handle. The mark, possibly made by water, was about half an inch from the end of the cane. Dinara studied the fish tank more closely and saw something glinting among the tiny pebbles heaped on the bottom.

She picked up the net and put it into the tank, handle first. She used the end of the bamboo to clear some of the pebbles and saw a brass button not much wider than the cane. She centered the handle over the button and pushed. The button depressed about half an inch, and the edge of the housing rubbed the cane where the faint mark was. Something clicked in the base of the tank, and a concealed compartment opened. Dinara pulled it wide.

"I've found something," she said, peering inside.

Leonid hurried into the room as Dinara reached into the secret compartment that stretched the length and width of the tank. She pulled out a silver laptop and her mouth widened as she saw the sticker on the machine.

"What is it?" Leonid asked.

Dinara held the computer sideways so he could see the sticker. It said "Otkrov" and they both understood its significance immediately. It was short for *otkroveniye*, the Russian word for revelation. Otkrov was the pen name of Russia's most notorious conspiracy blogger, a thorn in the Kremlin's side and a source of alternative news and sensational stories for dissidents and malcontents all over the country. Such stickers were sold in vaping stores across Moscow and were popular with young rebels who wanted to stick it to the establishment, but there was something about the way this laptop had been hidden …

"Don't even think it," Leonid said. "She can't have been. Look around you. Otkrov's stories don't come from a place like this."

Dinara wasn't so sure. "We should go. We need to find out what's on this machine."

CHAPTER 26

I WAS SITTING at the bar, drinking a highball. Mo-bot had gone to Private New York to make use of the tech systems that would help her open Karl's computer. I knew she preferred to work without someone at her shoulder, so I'd returned to the Nomad, the hotel Jessie's assistant had booked us into.

A middle-aged couple at a nearby table were having a conversation in hushed but strained tones. The woman looked as though she might cry. At the other end of the long counter, a couple of guys sat side by side, drinking beer wordlessly as they watched an NBA game on an iPad. The Library at the Nomad wasn't a sports bar, but the Knicks were playing the Wizards, and the New Yorkers were running away with the game, so the barman cut the pair some slack and let them watch with the volume down. There weren't many customers to complain about them lowering the tone of the grand drinking hole. The tables on the gallery level that ringed the bar were all empty, and only a couple of the booths that nestled among the high bookcases were occupied. If the bar was anything to go by, the hotel was experiencing a post-Christmas lull, but the quiet suited me. Free from distraction, I was thinking about what we'd discovered in Karl Parker's secret basement. What had my friend been doing?

Karl had gone to great lengths to set up a trail designed specifically for me, which meant he didn't want anyone else, not even Victoria, knowing his secret. I hoped my old friend hadn't got caught up in anything illegal. I was already struggling with his loss and didn't want to have to face anything that might tarnish my memories of him. I wanted to remember Karl as an honorable man who'd served his country with distinction, but the cache of false passports, weapons and money led me to suspect I was clinging to false hope.

"I know that face," Justine said, sliding onto the stool beside me. "Something bothering you?"

She was a welcome sight. Truly the only person I wanted to be with at this moment.

"We found weapons, fake passports and foreign currency that might have belonged to Karl Parker," I replied. "Not the sort of stuff the average CEO has lying around."

Justine pursed her lips.

"Can I get you anything?" the barman asked.

"I'll have what he's having," she replied.

"One highball," the barman said, before stepping away to prepare her drink.

"You think he might have been Agency?" Justine asked.

I'd clutched at that hope too. The CIA recruited from the armed services, and had a track record of supporting businesses of strategic importance. Karl's firm, Silverlink International, certainly fit that category.

"Maybe," I replied. "But he's dead. Why go to all this trouble? If he was Agency, why not just leave a note?"

"To protect a source or a mission maybe?" Justine suggested.

I smiled. I knew she was trying to make me feel better by suggesting a scenario that didn't involve my friend being a bad guy. She looked at me and the light caught her eyes, making them shine. I thought of the times we'd spent together and wanted to feel her in my arms.

"I know that look," she said, laughing and turning to the barman as he brought her drink. "Thanks."

"We weren't so bad together, were we?" I asked as she took her first sip.

"Not bad," she replied. "Just complicated. Grief can do strange things, Jack. It makes you yearn for things that are gone."

She looked at me pointedly, and I held her gaze. She was right. Death had a way of distorting emotions, but my feelings for Justine had nothing to do with Karl's murder. I'd often thought about how good the two of us were together.

"I don't want to complicate what we have." Justine reached out and put her hand on mine.

Her touch was exactly what I needed. Reassuringly familiar and gentle.

"Justine . . ." I began.

"I don't think we can afford the confusion, Jack," she said, cutting me off. She looked as though she was about to say something else, but she never got the chance.

"You would not believe the day I've had," Sci said, appearing suddenly at our shoulders. "It's brutal out there."

Justine withdrew her hand, and Sci shot me a questioning look.

"You find anything?" I asked.

He shook his head. "Nothing useful yet. Footage shows the shooter wore gloves throughout, and traffic cameras picked him up coming out of the Broad Street subway station. We tracked him back to Classon Avenue in Brooklyn, but after that the trail runs cold."

"Same with the chopper," Justine said. "It crashed with three on board. It was chartered by a service company acting for Antares Futures and Investments, a corporation based in Belize. NYPD has asked for FBI support, and the Bureau is trying to find out who owns the Belize firm."

"So we've got nothing?" I asked.

Justine glanced away, and I wondered whether she thought I was talking about the case, or our relationship. She'd been right. It had the potential to get complicated, and right now my mind wasn't completely on the investigation.

"Sorry, Jack," Sci replied. "I'll get back on it first thing."

"Thanks. I'm calling it a day," I said, getting to my feet.

"Aren't you going to finish your drink?" Justine asked.

"Another time, maybe," I replied.

"Night," Sci said.

"Night, Jack," Justine added, and I could have sworn I felt her eyes on me as I left the bar.

CHAPTER 27

I COULD STILL taste the highball when a phone call woke me at six thirty. I saw Mo-bot's name light up the screen, and answered: "Yeah."

"And good morning to you too," she responded cheerfully. "I found something. When can you get here?"

"You still at the office?" I asked.

"Sleep's overrated," she replied.

"I'm on my way," I said, hanging up.

I got out of bed, dressed quickly, brushed the whisky from my mouth and left the room. I thought about waking Justine, but after the previous evening I wasn't sure why I wanted her with me. For her professional insight? Or for something far more personal? It irritated me that she had been right.

I left Justine and Sci sleeping and took a cab from the Nomad to the Madison Building. They could follow me later in the Private staff car.

When I arrived, the office was almost deserted, save for a couple of investigators who were at their desks in their sweat-soaked jogging gear. It was a Sunday, but the Parker case meant we'd called people in. The two early-morning joggers stiffened when they saw me, and we exchanged greetings as I hurried through.

I found Mo-bot in one of the conference rooms. Her gear was spread across a large table along with discarded Chinese takeout boxes, files and handwritten notes. She sat in front of the laptop we'd recovered.

"Morning," Mo-bot said. "I cracked the computer. I also found out who owns the building where we found it. Mahmood Hannan, a Lebanese national who's been living in America for twenty years."

"We need to speak to him," I said.

"I already have. At three forty-seven this morning. He was eager to talk when I threatened to set the IRS on him. Said the warehouse was rented by a company in Belize. The same one that chartered the chopper the assassin used to escape, Antares Futures and Investments."

I was stunned by the revelation. Karl Parker had led us to a building rented by the people who'd killed him.

"See if you can track down the owners of the Belize corporation," I said.

Mo-bot nodded and turned the laptop to face me. "There's some interesting stuff on here." She opened a text document. "This was in a folder marked personal."

I read the document, which amounted to a single sentence.

Sometimes the only way out is a dead end.

KP

It was a bleak message that could have been a suicide note or an admission he'd known he'd been targeted for death. But if he'd known he was a target, why hadn't he done anything about it?

"I also found this," Mo-bot said.

She opened another document from the same folder which contained a web link. She clicked the link and went to an MSNBC page that told the story of Robert Carlyle, a Washington, D.C., financier and fixer. Carlyle had died less than two weeks ago in a single-vehicle car accident. According to the article, his Mercedes S-Class had come off the road at speed and wrapped itself around a tree.

"Is Karl saying this incident is linked to his death?" I asked.

"That was my guess too. I haven't found anything to connect Carlyle to Mr. Parker, but I'll keep looking," Mo-bot said. "There's something else."

She switched back to the document and scrolled down the next page until she came to another link, which took us to the executive biography of Elizabeth Connor, the owner of the *New York Tribune*, one of the city's most successful newspapers. Connor was a reclusive billionaire and a clear-cut member of the 1 percent.

"Any idea how she's involved?" Mo-bot asked.

I studied Connor's photograph and tried to get inside my friend's head. "I think Karl Parker might have just identified the next target."

"There was one other thing on the machine," Mo-bot said, switching to the explorer window.

She opened a text file called "Morgan.txt."

The message was short and simple.

You can't trust the cops. You can't trust the Bureau.
You can't trust the Agency. Your life is in danger.

CHAPTER 28

I WAS ON my way out of the office when I ran into Sci and Justine.

"Early start?" Sci asked as they emerged from the elevator.

"Mo cracked Karl's machine," I replied. "We think he's identified the next target."

"Who?" Justine asked.

"Elizabeth Connor, the owner of the *Tribune*," I said. "I'm on my way to see her now."

"You want company?" Sci asked.

I shook my head. "Mo-bot is looking for links between Karl Parker and Elizabeth Connor, but there was another death Karl pointed us in the direction of: Robert Carlyle—"

"The financier?" Sci interrupted.

"Yeah," I replied. "Car crash twelve days ago. Police say he lost control of the vehicle, but I want you to see whether there was any foul play."

Sci nodded. "I'll get right on it."

He left Justine and me in the lobby, and headed into the main office. We endured a moment of uncomfortable silence.

"Why don't you come with me?" I suggested. "I could use your read on what we know about the killer so far."

Justine hesitated.

"Sure," she said, and we took the elevator to the parking garage. "Where are we going?" she asked as we approached the staff car.

"Elizabeth Connor keeps an office at the *Tribune*. She's there seven days a week. We had no luck reaching her by phone, so I'm going to try the personal touch."

"Irresistible," Justine said, sliding into the driver's seat. She pressed the Nissan's ignition as I got in beside her, but paused for a moment. "Sorry, Jack," she said. "I didn't mean anything ..." She hesitated.

"It was a joke, Justine. I get that," I reassured her. "Nothing's changed between us."

That wasn't true. Revisiting the past last night had altered everything. The easy rapport we usually had was gone, replaced by a sense of awkwardness.

"What's your read on the shooter?" I asked, changing the subject.

She put the car in gear and thought about the question as she drove out of the garage and joined the traffic on East 26th Street.

"The gloves, the disguise and the planning that went into the shooting all suggest someone extremely methodical. The chopper and the size of his support team point to a well-resourced organization," Justine said as we crawled along the frozen street.

"And the Ninety-nine?" I asked.

"If Elizabeth Connor is the next target, that would fit their one percent motive, but terrorist organizations don't spring out of nowhere. The FBI or NSA would have picked up some chatter. Heck, even local police intelligence would have some reference to the group, but there's nothing."

"Which suggests it's a cover," I remarked.

Justine nodded. "Criminal gang, or some other political group hiding their involvement."

"Or a foreign power," I suggested.

Justine nodded. "Motive is key," she observed. "Find out why Karl Parker was killed and the truth of who was behind it will follow."

I nodded and studied her face as she drove. She was as beautiful and smart as ever. She caught me watching her, and smiled. Maybe Karl's death had knocked me off center, but watching her face light up made me want her more than ever.

CHAPTER 29

THE *TRIBUNE'S* OFFICES were located on 6th Avenue in a towering skyscraper that occupied the block between 48th and 49th Streets, a short distance from the *New York Times*. The two papers had a longstanding rivalry which had been exacerbated when Elizabeth Connor had purchased the *Tribune* ten years ago. Taking her cue from Fox News, Connor had shifted the paper's editorial stance, transforming it from broadly centrist into a partisan conservative publication that chased controversy at every opportunity. She'd famously said she'd never rest until every American had been saved from the disease of social liberalism. It had been a brave stance to take in a largely Democrat city, but it had worked and the *Tribune's* circulation had jumped 25 percent since Connor had taken charge.

Justine and I managed to get past the main front desk located on the first floor and made it to the *Tribune's* lobby on the thirty-fifth floor. The paper's editorial position was reflected in the décor of its office. A huge Stars and Stripes hung behind the lobby desk, alongside photos of every Republican president since Eisenhower. A six-foot-high sculpture of a bald eagle stood guard beside the secure double doors that led to the main office. The *Tribune* was a 24/7 operation, and beyond the doors there was no sign of reduced activity because it was a Sunday.

"Good morning," the desk clerk said. He was a smartly dressed guy with the fresh face of someone just out of college. "How can I help?"

"My name is Jack Morgan. This is my colleague Justine Smith. We're from Private, the detective agency, and we'd like to see Elizabeth Connor."

"Do you have an appointment?" he asked.

His smile didn't waver, but his demeanor shifted. Very few people got in to see the reclusive Elizabeth Connor and those who did probably didn't come through the front door.

"We're investigating the death of Karl Parker," I replied. "She's going to want to hear what we have to say."

"Take a seat," the clerk said, pointing us toward a long leather corner couch beneath framed front pages that were stuck to the lobby's bare brick walls.

Justine and I walked over, but we didn't sit; instead we milled around while the clerk made a phone call.

I got partway through a front page from 26 October 1983, broadly supporting President Reagan's intervention in Grenada. The paper's take on events was gentle and measured and a far cry from the partisan editorial of today's editions, but the photo and headline helped sell the narrative that the *Tribune* had always been a deeply conservative newspaper. My reading was interrupted by a silver-haired man in a dark tailored suit that was cut a little too short for him.

"Mr. Morgan," he called out as he stepped through the double doors.

I walked over, and Justine followed, and we exchanged greetings.

"My name's Clancy Fairbourne," the man said. He had a thick Texan drawl. His smooth, angular face looked as though it had been chiseled into shape by skilled plastic surgeons. Like a snake who knows no better, he had a permanent smile fixed to his face.

I disliked the man immediately.

"I'm general counsel for the *Tribune*. Is there something I can help you with?"

"We're investigating the murder of Karl Parker. We'd like to talk to Miss Connor about—"

"Let me stop you there, Mr. Morgan," Clancy said. "Miss Elizabeth Connor denies all knowledge of Karl Parker and if you or any of your associates assert otherwise, she will have no alternative but to take action."

I took a step closer, just to make it clear I wasn't going to be intimidated. "What kind of action?"

"She would be forced to take legal action," he replied.

I smiled. I'd been threatened before, but never had a situation escalated so quickly and without any provocation.

"We believe her life is in danger," Justine said.

"Miss Connor's life is always in danger, little lady," Clancy responded.

"My name is Justine Smith. I'm a forensic profiler with enough experience to spot a front man working hard to neutralize a potential scandal. What's your boss hiding, Mr. Fairbourne?"

"Well, Miss Smith," Clancy said, drawing close to Justine. "I apologize for assuming you were Mr. Morgan's assistant, but it was understandable. You're just so young and pretty."

I felt Justine bristle and stepped between the two of them. This guy was testing my patience and it was clear he was hoping to provoke a response. I just couldn't figure out why. As far as I could tell, Elizabeth Connor wasn't under suspicion of anything.

"A group calling themselves the Ninety-nine has claimed responsibility for the murder of Karl Parker, and we have reason to believe that Miss Connor is next on their list of targets," I said.

"Then I hope you've shared that information with the proper authorities," Clancy replied. "Miss Connor gets threats from the liberal establishment every day, and we take great care to protect her from those. So I hope you won't consider me impolite when I say we have nothing more to talk about." Clancy fixed me with a look that was all daggers beneath his big smile. "Even if there was something to discuss, Miss Connor isn't here. Now you'll have to excuse me. The news never stops, not even on the Lord's day. You know your way out, Mr. Morgan, Miss Smith."

Clancy headed for the office and Justine and I watched him leave. Puzzled, I called an elevator.

"What just happened?" Justine asked as we stepped inside.

"He just waved the biggest red flag I've ever seen," I replied. "When we got here, I wasn't sure Connor and Karl were connected, but I am now."

"So what next?" Justine asked.

"We're going to talk to Elizabeth Connor and find out exactly what she knows about Karl Parker's death," I said as the elevator doors slid shut.

CHAPTER 30

THE RICH SMELL of solyanka soup announced Leonid's arrival before he rounded the corner. Dinara was sitting at her desk in Private Moscow's open-plan office on the second floor of the Schechtel Building on Lyalin Lane, a street of beautiful old residences that had been robbed of their majesty by the revolution. Grand old villas had been turned into industrial yards, and ornate apartment blocks had been converted into functional offices. The Schechtel Building was a Russian Revival villa, an imposing, traditional structure of columns and arches that looked more to Russia's past than its future. The lease had been agreed by Lev Vesnin, the former Russian Army officer who used to run Private Moscow, and Dinara longed for the day she could leave the dilapidated offices and move to surroundings that were more in keeping with Private's cutting-edge international brand.

The office was just one of many issues that had resulted in Lev falling out with Jack Morgan. The most significant source of contention was Private Moscow's precipitous decline in fortunes. At its peak, the Moscow office had employed twenty-three people, but by the time Dinara joined, they were down to two investigators and Elena Kabova, the middle-aged administrator and office manager, who kept everything ticking over. The two investigators had objected to working for a woman and left, so Dinara had hired Leonid to replace them. Business hadn't picked up enough to employ anyone else.

Dinara couldn't help feeling as though the Yana Petrova case was her last roll of the dice. If they didn't solve Petrova's murder, the office would have to close. Jack Morgan couldn't keep subsidizing them forever.

Leonid sauntered over with a plastic bag full of food containers.

"One solyanka," he said, taking out a plastic bowl and wooden spoon.

Elena left her desk in the little corner space they'd turned into a lobby, and joined them.

"Solyanka with chilli sauce," Leonid said, handing her another container and spoon.

"Thanks," Elena said.

Dinara had a lot of time for the quiet office manager. She never complained, always smiled, and went out of her way to make their lives easier. Firing Elena would be much harder than letting Leonid go.

Dinara took the lid off her soup and checked the progress of the cracking program Maureen Roth had sent her. It was crunching its way through the laptop they'd discovered in Yana Petrova's apartment, trying to force its way to her password.

Elena and Leonid each sat at an empty desk, and Dinara turned to face them. She'd instituted team lunches in an effort to keep up morale, but now they just seemed like sad little daily interludes, and the three of them often had to search for something they could all talk about. At least they had a case today.

"Any luck?" Leonid asked.

Dinara glanced back at the laptop, which was still refusing to yield to the cracking program. She shook her head.

"It's good to have a case," Elena said. "Even one that's a secret."

Elena's pointed remark wasn't lost on Dinara or Leonid. As their administrator, she'd always had the details of investigations so she could process paperwork and assist with low-level background, but this case was different. Maxim Yenen was connected and if Yana Petrova really was Otkrov, or had some link to the conspiracy blogger, they'd be on extremely dangerous ground. Elena's ignorance might help keep her safe.

"We'll give you the details when we can," Dinara responded. "It's nothing personal, Elena."

A low tone signaled the cracking program had succeeded and Dinara turned to see the laptop come to life. The computer's background image was a photograph of Yana Petrova holding a white card that read, "#IAmOtkrov."

"Otkrov?" Elena asked, craning toward the machine.

"Lots of kids posted pictures of themselves with this hashtag," Dinara noted. "Can you give us a minute?"

Elena picked up her soup and reluctantly returned to the reception area around the corner.

Dinara clicked the Explorer icon and found a list of folders. She opened one called "Completed Cases" and discovered a number of sub-folders. She recognized many of them as significant stories Otkrov had published: a Kremlin corruption scandal; the "truth" behind a nuclear-submarine accident; a military sex ring; and so on. There were other stories Dinara hadn't heard of, but she wasn't an avid follower of Otkrov's blog.

"I recognize some of these," Dinara said.

"Me too," Leonid replied. "Looks like it could be her."

Dinara went up to the main folder level and ran the cursor down the sub-files until she came to one called "Pending Cases." When she clicked the icon, she discovered the Pending Cases sub-folder contained only one file called "Boxing." Dinara opened it and found pages of typed rough notes.

"It looks as though she was investigating match-fixing," Dinara said as she skimmed the text.

Leonid leaned over her shoulder. "She seems to think Spartak Zima threw his world championship title challenge, and that the mob was behind it. Solntsevskaya Bratva, maybe?"

"And they have the means and motive to have killed her," Dinara said.

"The mob ..." Leonid said the word dreamily, as though his mind was elsewhere.

"Problem?" Dinara asked.

He shook his head. "Nothing's ever really a problem. Not if you've got enough firepower."

CHAPTER 31

ELIZABETH CONNOR WAS attending a charity lunch at the Beekman, the luxury hotel where I'd met Karl Parker the morning he'd been shot. Her schedule was closely guarded, but Mo-bot had managed to hack into Connor's assistant's computer.

Justine and I drove south to the hotel and parked the car a block away on William Street. We hurried through the quiet, frozen streets and entered the hotel without incident, but once inside the grand lobby, we saw heightened security everywhere. Hotel guards eyed everyone coming into the traditionally decorated redbrick building, and their presence was augmented by the addition of private security personnel, who were easy to spot with their dark suits and discreet earpieces. They congregated at the edge of the lobby, by the entrance to the first-floor bar, which had been closed to the public.

"This way, honey," I said to Justine, gently steering her toward the bar.

Playing the part of a couple of gawking tourists, we peered past the security personnel into the large space beyond. Dozens of people sat at ornately decorated circular tables, and at the very end of the room was a long table on a raised dais where twenty VIP guests sat. Elizabeth Connor was seated in the middle of the table and had two guards standing behind her, flanking either side. The room was a beautiful example of nine-teenth-century architecture, with tiled mosaics, decorative arches and wood paneling everywhere. But the most impressive feature was the nine-story atrium that was capped by a huge skylight. The balustrades of the nine balconies that overlooked the bar were made of ornate metalwork, and wherever you looked there was a beautiful feature to catch the eye.

"Can I help you, sir?" one of the suited men asked as we spied what was happening inside.

"We were hoping to have a drink at the bar," I said.

"It reopens at five, sir," the man replied.

"Let's go to our room," I said to Justine, and we headed for the elevators.

"It's like they're protecting the President. How do we get to her?" Justine asked.

"I'm working on it," I replied, calling the elevator.

We stepped inside one of the three cars and I looked at our reflections in the smoked mirrors. I was in a lounge suit, and Justine wore a pullover and jeans. We were hardly dressed for a high-society lunch.

The elevator doors opened on the seventh floor and we moved along the corridor to the rectangular balcony that edged the atrium and overlooked the bar. The lunch was in full flow and the hubbub cascaded up to the skylight. I caught sight of a chambermaid in one of the corridors leading off the balcony. She was at her housekeeping trolley, going over a checklist. I put my arm around Justine and started tickling her playfully as we moved toward the chambermaid.

"What the—?" Justine said. "Get off me."

She pushed me away, and I collided with the chambermaid, knocking her into her trolley.

"I'm so sorry," I said.

"That's OK, sir," the chambermaid responded as I steadied her.

"What the hell was that?" Justine asked as we walked on.

"A little misdirection," I said. "Sorry."

I showed her the maid's keyring, which included a hotel master key.

"Nicely done," Justine remarked.

We went round a corner and found a double door marked "Service Area." The chambermaid's master key got us inside a twelve-by-twelve-foot space that contained racks of linen and a couple of housekeeping trolleys. There was also a service elevator, which I called using the stolen key card. Justine and I stepped inside and I pressed the button for the first floor.

We descended in silence and as the floors counted down, my body crackled with anticipation. We had no idea where the elevator would bring us out, but I was almost certain there would be a guard posted nearby, and if we couldn't bluff our way past, I'd have to take a more direct approach. I looked at Justine and could read the tension on her face. She offered the faintest smile, but it was forced through layers of stress.

"It's going to be OK," I told her, steeling myself as we reached the ground floor.

The doors slid open, and we stepped into mayhem.

Staff were running through a vast kitchen and a couple of close-protection personnel were trying to maintain order by a set of double doors. Guests were screaming and pouring through the doors, joined by servers and other hotel staff. Justine and I pushed against the flow of people until we were able to see into the atrium bar.

At the far end of the chamber, on the raised dais, a crowd had gathered around the chair at the center of the table.

"She's dead," I heard a voice say. "Elizabeth Connor is dead."

Instantly, I searched for an anomaly. Most staff and guests were streaming out of the bar through the main exit or the kitchen, where we were, but there was one waiter on the other side of the room who only started to move when he heard that pronouncement. His face was unfamiliar, unnatural and distorted by a prosthetic mask, and when he caught sight of me, I saw a flash of recognition in his eyes.

It was the man who'd killed Karl Parker.

I started running, and an instant later so did he.

CHAPTER 32

I RAN ACROSS the room as the assassin made it to a fire door. He glanced over his shoulder and caught sight of me through the crush of people. I held his gaze for a moment before he sprinted into the corridor and the fire door slammed shut. I fought my way through the noisy crowd and followed.

The corridor was capped by another fire door and when I stepped beyond it I could hear street noise and saw a fire exit, which was wide open. The assassin had fled the building. I sprinted toward the sound of an engine rumbling in the snow-filled alley. I cast around for a weapon and spotted a CO_2 fire extinguisher near the door. I grabbed it as I raced outside.

I burst into an alleyway and was immediately confronted by a Dodge Challenger racing toward me. The assassin was in the passenger seat. He was being driven by a man whose face was covered by a skull mask.

The car's engine roared and its wheels spun on ice as it surged forward. I hurled the heavy extinguisher at the windshield and leaped back through the fire exit as the metal canister smashed the glass. The car collided with the fire door, clipped the hotel wall and veered across the alleyway before striking the adjacent building and coming to an abrupt stop.

I ran through ice and slush and crossed the freezing alleyway. The driver was trying to get out, but I grabbed the fire extinguisher that had fallen beside the car and shoved the nozzle through the open door and pulled the trigger. The car, already white with airbags and silicon dust, filled with gas and foam.

The sound of a gunshot rattled off the walls and a bullet shattered the driver's window. A voice yelled in what sounded like Russian.

As I jumped back, the door swung open and the masked driver leaped out, gun in hand. He pointed the pistol at me, but I moved in and knocked the weapon away. The gun hit the ground and skidded across the alley, disappearing into a deep drift.

Another gunshot from the assassin's pistol sent me dodging back. The driver rushed forward and tackled me hard. We barreled back out of control and I lost my footing when the two of us tumbled through the open fire exit into the corridor beyond. We hit the deck hard.

Outside, I saw the assassin slide into the driver's seat, but there was nothing I could do about him. The masked driver was on me and it took all my energy to block his ferocious blows.

I heard the engine roar and glanced beyond my formidable opponent to see the Dodge speed along the alleyway, heading for Beekman Street.

CHAPTER 33

I KNEED THE driver in the gut and he tumbled forward and rolled off me. I snapped to my feet and aimed a punch at his head, but he turned and I caught his shoulder. He fell backwards and I ran into the alleyway to see the Dodge's burning taillights arc round the corner and vanish north on Beekman Street. I had no hope of catching the assassin, but the getaway driver was still within my reach.

I ran into the building to find him on his feet, sprinting along the corridor. He burst through the fire door leading inside and bounded up the stairs. I raced after him and shoved the fire door so hard the sound of it crashing into the wall startled the man. He glanced down at me from one flight up, and redoubled his efforts. I bounded up the steps two at a time, and pushed myself off the wall when I came to the first landing. The driver was a little over a flight above me, and I could hear his labored breaths between his pounding steps. He was getting tired and I was gaining on him.

We ran on, climbing the stairs at a punishing pace. My legs burned and my lungs screamed at me to stop, but there was no way I was giving in. This man was a living connection to the assassin who'd murdered my friend. I pushed myself on and finally closed the gap when we reached the landing between the seventh and eighth floors.

He glanced over his shoulder, saw me coming and tried to lash out with a kick, but mistimed it, so I sidestepped his attempt and surged forward, grabbed him around his midriff and put my bodyweight against it. He toppled over and hit the deck and we got right to it.

I drove a fist into his face as he tried to get up, and he went down again, but he wasn't out. He sprang to his feet and caught me with a knee to the ribs that knocked the wind from my chest. I stepped back and he scrambled up the steps. This was no street brawler. Some of his moves were Krav Maga; others were aikido. Not the repertoire of a political activist.

I raced on, following him up the stairs, and when he reached the eighth floor he yanked the fire door open and sprinted into the carpeted corridor beyond. I chased him through one of the hotel's executive floors and he tried to block the corridor by pulling over marble-topped tables and pot plants. I jumped the obstacles and followed him into a stairwell on the other side of the building. As I bounced off the bannister, I heard a voice yell, "Jack!"

I glanced over the rail and saw Justine a long way down.

I sprinted on. We were near the roof now, and I heard the metallic rattle and clang of the stairwell door opening. I ran up the last flight and burst through the metal fire door onto a wide, flat roof.

A blinding flash and an explosive ringing in my ears told me I'd been hit, even before the pain started, and as I staggered forward, I turned to see the driver wielding a chair, taken from a stack behind the stairwell. He swung again, but I jumped out of range. I slipped on a layer of ice that lay beneath the soft powder covering the rooftop, and my sudden stumble saved me from another blow. As the chair whipped over my head, I powered forward and tackled my assailant. He fell backwards and dropped the chair as he hit the deck. I punched him in the ribs and the second time I did it, I felt something crack, and he yelped in pain.

I swung again, but he kicked me, catching me in the chest. I staggered back and he got to his feet. I grabbed the chair and drove its legs forward. One of them struck him in the face like a pool cue and his nose gushed blood. He pulled his mask off and I saw the mess he was in. His face was bloodied and he'd lost a number of teeth. His eyes were rolling and he was having trouble focusing.

"It's over," I said.

He wiped his bloodied face with his hand and I noticed the scar of an old bullet wound on his cheek. This was a man who'd survived being shot in the face.

"It's never over," he said with a grotesque grin. As with the assassin, there was no mistaking this man's Russian accent.

He fumbled in his pocket for something, and, thinking he was going for a weapon, I lashed out with the chair. One of the legs caught him on the ear and he dropped whatever had been in his hand as he stumbled. I looked down and saw something small and black in the snow. A plastic square about the size of a book of matches. The driver was looking at it too. He tried to lunge for it, but I hit him again and he fell back.

"Give up," I said.

He reached a decision and suddenly ran away from me, toward the giant rooftop skylight that hung over the bar.

"No!" I yelled.

He jumped, sailed through the air and crashed into the skylight. The glass shattered, the frame splintered, and I ran over and watched him flailing as he fell nine stories and smashed into one of the ornately decorated banquet tables far below.

CHAPTER 34

I DROPPED THE chair, picked up the small black device and ran to the fire door. I raced into the building, down the fire stairs and into the eighth-floor guest corridor. I could hear commotion rising through the huge atrium and pressed the elevator call button. Burning with adrenalin, I paced the elevator lobby and caught my breath. I looked over the edge of the balcony and saw a crowd gathered around the fallen man's body. Snow was being blown off the roof through the hole in the skylight, glinting as it floated down toward him.

The elevator tone sounded its arrival and I hurried over to the middle car and waited impatiently for the doors to slide open. I stepped inside and hit the button for the ground floor. The ride down seemed to take an age and I used the time to study the square device the driver had dropped. There were two buttons and a small LCD screen that reminded me of an old calculator. I pressed the buttons, but nothing happened. What was this thing? Why had he been reaching for it?

I glanced in the mirror. My eyes were wild, my hair disheveled and my face dirty and bruised. My right ear was glowing red, the legacy of where I'd been caught by the chair. My clothes were soaked with melted snow, and covered in stains. I certainly didn't look like a winner, and the loss of the assassin and the driver meant I didn't feel like one either. As the adrenalin subsided, aches and pains began to make themselves known.

When the doors opened, I rushed across an almost deserted lobby to the bar, where I found a few uniformed members of staff and a couple of well-to-do guests milling around near the entrance. Police and paramedics were on scene. One team was clustered by the long table at the podium. Another group had surrounded the Russian driver, who was spread-eagled in the wreckage of the collapsed table.

"Jack!" Justine called out from across the room.

She ran over and surprised me by throwing her arms around me.

"I thought it was you," she said. "When I first saw him, I thought it was you."

She looked up, and tears glistened in her eyes.

"It's OK," I said. "Take this." I handed her the black device. "Give it to Mo. See if she can figure out what it is."

"I've got a pulse," a voice announced.

Justine and I turned to the group around the driver, and sensed new urgency from the paramedics. I pushed my way through the gathered people and was soon beside the injured man. His eyes were glazed, and flecks of blood and spittle were rasping from his mouth with each labored breath. He didn't have long.

"We've got to get him out of here," the attending paramedic said. "Bring over the gurney."

Another medic ran for a gurney that was parked by the lobby entrance. I'd seen enough endings to know the Russian had the cold shadow of death on him. It was now or never.

I sensed collective shock and disbelief as I knelt beside the injured man and grabbed his collar.

"Who sent you? I demanded.

The paramedic tried to push me away. "Hey! What the hell do you think you're doing?"

I resisted, and kept my focus on the Russian. "Who sent you?" I repeated.

I felt hands on me, but I fought their pull and pressured the driver.

"Tell me!" I yelled.

The man muttered something in Russian and his eyes focused briefly.

"Get off him!" an angry voice yelled, and it was joined by others.

The hands were pulling harder now. I couldn't resist for much longer.

"Give me a name!" I demanded.

The driver smiled darkly.

"Who's next? Who's your next target?" I pressed my hand against his broken ribs, and the sudden jolt of pain brought the getaway driver out of his stupor.

"You've failed, American," he moaned. "You've failed."

I was hauled off the dying man and heard one of the uniformed cops utter the words, "You have the right to remain silent," as hard steel was tightened around my wrists.

CHAPTER 35

"WE ARE THE Ninety-nine. Elizabeth Connor's time is at an end and her riches will go to others. We will continue to strike at the one percent, and you must choose: your money or your lives. If you want off our list, unburden yourself of your deadly wealth. We are the Ninety-nine and we shall punish all those who live so greedily while others starve and suffer."

The masked man sat in front of a large anarchy symbol, a new innovation since the last video. His voice was disguised and the table in front of him prevented an accurate assessment of his size and weight.

Rick Tana, the NYPD detective leading the investigation into Karl Parker's murder, minimized the window and pushed the tablet computer to one side. We were in the same interview room in One Police Plaza that I'd been taken to after the shooting at the Stock Exchange.

"Hotel surveillance footage corroborates your story," Tana said. "And this video has sent the media into a tailspin. Fringe groups like the League of Radical Communists are saying this is the beginning of a second American revolution."

"It's bullshit," I replied. "It's a smokescreen. The assassin is methodical and highly trained, and the getaway driver was an expert in martial arts. This Ninety-nine cover is designed to confuse and divide."

"Well, it's working," Tana remarked. "Talk radio is full of people calling in saying these guys have a point. How come so many people have so much?"

"My buddy worked his whole life for everything he had," I snapped. "Just like me. Just like you."

I took a breath and tried to let go of my anger at the divisive politics.

"We're working on identifying the getaway driver, the motor-cyclist who died outside the Stock Exchange, and the three killed in the helicopter crash, but so far we've come up blank," Tana said.

"Did the getaway driver say anything to you before he died?" Tana asked.

The Russian had passed away en route to the hospital.

"No," I said, inwardly cursing myself for not having done more to prevent the guy jumping.

Tana sighed. "Since your story checks out, there's no reason for me to hold you."

"I told you that three hours ago," I countered, but some of my pent-up tension ebbed away. Tana wasn't a bad cop; he was just doing his job.

"If you keep showing up at murder scenes, we'll keep bringing you in," Tana said.

"I like our little talks, but maybe try to catch the killer next time?" I said, getting to my feet.

Tana walked me through the building to central booking, where Justine waited with Jessie Fleming and Mo-bot.

"Are you OK, Jack?" Justine asked. She looked far more composed than when I'd last seen her.

I nodded.

"Stay in touch, Mr. Morgan," Tana said, before walking away.

"The Ninety-nine claimed responsibility again," Jessie said.

"I think that's a smokescreen. The guy I fought was trained in martial arts, and he spoke with a Russian accent," I responded. "It feels like a foreign intelligence operation."

"This little doohickey you found would back up that theory," Mo-bot said, producing the small black device the getaway driver had dropped. "It's a satellite communicator, encrypted and daisy-chained to a network of other devices."

"English," I said a little too tersely.

Mo-bot feigned hurt. "It's like a pager," she replied. "But instead of a phone number, it sends a set of coordinates. My guess is your man was planning to destroy it before he jumped. Someone tried a remote wipe, but I was able to recover the data from the drive. Four sets of coordinates. Robert Carlyle's headquarters in DC, Karl Parker's in New York, and Elizabeth Connor's office on Sixth Avenue."

"A list of targets," Justine remarked.

Mo-bot nodded. "My guess is they get a new set of coordinates when they make a kill."

"A hit squad," I suggested. "But how do they know who their
target is?"

"The identity must come separately. Or maybe they already
know who they need to kill, they just don't know where the
target is located," Mo-bot replied.

"You said there were four sets of coordinates," I remarked.

"The data packet time stamp shows the latest set was sent
just after news of Elizabeth Connor's death broke," Mo-bot revealed. "The next target is based at the American embassy in
Moscow."

CHAPTER 36

GROM BOXING, THE home of Spartak Zima. The huge sign didn't offer even the slightest concession to subtlety. Spartak's head and sweaty torso must have been at least thirty feet high, and next to the flashy red text was the huge image of his jewel-encrusted Russian title belt. The gigantic billboard was fixed to the side of a converted Soviet-era redbrick warehouse that loomed over Leonid's car.

Dinara and Leonid had spent the day trawling the files on Yana Petrova's computer. There seemed little doubt the dead customer-service agent was Otkrov. The admin folder contained log-in details for Otkrov's servers and information on the no-torious blogger's secure communications tools. The only open case had been the investigation into match-fixing, and Yana's notes had identified Makar Koslov, Spartak's trainer, as a person of interest. When they'd got up to speed on the background of the investigation—the alleged throwing of a world title bout with heavyweight champion Larry Kenler—they'd driven across Moscow to Tagansky, a working-class neighborhood southeast of the city.

Dinara pulled her coat collar tight as she stepped into the bitter night. Moscow seemed to grow colder with each passing winter. Or perhaps age was eroding her resilience?

You're only thirty-three, she told herself, stowing her dark thoughts as she hurried across the busy parking lot. Leonid was a couple of paces behind.

They stepped through a large metal door into a lobby that was decorated in an industrial style that majored on exposed brickwork, ducts and copper piping. There was no one at the front desk, so Dinara went through a set of double doors and entered the gym.

There were more than thirty boxers training on maize balls, heavy bags and ropes, and sparring in the ring. They all had closely shaved heads and the same hunger in their eyes. A few of those nearest turned as Dinara walked into the room, and they stared at her with undisguised hostility.

Spartak Zima wasn't in the gym, but Dinara recognized his trainer, Makar Koslov, from the photos on Yana's computer. The former middleweight champion was leaning over the ropes, shouting instructions to the duo sparring in the ring. Koslov was a long way from his fighting prime. A large gut strained the seams of his Grom Boxing T-shirt, and his black sweatpants clung to a couple of tree-trunk legs. Narrow eyes, a broken nose and permanent fat lip did little to enhance the looks of a man whose broken face had taken far too many beatings. He wiped a hand over his bald head and, when one of his fighters gestured toward Leonid and Dinara, he glanced over.

Koslov stepped down from the ring. "Yes?" he said.

"We're investigating a murder," Leonid replied. "We'd like to ask you some questions."

Koslov sneered, but Dinara's eyes shifted beyond him. The young boxer who'd pointed them out hurried into the far corner of the room where another trainer sat with a gray-haired man who wore a black jacket and a matching black T-shirt that had the number "100" outlined against the dark background. It was subtle, but those who understood its significance would know the man was a member of the Black Hundreds, an old ultra-nationalist group that had recently been revived by a group of self-proclaimed patriots. Dinara had received briefings on the Black Hundreds while at the FSB. They had a lot of former priests, politicians and soldiers in their ranks, and commonly used boxing gyms and football and martial arts clubs as recruiting grounds.

"Who are you? Either you're a cop who's here without authority," Koslov remarked, closing on Leonid, "or you're someone who shouldn't be here at all."

"I'm interested in joining. I think I've got what it takes to become a champion," Leonid replied, toeing the line with the former middleweight champion of Russia. "So far I'm not impressed with how you welcome prospective members."

Koslov glowered, and Dinara stepped between the two men.

"Makar, I'll attend to this. Get back to your training."

Dinara glanced over the large man's shoulder and saw the silver-haired member of the Black Hundreds approach. He had the upright posture of a military man, and the cold eyes of someone who couldn't care less about the feelings of those around him.

Koslov backed away, eying Leonid until he reached the ring.

"Keep working," he yelled at the two sparring fighters, who'd paused to watch.

The men resumed trading blows.

"This is a members' only gym," the silver-haired man said. "And we're not accepting new applications."

"And you are?" Dinara asked.

"If you don't already know, it means you're not meant to," the man replied.

"Is that some kind of parable?" Dinara countered.

"It's a truth," he replied. "We welcome friends here." He looked them up and down. "And I don't think you're friends."

"We're investigating a murder," Dinara said.

"A terrible sin," the man replied. "I was a priest before I found a better way to reach my flock. I know all about sin."

"I'm sure you do," Leonid said.

"But I know nothing about murder," the man remarked without missing a beat. It was as though Leonid hadn't spoken. "So if there's nothing else, I must insist you leave."

"You haven't even asked us who was killed," Dinara observed.

"Because I don't know about any murder," the man said.

He stepped closer to Dinara and tried to jostle her back. She could feel Leonid bristle, and sensed a shift in the atmosphere.

She glanced past the silver-haired man to see every fighter in the place watching them.

"Come on," Dinara told Leonid. "Let's go."

She tried to move her partner, but he held firm and glared at the Black Hundreds member. Finally, Leonid gave ground and allowed himself to be ushered to the door. Dinara felt the boxers' hostile eyes on her as they left the room.

"You should have let me—" Leonid began.

"No need," Dinara cut him off. She flashed the wallet she'd lifted from the man's pocket. "Erik Utkin," she said, reading from the identity card she found inside. "Let's do our research before we do our fighting."

She used her phone to take pictures of the man's ID, bank card and old Army personnel pass, before tossing everything in the snow.

"At least now we know who we're dealing with," Dinara said.

Leonid smiled. "We might make an investigator of you yet," he said, and Dinara punched him playfully as they headed for his car.

CHAPTER 37

DINARA COULD SEE flecks of congealed white fat in every mouthful. She didn't understand how Leonid could face cold solyanka soup, but he often finished their lunchtime leftovers whenever they worked late. He was leaning back in his chair and had his feet on his desk as he dug into the remnants of Elena's bowl. The office administrator was long gone, but she knew better than to throw away her leftovers if Leonid was working a case.

Dinara's phone rang and she answered the call from Anatoli Titov, an old FSB contact.

"Anatoli," she said, forcing herself to sound pleased to hear from him. "What have you got?"

Anatoli had had a thing for her when they'd both worked counterterrorism, and he'd since married and had a child, but the way he'd responded to her flirtatious request for a favor suggested the flame of desire hadn't quite been extinguished.

"I have got something," he replied. "Erik Utkin is a former army captain who was pensioned out with an injury he picked up in Chechnya. He retrained as a priest, but quit the church three years ago to join the Black Hundreds as a recruiter. We think he's connected to some small-time criminals."

"Anything else?"

"Always greedy. How about we get together for a drink?"

"Now who's greedy?" Dinara asked. "Aren't you married?"

"So?" Anatoli said. "You wouldn't ask a man to eat dinner at the same restaurant for the rest of his life."

"You're lucky you're not starving," Dinara replied.

Anatoli scoffed and was about to speak, but she cut him off.

"Thank you, Anatoli. I owe you a professional favor."

She ignored his grumbling and hung up.

"Well?" Leonid asked, wiping his mouth with the back of his hand.

"Former army captain, former priest, maybe a minor criminal," Dinara replied.

"Minor, as far as they know," Leonid observed.

Dinara nodded. The FSB was thorough, but it wasn't omniscient. There was a thin line between minor and major crime, and the murder of a blogger would definitely buy someone passage across it.

"What now?" Leonid said.

"Asking for guidance? It's almost as if you finally recognize me as your superior."

"I was talking to the soup," he replied, gesturing with his spoon.

"We run surveillance on Erik Utkin and see what he's really hiding," she replied, but before she could go any further, her phone rang, and the words "Private New York" flashed on screen.

"Hello," she said in English.

"Dinara? It's Jessie Fleming of the New York office."

Dinara hadn't had much contact with the head of the New York branch but she recognized the name.

"Sorry to call on a Sunday, but it's an emergency."

"No problem. I'm in the office too," Dinara replied. Her FSB training had made her fluent in four languages, and, next to Russian, English was her favorite. "What's going on?"

"Check your email," Jessie said. "Call me if there are any problems."

"Will do," Dinara said, before hanging up.

"What was that? Leonid asked.

Dinara woke her laptop and logged into the company's encrypted email server. "We weren't on a secure line, so she couldn't tell me what it was about." After entering her personal decryption key, she read the message Jessie had sent her, and leaned back in her chair. "He's coming to Moscow," she said.

"Who?" Leonid asked.

"Jack Morgan."

CHAPTER 38

THE WOMAN ACROSS the aisle was dreaming. Her eyelids flickered and she muttered something in her sleep. Her face was in shadow, which gave her a ghostly appearance, and her body was tucked beneath one of the blankets I'd refused. I was too busy reviewing the case file Sci had prepared to even consider resting. I was also waiting for a call on the satellite phone Mo-bot had given me.

We were investigating three deaths. Robert Carlyle, a Washington fixer and financier who'd been killed in a car crash, Karl Parker, shot in the New York Stock Exchange, and Elizabeth Connor, who it seemed had been poisoned by a man posing as a hotel waiter. There was no apparent link between the three victims, other than their wealth, which made the Ninety-nine's claims of responsibility plausible. Except they hadn't taken credit for Robert Carlyle, and the only thing connecting him to

Karl Parker and Elizabeth Connor were the clues left on Karl's secret laptop. As far as we could tell, they'd never met, nor had they ever done business together.

Sci was going to Washington, D.C., to review the evidence from the scene of Carlyle's crash. Justine had driven me to the airport to catch that day's last commercial flight to Moscow. For a moment my attention drifted from the investigation to the memory of her reaction at the hotel. Her relief, the tenderness of her embrace and the tears in her eyes all told me she still felt something beyond friendship. She'd wanted to come to Moscow, but I needed her in New York, working with Jessie and Mo-bot to identify the dead getaway driver and chase down links between the three dead victims.

My satellite phone vibrated and I answered the call. At altitude, the signal was clear and didn't suffer with the interference issues often caused by trees and buildings.

"Mr. Morgan, this is Master Gunnery Sergeant Marlon West. I got a message to call you."

West was the commander of the Marine Corps security detachment at the US embassy in Moscow. I'd reached out to him via Lieutenant Colonel Edward Frost, an old buddy, who was now stationed in Frankfurt and ran the Marine Corps Embassy Security Group for Eastern Europe.

"Master Sergeant West, I'm calling to make sure you got the intelligence regarding a possible attempt on the ambassador's life," I said quietly.

When Mo-bot had revealed the location of the next target, I'd called Detective Tana and shared the information on the understanding he alerted the State Department. We were working on the assumption the next target was Ambassador Thomas Dussler, the President's high-profile billionaire appointment to Moscow.

The woman opposite me shifted in her sleep, but none of the other passengers in the first-class cabin gave any sign the call was disturbing them.

"We received a flash alert, yes," West replied. "And we're taking steps."

"Good," I replied, relieved the message had got through. Tana seemed honest, but I wasn't taking any chances.

"Is that everything, Mr. Morgan?" West asked.

"Yes," I replied. "Sorry to have troubled you."

"No problem," West said. "Lieutenant Colonel Frost speaks very highly of you, and I appreciate the vigilance."

He hung up and I returned to the case file Sci had prepared. As I studied the notes, I prayed the ambassador would be alive when I reached Moscow. Right now, he was my only link to the man who'd killed my friend.

CHAPTER 39

WHEN DINARA LEFT her apartment building, she found Leonid using the EMF detector to sweep his car for bugs. A steady flow of morning traffic rolled though the gray snow and swerved round Leonid's Lada, which had two wheels propped on the pavement.

"Anything?" Dinara asked as she approached.

Leonid shook his head. "And no eyes on us either," he said, glancing round the frozen square in front of Dinara's building.

"At least none you can see," Dinara remarked playfully as she climbed in the passenger seat.

Leonid put the EMF detector in the boot and got behind the wheel.

"Any word on what brings Jack Morgan to Moscow?" he asked as he started the engine.

"No," Dinara said.

Maybe this was it. The final visit to thank her for her efforts and shut down the office.

"Don't look so nervous," Leonid said, pulling into traffic. "If it was bad news, he would have emailed."

Dinara smiled as the Lada headed north toward the Garden Ring. A few minutes later, they were crawling along the wide beltway with hundreds of other slow-moving vehicles.

"I checked with an old friend," Leonid said. "Grom Boxing is paying for police protection."

"How high up does it go?" Dinara asked.

"My friend doesn't know."

"Then it's high."

"You're as smart as you are beautiful," Leonid quipped.

"And you're as condescending as you are arrogant," Dinara replied. "Why would a boxing gym need high-level police protection?"

"We could be finding out, if we weren't busy taxiing the big American," Leonid muttered.

"Otherwise known as our boss."

"If you want to get technical," Leonid scoffed.

They drove north toward Sheremetyevo International Airport, and passed the time discussing what little they knew about Yana Petrova. Dinara had spent much of the night going through the blogger's computer, trawling Yana's extensive background research for each of her published articles for anything that might point them toward a suspect.

"She was unremarkable in school," Leonid said. He'd dug into Yana's background. "Her reports say she showed no aptitude for

anything, and she took a mundane job with Moesk after gradu-
ating with a degree in economics from St. Petersburg Polytechnic.
Nothing about her says enemy of the state."

"Which is why she went undetected for so long," Dinara
observed.

They continued discussing Yana and speculating about her
fight-fixing investigation. After forty minutes, they reached the
MKAD, the outer beltway, and joined it heading west. The rush-
hour traffic had eased up, but the highway was one of the main
routes to the airport, and was always busy. The winter storm
had only made things worse.

They turned off at junction 79, and drove along a narrow
furrow that had been plowed between two cliffs of frozen snow
to join the slip road.

Out of nowhere, a truck appeared alongside them, tearing
through the snow, spraying it everywhere.

"Hold on," Leonid said, the instant before the truck side-
swiped them.

The Lada spun into the drift to their right and careened
wildly out of control before coming to a sudden halt when it
crashed into the metal safety barrier. The airbags popped and
Dinara's training kicked in.

Move, she thought, *keep moving.*

Everything was white, and her head was pounding, but she
reached for the handle and pushed the door open. Her senses
returned and she saw a gang of men in ski masks emerge from
the back of the truck that had hit them. The men ran toward
her, and one held a gun, but it wasn't pointed at Dinara. She

turned to see Leonid emerge from the battered driver's side of the Lada, and realized he was the target. His head was bloody and he took two faltering steps before the masked gunman shot him three times in the chest.

Leonid fell back into the thick snowdrift and Dinara's world spun as she registered the full horror of what was happening.

Gloved hands grabbed her and she tried to fight them off. As she struggled against the three men who were dragging her away, she caught the cuff of one of their gloves and saw a tattoo she recognized. It was a snake wrapped around a dagger, and she had last seen it on the wrist of one of the fighters who'd been sparring in the ring at Grom Boxing.

"Help! Help me!" Dinara shouted to the onlookers, who'd started to emerge from the line of cars backed up behind the crash.

The gunman brandished his pistol. "Stay back," he yelled, and no one argued with him.

How had I not noticed the truck? Dinara asked herself as the strong men dragged her toward the waiting vehicle. The gunman jogged behind her, and she stared into his eyes, swearing they would witness her revenge.

CHAPTER 40

DINARA GLANCED OVER her shoulder to see a female driver yelling at other onlookers.

"Stop them! What's the matter with you? Help her!"

"He's got a gun," a nearby motorist shouted back.

No one was going to help her and Dinara couldn't blame them. There were two masked men waiting by the back of the truck and three hauling her toward them. There was a driver and an accomplice in the cab, and then there was the shooter, the man who'd killed Leonid. This was a formidable, organized group. If she was to escape, she would have to save herself.

Dinara lashed out, kicking the man immediately to her left. She caught him in the shin and he let go of her. She swung her fist at the man to her right, but he dodged it, and she heard rapid footsteps crunching in the snow, and felt the muzzle of a gun pressed against her temple.

"Be good," the gunman said.

The man she'd kicked slapped her, and took hold of her arm. She looked at him defiantly, memorizing another set of eyes that would one day look upon her revenge.

The gunman took the muzzle away, and the men continued pulling her toward the truck. She wanted to scream with grief and anger, but she refused to give her assailants the satisfaction of seeing how much they'd hurt her, so she stayed grimly silent.

The gunshot shocked Dinara and startled the men holding her. She couldn't believe what she was seeing when the gunman went down with a bullet wound in his leg. Then she looked round to see Leonid standing there, seemingly back from the dead, with gun drawn. Dinara was astonished, but this grim-faced Lazarus seemed unaffected by his journey to the other side, and carried on with his dirty work.

Leonid shot the man to Dinara's left, and the bullet hit him in the leg, almost exactly where she'd kicked him. He fell away, moaning and clutching the wound. Another shot hit the man to her right in his left arm, and Dinara pulled free of him as he cried out in pain.

The gunman was hauling himself up, and Dinara lunged for him and wrestled him for his weapon. As they struggled, Leonid rushed over and delivered a heavy pistol blow to the head, knocking the gunman out cold.

Leonid grabbed Dinara. "Come on!"

They started running as one of the masked men retrieved the pistol from the unconscious gunman and opened fire. The bullets hit the wreckage of Leonid's Lada as he and Dinara dashed behind it.

"Keep going," Leonid said, dragging Dinara on toward the safety barrier.

They jumped the metal rail, sailed through the air and hit a steep snow-covered bank. Dinara couldn't stop herself; she tumbled forward and rolled down the steep slope. She was dimly aware of a mass of arms and legs falling beside her.

Dizzy and disorientated, she finally came to a halt near a copse of trees and helped Leonid to his feet. They ran for cover as bullets chewed the trunks of the surrounding trees. They ducked behind a large elm and peered up at the slip road.

A couple of the masked men were eying the tree line.

"We have to go after them," Dinara heard one of them say.

"Are you crazy?" the other replied. "The cops are almost here. Help get the guys into the truck."

The speaker withdrew from sight, and a moment later, so did his gun-toting companion.

Dinara took the opportunity to catch her breath.

"How?" she asked between lungfuls of freezing air.

Leonid opened his jacket and pulled his shirt apart to reveal a concealed layer of body armor.

"Some call it paranoia," he said. "I call it common sense."

Dinara stared at him in awe.

"Come on," he said. "We'd better get moving, or we'll be late."

He ran into the trees, and a moment later a bemused but jubilant Dinara followed.

CHAPTER 41

IN THE END, I managed a couple of hours' sleep on the plane, but by the time I arrived, my eyes were gritty and my body ached with the ground-in fatigue that was commonplace after transatlantic flights. But no matter how rough I felt, I knew I didn't look as bad as my two employees. I'd hired Dinara Orlova because she was highly experienced and extremely intelligent. Every time I'd met her she'd been exceptionally composed and immaculately presented. But right now her long dark hair was lank and matted, and her normally flawless skin was scratched and marked by dirt. Her trousers and coat were soaked with ugly stains. Her companion, Leonid Boykov, a grizzled former cop who oozed roguish charm, looked even worse.

I crossed the Sheremetyevo arrivals hall, which was busy with the early-morning crowds associated with the arrival of a flurry of transatlantic red-eye flights. As Dinara and Leonid came to meet me, I noticed the former Moscow cop was scanning the terminal nervously.

"Thanks for coming," I said, shaking Dinara's hand.

"Good to see you, Mr. Morgan," she replied in English. "I'm sorry for our condition. We just escaped an abduction attempt."

"Abduction for you," Leonid said. "Murder for me."

The former cop had been Dinara's hire and I didn't know him well enough to be certain he wasn't joking. I glanced at Dinara, who confirmed the statement with an emphatic nod.

"What the hell happened?" I asked. "Where's the car?"

"About seven kilometers that way," Leonid replied. "Blocking a major exit on the highway."

Dinara frowned at him. "We need to take a taxi."

She ushered me toward one of the doors, and I glanced at Leonid, who was looking from wall to wall, like a bird of prey. As I studied him, I finally registered the holes in his jacket.

"Are those—"

"Yes," he cut me off. "Bullets. Three of them."

"We were lucky," Dinara said.

"A bulletproof vest is not luck," Leonid responded. "It is the correct preparation."

Struggling to get my head around the news, I steered them away from the doors to a quiet part of the arrivals hall where we wouldn't be overheard.

"You'd better tell me what's going on," I said.

With the occasional interjection from Leonid, Dinara briefed me on the death of Yana Petrova, their meeting with the Kremlin-connected oligarch Maxim Yenen, and the discovery of Yana's second life as the conspiracy blogger Otkrov. Then they told me about Grom Boxing and Dinara's belief that one of their assailants was a boxer she'd seen at the gym the previous night. After months in the wilderness, it sounded as though Private Moscow had finally scored a truly challenging case.

"And why are you here?" Leonid asked when Dinara had finished.

I didn't know either of my Russian employees well enough to trust them with full disclosure, but saying nothing would have been counterproductive.

"I'm investigating the murder of Karl Parker," I replied. "He was a friend."

"I'm sorry," Dinara offered.

"I appreciate it," I replied. "We'd better go. It sounds like you've got to clear up this morning's mess."

"Not a problem," Leonid said. "The police in Moscow are experts at making things vanish. My old friends on the force will know how to handle this. As long as I can get my car insurance to pay up. I'm not sure it covers hijacking and gun fights."

"If it doesn't, I'll make sure you don't lose out," I said.

"Thank you, Mr. Morgan," Leonid replied. "That means a lot."

"Not a problem. And please, both of you, call me Jack."

I followed Dinara and Leonid through the terminal and we were soon outside with the ice and snow. I couldn't say whether Moscow or New York was colder. Both had been hit by vicious snowstorms and were still in the grip of a big freeze.

The cab driver took my suitcase and put it in the trunk of his Volkswagen Passat while Dinara and I climbed in the back, and Leonid took the front passenger seat.

The driver jumped behind the wheel and slammed the door. He removed his gloves and blew on his hands, before saying something in Russian.

"Where to?" Dinara translated.

"The American embassy," I replied.

CHAPTER 42

TWO HOURS LATER, I was finally shown into the office of the US Ambassador to Moscow, Thomas Dussler. He was from old Wall Street money and it showed in the traditional furniture and dark bookcases that lined the walls of the room. The décor was out of keeping with the rest of the contemporary nine-story building, which lay in a heavily fortified compound a few miles west of the Kremlin. There was the obligatory photograph of Dussler with the President, and framed artwork that dated from shortly after the Revolutionary War. The antique furniture was designed to impress, as was the view, which took in a few snow-capped high-rise hotels and the Moscow River, but I wasn't much interested in the trappings of power: it was Dussler's life that concerned me.

Master Gunnery Sergeant Marlon West had taken the threat very seriously, but hadn't been able to convince the ambassador to change his schedule in light of the intelligence, and I got the impression I was West's last hope at convincing Dussler to recognize the danger.

"Ambassador," I said.

"Mr. Morgan," he replied, rising from behind his large desk. "I know your firm by reputation. You have quite a record."

"Thank you," I responded. "This is Dinara Orlova, the head of Private Moscow, and one of our investigators, Leonid Boykov."

We'd stopped at the Private Moscow office en route from the airport, so both of them could shower and change. Dinara was in a dark trouser suit, and Leonid wore chinos and a tweed jacket.

"Pleased to meet you," Dussler said, shaking our hands. "Have a seat."

He ushered us toward a long conference table.

"This is my security adviser, Carrie Underwood." He introduced us to a somber woman in a formal navy blue dress. "And you know Master Gunnery Sergeant West."

I nodded at the Marine as Dinara, Leonid and I took seats at the table. West had a hopeful look in his eyes.

"Master Gunnery Sergeant West tells me you're the source of the intelligence report indicating there might be a threat on my life," Dussler remarked with a smile.

"That's right, sir," I replied. "I got the information from a device we found on a man who was involved in the assassination of Elizabeth Connor."

"Tragic," Dussler observed.

"We believe Miss Connor's death is also linked to the shooting of Karl Parker," I said.

"Ah yes, the Ninety-nine," Dussler remarked.

"No, sir," I replied. "I don't think so. The man I apprehended, well, he was Russian."

"And you found my name on this device?"

I hesitated, imagining how this conversation had played out with West. "No, sir," I replied at last.

"Then you don't know I'm the target," Dussler countered.

"You fit the profile, sir," I said.

"Thomas, for the last time, we need to revise some of your engagements." Carrie Underwood's concern was palpable. Another person taking the threat very seriously.

Dussler smiled like a parent indulging a child. He had the superior air of someone who didn't think the world's mundane concerns should trouble him. "And should we jump every time a ghost goes bump in the night?"

"If that ghost is leaving a trail of bodies," I replied.

"What was on this device?" Dussler asked.

"Coordinates," I said. "The coordinates for this embassy."

Dussler sat back and his indulgent smiled widened. "Hundreds of people work here. Even if this information is reliable, the target could be any one of them."

"Mr. Parker, Miss Connor, these were powerful, well-protected people. They were hard targets, just like you, sir," I protested.

Dussler wavered and the confident smile fell for a moment before returning with a fresh shine. "I don't have the luxury of being a private citizen," he said. "I have duties, Mr. Morgan. America is counting on me. I'm sorry, I can't change my schedule because you found the embassy's address on a bad guy's Nintendo." He grinned at his own joke. "Besides, I have my Secret Service detail and Master Gunnery Sergeant West to keep me safe."

"Sir," West began, "there's only so much—"

Dussler interrupted him. "Only so much you can do to protect me. Don't worry, Master Gunnery Sergeant, I won't hold you responsible."

West shook his head with resignation.

"Listen, Mr. Morgan," Dussler said as he stood. "You share what you've got with my chief of staff, Ernie Fisher, and if he recommends changes, I'll listen."

"OK," I said, exchanging a look of defeat with West and Underwood. Dussler was giving us the brush-off.

"Where is Ernie?" the ambassador asked. "He should be in on this."

Dussler crossed the room and opened his office door.

"Where's Mr. Fisher?" he asked the nearest of his three assistants.

"He said he had to go home, sir," the assistant replied. "Mr. Fisher said he'd forgotten something important."

"When was this?" I asked, my hackles rising.

"About an hour ago," the assistant replied. "He should have been back by now."

I turned to West. "Where does Fisher live?"

"About ten minutes away," he replied. "Near Russian Federation House."

"What's going on?" Dussler asked.

"Conspirators fearing exposure often run," I told him.

"Are you serious? Ernie Fisher a conspirator?"

"Or a target," I conceded. "Either way, we've got to check anything out of the ordinary. Can you take me there?" I asked West. He nodded.

"I'm going to put you in lockdown, sir," Underwood said. "Until we know what's going on."

"Leonid, alert the Moscow police. Send them to Fisher's home," I told the former cop as I got to my feet. "Dinara, you're coming with us."

CHAPTER 43

THE PLACE STANK of alcohol, but it was only now that Ernie Fisher registered the full extent of the stench. He was turning over his own apartment, desperately searching for the key that would keep him alive.

You've become sloppy, he told himself. *All your training, all your discipline lost at the bottom of a bottle.*

He'd become a drunk. A functioning one, but a drunk nonetheless. He'd hidden it from the ambassador, but his day job wasn't that demanding. Not compared to his real work, the task he'd spent decades preparing for.

He needed the key. The key he'd hidden years ago when he'd first come to Moscow and taken the grand tenth-floor apartment overlooking the river. It was the key he'd told himself he'd never need.

Ernie pulled books from his shelves. He'd amassed a collection of political history and theory, but had hardly read any of them. But books helped sell the image, and made people think he was a savvy political operator, a high-flying Ann Arbor alumnus who had his finger on the pulse. He tossed the heavy books on the Persian rug he'd bought in the Novopodrezkovo Market, and for the very first time, he saw it with a stranger's eyes. It was covered in stains, tiny droplets spilled during his many vodka-infused rants against how unfair life was. The dark reckonings he held with himself in the early hours, when no one but the witches and wolves were around to hear.

You're losing your mind, he told himself. *Lost. Past tense,* he thought.

He turned from the shelves to an armoire he'd picked up in an antique store on Year 1905 Street. He pulled out the drawers and emptied the contents everywhere. He'd already wasted so much time and was getting desperate. He'd made a cursory search of the apartment and had given up, telling himself he could break into the safe without the key. But when he'd gone to his little bolthole, he'd found the safe impossible to crack and it had chewed up his drill. He'd returned to his apartment, convinced he'd be walking into the jaws of death, but he'd found nothing out of the ordinary, and had resumed his desperate search for the key.

He got on his hands and knees and rummaged through the contents of the drawers, but there was no sign of the key. Frantic, Ernie sat up, ran his fingers through his hair, and dragged them down his face.

"I wasn't expecting to find you so easily," a voice said in English.

The words were like nails on a chalkboard and sent a shiver down Ernie's spine. He turned to face the speaker, and that's when he caught sight of it. A flash of brass, the key taped to the underside of one of the compartments that housed the drawers. His heart leaped. That's where he'd put it all those years ago. He could escape. If he could just get past death's messenger, he could flee.

The man standing in the doorway wore the dark green urban combat uniform of Russian Special Forces. It was common to see such soldiers around Federation House, but what was uncommon was the ski mask covering his face and the tactical vest protecting his torso. Ernie was surprised not to see a gun in the man's hand. Instead, he caught the glint of piano wire looped at either end around the man's gloved hands.

Ernie slowly got to his feet. This man was a trained killer, but so was he.

Older, out of shape, and carrying the weight of drunkenness, he thought.

He was dead either way, but if he fought, at least he'd have a chance, and it was better to die with hope.

"I thought you would have run," the masked man said. "But then, according to our intelligence reports, you have become ineffective. Careless."

Ernie felt the embers of pride flare. He was many things, but he wasn't careless.

You missed your chance to escape because you forgot where you hid the key, he told himself. *You're a drunk. That's as careless as it gets.*

He flushed with embarrassment.

"Will the Ninety-nine claim credit for me?" he asked.

The masked man shook his head. "You are no billionaire, Mr. . . . What shall we call you?"

"Fisher," Ernie said.

"Fisher," the masked man sneered. "You will just be another statistic. A miserable drunk who took his own life. No credit will be claimed."

The embers of pride rose into a fire of indignation. He would not die here in his own apartment at the hands of this arrogant man.

Ernie rushed at the masked man and launched a side kick at his ribs, but his leg was too slow, and his opponent stepped in and wrapped the piano wire around Ernie's neck. He tried to get a hand between the coils, but he wasn't fast enough, and the metal snapped tight and bit into his Adam's apple. The pain was excruciating, and Ernie fought it with everything he had. His arms and legs flailed wildly, but they found no purchase and slowly the pain gave way to numb realization.

There was a noise in the distance. Raised voices and a crash, but the sounds must have been from the memory of a dream, because nothing in Ernie's reality changed, and a moment later his world turned completely dark.

CHAPTER 44

DINARA HAD PICKED the locks on the main entrance to get us into the building, but Ernie Fisher's apartment on the ninth floor was more challenging.

"I can get it. I just need a few minutes," she said as she crouched over a mortise lock that was designed to be impossible to pick.

I could hear the sound of sirens getting closer, and guessed it was the police responding to Leonid's call.

Dinara was making fine adjustments with her lock-picking tools. "If I can just ..." There was a faint snapping sound. "Damn!"

She pulled out a broken single hump Bogota pick, and looked at West and me with pure frustration.

"Stand back," I said, and when Dinara stepped out of the way, I aimed my heel at the lock and kicked hard.

The lock popped, but a full-length security bar prevented the door from opening.

I was convinced I heard movement inside the apartment. "Come on," I said, and West and I put our shoulders to the door and barged with our full combined force. The security bar made a terrible noise as it tore away from the screws embedded deep in the frame.

We burst into the grand apartment and I immediately saw the place had been turned over, and on the far side of the apartment Fisher was hanging by a window that overlooked the Moscow River. A length of piano wire was attached to a curtain rail and the other end was lost in the folds of his neck.

Dinara and West rushed over and started trying to get Fisher down. I was about to join them when a noise caught my attention. I ran into a large kitchen and saw an open door on the other side of the room. I crossed the white tiled floor and approached the door, which led to a metal fire escape. I could hear footsteps echoing off the walls and pulled the door wide. When I stepped through and glanced down, I saw the fire escape was built into a well that cut through the heart of the old building. Tiny balconies joined every apartment to the stairs that ran all the way down to the ground. Many of the balconies were cluttered by washing lines, toys, garden furniture and junk, which would have made escape a nightmare if there ever were a fire. I could see no sign of the source of the noise, so I looked up.

There, frozen almost directly above me, standing next to the balustrade that marked the edge of the roof, was a masked man in special forces gear. We stared at each other and I recognized his eyes. It was the man who'd murdered Karl Parker and Elizabeth Connor in New York.

He drew a pistol and opened fire, forcing me back into Ernie Fisher's kitchen. Bullets flashed off the metal fire escape like tiny bolts of lightning and the thunder crack of the shots echoed around the well. A moment later, the shooting stopped.

"What the hell is happening?" West yelled from the living room, but I didn't hang around to answer.

I ran outside and bounded up the fire escape, racing to the roof. When I reached the top of the stairs, instead of being confronted by the formidable assassin, I found nothing but footsteps in the deep snow. I followed them to the rear of the building and, concealed in a thick drift, I discovered an anchor and tactical rope that vanished over the low concrete barrier that marked the edge of the roof.

I glanced over and saw the assassin completing his rappel down the side of the building. He landed on an unmarked gray van and, in one fluid move, rolled off the roof and slid through the open passenger door onto the front seat. He slammed the door, and the van drove away. I considered the rope and wondered whether there was anything to be gained by following him down using a makeshift abseiling loop. Could I make it down before the van reached the end of the alleyway?

The decision was taken out of my hands.

"*Stoy!*" a voice yelled, and I turned to see three Moscow police officers moving toward me, their guns trained in my direction as they crossed the roof.

I glanced down and burned with frustration as I saw the gray van leave the alleyway and turn right onto the road that ran alongside the vast riverside government complex that was officially known as Federation House.

Once again, the killer had escaped.

CHAPTER 45

I'D HAD THE royal treatment for almost twenty-four hours. The police had cuffed me, and when Dinara had come up to the roof to see what was happening, they'd arrested her too. The cops had tried to take Master Sergeant West, but he'd flashed his diplomatic credentials, which were respected no matter what the state of relations were between Moscow and Washington. No beat cop would risk a diplomatic incident.

Dinara had told me we were being arrested on a murder charge before we were put in separate vehicles and taken away. She'd been pushed into a patrol car, while I'd had a disorientating ride in the back of a windowless van. I don't know if she was taken to the same place as me, but I saw no sign of her when I was booked, stripped of my belongings and left to stew in a cell for the best part of a day and a night.

Finally, late Tuesday morning, the door to my cell opened and a uniformed police officer barked a command in Russian and gestured at me to get off the fold-down metal bunk. If I never saw the rusting toilet, or tasted the overly boiled food ever again, it would be too soon.

I followed the officer through the cell block. He unlocked a clanging metal gate and took me into a long corridor with rooms either side. The cop stopped at the first door and knocked. A voice inside replied in Russian and the cop opened the door and waved me in.

I walked into a windowless interview room and found two women sitting at a metal table that had been scored with graffiti.

"Please sit down, Mr. Morgan," the younger of the two women said. "My name is Anna Bolshova and I am an officer with the Criminal Investigations Department currently assigned to the Interior Ministry."

I had no idea what that meant. Was she a cop? Or a spy? She wore a severe dark blue, almost black jacket, and a pencil skirt. Her companion was an older woman who was in a skirt and blazer that looked as though they could have been beamed from the 1980s. The navy blue jacket had huge shoulder pads, brass buttons and gold brocade, and beneath it was a busy floral blouse.

"This is Zoya Popova, our official translator," Anna said. "My English is good, but just in case."

Zoya looked decidedly unhappy; perhaps she was annoyed at being made redundant.

"Please sit."

Anna gestured at a chair opposite the two of them, and I took a seat.

"No lawyer?" I asked.

"Do you need one?" Anna responded. "It's early days. We should get to know each other first."

I smiled. Her short black hair was styled with a parting that made her look tomboyish, but her features were soft and her makeup accentuated her femininity.

"I didn't realize we were here to make friends," I said. "I thought I'd been arrested for murder."

"Even so," Anna replied. "This is an opportunity for you to tell your story without a lawyer confusing fact and fiction."

"Is that what they do?"

"Sometimes."

"Is this standard Moscow police procedure?" I asked.

The translator shifted in her seat.

"Nothing about this investigation is standard, Mr. Morgan," Anna replied. "You worry about your rules and I will worry about mine. Shall we begin?" She reached into her jacket pocket and took out a digital dictaphone. She put it on the table and pressed record. After a preamble in Russian, she said, "State your name."

I stayed silent.

"Your name, please," she tried.

I said nothing.

"I'm with Mr. Jack Morgan, the owner of Private," Anna spoke into the recorder. "Mr. Morgan, why don't you tell us in your own words what happened in the apartment of Mr. Ernest Fisher, chief of staff to the American ambassador here in Moscow?"

"I have no comment," I replied. "I would like to see a representative of the US embassy or a lawyer."

Anna smiled, but I could tell she wasn't happy. She ignored my response and reached beneath the table. After a short time spent ferreting in a large satchel, she produced a sheaf of printouts which she pushed toward me.

"This is the translation of an article that was published today on the Otkrov blog, stating that Private is working with a group called the Ninety-nine to target members of America's elite," Anna said.

I glanced at the printout of the original piece before turning to the translated article and reading it with growing dismay. A mix of conjecture and wild allegation, it suggested that after years investigating and covering up the excesses of the very wealthy, I'd had enough and had secretly conspired with the Ninety-nine to assassinate members of the 1 percent. The article pointed out that I'd been caught at the scene of both murders that the Ninety-Nine had claimed responsibility for and said that members of the Private team were colluding to help me in my objective.

"As you can see, the article says you murdered Mr. Fisher because he had evidence linking you to the conspiracy," Anna said, fixing me with a triumphant stare. "Now, Mr. Morgan, perhaps you would like to comment?"

CHAPTER 46

I STUDIED ANNA, wondering whether she was in on the lies or if she was simply being manipulated.

"Well, Mr. Morgan?" she pressed.

Dinara and Leonid had told me the woman behind the Otkrov blog had been murdered, so I found myself asking whether the blog had been written by more than one person, or if it had been hacked and compromised for disinformation purposes. Dinara had spoken highly of the blog's record for accuracy, and I was leaning toward the latter theory because I knew what was being alleged was completely untrue. No one interested in telling the truth could have published that article. With Yana Petrova, the supposed true author of the blog out of the way, the Otkrov platform had become a powerful and vacant tool for someone wishing to spread propaganda.

"When your officers arrested me on the roof, I was in pursuit of a suspect," I said.

"We found no evidence of anyone else," Anna replied. "Just a rope that you'd set up for your escape."

"If your people hadn't contaminated the scene, they would have found another set of footprints in the snow," I pointed out. "This story is a complete fabrication. I attended the property with two witnesses."

"Yes," Anna agreed. "Dinara Orlova, one of your employees, and Marlon West, an American Marine who may or may not be an intelligence operative. I'm not sure how you can expect us to consider these people impartial witnesses."

"Then why are you interested in anything I've got to say?" I asked. "I'm not impartial either."

Ernie Fisher's death troubled me for more than the obvious reasons. He wasn't wealthy and could scarcely be classed as part of the 20 percent, let alone the 1 percent. He simply didn't fit the profile of the other victims, which confirmed my suspicion that the idea of a radical group targeting America's wealthiest people was merely a cover story. I guessed that was part of the motivation behind the false flag article supposedly written by Otkrov. The killer had obviously staged the murder to look like a suicide, so wasn't planning to credit it to the Ninety-nine. When I discovered him on the scene, he realized the suicide set-up wasn't going to fly, so he needed a story that maintained the Ninety-nine cover, while throwing people off his trail. Blaming me for the anomalous kill would achieve both aims perfectly.

"This is an opportunity for you to explain," Anna said.

"Lawyer," I replied. "Or US embassy."

"Mr. Morgan, be reasonable, please. If you won't talk, then I will be forced to hold you while we complete our own inquiries. That could be weeks."

"Lawyer," I repeated.

Anna shrugged and said something in Russian to the translator. Zoya responded with a mocking laugh.

"I give you one last chance, Mr. Morgan," Anna said.

"Lawyer," I replied.

"OK," Anna responded, getting to her feet. "Then you must go back to your cell."

She stopped the recorder and knocked on the interview-room door. The cop who'd escorted me stepped inside, and Anna said something to him in Russian.

"Come," he said, taking my arm and hauling me to my feet.

We were on our way out of the room when a police officer entered. My escort snapped to attention, as did Anna. Even the translator got to her feet. The newcomer was a gray-haired man with a line of ribbons across his chest. It was clear he was a senior officer. He gave me a cursory glance before barking something at Anna.

The moment he'd given the command, he turned on his heel and left the room. Like a sudden violent storm, the officer had changed everything. Anna's demeanor shifted from confident and controlling to one of dejection.

"It seems you are to be released, Mr. Morgan," she said. "And I am to apologize for any inconvenience," she added grudgingly.

She said something to my escort and he let go of my arm.

"You're free to go," Anna told me, gesturing at the open door. I didn't have to be a mind reader to know she wasn't enjoying the crow her superior had forced her to eat. "My colleague will show you out."

CHAPTER 47

I WAS TAKEN out of the cell block to a booking hall where I was processed and got my things back, including my satellite phone. Feeling grubby and disheveled, I left what I'd thought was a police station—I'd only seen the rear entrance when I'd been pushed out of the police van—but when I finally stepped outside I discovered I'd been inside a huge government building. A courtyard lay between three six-story wings, each of which featured grand columns and high, arched windows. I walked along a path that bisected the snow-covered courtyard, toward a concrete gatehouse, where two uniformed guards kept watch. I passed through the high gate without incident and found myself on an unfamiliar street. There was a grand building and parkland behind a high wall on the other side of the busy road, and as I looked to my left and right, I saw no landmarks I recognized. There hadn't been any fresh snow while I'd been inside, and everywhere was covered in icy, graying slush that made the city feel just as drab and shabby as me.

I was about to call Justine when I noticed exhaust fumes coming from the tail pipe of a small SUV parked in a bay on the opposite side of the street. I got the sense the occupants were watching me, but couldn't see them clearly because the windows were steamed up. A hand wiped some of the moisture from the windshield and a moment later the passenger and driver doors opened. I was about to start running when I recognized the two figures that emerged as Leonid Boykov and Dinara Orlova.

"Jack," Dinara yelled over the passing vehicles.

Relieved, I picked my way through the traffic, and joined them by the vehicle, a Lada Niva, a Soviet-era SUV that must have been at least thirty years old. As I approached, I could hear the engine ticking over unevenly, revving high and then running low, almost to faltering point.

"Yes, it sounds like a dying bull," Leonid said. "But it moves. It's my uncle's car."

They got in the front and I climbed in the back. The interior wasn't much warmer than the street.

"The heater's broken," Leonid explained, wiping the windshield again.

"How did you get out?" I asked Dinara.

She nodded at Leonid. "It pays to have powerful friends."

"I'm sorry it took so long for you," Leonid said to me. "It's one thing getting a former FSB agent out of a police station, quite another thing securing the release of a foreigner from the Ministry of Internal Affairs."

I looked at the grand building. "You got me out of there?"

"Of course." He nodded. "There are still some members of the Moscow establishment who whisper the name Leonid Boykov with pride."

"Thank you," I said. "I'd better check in with New York."

I dialed Justine's number, but it went straight to voicemail. It was just gone eleven in Moscow, which meant it was a little after 4 a.m. in New York. I left a message, letting her know I was OK and asking her to call. I also tried the New York office in case Mo-bot or anyone else was working through the night. I got the company message service and left one for Jessie.

"I spoke to Miss Fleming yesterday," Dinara said after I'd hung up. "I let her know what happened. She was worried about you, but I was able to put her mind at rest."

"Thanks," I said. "Any leads from yesterday? I saw the killer get into a van which went down the alley toward Federation House. It turned right onto the street that runs to the river."

Leonid shook his head. "Federation House is even more secure than the Pentagon. They have surveillance everywhere. There are two government cameras in the alleyway behind Fisher's building, but when I made a request, they said they have no footage of the incident."

"Without evidence, it's going to be difficult to prove what you saw," Dinara said.

"And it's clear there are people who don't want you on the street," Leonid remarked.

"The Otkrov article?" I guessed.

Leonid nodded.

"What's your read on that?" I asked. "Has there always been another writer? Or was the blog hacked?"

"Hacked would be my assessment," Dinara replied. "The writing style is different to any of Otkrov's previous posts. Whoever did it must know Otkrov is dead and won't take down the post or interfere with the fake news."

"Which means our investigations might be connected," I observed.

"Possibly," Dinara conceded.

"Feels like FSB," Leonid said. "Dirty sneaks with some big plot, trying to control what people think." He glanced at Dinara. "No offence."

"Of course," she replied generously. "I'm no longer FSB, and even if I was, do you think the opinion of an unimaginative beat cop would have mattered to me?"

"Beat cop?" Leonid scoffed.

"Whoever is behind these murders, it's clear you've made powerful enemies, Jack, so we're going to take steps to keep you safe," Dinara said.

"How?" I asked.

Leonid glanced in the rear-view mirror and gave me a wry smile. "We're taking you somewhere even the FSB wouldn't dare go."

CHAPTER 48

WE DROVE FOR an hour, passing through the city center and out east to a place called the Kuzminki District. We'd driven through areas of wealth and plenty where high modern apartment blocks mixed with classical villas, but Kuzminki was a blue-collar neighborhood with dormitory blocks inhabited by working Russians. We turned off a six-lane overpass and drove under the busy highway. A group of teenagers were racing minibikes in the space beneath the overpass. We crossed a major slip road and went up a tree-lined street, past a large red church with a golden dome, which dazzled in the crisp January sunlight.

"This is Kuzminki," Dinara explained. "It was where the Soviet government housed people it considered undesirable. If the Central Committee didn't like you, this is where you lived."

"Here or the gulag," Leonid added.

We drove past huge estates of high-rise apartment blocks, some dating from the Soviet era, others more recent, and no more than ten minutes from the highway we turned north onto a service street that ran between two sprawling estates. A group of young men stood in a clearing in the snow, huddled around an oil-drum fire. They eyed us as we drove by. Up ahead, beyond the gardens that lay behind the tower blocks, the road was cut short by a gate, and next to it was a small hut. A grim-faced man in a heavy black coat emerged as the old SUV rattled to a halt. When Leonid wound down the window, the guy smiled warmly.

"Leonid Boykov!" he exclaimed.

The rest of what he said was lost on me as he and Leonid conversed in Russian. The tone was light-hearted and friendly and I got the impression these men knew each other well.

"Welcome, welcome," the man said to me as he raised the gate.

"That was Evgeniy Ertel. He used to be a captain in the riot police," Leonid said as he drove on. "Tough as army boot leather," he added as we turned into a large parking lot full of vehicles.

Beyond it stood a huge two-story concrete building that dominated the heart of a ten-acre lot. It looked like an old school or hospital. A handful of men and women gathered outside the main entrance, smoking cigarettes.

"This is your new home," Leonid said. "Well, our new home."

Dinara replied in Russian.

"Of course," he said. "We can't go home any more than he can. Not until we know what we're up against."

"What is this place?" I asked as Leonid pulled into a parking space.

"We call it the Residence. It's where my brothers and sisters live," he replied cryptically. "It's like a retirement home for cops. A hospital too. If you don't have family or money, this is where you come."

"Like a veterans' home?" I asked, getting out of the SUV.

"Maybe," Leonid said. "It was a school, but the government doesn't have so much money for schools, so they rented it to the people who run this place."

I quickly realized this place was nothing like a veterans' home as we approached the smokers. A dozen men and women: they must all have been under the age of fifty, and had the hard, incisive eyes of competent police officers. Inside, there were a couple of young men in wheelchairs, reading in the lobby, and I could see two recreation rooms off the large space, where former police officers between the ages of thirty-five and sixty played games, watched TV, drank, talked or sat with their heads in books or magazines. This was part convalescence home, part hospital, part social housing, part private members' club, and I'd never seen anything like it.

"Boykov!" a booming voice yelled.

I turned toward a huge bear of a man with bushy brown hair and a matching beard. He hurried over to us, wearing jeans, open-toed sandals over thick black socks and a bright blue painter's smock that was covered in splotches of color.

"Feodor Arapov!" Leonid replied, and the pair embraced.

'Feo, this is Jack Morgan and Dinara Orlova, my colleagues.'

I offered Feo my hand, but he brushed it aside and gave me a hug that hinted at his strength.

'Welcome, American,' he said. 'Boykov says you're OK.' He released me, and shook Dinara's hand. 'Never cuddle a lady without invitation,' he said.

'Very wise,' Dinara observed.

'I have arranged rooms for each of you in the west building,' Feo said. 'Come. Come.'

He headed into the large building, and Leonid, Dinara and I followed him into our new, unconventional home.

CHAPTER 49

"WHO PAYS FOR this?" I asked, gesturing at the huge dining hall.

Leonid, Dinara and I had settled into our rooms. I'd found my holdall on my bed. Leonid had retrieved it from the office where I'd left it when we'd stopped off en route to the US embassy from the airport.

My little room reminded me of a priest's cell. There was a single bed, a battered old closet, a window that overlooked the snow-covered grounds, an ancient radiator that was scalding hot, and a small sink. The bathroom was shared with eight other residents. I'd taken the opportunity to shower and change immediately, and had emerged feeling much more myself. Dressing in a black sweater and jeans, I'd joined Leonid and Dinara for lunch in the vast dining hall.

"Each according to his means," Leonid replied. "Everyone gives what they can, and we get money from charity and families, and the government gives a little and the police pension some more. Piece by piece a community is built. Some of the men and women here have jobs, and they pay more."

He looked at his former colleagues. There must have been over one hundred of them tucking into a rich beef stew with dumplings and potatoes.

"Everyone wants this place to stay open, so we all pay what we can," Leonid remarked.

"We?" Dinara asked.

"A small contribution buys a lot of goodwill," he replied.

"I never thought you were sentimental," Dinara said.

"Not sentimental. Just good old-fashioned self-interest," he objected, but I could tell he was lying.

His admiration and love for the place was palpable, and with good reason. There was a sense of camaraderie and community that was one of the things most often missed by former cops or service personnel. As I looked at the people seated at the long tables that were spread across the hall, I noticed that no one was being left out. Every single resident was talking to someone and there was no one who didn't seem to belong.

"Otkrov's story has found some admirers," Dinara said, showing me her phone.

She swiped through a number of Russian news sources and a couple of small American ones that had run variations of Otkrov's sensational allegations that Private was engaged in assassination. "Murder Detectives on the Rampage," said Citizen's

Bulletin, an alternative news site, and I felt my anger rise as I scrolled through the tawdry article. I'd spent years building Private into the world's number one detective agency, and all my efforts were being jeopardized by a single, unfounded allegation. If the mainstream media picked up the story, Private could be in real trouble.

My satellite phone buzzed and I pulled it from my pocket and answered.

"Jack, it's me," Justine said. "We heard what happened. Are you OK?"

"I'm fine," I assured her. "You seen the stories about Private?"

"Yes," she said. "People are just waking up here, so . . ."

"It's going to travel further," I finished her hanging sentence.

"Probably," she replied. "Our client list makes us newsworthy, and even if the allegations aren't true, they're sensational, which is what counts nowadays."

I couldn't let anonymous lies threaten everything I'd built.

"Talk to Rafael. See what he can do to shut this story down," I suggested. The First Amendment protected free speech, but there might be something Private New York's attorney could do to stop the spread of fake news. "And ask Mo-bot to check the server logs of Otkrov's blog. See if she can find out who published the article."

"Will do," Justine said. "We got a hit on the driver who threw himself off the roof of the Beekman Hotel. His name was Major Ivan Shulgin. He's a former officer with the First Guards Tank Army. I've emailed you his details. His service record fits the profile of an SVR asset."

"Thanks," I replied, grateful for our first solid lead.

"Are you sure you're OK, Jack?" Justine asked. "These are serious people."

"I'm safe," I assured her. "I'm with Leonid and Dinara."

"Dinara?" she asked.

Was that jealousy in her voice?

"Yeah," I replied. "We're with friends."

"Make sure you come home in one piece, Jack," Justine said.

"I'll do my best," I replied. "I'll be in touch," I added, before hanging up.

"Everything OK?" Dinara asked.

"Looks like the guy from the hotel was SVR," I replied.

I considered the revelation in light of everything that had happened. If our information was correct, I'd fought and chased a highly trained Russian intelligence operative.

"I think we need to know why we were hired to investigate the death of a customer-service supervisor," I said. "My guess is our client knew Yana Petrova was Otkrov. I want to find out how he came by that information and what he knows about her killer. I want to meet Maxim Yenen."

CHAPTER 50

"LET'S ARRANGE THE meeting from the car," Leonid said, getting to his feet. "We also have some other business we need to attend to."

Dinara was bemused until he added, "Murder. Abduction."

She rose hurriedly. "Of course."

In the turmoil of their arrest and securing Jack Morgan's release from police custody, Dinara realized they'd done nothing more about the previous morning's shooting and attempted kidnapping, other than giving statements to the police, explaining how Leonid's car came to be riddled with bullets and stuck on a highway.

"I would like to pay our friends at Grom Boxing a visit," Leonid said.

"I'll come with you," Jack said.

Leonid hesitated. "These men don't take well to outsiders."

"Doesn't sound like they took too well to you either," Jack shot back.

Dinara's limited dealings with the owner of Private simply hadn't prepared her for the sheer presence of the man. He wasn't particularly tall or broad, but there was a quiet assuredness about him, as though he could handle anything the world threw at him. There was no sense of him being a stranger in a foreign land. He was taking everything in his stride and behaving with the confidence of a local investigator. Dinara wondered just what it took to shake Jack Morgan.

"I'm not sitting this out when two of my team have been attacked," he said.

Leonid shrugged. "As stubborn as a Russian," he joked.

"And then some," Jack responded.

They went back to their rooms to get their coats and gear. Leonid was at the end of the corridor, in what Dinara mockingly called the suite, because it had two windows. Dinara and Jack had rooms opposite each other, and there were another five on the wing, all of which were occupied.

"Do you need a gun?" Leonid asked Jack.

"What's the law say?" he replied.

"As a visitor, if you get caught ..." Leonid did a swift intake of breath and held his hands out as though he was being cuffed. "Long jail time."

"Pistols are prohibited in Russia, unless by special decree, or an award from a military or federal authority," Dinara said as she grabbed her coat and a Makarov pistol from her overnight bag.

After the incident on their way to the airport, there was no way she was going back to the gym unarmed. "My license is signed by the Prime Minister himself."

"I only have one from the Minister of Internal Affairs," Leonid responded as he left his room.

"Then I'd better let you carry the hardware," Jack said, pulling on his coat as he joined them in the corridor.

Wrapped up for the freezing weather, they left the Residence and took the old SUV across the city to Grom Boxing. It was a little after 4 p.m. when they arrived and there were a handful of vehicles in the parking lot. Leonid reversed into a space near the door.

"For a quick escape," he explained as he got out. He leaned down and placed the keys on top of the front tire. "In case something happens to any of us. The others can still get away."

"I thought I was paranoid," Dinara said.

"Preparation prevents desperation," Leonid responded flatly. "Come on."

He led Dinara and Jack inside. Once again, the lobby area was deserted, but Dinara heard the sounds of men training in the gym beyond. She looked at Jack and Leonid, and both men nodded, so she pulled open the door and went inside.

There were a dozen fighters in the gym, along with the large trainer, Makar Koslov, and Erik Utkin, the Black Hundreds organizer. Every single man in the place stopped what he was doing and stared at the visitors. The man closest to them, a lean fighter who'd been using a heavy bag, was the owner of the snake and dagger tattoo Dinara had seen during the highway attack. She was convinced she saw a flicker of shame in his eyes and she caught him glance uncertainly at Erik Utkin. The older man strolled over casually.

"Why would you come back?" Utkin asked in Russian. "You know who I am. We found my wallet outside in the snow."

Jack couldn't understand a word, but Dinara would never have known by the way he carried himself.

"That's real interesting, Erik," Jack said, striding forwards. "But what I want to know is who's going to compensate my colleagues for the losses they've suffered?"

"Ah, Yankee Doodle," Utkin sneered. "Thinking you can come in here, like some buck rooster with a puffed out chest and a big, empty ego."

Jack and Utkin met near the ring and the fighters clustered round. If Jack was afraid, Dinara didn't pick up the slightest indication.

"I'm guessing that since you're the one doing all the talking, you're the one calling all the shots," Jack replied. "So you're the one responsible for what happened to my associates."

"American asshole," Utkin jeered in Russian, and the fighters laughed.

"I'm sorry, I didn't catch that," Jack said. "You carry on impressing your little boys here."

Some of the men must have spoken English, because Dinara felt them bristle at Jack's remark.

"I'm betting that since you're willing to abduct and kill people in broad daylight for simply coming here and asking questions, you've got some big things to hide," Jack said, and Utkin's mood changed instantly.

He looked beyond Jack to Dinara and Leonid. "Like I said before, why would you come back?" he asked in Russian. "It's going to cost you and your American friend your lives."

CHAPTER 51

THE GUY STANK of villainy. I'd encountered enough of it in my life to be familiar with the smell. Everything about him, from his oozing, showy confidence to the arrogant way he assumed he had the upper hand, from the court of minor league villains who surrounded us, to the tacit admission he'd been behind the abduction and murder attempt.

I couldn't understand what he'd said to Dinara and Leonid, but I sensed menace in his words. Equally, he hadn't understood my true purpose. I'd played up being an arrogant, loudmouth American because I'd suspected it would provoke a reaction, and it had. We now knew beyond any doubt that Erik Utkin and some or all the men in the room were involved in serious criminality they were willing to kill for.

I sensed movement to my right. One of the boxers came for me, a fit, muscular man about an inch shorter than me. He'd been on a heavy bag when we'd entered, and was marked with the dagger and serpent tattoo Dinara had recalled seeing during her abduction.

He was quick, but I dodged his first swing and pushed him past me, so he stumbled into some of his buddies. I took off my coat as he turned to face me.

A shaved head, narrow, hostile eyes, muscles that glistened with sweat, the guy wore shorts and an old Lokomotiv Moscow T-shirt. His hands were protected by light training mitts.

"Jack," Dinara said anxiously.

I looked at her and Leonid and signaled them to stay out of this.

"OK," I said, adopting the thinking man's pose. "Let's do this."

My opponent sneered and said something in Russian that made the other fighters laugh. Erik Utkin and an older, larger man, who I guessed was Makar Koslov, didn't find any humor in the remark and remained stony-faced. Maybe they were sufficiently experienced to know that my unconventional stance might look strange to a trained boxer, but that it was very effective in a street brawl.

My opponent assumed a southpaw stance and came forward. He threw a probing jab, and I taught him a swift lesson about the difference between boxing and street fighting. I deflected the punch by raising my left hand to meet his forearm with my elbow. My right hand, which had been balled in a fist beneath my chin, whipped out and went crashing into the man's nose.

He staggered back, dazed, and I felt the other fighters close in on us. Those to his rear pushed him forward and as he came toward me, I lashed out with a heel kick to his shin that made him yelp. Natural pain response sent his hands darting toward the injury, and I had my opening. I hit him with a jab that disorientated him, and followed up with a hammer blow to his clavicle. The fragile collarbone only requires about nine pounds of pressure to break, and my fist must have delivered over thirty.

The man went down, groaning and clutching his shoulder, and his companions, who'd been so full of laughs and jeers only moments ago, were silent. Brimming with anger and humiliation, they clustered around me and a couple grabbed my arms.

"You come in my place," Utkin said. "And you do this?"

He gestured at the injured fighter, who was being led away by Koslov and another boxer.

"I'll do it again and again, until we get through all the men involved in what happened," I said. "So take a number."

Utkin snarled and barked a command in Russian. There was a flurry of movement, and the other fighters swarmed toward Leonid and Dinara.

They stopped the moment Leonid produced his pistol, and a second later, Dinara was brandishing hers.

They both yelled in Russian and the fighters backed up. The three men who had hold of me released their grip. All ten of the hard-faced, lean fighters moved away and formed up around Utkin, who glared at us.

"You and your friends made a big mistake coming here, American," Utkin said. "The best thing a man can do when he meets a bear is run. Only a fool goes to its cave and bothers it with a stick."

"I don't see any bears here," I replied, backing away. "Just little cubs."

"Come on," Dinara said, tugging at my arm.

I held Erik Utkin's gaze until the last possible moment, and once we were through the double doors, we turned and ran for the car.

CHAPTER 52

ADRENALIN WAS STILL surging through my system when we joined the highway and headed toward the city center.

"That was unexpected," Leonid said.

"It was your idea to go there," Dinara responded.

"To ask questions. Maybe encourage one of them to talk," Leonid said. He glanced in the rear-view mirror. "*V tihom omute cherti vodyatsa.*"

I looked at Dinara, who smiled.

"In quiet lagoons, devils dwell," she translated. "He thinks you're dangerous. Unpredictable."

"They strike you as the kind of people who talk?" I asked Leonid.

He shrugged. "I guess not. So what now? The soft approach is dead."

"This is about much more than fixing fights," I replied. "Erik Utkin looked like I'd hit him with a cattle prod when I said they were covering up something big. I want you to stay on the gym," I said to Leonid. "Follow Utkin. See if you can find out where he goes, what he does."

"Alone?" Leonid asked.

"Dinara and I will take the other strands, Ernie Fisher's death and Maxim Yenen."

I could see Leonid consider the suggestion as he slowed to join a line of rush-hour traffic.

"Maybe we have some budget for support?" he suggested.

I looked at Dinara.

"Yenen's given us a blank check," she said.

"Good. Then I can buy some help," Leonid responded.

"Who?" I asked.

"Our new housemates," he said. "My old police friends."

We had a pool of experienced police officers at our disposal, many of whom were time rich and cash poor. It made sense, as long as they could be trusted.

"OK," I said, "but choose your people carefully."

"Of course," Leonid agreed.

Dinara's phone rang and she answered. She listened for a moment and hung up without saying a word.

"Maxim Yenen will meet us tonight," she said. "Eleven p.m., Bolshoy Moskvoretskiy Bridge."

"Is he crazy?" Leonid asked. "That's by Red Square. Not exactly a private spot."

"He said it's there or nowhere," Dinara replied.

Leonid shook his head disapprovingly.

"We'll be careful," I assured him. I turned to Dinara. "That gives us time."

"For what?" she asked.

"I want to take a look at Ernie Fisher's apartment. See what we can learn about the man."

CHAPTER 53

NIGHT WAS FALLING by the time Leonid dropped us off in Rochdelskaya Street, two blocks from Ernie Fisher's riverfront apartment building. Warning us to be careful, Leonid drove off in the spluttering Lada to muster a surveillance team made up of ex-cops from the Residence.

Dinara and I walked the icy streets toward the river. The buildings on the other bank were lit up and the freezing mist that rose above the water made their lights shimmer like stars.

It didn't take Dinara long to pick the front door again, and we were soon inside.

"Where did you learn how to do that?" I asked.

"FSB training module," she replied. "Everywhere we go, we meet closed doors. I thought it would be useful to know how to get through them."

She flashed me a smile, and I replied in kind. She was strong, capable and beautiful and in different circumstances, perhaps ...

I killed the idea before it took flight. Had Karl's death hit me so hard I'd become desperate for human connection? Or was I just lonely? I lived a difficult, solitary life. Was I secretly longing for someone to share it with?

I followed Dinara through the grand old building. It was located in the heart of the government district, next to one of the centers of Russian power, Federation House, and, according to Leonid and Dinara, it was inhabited by mid-level civil servants, politicians and diplomats. The richly patterned, worn carpet, grimy old chandeliers and cracked marble trim pointed to people who liked the trappings of power, but lacked the funds to maintain them.

I followed Dinara into an elevator and we went to the ninth floor. The corridor was deserted and when we got to Fisher's apartment, we discovered it had been sealed by a temporary metal security door that was covered in warning signs and padlocked to the wall.

"'Moscow Police. Keep Out,'" Dinara read, reaching for her lock picks.

She pulled a couple of tiny tools from a neat leather case and opened the padlock in less than a minute.

"If they were serious about keeping people out, they'd buy better locks," she said, pulling the door wide.

I hadn't noticed it the day before, but the smell of stale alcohol hit me the moment we stepped inside the cold apartment. I closed the security door behind me and we moved further into Fisher's home.

The place was otherwise as I remembered. It looked as though it had been turned over by someone in a rush. Books and papers were scattered everywhere and everything from clothes to cutlery had been strewn about the apartment. The only noticeable difference since our last visit was dark finger-print dust covering almost every smooth surface from the win-dowsills to the shelves.

"Why don't I take the bedroom?" Dinara suggested.

"I'll search in here," I replied.

Dinara carefully picked her way through the mess and I watched her go into a dark corridor before I started my search.

We kept the lights off so we wouldn't draw attention to our presence, and had to rely on ambient light from the city to illu-minate the apartment. The gloom made the place seem even more tragic, and as I scoured the living room, I found evidence that Ernie Fisher might have been a big drinker. There were stains and spillages everywhere, and half-empty liquor bottles littered the floor.

We spent an hour carefully picking over the place, but I found nothing to link Ernie Fisher to Karl Parker, Elizabeth Connor or Robert Carlyle. Dinara emerged from the corridor, carrying a small suitcase.

"Anything?" she asked.

I shook my head. "You?"

"This was on the bed. It's full of clothes and toiletries, like he was packing for a trip," she replied. "But I can't find a passport."

"Maybe it's at the embassy," I suggested.

"Possibly."

"Anything else?" I asked.

"Nothing," she said. "Just some empty vodka bottles under his bed."

"Yeah, I think he had a drink problem."

"A guilty conscience, perhaps," Dinara suggested.

"Maybe," I said. "I think we're done here. Let's go."

We started for the door, but as I stepped over a small broken mirror, I caught the fractured reflection of something gold in the shattered pieces. I crouched down and followed the line of sight to discover a brass key strapped inside an armoire. The key was attached to the top of a compartment that would have housed one of three drawers scattered about the room.

"What is it?" Dinara asked.

I reached in and pulled at the tape that held it in place.

"A key," I said as I stood up and showed her the tiny discovery.

CHAPTER 54

THE KEY DIDN'T fit anything in the apartment and we found nothing else of interest, so we left and caught a cab round the corner from Ernie Fisher's place. Both of us sat in the back, and I watched the city roll by as we headed to the Residence.

"Is it much like America?" Dinara asked.

"You've never been, right?" I recalled her mentioning a desire to visit the US at our interview.

She shook her head. "London is my furthest west."

"Different architecture"—I gestured to the brightly lit bronze dome of an Orthodox church—"but it's much the same. Fast-food joints everywhere, just like here, fewer European cars on the streets, same freezing weather in the north, heat in the south. Cities full of people just trying to get by. Beneath the surface, I don't think any country is that different, because people aren't that different. Most want health, happiness and a good life for their family."

"And you?" she asked pointedly. "What do you want?" Her eyes shone in the light cast by oncoming cars.

"I want people to have justice."

"And family?" Dinara pressed. "For yourself?"

"I don't know," I replied honestly. "Maybe one day."

The rest of the journey passed in silence, and when we reached the Residence, I asked Dinara whether she'd help me try to identify the key. A building full of former cops was as good a place as any to start the search.

We went into one of the recreation rooms that lay off the lobby and spoke to half a dozen residents. A couple spoke English, but most needed Dinara's translation. They didn't recognize the key and couldn't help, but when we sat opposite the seventh ex-cop, and showed it to him, his eyes flashed knowingly.

"It's for a Mauer keylock. They use them on Kaso safes," the man said in fluent English.

"Are you sure?" I asked.

"Of course," he replied, almost insulted. "I worked burglary for fifteen years. Valentin Popel," he said, offering me his hand, which I shook.

Popel must have been in his mid-fifties and had curly gray hair that fell around his ears. He'd been sitting alone, reading a book when we'd approached him, and was wearing slippers, slacks and a cardigan. He looked more like someone's grandfather than a hardboiled cop.

"How big is one of these safes?" I asked.

"About the size of a small refrigerator. Maybe bigger," he said.

I glanced at Dinara. There was nowhere in the apartment Ernie Fisher could have concealed something that size.

"Are these things rare?" I asked hopefully.

"Kaso? No. They sell them all over the world. It's a very good safe."

"Could it be in the American embassy?" Dinara asked.

Popel shook his head. "American embassies only trust American safes. No, this thing would not be there. Unless it was unofficial."

"Spying?" Dinara suggested.

"A spy with a four-foot-tall safe," Popel scoffed. "Not very subtle. This is a big thing to hide. Not something anyone would be able to conceal in an embassy."

I glanced at Dinara. "Thank you, Mr. Popel," I said to the man. "Please excuse me. I need to make a call."

I left him and Dinara and went to my room where I phoned Justine. I brought her up to speed and told her about the key, which I hid in a crack beneath my windowsill.

"We think it's for a safe," I explained. "We need to find out where it's located. Can you ask Mo-bot to go through Ernie Fisher's personal history and employment records for any possible sites? Also check his bank accounts and credit cards. See if there's a record of him buying a safe. Also look for anywhere he's visited regularly."

"Will do," she replied.

There was a brief pause.

"How are you coping out there, Jack?"

"Fine," I replied. "I'm with good people."

"Dinara?" she asked, her voice strained with jealousy.

"I thought we weren't going to complicate things," I said.

My remark was greeted with silence. Then came a knock at the door.

"I've got to go," I said.

"Be safe," Justine replied, before I hung up.

I opened the door and found Dinara waiting.

"We have to leave," she said. "It's time to meet Maxim Yenen."

CHAPTER 55

MAXIM YENEN'S DECISION to meet near Red Square surprised Dinara. It was one of the most heavily monitored parts of Moscow, and if the billionaire was trying to downplay his links to Private, the location was an odd choice.

They'd taken a taxi from the Residence to Pyanitskaya Street, where they'd joined the meager groups of tourists who'd braved the late hour and freezing temperatures to see the grandeur of St. Basil's Cathedral and Red Square. As they reached the Bolshoy Moskvoretskiy Bridge, Dinara could see the distinctive outline of the cathedral, and the spires of the surrounding buildings. The brightly colored structures rose from the snow-covered landscape and were floodlit against the dark sky. The cathedral's rainbow of domes, pattered like whipped ice creams gave the district a fairy-tale quality, but the charm of this building was dangerously disarming. It was easy to forget the violence and oppression this place had witnessed. Bad things had happened here.

Dinara and Jack walked north across the bridge. There were a few tourists milling around here and there, taking pictures of the landmarks. Jack said nothing as they crossed the river, his eyes set firmly ahead. Dinara had been impressed with how he'd tackled the fighter at Grom Boxing, and found herself wondering whether he'd been particularly hard on his opponent because he'd been one of the men who'd tried to abduct her.

He's not your knight in armor, Dinara told herself. *He's your boss and he did what he thought best for the investigation.*

Still, it didn't hurt to dream, and there were far worse things to imagine than a life with Jack Morgan. He was handsome, strong, intelligent and capable.

Dinara's attention was drawn to a group of six men crossing the bridge in the other direction. She recognized Yenen's bodyguards and saw the man himself at the heart of the entourage. He wore a tuxedo and a long woolen coat, and carried a tumbler of amber liquid.

"You've been making a lot of noise for a company called Private," he said in Russian.

"It was necessary," Dinara replied. She switched to English and said, "Maxim Yenen, this is Jack Morgan, the head of Private."

"I know who Mr. Morgan is," Yenen responded in perfect English. "His name is being whispered all over the Kremlin."

"I'm flattered by the attention," Jack said. "But I'm not interested in fame. I want to know why you hired us. I want to know who Yana Petrova is."

Yenen looked irritated and he waved his guards away.

"Give us a minute," he instructed them in Russian, and the five large men backed away.

"I thought you were discreet," Yenen said, rounding on Dinara.

"Take it easy," Jack interjected, putting himself between the two of them. "Did you know Petrova was—"

"Don't even say that name," Yenen interrupted, looking round nervously.

Dinara was puzzled. This wasn't the confident billionaire they'd met days earlier.

"Why did you hire us? Did you know her other identity?" Jack asked.

"Who knows who anyone really is?" Yenen replied cryptically. "Truth. Lies. Does any of it matter?"

"Yes," Jack snapped back instantly. "It all matters. The lies someone's spreading right now are destroying my business. What do you know about that?"

"You've been making too much noise," Yenen replied. "That's all I know."

"Was Yana Petrova making too much noise?" Dinara asked.

"They made an example of her," Yenen said. "To discourage others."

"Others?" Jack asked.

"Maybe I made a mistake," Yenen responded. "It was wrong of me to involve you. I don't know why I did it, but then who knows why I do half the things I do?"

"Mr. Yenen, is there something you want to tell us?" Jack asked.

Dinara thought he must have been picking up the same cagey feeling from the man. They were in the presence of someone who was desperately trying not to show how frightened and confused he was.

"I want to tell you to stop your investigation," Yenen said. He drank from the tumbler. "Scotch," he added, raising his glass. "Thirty-year-old Glenfarclas. Good for the soul."

Dinara and Jack exchanged puzzled looks.

"Yes," Yenen went on. "I want to end the investigation. Shut it down. My lawyer will settle your bill."

"Mr. Yenen," Jack began, but the powerful Kremlin insider raised his hand.

"Shut it down, Mr. Morgan, Miss Orlova. Shut down the investigation and close the file."

CHAPTER 56

I WATCHED THE Russian stagger over to his bodyguards, who quickly surrounded him as he walked toward St. Basil's Cathedral. The guards were like limbs, extensions of the man and manifestations of his power.

Or the bars of a cage, I thought darkly.

I looked at Dinara, who was equally puzzled. Why did he bring us here to fire us? Here of all places ... unless ...

I glanced at a group of tourists gathered at the north end of the bridge. Three men and two women busy taking selfies with the brightly lit cathedral in the background. As Maxim Yenen and his entourage passed, the tourists put away their phones and started toward us.

Almost directly opposite us on the other side of the bridge, a middle-aged couple were watching us closely. Every inch of me suddenly came alive with adrenalin.

"We need to get out of here," I said.

Dinara had spotted them too, and nodded.

We turned around and headed south across the bridge. A trio of drunks came toward us, young men with their arms around each other's shoulders, singing jovially. But there was something wrong; their movements seemed forced and their slurring artificial.

"You got your gun?" I asked.

"Yes," Dinara said, and she slipped her hand into her coat pocket.

We walked faster, and when I glanced over my shoulder, I saw the quintet of selfie-takers had matched our pace. The couple on the other side of the bridge were tracking a few yards behind us. And on came the trio of drunks, their singing growing increasingly loud.

I sensed Dinara's anxiety, and it magnified my own. I saw her arm shift slightly. She was probably adjusting her grip on her pistol. My breathing grew rapid and shallow and my head was pounding with the rush of blood being pumped by my thundering heart. I took my hands out of my pockets and pressed the fingers of my gloves tight as we drew near the three men. They were ten feet away.

Then five.

One of them glanced at me and I thought I saw a flicker of recognition. I steeled myself for the inevitable confrontation.

But they passed us and kept on going, singing and swaying their way across the bridge. I glanced back and saw the couple had stopped and were looking over the barrier at something in the river. Even the quintet of men and women had halted and were taking selfies in the middle of the bridge.

I looked at Dinara, who was visibly relieved. She shot me a smile and I grinned in reply. We'd let out imaginations run wild.

When we reached the southern end of the bridge, I heard steps behind us and turned to see the trio of drunks sprinting toward us. There was a roar and a screech ahead of us, and a white van came racing along the bridge, and skidded to a halt beside us.

Dinara had her pistol out and trained it at the masked driver, but the side door slid open and another masked man jumped out, brandishing an assault rifle. He pointed the barrel of the gun directly at me. He yelled something in Russian.

"He says he'll kill you this time," Dinara translated.

I studied the gunman's eyes and recognized him as the assassin I'd followed from New York. The man who'd killed Ernie Fisher, Elizabeth Connor and Karl Parker. He was probably also responsible for Robert Carlyle's death.

I glanced over my shoulder at the trio of drunks who were almost upon us. Behind them, the quintet hurried in our direction, talking into radios. They were all part of what was about to happen to us. Only the middle-aged couple were innocent, and they fled the scene hurriedly.

I heard a familiar hum above us and looked up to see a chopper sweep over St. Basil's Cathedral and shine its powerful spotlight on us. There was no escaping this. Our instincts had been right. Maxim Yenen had walked us into a trap.

Why? I asked myself.

It was my last coherent thought. One of the drunks ran up behind us and struck me on the back of the head, and the world went black.

CHAPTER 57

I COULD HEAR the crash of distant waves and felt the beat of the sun on my face. I was lying on warm sand and could almost taste the brine in the baking air. Part of me was puzzled by my circumstances, but there was nothing I could do about them. I couldn't even move, which was troubling because I could feel the soft touch of a woman stroking my hair. I couldn't see her face, just the edge of her wide-brimmed straw hat, which intermittently blocked the blinding sun that blazed in an unblemished sky.

Then it was all gone, replaced by darkness. I'd been dreaming, and woke to a pounding headache and a bitter taste in my mouth. My eyes adjusted to the dim light and I realized I was in an empty apartment high above the city. The windows were covered in some kind of blackout material, but it had curled at the edges to create tiny gaps that enabled me to see the twinkling lights of Moscow spread out far below. These gaps were the sole source of light, and only cast enough to discern wall from floor and space from solid shape.

My arms were stretched above my head, and when I looked up I saw my wrists were secured in fabric cuffs that were attached to a chain, which hung from a hook. My feet were bound together by similar fabric cuffs and attached by chain to a hook in the floor. I'd been stripped to my underwear.

I was suddenly assaulted by loud noise, death metal music, and blinding light dazzled me. I squeezed my eyes shut and desperately tried to pull my arms down to cover my ears, but they were chained tight and the light was so bright it blazed through my lids. Then the light and noise were gone, replaced by darkness.

"Are you with us?" a voice asked.

It was a voice I'd heard before, belonging to a man with a Russian accent, the killer I'd chased from New York.

A light went on behind me and illuminated the space ahead. I saw my shadow cast on the concrete floor, pathetic and helpless. I looked away from it and noticed the walls had also been stripped back to concrete, but they were covered with graffiti, scrawled in what looked like dried blood. It was a nightmarish scene, and I was at the heart of it.

I heard footsteps to my rear and the man I'd pursued from New York stepped into my field of vision. He wasn't wearing a mask or a disguise, which was bad news because it signaled he had no intention of letting me live.

"Where's Dinara?" I asked. My voice was dry and rasping. I cleared my throat. "What have you done with her?"

He stepped forward and I got a good look at his face. He had short brown hair, a flat nose, almond eyes and a square jaw. Handsome, but those who knew what to look for would notice an ugly cruelty in his eyes. He wore black combat trousers, a matching T-shirt and boots, and looked every inch the highly trained soldier I'd suspected he was when I first encountered him in New York.

"They call me Veles," the man said. "It has been interesting to finally encounter someone who can almost keep up with me."

"Let her go," I said. "You have me. There's no need to hurt her."

"But there is," Veles replied.

He yelled something in Russian, and I heard movement behind me. I strained to turn my head as footsteps approached. Two sets, I thought, dragging something across the concrete.

It was two men in the same uniform as Veles, and they were pulling Dinara. She too had been stripped to her underwear and was bound at her ankles and wrists. Her feet had been grazed by the concrete and were bloody, and she had a gag over her mouth. Her eyes met mine, and they shimmered with fear.

"Jack Morgan. Marine. Detective. Fighter. Survivor," Veles said. "Not the kind of man who cares about his own suffering. But the suffering of another ..."

He walked over to Dinara and caressed her shoulder.

"Leave her alone!" I yelled.

"What do you know, Mr. Morgan?" he said. "Tell me everything. And then tell me what your team knows, and we can decide who has to die." Veles produced a butterfly knife from his pocket, flipped it open and pressed the point against Dinara's exposed sternum. "And we can decide *how* they have to die. Quickly and kindly. Or slowly. In unimaginable pain."

CHAPTER 58

I STRUGGLED AGAINST my restraints but they held firm. Dinara was defiant, but there was terror in her eyes.

"Don't do this," I said. "Just let her go."

Dinara's tough veneer was starting to crack and I could see tears forming. Blazing with anger and frustration, I struggled again, but there was nothing I could do.

Suddenly, a gunshot erupted from somewhere behind me, followed by the thunderous sound of footsteps and the crash of a door being slammed against a wall. I heard heavy boots tramp into the room, and urgent cries filled the air. I couldn't believe it when Veles dropped the butterfly knife, and he and the two men holding Dinara raised their hands, and backed toward the windows.

The room filled with gun-toting police officers, who trained their weapons on our abductors. A female officer untied Dinara's gag, and she began yelling at Veles, who ignored her and instead barked angry commands at the police. But they paid no attention to his instructions, and handcuffed him and his accomplices. The female officer used the discarded butterfly knife to cut Dinara's bonds, and she ran over to me, just as Anna Bolshova, the Moscow detective who'd tried to interrogate me, entered the room.

She seemed to be in command of the raid, and was barking instructions at the dozen or so officers in the large apartment. Two of them hoisted me off the hook and cut the bonds around my legs so I could stand freely.

Dinara leaned against me, trying to control her emotions.

"I'm sorry," she said. "I should have known it was a trap."

"Me too," I said.

Veles exchanged angry words with Anna as he and his two men were frogmarched out of the room.

Anna seemed unsettled when she came over. "Asshole!" she remarked. "Are you OK?"

Dinara nodded.

"How did you know where we were?" I asked.

Anna looked over my shoulder, and I glanced round to see Feodor Arapov, the huge bear of a man from the Residence, pass Veles and the other two prisoners as they were led from the room.

"Hello, American," he boomed. "Did we spoil your fun?"

"How ... ?"

"Leonid asked some of us to keep an eye on you," Feo said. "The couple you spotted at the bridge. They were our guys. We saw you get taken and followed you here."

"And they called me and said you'd been abducted by a drugs gang," Anna added.

Feo looked sheepish, and my expression must have given something away, because Anna suddenly realized she'd been played.

"You mean that man really was SVR?" she asked nervously.

None of us said anything.

"He told me we were disrupting an intelligence operation," Anna said. She looked at us searchingly. "Oh, come on! You said they were part of a gang."

"They are," Feo replied. "It's just a very powerful gang." He took my arm. "Come," he said. "Time for us to go, before she rethinks who the villains are."

"What about a statement?" Anna asked.

"Those men abducted us," I replied. "If you hadn't arrived, they were going to torture and kill us."

"They can help you fill in the blanks tomorrow," Feo said. "If you manage to hold those men for longer than a couple of hours. For now, these two need medical attention."

"SVR? This is going to cause real trouble," Anna said.

"You saved our lives," I replied. "I owe you one."

Dinara added her own response in Russian, but neither of us seemed able to lift Anna's spirits. She had a rough night ahead.

As we followed Feo from the room, he took off his coat and wrapped it around Dinara's shoulders.

"They found your clothes in another room," he said.

"Thank you," she replied.

"I owe you," I told him.

"You're welcome, American," he said, patting my back. "Now let's get you both home."

CHAPTER 59

FEO TOOK US back to the Residence in his brown UAZ Pickup truck. Dinara sat in the second row and said nothing as we drove through the quiet city. It was a few minutes after two in the morning, and the roads were almost deserted. The apartment where we'd been captives was in a rundown estate in Solntsevo, to the southwest of the city. Our journey to Kuzminki took twenty-five minutes, and Feo tried to start a couple of conversations, before eventually reading the mood. He turned on the stereo, which played a Pink Floyd compilation.

Dinara looked shell-shocked, and she avoided meeting my gaze whenever I glanced back at her. We'd found our clothes and got dressed, but she looked as though she still felt exposed. We'd shared an extreme experience and had been forced to confront death. I felt ashamed I hadn't been able to do anything to protect her. Did she think me weak? Did she hate me for my failure?

When we reached the Residence, Dinara made to go straight to her room without saying a word, but Feo grabbed her and uttered something in Russian.

She still looked distressed, but she nodded and went into the smaller of the two recreation rooms that lay off the lobby.

"I told her she needed medical attention," Feo explained. "And so do you. Then you can rest."

I didn't object when he steered me toward the recreation room. As we got closer, I heard the rowdy chatter of a large group, and when we stepped inside I saw fifteen men and women seated around a large table. They were passing four large bottles of vodka between them. Dinara had taken a seat at the table, near Leonid, who noticed me enter.

"American! Boss man!" he yelled, clearly drunk. "I hear you had some problems."

I looked at Dinara, who turned away.

"No matter," Leonid said. "Vodka will fix you."

"Medical attention," Feo explained mischievously.

There were shouts of approval as I took a seat at the table almost directly opposite Dinara.

Someone passed me a shot glass, and my neighbor, a bald man with rough stubble, filled it. I necked the shot and immediately felt its warmth spread throughout my body. The glass was refilled to murmurs of approval, and I knocked back a second shot.

My glass was refilled a third time, and I realized this process would continue as long as I kept drinking, so I left the glass alone and the bottle moved on.

"I owe you my thanks," I said to Leonid.

"Of course," he replied loudly. "And to Lera and Kiril." He gestured at a man and woman to his left, and I recognized them as the middle-aged couple from the bridge. "They did the real work."

"Thank you," I said.

My neighbors turned to the people on the other side of them, and I was left alone. Dinara threw a couple of furtive glances in my direction, but otherwise I sat surrounded by chatter I couldn't understand. The alcohol eased its way into my system, and the tension I'd felt all night melted away. As I replayed events in my head, I found myself struggling to hold on to a memory long enough to blame myself for what had happened. Everything was foggy and distant and I glanced down at my shot glass and wondered just how strong the vodka was. Realizing I'd had enough, I got to my feet.

"Goodnight," I said.

Everyone jeered.

"Never leave a full glass on the table," Leonid yelled above the noise, and his words triggered fresh derision.

I raised the brimming shot glass and downed it in a single gulp. The jeers turned to cheers and I left the room to the sound of their drunken approval.

I walked through the building to the quiet residential wings and found my way to my room. I'd just stepped inside when there was a knock on my door.

I opened it and found Dinara outside. She looked up at me and hesitated.

"I'm sorry," she said.

Her eyes were glassy and unfocused, and if she'd had any-where near as much vodka as me, I could understand why.

"What for?" I asked.

"I should have seen it was a trap," she replied. "I should have ..."

I thought she was going to break down, so I held her by the shoulders.

"I shouldn't have let us get in that situation," I said. "It's on me."

We stood staring at each other, both blaming ourselves for what had happened. I could feel the warmth of her body beneath my fingertips.

"Make up your minds," Leonid slurred as he staggered into the corridor. "Your room or hers."

I took my hands away, and Dinara backed up.

"I'm going to ignore that because we owe you our lives," she said.

"Too right," he replied, passing between us.

"Shouldn't you be on a stakeout?" I asked.

"I have my underlings watching Utkin," he replied. "A chief doesn't work the night shift. Goodnight to you both," he said.

He stepped inside his room and shut his door, and Dinara and I stood there eying each other for a moment. I realized I was caught up in the emotions of what had happened and my pro-fessional judgment was in danger of being swept away on a tide of vodka.

"I'd better ..." I said, taking a step back.

"Me too," Dinara agreed.

She crossed the corridor.

"Goodnight," she said, and she went into her room and quickly shut the door.

I did likewise, and collapsed on my bed, laces tied, clothes on. Within moments, I was deep asleep.

CHAPTER 60

MY PHONE WOKE me from a dreamless sleep at 9:15 the next morning. My eyes were raw and my head pounded. My arms ached from having been suspended in a stress position, and I winced as I answered the call.

"Jack?" Justine said.

"Yeah," I croaked. "What time is it there?"

"Quarter past two in the morning. We're working round the clock," she replied.

I rubbed my face and sat up.

"What's been happening over there?" Justine asked. "I couldn't get hold of anyone."

I should have told her about my abduction by Veles, but I didn't want her to worry.

"We're following up some leads," I replied blandly. "We caught a name: Veles. Probably Spetsnaz or Russian intelligence. Can you ask Mo to run an alias search? See what it flags up."

"Will do," she said. "I've sent Dinara everything we could get on Ernie Fisher, Robert Carlyle, Karl Parker and Elizabeth Connor. Personnel records, school transcripts, service histories."

"Thanks."

"Are you with her?" Justine asked.

It was a loaded question, and after the events of the previous night, I just couldn't face it head on.

"Not right now, no," I replied. "Anything else?"

There was a pause.

"No," she replied at last.

"Stay in touch," I said, before hanging up.

Twenty minutes later, I'd showered and got dressed, and, feeling a little more human, left my room and knocked on Dinara's door. There was no answer, so I tried Leonid's, but his room was also silent.

I went into the main building and found a few late risers finishing breakfast in the dining hall. I recognized some of them from the previous night's vodka session, and when they waved at me, I nodded in reply.

I finally found Dinara in the library, where she was working alone, hunched over her computer. She looked fresh, free of any sign of her abduction and traumatic ordeal.

"Morning," I said.

She looked up and shifted awkwardly. "Good morning," she replied. "Justine has sent us some information on Ernest Fisher and Robert Carlyle. I've been pulling out the highlights."

"Mind if I take a look?"

She shook her head, and I grabbed a chair. The library was one of the few rooms that didn't look as though it had undergone any refurbishment since the place had been converted from a school. Books were arranged on low, child-friendly shelves, and classroom tables had been pushed together in clusters of four to create reading areas.

Dinara was at the cluster nearest the windows, overlooking football goals and a playing field that was buried beneath snow. She had a series of applications open on her laptop, but she was currently working on a simple document that listed key moments in Ernie Fisher's life, from his birth in Featherville, a tiny settlement in Idaho, to his appointment as the US ambassador's chief of staff.

"That's interesting," I remarked. "He and Karl Parker were both born and raised in small Midwest towns."

"And both enlisted in the Marine Corps within two years of each other," Dinara observed.

"Fisher was a couple of years older than Karl," I said. "Similar academic profiles too. Solid but nothing flashy. Certainly nothing to indicate their later achievements."

"What about Robert Carlyle?" I asked.

Dinara opened a similar document and showed me the Washington financier's potted history. "Born in Arminto, Wyoming, enlisted in the Marines aged eighteen," she said.

"There's a pattern," I remarked.

I thought about the key I'd found in Ernie Fisher's apartment.

"What if their similarities aren't just in the past?" I asked. "What if the key is for a safe in a warehouse like the one Karl Parker had? Someplace secret. Completely off the books."

"He was planning to leave," Dinara remarked.

"So his next stop was going to be to collect his passport and whatever else he needed," I surmised. "It will be somewhere close by. Like Karl's, it will be in the city, someplace Fisher could get to quickly.

"Any idea how we find it?"

"Old-fashioned detective work," I replied. "We canvass. It's time-consuming, but I don't see any other way. We start at the epicenter, Fisher's home, and work our way out."

CHAPTER 61

LEONID REGRETTED EVERY sip of vodka he'd had the previous night. His tongue felt like an old babushka's pumice stone and his head was as tender as a steak put through a mangle. But he'd needed to blow away the residue of his brush with death. An inch or two above his protective vest and his drinking buddies would have been toasting his memory.

He'd blustered his way through the experience and brushed off Dinara's concerns for his wellbeing, but deep down he'd been shaken. Why was he in this job? He could easily have got a quiet desk job as head of security for a big firm, but instead had chosen to put himself back on the front line without any real support.

Who wants to live forever? a small voice inside him asked.

Was that it? Did he have a death wish?

Leonid shook the thought from his mind, and focused on Erik Utkin's apartment building. The Black Hundreds' recruiter lived in Meshchansky District, on Shchepkina Street, in a traditional villa that had been split into large apartments. It was a lovely home in a great neighborhood, one that was beyond the reach of most Muscovites.

Leonid had relieved Larin, one of the ex-cops who lived at the Residence, and who'd staked out Utkin's place overnight. Leonid had been parked fifty meters along the street from the yellow-fronted building for an hour when Erik Utkin finally emerged and climbed into a black BMW 6 Series.

Leonid followed Utkin across Moscow to Kapotnya, a neighborhood almost twenty kilometers from the city center. Kapotnya was one Moscow's most crime-ridden, poverty-stricken areas, and even in the arctic conditions, there was clear evidence of drug use on the streets. Leonid drove by a group of scrawny men gathered around an oil-barrel fire, sharing a crack pipe. Soon afterwards he passed a couple of skeletal men shooting up in a bus shelter.

Erik Utkin finally stopped on the corner of Kapotninskiy Passage and Kapotnya Block, and Leonid pulled over a short distance behind him. Filthy tower blocks rose either side of the street, and the bare branches of the trees that lined the road looked like jagged scars against the ugly buildings. Utkin kept his engine running, but Leonid cut his to avoid the vapor of exhaust fumes attracting unnecessary attention.

Leonid could see the Black Hundreds' recruiter through the BMW's rear window. He had his head turned toward a gray high-rise apartment building to their right.

Soon, three men came out. Two of them wore hooded tops beneath heavy coats, but Leonid recognized them as fighters from Grom Boxing. They were scowling as they were accosted by the third man, who was gaunt and covered in sores. He didn't have a coat and shivered as he capered around the two boxers. His face was grubby and pinched and his hollow eyes spoke of years of drug addiction. He chattered away, oblivious to the boxers' rising anger, and even at a distance Leonid could sense the desperation of an addict.

Finally, one of the boxers ferreted in his coat pocket and produced a small plastic bag, which he handed to the gaunt man in exchange for crumpled notes. These two boxers were dealing drugs, and unless Leonid was very much mistaken, they were doing it with Erik Utkin's approval. Sitting in his BMW, the man had watched the trade without emotion.

The addict ran off, and the two boxers approached Utkin, who opened his window. Clouds of vapor escaped their mouths as they exchanged greetings in the cold, and after a minute or so of chatter, Utkin popped his trunk. One of the fighters went to the rear of the BMW and removed a plastic bag from the car, while the other man handed Utkin an envelope.

Erik Utkin was giving these men more than his approval; he was supplying them with product.

Leonid pulled his phone from his pocket and made a call.

"Dinara," he said when she answered. "I think I've found Erik Utkin's secret. It looks like he and his men are dealing drugs."

"But the Black Hundreds would crucify him if they found out," Dinara replied. "They kill dealers."

"I know. He's gambling his life," Leonid agreed. "Which is why he didn't want us digging around. You want me to stay on him?"

"Can you arrange for someone else to pick up his tail?"

"Of course," Leonid replied. "Why?"

"We could use your expertise," Dinara said. "Meet us at Ernest Fisher's apartment as soon as possible."

"OK," Leonid said, hanging up.

Sava Efimov was due to relieve him at 3 p.m., and almost certainly wouldn't appreciate being summoned early.

"*Da*," Sava grunted as he answered the call. He'd been one of the previous night's biggest drinkers.

"I need you to take over early," Leonid said. "Duty calls."

Sava groaned. "I should never have agreed to help. This is why I left the force."

"You left the force because someone shot you in the gut and you got pensioned off," Leonid corrected the man. "You love this and you miss it."

"You're a jerk, Leonid Boykov."

"I'm also right," Leonid replied. "Hurry up and get dressed. Head for Kapotnya. I'll call you with the final location when you're nearby."

"OK," Sava said, and Leonid hung up.

Up ahead, Erik Utkin bid the two fighters farewell and drove away. Leonid followed. He'd stay on the man's tail until Sava arrived.

Maybe that's why you do this, he told himself. *Same as Sava, you love it and you'll miss it when it's finally gone.*

CHAPTER 62

DINARA AND JACK waited in Feo's UAZ Pickup. The larger-than-life former cop had insisted they take his truck, and Jack had agreed but only on condition Private paid a fair hire charge for it. They were parked behind Ernie Fisher's building, waiting for Leonid to arrive, and they'd exhausted all their small talk. Neither of them had addressed what had happened the previous night, and Dinara wished she could take it all back. The rush of emotions she'd experienced after escaping from Veles, combined with the vodka, had impaired her judgment, and Jack Morgan—handsome, strong, successful Jack Morgan—had seemed irresistible. But he was her boss, and they had a job to do.

"How do we handle billing this?" Dinara asked, trying to re-establish their professional relationship. "This truck, the surveillance team, any other costs we incur. Maxim Yenen has terminated our contract."

"I'm going to cover everything personally from here on," Jack replied. He turned up the heating, which was preventing the windshield from misting over. "Maxim Yenen hired you to investigate a woman whose blog was just used by the people who killed Ernie Fisher to try to discredit Private's investigation into the deaths of Karl Parker and Elizabeth Connor. I don't know whether that was opportunism, or if the two investigations are connected. Until we have answers, we're keeping both cases live."

Dinara nodded. She didn't dare ask what would happen after these cases. Partly because she didn't want to add to Jack's concerns, partly because she was afraid of the inevitable answer. Without clients, Private Moscow couldn't stay in business. Dinara didn't want to think about how she'd deal with what would be a serious personal and professional failure. Jobs like this were hard to come by, particularly for people who ran their last business into the ground.

"There he is," Jack said, indicating Leonid's old Niva, which was turning onto Rochdelskaya Street.

Leonid parked a few cars away, hurried over and climbed in the back. "Feo loaned you his truck?" he asked in Russian.

"For a price," Dinara replied in English.

"Apologies," Leonid said immediately. "I forgot you don't speak Russian, Mr. Morgan."

"My problem, not yours," Jack responded. "So you caught Erik Utkin dealing drugs?"

Leonid nodded. "It seems so. I couldn't see what was in the bag, but a couple of his fighters were definitely selling narcotics of some kind."

"The Black Hundreds would punish him severely," Dinara observed.

"Unless they've branched into new ways of making money," Jack said.

Dinara shook her head. "Not these people. For them patriotism is bound up in the preconception of a wholesome life. God, country, family. Drugs would attack the very core of what they stand for."

"It wouldn't be the first time the actions of an organization like this don't match its words," Jack replied. "But let's assume you're right for now, unless we find anything to suggest otherwise."

"What about Fisher?" Leonid asked.

"We think he had a safe somewhere in the city, possibly a warehouse similar to Karl Parker's," Jack replied. "We're going to canvass his neighbors and nearby businesses to see if anyone remembers him. Find out if he's got a place people saw him using. We'll start here and spread out. Put his photo in front of enough people and someone will recognize him."

"What's our search radius?" Leonid asked.

"We start here and keep going until we find something," Jack replied.

"The whole city?" Leonid remarked in disbelief.

"I don't think it will come to that," Jack said flatly. "But we keep going until Justine and the team in New York come up with a better angle."

"What's the matter?" Dinara goaded Leonid. "You're not afraid of a little hard work, are you?"

He replied in Russian.

"What did he say?" Jack asked.

"Something about how cold it is," Dinara replied, frowning at the old cop. "The rest of his words I won't translate, because they belong in the gutter."

Jack laughed. "Come on," he said. "Let's go."

CHAPTER 63

I FELT JUST shy of useless. A detective who couldn't speak the language wasn't much good at canvassing, and I found myself standing idle as Dinara spoke to storekeepers on Year 1905 Street.

We'd drawn the short straw. Leonid was inside Ernie Fisher's building, speaking to the man's neighbors, while Dinara and I trudged the snowy streets, checking with desk clerks, restaurateurs and the managers of local stores. We'd been on the hunt for five hours, and my feet ached and my head was pounding worse than ever.

"You look like you could use a break," Dinara said as we left an antiques dealership.

"I'm fine," I told her. It was bad enough being useless. I was determined I at least wouldn't be the one to slow us down.

"The owner recognized Ernest Fisher," Dinara told me, gesturing toward the double-fronted store on the ground floor of a large redbrick building. The shop's windows were full of old Russian and Ottoman furniture and art. "He said Fisher bought an armoire from him a few years ago. He came in to have some restoration work done to one of the drawers shortly after buying it."

"Might have been the one the key was hidden in," I remarked.

"Maybe," Dinara agreed. "The owner hasn't seen Fisher since."

We walked down the street a little and stood near the corner of Krasnopresnenskaya Naberezhnaya, the Embankment. The light was fading quickly, and the buildings on the other side of the river were already twinkling in the last of the sunshine. It would be dark soon and the stores would close for the day, and we'd be left with restaurants and bars. Despite the canvass being my idea, I couldn't help but feel we were clutching at straws.

I looked around, searching for inspiration. We'd already canvassed most of the nearby businesses and would soon need to widen the area of our search. I glanced at Dinara, who was pale. The legacy of her ordeal at the hands of Veles and his associates? Or had her hangover finally caught up with her? Or was she simply feeling the effects of a long day trudging the frozen city? We couldn't carry on for much longer.

I looked down Year 1905 Street and saw a taxi pull into a spot near the corner of the Embankment. It was soon followed by three others, and the four drivers got out and clustered on the sidewalk. Three of them lit cigarettes and the fourth used a vape.

"Come on," I said to Dinara, and I felt her spirits lift when she registered where we were heading.

The taxi drivers looked as though they were from Central Asia. They all wore heavy woolen coats and thick beanie hats and were laughing and chatting, but when one of them spotted us, he signaled the others and they fell silent.

"Taxi?" the nudger asked.

Dinara replied in Russian, and the man looked blank and held up his hands in the universal gesture of incomprehension.

"English?" I tried.

"Is better," the man replied.

"Where are you from?" I asked.

"Uzbekistan," he said uncertainly.

"Do you work this neighborhood?" I said.

One of his companions muttered something and the nudger clammed up.

"Talk is trouble," the mutterer said. His dark skin was puckered around his mouth and eyes, and his bushy black eyebrows were flecked with gray that almost matched his patched coat. I placed him in his mid-forties, but his eyes seemed older, as though they belonged to someone who'd seen a lifetime of misery.

"We're not looking for trouble," I replied. "We're trying to find people who recognize this man."

I produced a photograph of Ernie Fisher and showed it to the group. The mutterer took a drag of his cigarette.

"How much?" he asked. "If my eyes see him. How much you pay?"

"If you can give us useful information, we can come to a deal," I said.

"Deal not money," the mutterer said, backing toward his cab, an old Skoda. "Time is money."

"A hundred US dollars," I offered. "More if you give us something worthwhile."

He took another drag of his cigarette. "OK. Come," he said. "Come in taxi."

"Jack ..." Dinara interjected, her concern evident in her voice.

"It's OK," I replied.

"Come," the mutterer repeated. "We take a ride."

CHAPTER 64

THE OPPRESSIVE DARKNESS of a January night set in during our journey across the city.

"What's your name?" I asked the mutterer, who drove with two fingers on the wheel.

"Ghani," he replied, glancing back at Dinara and me. "From Afghanistan. You know it?"

I knew it all too well. The memory of my last day on the battlefield was still seared in my mind. I'd lost so many friends, and our driver might have sympathized with the people who'd killed them. Heck, he might have been one of them.

"No," I replied. It was simpler to lie. "I've never been."

"I have," Dinara replied, surprising me. "A long time ago. In Kabul."

The driver nodded, and I got the sense he knew better than to pry. Had she been there with the FSB? As a Russian operative?

Or simply as a traveler? It was a part of the world that was so damaged a simple conversation risked opening a sectarian can of worms.

"When did you last see the man in the photograph?" I asked.

Ghani sucked on his cigarette. He'd taken off his hat and rubbed a hand through his thick salt and pepper hair. He exhaled a cloud of smoke, which I tried my best to ignore in the confined, warm cabin of his rattling Skoda.

"The day after yesterday," he said.

"The day before yesterday?" Dinara qualified.

Ghani nodded. "Yes, yes."

I glanced at Dinara and saw that she was also alive with the thrill of a lead.

"What time?" I asked.

"Morning," he replied. "Maybe ten o'clock."

That was roughly an hour before Ernie Fisher was murdered.

"He ask me to take him to Lefortovo. To a fun house. He tell me wait then we go to airport," Ghani said. "But we never go airport. When he come out of fun house, he angry. Mad. Tell me take him home. He forget something."

"The key?" Dinara guessed.

Ghani looked at her blankly.

"Fun house?" I asked.

"You know," Ghani replied. He arched his eyebrows, sucked on his cigarette and glanced at Dinara. "For girls."

"He means a brothel," Dinara clarified.

"Fun house," Ghani repeated. "Is where I take you."

He drew in another lungful of smoke and exhaled slowly, filling the velour-covered cabin with a thick cloud.

"You married?" he asked us.

"No," Dinara replied. "We work together."

"Why no?" Ghani asked. "You very beautiful," he told Dinara. "And he got the eyes of a mountain man."

"Is that good?" I asked.

"Yes. Is very good," Ghani replied. "You keep woman safe. You dangerous."

CHAPTER 65

A GROUP OF four rowdy men rounded the corner. They were pushing each other and jeering as they made their way along Energeticheskiy Passage.

Ghani was crawling along the road, which enabled Dinara to take in the neighborhood. They were in Lefortovo District to the east of the city, one of the most deprived parts of Moscow. Energeticheskiy had to be one of the low points of the area. The tall blocks that flanked the street were crumbling and covered in graffiti. One wing of the huge apartment building on the corner had been gutted by fire and the windows had been blown out, but the rest of the structure was still inhabited. Discarded food containers, empty bottles, nitrous canisters and needles littered the gray slush that covered the pavements.

Ghani's taxi was crawling along because there was an old Mercedes ahead of them, cruising the street, the driver examining the women who stood in lit apartment windows, or who braved the freezing conditions in faux fur coats and little else.

The four rowdy men on the sidewalk chatted to a couple of fur-clad women and went into one of the rundown Soviet-era blocks. There was little doubt what this particular street was famed for.

The Mercedes stopped and the driver, a bald man in his sixties with a jowly face, beckoned a young woman who couldn't have been more than twenty.

Ghani tooted his horn, but the jowly man ignored him.

"He's doing business," Ghani said.

Dinara looked at Jack and saw him frown. Was he wondering the same things she was? As the woman leaned through the driver's window, what went through her mind? What did she really think of this older, unattractive man and the things he was asking her to do with him?

The woman didn't look happy, but she nodded, and rounded the back of the jowly man's car where her haunted eyes were caught in Ghani's headlights. She climbed in the passenger seat of the Mercedes and the car sped away.

"Sad girl," Ghani observed as he continued along the street.

"This is it," he said, stopping his taxi outside a decrepit old villa. "The fun house."

"Can you wait?" Jack asked as he opened the door.

"Sure," Ghani replied. "No problem."

Dinara shivered as she and Jack got out of the taxi and approached the brothel. Ghani pulled into a space a short distance up the street.

The fun house was an old imperial villa that had somehow survived the vast Soviet-era developments that had been constructed around it. Fifteen-story blocks loomed either side of the villa's small garden, and the patches of damp that blackened the building suggested it rarely got any light. Fitting, because it was immediately obvious it was home to the kind of business that thrived in darkness. A woman wearing nothing but her underwear lounged on a recliner in one of the upstairs windows. The room was backlit in crimson, and she eyed Dinara and Jack suggestively as they approached the building.

They passed a once grand wall that had crumbled long ago. The ruins poked through the thick snow, which covered the small front garden. A couple of mangy, leafless trees were the only things to protrude from the white blanket and their branches reached skyward like the bony fingers of a dying animal. The house itself was also crumbling. The window frames were rotten, the painted façade cracked and flaking and the guttering was broken.

Dinara followed Jack up the steps and he tugged on an ancient bell pull. Moments later, the door was opened by a huge man in a dark suit with a shaved head.

"Come in," he said in Russian.

"Welcome, darlings," a voice chimed, and Dinara saw a large woman sashay along the hallway. She wore a billowing outfit of many folds and colors, a dusty blond wig, and her face was caked in thick makeup, which made her age difficult to guess. She could have been anywhere between fifty and eighty.

"A couple," the woman remarked. "Very adventurous, my dears."

The interior of the house was almost as much of an assault on the senses as the woman's dress. Brightly painted walls, erotic sketches and photographs, nude sculptures, gaudy cushions, throws and drapes of every hue collided to ensure the mind was equally amused and disgusted wherever the eyes fell.

"My name is Madame Agafiya," the woman said in Russian. "Welcome to my humble house. Tell me, do you want one girl, or two? Or maybe a man?"

Dinara looked at an uncomprehending Jack, and blushed. "None, thank you," she replied in Russian. "We're here to ask some questions."

"Police?" Agafiya asked, suddenly on edge.

"No," Dinara replied.

"What's the matter with him?" Agafiya asked, gesturing at Jack. "Doesn't he speak?"

"He's American," Dinara replied, and Agafiya's eyes lit up.

"Ah, American," she said in English. "We have many American friends who visit us here. Our girls speak excellent English for the best intimate moments. My name is Madame Agafiya, American friend, and I welcome you to my house."

"We're just here for answers," Jack said. "Nothing else."

Agafiya's smile fell away. "We don't give answers," she said bitterly. "Only pleasure." She looked at the huge bouncer. "Show them out," she commanded in Russian.

The bouncer put his hand on Jack's shoulder, and Dinara saw from the change in her boss's expression that the man had made a serious mistake.

Jack grabbed the bouncer's hand and twisted his fingers to breaking point, forcing the huge man to his knees and making him groan in pain.

Jack fixed Agafiya with an unflinching stare. "Answers are our pleasure," he said.

CHAPTER 66

"PLEASURE COSTS," MADAME Agafiya said.

"We're willing to pay," I replied, releasing the big man's hand.

He backed away with the insolent look worn by all defeated men: *I could have beaten you if I'd really been trying.*

I paid him no mind. He could have his bravado and I'd keep my victory.

"Then let us get out of this cold hall and go somewhere warm," Madame Agafiya said.

She led us into a parlor off the hallway. It was a large room with high ceilings and was furnished with every piece Moscow's flea markets had to offer. Or at least it seemed that way. There was clutter everywhere, and two green fabric couches stood as islands among a sea of pictures, photos, figurines and tiny collectibles. Was it designed to disorientate her patrons? Or simply to mask the decayed state of the building?

"Sit." Agafiya gestured at the couch nearest the window.

She settled on the one opposite, and her bouncer watched us from the doorway. Dinara and I did as instructed, and I felt the old springs give as I sat on the frayed couch.

"What answers? And how much?" Agafiya asked as she arranged the layers of her multi-colored dress.

"We'd like to ask you about Ernest Fisher," Dinara replied. "We were told he came here."

Agafiya's hands froze and she studied them as though they were suddenly the most interesting things in the world.

"I don't know this man," she said.

I ignored the obvious lie and produced a photograph and showed it to her. "Ernie Fisher," I said, "but it's possible you know him by another name."

Her eyes flashed with indignation when she looked up. Her gaze softened as it shifted from me to the photograph.

"I've never seen this man before," she lied. "Who are you people?"

"Would it make a difference if you knew he was dead?" I asked.

Agafiya looked as though she'd been slapped in the face. "You lie," she said.

Dinara produced her phone and showed the stunned Russian madam a news article based on the Otkrov blog piece. It featured a photo of Ernie Fisher and gave an account of his death.

"Why would someone do this?" Agafiya said at last. "Ernst was a nice man."

"So you did know him," I remarked.

She nodded, and tears formed in her eyes. "He was an old friend. He told me never to say I knew him or that he was here."

"Where did you meet?" I asked.

"Many years ago. I worked in a bar. He was a customer," Agafiya said. "Long time ago."

"How long?"

"Maybe thirty years?" she said.

"In Russia?" I asked.

"Of course," Agafiya replied. "I've never been to another country."

I was surprised. There was nothing in Fisher's history to suggest he had any contact with Russia prior to his chief-of-staff posting.

"Did he have a room here?" I pressed. "A private space?"

Agafiya shifted uncomfortably.

"He's dead," I said. "Your silence doesn't protect him anymore. It just protects the people who killed him."

Agafiya eyed me uncertainly.

"If you help us, we might be able to find the man who murdered Mr. Fisher," I assured her.

She nodded. "Downstairs. But there's nothing there."

"Nothing?" Dinara asked.

"He told me never to go inside, but I did. Just to see, you know," Agafiya said. "The room is totally empty."

"Can you show us?" I asked.

CHAPTER 67

THE BASEMENT WAS a vast, damp, dingy space which was accessed through a heavy locked door and a staircase that ran down from the kitchen. The place was ripe with decades of rot.

"You see?" Agafiya said. "Nothing."

Knotted old floorboards and exposed stonework formed the outer shell of the basement. The house above was supported by rows of stone columns, which had been half encased in wood cabinets. There was nothing else in the room.

"Does anyone else have a key?" I asked.

Agafiya shook her head. "Me and Ernst."

"Who put the cabinets around the columns?" Dinara asked.

"Ernst," Agafiya replied. "He told me it was to protect them."

Dinara and I shared a look of excitement. The structural supports were slightly larger than the safe we were looking for.

"How many are there?" I asked.

She looked bemused. "You Americans can count, surely?"

"So you don't know?" I said.

"There are thirteen," Dinara remarked.

"Thirteen," Agafiya repeated emphatically.

I stalked through the basement, examining the floorboards around the supports, looking for any sign of disturbance.

I found it in the heart of the room. I crouched down and touched a scuff mark beside a column. Scored lines arced across the floorboards. I checked the cabinet around the support and was gratified to feel a catch at the top. I pressed it and the panel directly in front of me swung off a latch and eased open a little. I pulled it wide to reveal a Kaso safe inside the cabinet. I tapped the stonework directly above it, and heard a hollow sound. The stone rising above the safe was a façade designed to fool people into thinking this was just another structural support.

"What is it?" Agafiya asked, hurrying forward. "A safe? Why would Ernst need a safe?"

I produced the key I'd found in Fisher's apartment, and pushed it into the lock. I felt the satisfying clunk of the cylinders disengaging and the bolts drawing back.

Agafiya whistled when I opened the door. Like Karl Parker, Fisher had a stash of guns, documents and a huge amount of cash.

"For escape," Dinara observed.

I nodded.

"Why didn't he use it?" she asked.

I nodded toward a drill that was wedged between the safe and the surrounding panels. There were circular scores near the lock.

"I think he forgot his key," I replied. It was a mundane mistake, the kind that littered most people's lives. Unfortunately for Ernie Fisher, he had paid the ultimate price for it. "I think that's why he went back to his apartment."

"He was getting very forgetful," Agafiya said. "And sad. He drank too much."

"Do you know why?" I asked.

She shook her head.

"We'd better search it," Dinara said.

She crouched beside the safe and started sifting through the contents.

"What will happen to the money?" Agafiya asked.

"This is your house," I replied. "How you handle this discovery is up to you."

Agafiya brightened. "For the first time in many years, fate gives me pleasure."

I was only half listening. Dinara's shoulder had brushed against something that had been stuck to the inside of the door, and dislodged it. As it floated to the floor, I realized it was a Polaroid photograph. It landed face down, and when I picked it up and turned it over, I almost recoiled in shock.

The faded old image was of Ernie Fisher, Elizabeth Connor and Karl Parker as smiling teenagers, arms around each other's shoulders, the familiar pose of close friends caught in a moment of pure joy.

CHAPTER 68

"I TOOK THAT picture," Agafiya said wistfully. "I didn't know he had kept it."

I studied the picture, my mind in freefall as I tried to come up with a logical explanation for its existence. Two things shocked me about the image. The first was the Spartak Moscow top sported by Karl Parker, and the second was the Russian imagery and signs that surrounded them.

"That was the bar where I met Ernst," Agafiya continued, "where I used to work."

She took the photograph from me and stroked Fisher's likeness tenderly.

"I loved him very much," she said. "I was younger then. Not too much older than him, but enough. He told me I was his first."

Dinara had halted her search and looked at the photo in disbelief. "Ernest Fisher, Karl Parker and Elizabeth Conner knew each other," she remarked in astonishment. "In Russia?"

"I didn't know the others. Just Ernst," Agafiya said. "He was a fine young man. It's very sad what has happened to him." Tears welled in her eyes.

"Where was this?" I asked.

"Volkovo, north of Rybinsk," Agafiya replied.

"Do you know what they were doing there?" I asked.

She shook her head. "Ernst always said he could never talk about it. But he told me it was the biggest mistake of his life. Not then, but now. He said he regretted it every day."

Dinara and I shared a knowing look. Her theory about guilt being behind his drinking was starting to sound plausible. It seemed clear Ernie Fisher had been living a lie.

"But back then he was full of himself. He would come to the bar often and try to win me with his words," Agafiya said. "His friends only came once. When I took that picture. They were greedy for drink. Vodka. Like it was their last day alive."

"Were they talking Russian?" I asked.

"I don't remember about the other two, but Ernst definitely spoke to me in Russian," she replied. "How else could he hope to win my heart? I didn't learn English until I came to Moscow many years later."

"Were you still ... ?" Dinara trailed off, but Agafiya got her meaning immediately.

"No, no," she replied. "Our love is a memory. When he found me again, we were only friends. Not even that. I think he just wanted someone to listen to him while he drank. Or maybe he just wanted this basement."

I looked at the photograph she held in her pale hand, and struggled to make sense of what she'd just told us. My friend, the man I'd crossed half the world to seek justice for, wasn't the man I thought he was. The younger version of Karl Parker, who grinned up at me from the old picture, was a stranger who wasn't supposed to exist. Karl Parker had been raised in Clarion, Iowa, and according to all the information Mo-bot had been able to find, he had never once been to Russia.

"You said Ernie Fisher spoke Russian to you in the past. What about now?" I asked.

"Of course," Agafiya said. "What else would he speak? He was an office administrator for a trading company in Moscow."

"Didn't you read the article?" I asked.

She stared at me coldly. "Not beyond the headline announcing the death of my old friend," she said bitterly.

"Ernie Fisher was the chief of staff for the US ambassador to Moscow," I said.

"No," Agafiya responded. "That's not possible."

She looked to Dinara for confirmation, and my colleague nodded emphatically.

"We've got to go to Volkovo," I said to Dinara. "I need to find out what they were doing there. I have to know who Karl Parker really was."

CHAPTER 69

GHANI TOOK US back to Fisher's apartment building where Leonid was waiting. I paid the Afghan cab driver a couple of hundred bucks for his help, and he went away smiling.

"Where to?" Leonid asked.

"Volkovo," Dinara replied. "Yaroslavl Oblast."

"Really?" the former cop replied uncertainly.

I nodded. "Karl Parker, Elizabeth Connor and Ernie Fisher were there as teenagers. We need to find out why."

"OK," Leonid said. "But it's a long drive, especially in this weather."

It wasn't snowing, but the clouds were bruised and swollen and the air had sharp teeth.

"I'll call Feo and let him know where he can collect his truck," Dinara said.

"No," Leonid responded. "We'll take it. The heating in my uncle's Lada still doesn't work."

Soon we were inside Feo's truck with the heating on full as we sped through the city. While Leonid drove, I tried the Parker home in Long Island, but there was no answer. I dialed Justine and she responded almost immediately.

"Everything OK, Jack?" she asked.

"Yeah," I replied. "How are things there?"

"The Otkrov story has broken and we're catching some heat. Mainstream media is reporting the allegations, but some of the conspiracy bloggers are having a field day and digging through every high-profile case we've ever worked."

"And our clients?" I asked.

"No one's said anything," Justine replied. "At least not yet."

"No one will," I remarked. "We'll just get termination emails from their lawyers if things get too hot."

"Speaking of heat, NYPD has been leaned on," Justine revealed. "We're not getting their cooperation anymore. Rick Tana, the detective in charge, says it's come from City Hall, a precautionary measure in case Private really is in bed with the Ninety-nine."

I sighed. "The Ninety-nine probably doesn't even exist."

"The lack of cooperation is making Sci and Mo's lives more difficult, but they're fighting on," she said.

"I've got another battle for them. I need everything we can find on Karl Parker's childhood," I said. "And I want confirmation he never left America as a kid. Same goes for Ernie Fisher and Elizabeth Connor."

"Why?" Justine asked.

"We've found a photograph that puts them in a small town a few hours north of Moscow. It suggests they knew each other as teenagers."

"Photos can be faked," she countered.

"This one feels genuine," I replied. "And we have a witness."

"People lie, and the best fakes always seem real," Justine observed. "But I'll ask Mo to look into it. Sci is in Washington checking the evidence from the Robert Carlyle crash."

"Thanks," I said. "One last thing. I just tried to call Victoria Parker, but there was no answer. Can you ask her to phone me as soon as possible?"

"Sure," Justine replied. "What time is it there?"

"Ten," I replied. "We're heading out of the city to check out the place the photo was taken."

"Be careful," Justine cautioned, before hanging up.

"She doesn't think the picture is genuine?" Dinara asked.

"She's right," I conceded. "It could be a fake."

I took the photograph from my coat pocket. I'd put it inside a cellophane evidence bag to protect it. Everything about the old Polaroid seemed authentic, but Justine was right, it was not beyond the capabilities of a good forger.

"Of course, if it is real ..." Dinara trailed off, but she didn't need to finish her sentence.

I knew exactly what she was implying. If the photograph was genuine, there was a distinct possibility Karl Parker was a Russian agent. Was that what he'd wanted to talk to me about on the day he died? And if so, why now? I couldn't believe my old friend, a man who'd served our country with distinction, could ever betray it. There could be a more innocent explanation, but I was struggling to come up with what that might be.

The possibility continued to trouble me as Leonid drove north out of the city into the frozen wilderness beyond.

CHAPTER 70

WHAT SHOULD HAVE been a five-hour drive became ten. The bad weather turned a 250-mile straight line into a crooked route of road closures and diversions. We shared the driving, and I took the dawn shift after a few hours' bad sleep on the back seat. We'd passed Rybinsk and were traveling through the ancient pine forests of Yaroslavl, along a deserted single-lane road. Dinara was asleep on the back seat, and Leonid was dozing next to me. The truck's heater filled the cabin with warm air, but just looking at the huge icy drifts that had been carved by snow plows was enough to make me shiver. They were so cold, their edges were tinged a toothpaste blue and the air seemed to shimmer around them.

Halfway between Rybinsk and Volkovo, we passed the wreckage of an accident. Two overturned, burned-out cars lay at the edge of the vast pine forest, their scorched rusting shells half covered in snow, suggesting the accident had happened months ago. I wondered whether anyone had survived. Even if they'd lived through the crash, what chance did they have in such hostile conditions, so far from help?

The sun had risen by the time I drove into Volkovo, and the town was just starting to wake up. Less than a mile in diameter, Volkovo straddled an inlet that branched off the enormous Rybinsk Reservoir, which lay to our west, concealed by thick forest. The town was made up of a couple of hundred homes and a handful of businesses. Most of the wooden houses had been constructed on spacious lots and many of them were in a state of disrepair. Volkovo reminded me of an Alpine village without the money.

Every building was capped with a thick layer of snow, which had turned to ice in the freezing temperatures. The tracks and driveways that lay off the main road were lost beneath deep drifts, and the parking bays that lined the street were populated by hillocks of snow, each of which marked a buried car.

Agafiya had told us the bar had been on route P104, the main drag that ran through the heart of town, and I followed the directions given by my phone's GPS to the location. I slowed and turned right into a yard in front of a square white single-story building. Leonid and Dinara stirred when I brought the car to a halt near the bright green front door.

Leonid yawned and stretched, and as I looked past him, I saw the bar was gone. Judging by the contents of the misty windows that flanked the entrance, the place was now a bakery.

"This is it," I told the others.

"Wait here," Leonid said, before getting out.

The blast of cold air countered the soporific effects of the heater and revived me after the long drive. I looked around the deserted town and tried to picture Karl Parker here. He simply didn't fit, and the more I thought about it, the more I found myself drawn to Justine's suggestion that the photograph might be fake.

"What would an American be doing out here?" Dinara asked. "Even Russians don't come here. At least not willingly."

"It must be nice in summer," I observed, and she replied with a snort of derision.

Leonid emerged from the bakery with a fully laden plastic bag.

"Breakfast," he said, signaling the bounty of bread and pastries as he jumped in the car.

"I'm not hungry," I responded.

"Any kalach?" Dinara asked.

Leonid nodded and ferreted in the bag for a hooped bun, which he handed her.

"Head up the street and make the next left toward the waterfront," he said, before taking a bite from a glazed pastry. "The bar closed ten years ago, but the owner still lives in town."

Ten minutes later, we were in the living room of a small wooden house that overlooked the frozen inlet. Nikita Garin, the bemused former owner of the Novoko Bar, was in the kitchen and Dinara, Leonid and I sat on frayed green corduroy couches and exchanged furtive glances. They'd fast-talked our way into the house, but the gray-haired, puffy-faced ex-barkeep hadn't needed too much convincing. I counted six cats, a parakeet and three dogs, and got the sense this was a man in desperate need of company.

The old instincts of a host hadn't died and Nikita emerged from the kitchen with a pot of tea and four glasses. He sat next to me in his pajamas and a threadbare dressing gown, and spoke to Dinara and Leonid as he poured the tea. His English was limited to "hello" and "OK," which is what he said when he handed me a glass of milky sweet tea.

"Show him the picture," Dinara advised me.

I produced the photograph Agafiya had taken in the Novoko Bar and showed it to Nikita.

The old barman smiled and started talking.

"He says he remembers them. Well, the one in the middle, at least," Dinara translated as Nikita pointed to Ernie Fisher. "He would always come to the bar and try to impress Agafiya. He would hang around trying to get her to go on a date."

"Where was he from?" I asked. "Was he local?"

Dinara translated, and Nikita shook his head.

"No, not local. Not really," Dinara said. "Apparently Ernest Fisher got very drunk one night and Nikita had to drive him home. He took him to the gatehouse of Boltino, an army base six kilometers north of here."

My stomach lurched as my worst fears about my friend gained substance.

Dinara continued. "Boltino Army Base was shut down in 2002, but before then it was a key strategic installation. One of the most restricted places in all of Russia."

CHAPTER 71

IT TOOK DINARA and Jack almost an hour to cover six kilometers. Boltino Army Base was located northeast of Volkovo, and they almost missed the overgrown access road off route P104. The rusty way-markers were largely lost to snow, and only the very tips of the metal poles were visible.

The access road was buried beneath two feet of snow, and the truck's four-wheel drive struggled to cope with the conditions. Jack had to jump out every so often and clear a path with Feo's shovel where the snow had drifted higher in places.

Leonid had stayed in town. Nikita had given him the names and addresses of locals who'd worked at the base, and Leonid planned to quiz them for more information, and see whether anyone else recognized Karl Parker, Ernie Fisher and Elizabeth Connor.

Dinara tapped the steering wheel as Jack returned to the truck, tossed the shovel in the back, and climbed into the passenger seat. He was sweating and breathing heavily, which wasn't surprising. He'd just cleared a twelve-foot stretch of road. Dinara drove slowly forward, the car inching along the furrows Jack had dug, the chunky snow tires digging into the crisp powder. The trees were close on both sides, and cast everything in shadow. The edges of the road weren't clear, so Dinara simply stayed in the middle of the long thin scar that had been cut through the forest. The route banked right; then, after a long, sweeping turn, it straightened up, and Dinara saw the remains of a gatehouse ahead of them.

Beyond the derelict structure lay a dozen buildings, warehouses, silos and stores. Even with the cleansing blanket of snow, Dinara could see the extent to which the structures had decayed. There were dark holes in the roofs, and rust was eating every visible surface. Most of the windows were cracked or missing entirely, and steel shutters were either buckled or absent.

"The snow is getting deeper," Jack said. "Let's leave the car here."

Dinara nodded and slowed to a halt. She put the truck in neutral and pulled on the parking brake, but left the engine running.

"So nothing freezes," she explained as she and Jack got out.

They grabbed their coats from the back seat and trudged through thick snow to the deserted base.

Once they were away from the vehicle, the only noise came from their steps. Otherwise the place was eerily quiet. The snow deadened sound, but there was none to be heard. No animals, birds or people, not even a whisper of wind. The clouds hung low above them and didn't seem to move. Dinara shivered as she and Jack approached what looked like the main administration building, but she wasn't sure the chill she felt was entirely a result of the cold. She couldn't shake the sense they were being watched, and, out here, far from help, they were vulnerable.

If such fears troubled Jack, he didn't show it. His eyes were fixed with grim determination. Dinara could only imagine what he was feeling. Each new revelation would shake the foundations of his friendship with Karl Parker, so the need to discover the truth must be unbearable for him.

The faded sign beside the long three-story structure said "Central Command," and Dinara translated it for Jack. The main doors were locked but the floor-to-ceiling windows had been smashed, so they stepped over the rusting frames and went inside.

The only thing in the lobby was a broken office chair that had been gnawed by animals. Snow had fallen through a hole in the roof, and huge shining icicles hung from the ragged edges of the collapsed ceiling two stories above.

Dinara and Jack moved further into the abandoned building. None of the interior doors were locked, not even the three-inch-steel blast doors that had been designed to protect critical sections from any kind of attack. It was in one such section, in the east wing of the building, where they discovered an unusual set of rooms. They found four dormitories, each of which contained twelve concrete bunks. Any mattresses were long gone, but there was no doubt these were sleeping quarters.

"Soldiers wouldn't usually be housed in the command block," Jack observed. "Why are there sleeping quarters here?"

Dinara didn't have an answer, and they left the room and continued through the eerie, derelict building.

Further along the wing, they found a large room with panoramic windows that overlooked the rest of the base. The panes had been smashed and a high drift had been blown across the room. When they stepped inside, Jack noticed something protruding from the snow, and he pushed through it to reach a sheet of wood, which he struggled to lift. As she approached to help, Dinara realized the object was an old-fashioned school desk.

She and Jack pulled it free of the icy grip of the snow, and dragged it off the drift onto the concrete floor near the door. Jack opened the lid and found yet more snow, but when he dug around inside, he discovered a Captain America pencil case, and a frozen book that had almost rotted away.

He closed the desk, put the book on the lid and brushed the worst of the ice off the cover. Dinara made out a bright yellow masthead and a pair of blank eyes above a giant, gaping mouth.

"I know this," Jack said. "It's a *Goosebumps* book." He read the words at the top of the masthead. "R. L. Stine." His fingers tracked to the text at the foot of the cover. "*Night of the Living Dummy.*"

Jack stood upright and fixed Dinara with a puzzled look.

"Why is there a child's pencil case and an American kids' book in a maximum-security military base?" he asked.

CHAPTER 72

WE SEARCHED THE rest of the base as thoroughly as we could, but in the end the freezing conditions defeated us, and we left without going inside two of the hangars. The others had all been empty, and apart from the desk in what we assumed had once been a classroom, we discovered nothing of note.

I struggled to imagine what Ernie Fisher had been doing there, and had even more difficulty picturing Karl Parker at the base.

It was a little after 3 p.m. when we returned to the idling car, which was almost out of fuel. Our journey back to Volkovo took fifteen minutes. There had been no fresh snowfall and I'd dug out the worst drifts on our way to the base.

We found Leonid waiting in the bakery. He was sitting at a small table enjoying a coffee and pastry, chatting to the owner, who stood behind a display counter.

"Anything?" Leonid asked when we entered.

"We found a classroom and an old American children's book," I said. "Nothing else."

"*Kofe?*" the baker asked.

Finally, a word I could understand. I shook my head. "No, thanks," I replied. "We should get going," I said to Dinara and Leonid. "Get back to Moscow. See if we can pick up any leads. I want us to look into Ernie Fisher's work at the embassy."

Leonid got to his feet.

"You find anything?" I asked.

"No," he replied. "The people I spoke to were junior personnel. Gate guards, patrolmen. None of them knew about any of the classified activities at the base. And they didn't recognize anyone in the photo."

Leonid settled his check, and we left the bakery, got in the truck and headed south. We filled up at a gas station not far outside town, and as we sped toward Moscow in the fading light, I tried to put the pieces together.

Karl Parker had asked me to New York to tell me a secret, but he'd been killed before we could speak. If Madame Agafiya and the Volkovo bar owner's testimony was to be trusted, it seemed likely Karl knew Ernie Fisher and Elizabeth Connor, and that they might have met in Russia, where Fisher seemed to have spent some time in a maximum-security military base. If Fisher had been a Russian operative, why had he been killed by one of his own?

I sat in the back of the truck, turning over scenarios, while Leonid drove. After a couple of hours, he and Dinara traded, and another three hours later, I took the wheel. It was 9 p.m., and we were a little under one hundred miles from Moscow when my phone rang. I pulled to the side of the dark, deserted road and took the call.

"Jack, it's Victoria. Justine Smith said I should call."

"Victoria, how are you and Kevin holding up?"

She sighed. "It seems wrong, but you eat, you sleep, you do the mundane things that need to get done. I always thought grief was all-consuming, but life forces its way in."

"I'm sorry, Victoria," I said. "I wish I could have done something."

"You're doing enough," she replied. "Sorry it took me a while to return your call. Kevin and I have been staying with my folks."

"I wanted to ask you about Karl's childhood," I said. "He talk about it much?"

"Why do you want to know?"

I couldn't tell her what we'd discovered. Not yet. Not without more evidence.

"We're just running full background on all the victims," I replied.

"He didn't like talking about it," she said. "His parents died in a car crash when he was seven, and he didn't have any other family, so he went into the foster system."

"I didn't know that."

"Like I said, he didn't like to talk about it," she replied. "And he had his official records sealed by court order. I think he tried to erase as much of his childhood as he could. He just found it too painful."

I thought about her answer. Karl's behavior was compatible with the actions of a spy, or they could have been those of someone who wanted to forget a traumatic childhood.

"Anything else?" Victoria asked.

"Can you dig out any childhood pictures you have of Karl?" I asked. "Send them to Justine?"

"Sure," Victoria replied. "And Jack ..." She hesitated. "Thank you for everything you're doing."

"Don't thank me," I said. "I owe it to Karl to find out the truth."

"What did she say?" Dinara asked from the back after I'd hung up.

"He lost his parents young and went into care. He took steps to get his childhood history sealed."

"Either he suffered things as a child that he wanted to keep secret," Leonid remarked, "or he's a spy."

"My thoughts exactly," I said.

"I may have a way for us to find out what was going on at that base," Leonid said. He was leaning back in the passenger seat, which he'd set to recline, and looking at him made me think of a lazy snake. Languid and patient, but lightning fast and deadly when the time came to strike.

"It will involve us doing a deal with the devil," he revealed.

I shot him a skeptical look.

"Let's go," he told me. "I'll explain on the way."

I put the truck in gear and we headed into darkness.

CHAPTER 73

LEONID BOYKOV YAWNED and shifted in his seat. He'd told Dinara and Jack his plan during the drive back from Volkovo. He'd billed it as a deal with the devil, but that was melodramatic. In truth, he planned some mutual backscratching with a Moscow cop, and Jack had approved the idea.

They'd arrived back at the Residence shortly after midnight, and Leonid had resisted Feo's invitation to join him and a few reprobates in a backgammon tournament. Instead, Leonid had gone straight to bed.

He'd risen at 5 a.m., feeling tired and dull, but a coffee and the short walk to his car that had filled his lungs with ice-cold air shocked him awake. He'd driven through the quiet city to Zhitnaya Street and the Ministry of Internal Affairs. He'd parked nearby, and had gone inside. After introducing himself to the officer on duty, he'd taken a seat in the grand lobby and waited.

A call to an old colleague had revealed Anna Bolshova's shift started at 6 a.m., and when she arrived ten minutes early, she looked tired and miserable. Her mood darkened further when she caught sight of Leonid. He intercepted her as she crossed the expansive lobby.

"Whatever it is," she said, "I don't have time."

"I've got something for you," Leonid replied.

"Really," Anna said, feigning interest. "I'm so lucky to have you in my life."

"You are," Leonid responded.

Anna's mood soured. "Do you have any idea what you've done? They're talking about sending me back to regular duty for destroying an SVR investigation." She picked up her pace. They were almost at the security barriers.

"It's a big one."

Anna stopped in her tracks and turned toward Leonid. He felt waves of anger radiating off her.

"What have you got for me this time?" she asked. "Are you going to get me to raid the Kremlin? Or perhaps round up the government?"

"You're going to like this," Leonid said.

"No, I'm not," she replied. "Leave me alone, Leonid Boykov."

She turned away from him and marched toward the security barriers. She pulled a pass from her pocket and was about to scan it, when Leonid spoke up.

"What if I could give you a Black Hundreds recruiter?"

Anna stopped and looked at him skeptically. The offer had even managed to get the duty officer's attention, but he quickly went back to the paperwork he was doing at the front desk.

Anna slowly retraced her steps. "How?" she asked.

"He's got his chapter running a sideline," Leonid revealed when he and Anna were toe to toe. "Selling narcotics."

She whistled. "Even Black Hundreds' supporters within the force won't try to protect him if that's true."

"Exactly," Leonid said. "It's an easy win. You can arrest the entire ring, put away some rotten apples and do it without fear of political interference. The Black Hundreds might try to kill the man, but they certainly won't protect him."

"Who's the recruiter?" Anna asked.

Leonid smiled, and Anna backed away, exasperated.

"And here's me thinking this was payback for sabotaging my career," she remarked.

"What's one thing got to do with the other?" Leonid asked. "This is a new favor, and a new favor deserves a new reward."

"What do you want?"

"Your assignment to the Interior Ministry gives you access to information beyond the reach of a normal police officer," Leonid replied. "I need you to find out what Boltino Army Base was used for."

"Tell me who the recruiter is," Anna replied.

Leonid slipped a card into her hand. "Here's my number," he said. "Call me when you've got answers."

He backed toward the exit.

"I should have you arrested," she said.

"But you won't," he responded. "Find out what was happening at Boltino, and I'll give you a name that will put you back on the command fast track."

CHAPTER 74

I WAS IN the library with Dinara when Leonid returned to the Residence. We were checking through the photographs Justine had sent us of Karl Parker as a child. Victoria had taken his album of childhood pictures to Private New York, and Justine had had them scanned and sent to Dinara's secure email.

There were baby photos, pictures of Karl as a young child, then there was a gap that started when he was around seven years old, the same time as his parents' accident. The pictures resumed when he was a teenager, maybe fifteen or sixteen years old. I wondered what had happened to my friend in those intervening years, and kept returning to the image of him, Elizabeth Connor and Ernie Fisher in the Novoko Bar in Volkovo.

"I made the offer," Leonid said, taking a seat at the neighboring table. "Then I checked on the surveillance team watching

Erik Utkin. They say he's definitely supplying the dealers. He has eight teams selling drugs throughout Kapotnya."

"They documenting it?" I asked.

"Of course," Leonid replied. "Gathering everything they can on camera."

"And will Anna Bolshova get us what we need?" Dinara asked.

"I think so," Leonid replied. "She needs a win to get out of trouble with her superiors." He looked at his watch. "Anyone hungry?" he asked. "Lunch finishes soon. Or do you just live on clues and paperwork?"

Dinara smiled and got to her feet. I was about to follow when my phone rang. It was Justine.

"Go ahead," I told them. "I'll catch up."

They left the library as I answered.

"I managed to get hold of the chief of police of Clarion," Justine said. "He was the officer on duty the night Karl Parker's parents died. I've got him on the line now."

"Patch him through," I said.

"Hold on."

The line went dead, and a moment later I heard a voice.

"Mr. Morgan?" a man said.

"Yes."

"This is Chief Wilson. Your colleague, Miss Smith, left a message for me to call yesterday," he said. "I got tied up with one thing or another, so my apologies. You're first on my list today."

"Thanks for phoning, chief," I said. "Must be early."

"Six a.m.," he replied. "But you know what they say about a man being early to rise. Apparently it should make me wise as a hooting owl. How can I help you, Mr. Morgan?"

"I want to ask you about an accident that happened thirty-five years ago," I said. "The Parkers."

"Your colleague mentioned something about it in her message. I remember it vividly. It was the first fatal accident I attended as a rookie. You never forget your first fatality."

"Was there any evidence of foul play?" I asked.

"No. None. The other driver was drunk. He overtook a truck out on the thirty-five and hit the Parkers head-on. There were no survivors," Chief Wilson replied. "What's this about?"

"We're investigating the death of Karl Parker," I said.

"The New York Stock Exchange shooting? I saw that," Chief Wilson remarked. "That's odd. Is he related to them?"

I felt the hairs on my neck rise. That wasn't a question I'd expected. Something wasn't right.

"He's their child," I said. "His parents were Ken and Delores Parker."

"That's impossible," Chief Wilson replied. "Their son was in the back of the car when it was hit. Karl Parker died at the scene of the crash with his parents."

CHAPTER 75

I STAGGERED INTO the dining hall, stunned by my conversation with Chief Wilson. I clutched the childhood photos of Karl Parker tightly, as though holding them might keep me connected to a past I now knew to be a lie. Nothing about my old friend's life was real. Everything he'd ever told me about his time before the Marines was false.

I found myself at Leonid and Dinara's table, and dropped the photos, which scattered like leaves falling from a tree.

"What's the matter?" Dinara asked.

"I just spoke to the chief of police of Karl Parker's home town," I replied. "The real Karl Parker died in a car crash with his parents. It seems the man I knew stole the dead child's identity."

Saying it out loud somehow made it even more real. I sat down, propped my elbows on the table and put my head in my hands.

"I'm sorry, Jack," Dinara offered.

I glanced at her and Leonid, who offered a sympathetic nod.

"I thought I knew Karl," I said. "The guy trained me. We were friends."

"You think his wife knew?" Leonid asked.

"I'm not sure," I replied. "I don't think so."

"*Prizrak*," Leonid said to Dinara.

I looked at her for an explanation.

"Ghost," she said. "It's another word for a sleeper. A deep-cover agent."

I was reeling and refused to accept the possibility. "Karl—the man I knew—he served his country with distinction. He was no traitor."

Leonid's phone rang, and he stepped away from the table to take the call.

"How are you feeling?" Dinara asked.

I looked at her clear, penetrating eyes. "Honestly, I don't know. I came here and risked everything for a friend. And now it turns out I never knew him at all."

"I don't think we can ever truly conceal what we are," Dinara said. "Even when we're deep under cover, I think our true character shines through."

I took little comfort from her words. A man prepared to lie big was certainly willing to lie small. All his interactions, every moment, everything he was and everything he stood for was all an illusion. Nothing he'd ever done was beyond question.

"Can you email Justine?" I asked. "Let her know what the chief told me. I can't face explaining it again."

I slapped the tabletop in frustration. "I feel like a fool!" I exclaimed, drawing the attention of a handful of people lingering over their late lunches. "The head of the world's best detective agency couldn't figure out his own friend was a fraud."

"Assuming he was, he will have been trained by the very best," Dinara said. "I'll let Justine know. And Jack ..." She hesitated. "You weren't looking for it. That's why you didn't see the lie. He was your friend and teacher, and you trusted him."

Leonid returned before I could answer.

"That was Anna Bolshova. She says she's got something for me. She wants to meet."

"When?" Dinara asked.

"Thirty minutes, the Arts Park, by the river," Leonid replied.

"Want some company?" she asked.

Leonid shrugged. "Sure."

"Jack?" Dinara asked.

"I'm going to stay here," I replied. "See if I can figure out when the man I knew took over the real Karl Parker's identity."

"OK," Leonid said. "Hopefully we'll bring you back something useful."

Dinara got to her feet and followed the grizzled former detective out. I sat staring at the remains of their meals for a few moments, before I shook off my self-pity and headed back to the library.

CHAPTER 76

AN OLD WOMAN stood by the frozen edges of the river and tossed crumbs across the ice. A solitary robin flitted from spot to spot, pecking at the bounty, and the old woman chatted to the little bird as though it was a friend.

Dinara watched her, and wondered at her story. What kind of life had led her to this small park, where she sought the company of birds? Leonid shuffled on the spot and rubbed his gloved hands together before pushing them into his coat pockets.

It was only 3:45 p.m., but it was already gloomy. Heavy clouds had hung over the city for the past few days, threatening snow, but they were yet to deliver. They seemed to get lower and darker with each passing moment, and even though this winter had already seen more than enough snow to last a lifetime, Dinara wished they would shed their load and get the inevitable storm over with.

"She's late," Leonid observed, checking his watch.

Dinara caught sight of Anna Bolshova the moment the words had left Leonid's mouth. She was hurrying along the wide boulevard that ran alongside the roadway that led to Krymsky Bridge. She wore her police uniform and standard-issue long winter coat. The boulevard had been cleared of snow, but the park itself was buried. Dinara and Leonid stood where the boulevard met the embankment, near the bridge. The only other person around was the old woman feeding the friendly robin. High to Dinara's right, traffic rumbled over the bridge. To her left, the long pavilion, which usually housed hundreds of paintings by local artists, was empty. Robbed of vital people and civilizing artwork, the Muzeon Park of Arts seemed a desolate, foreboding place. The Interior Ministry stood approximately half a kilometer to the east, along Krymsky Bank, and Dinara was glad Anna hadn't arranged to meet any closer to the department.

"Sorry," the detective said as she drew near. "I was called in for another corrective meeting."

Dinara was puzzled.

"It's boss-speak for a reprimand," Leonid explained. "Dressed up as advice to help you improve your performance."

"What the hell are you people into?" Anna asked, glancing around the park.

Leonid shrugged, and Dinara couldn't think of a good way to answer the question.

"That base," Anna went on. "I made a couple of calls and I was told that it never existed. So I called a friend in Army Intelligence and he said I was playing with fire."

"Did he say anything else?" Dinara asked.

"Are you kidding? He was terrified even talking to me," Anna replied.

Leonid shook his head with resignation. Dinara knew what he was thinking. They'd hit a dead end.

"Give me the name," Anna said. "I did as much as I could. Keep your side of the deal, Boykov."

He sighed. "OK," he conceded. "The Black Hundreds recruiter is a man called Erik Utkin. He runs a group out of a gym called Grom Boxing. It's where Spartak Zima trains."

Anna whistled.

"The fighters are dealing for him," Leonid continued. "We've been conducting surveillance on them. I've asked my team to send you everything we've got."

"Really?" Anna asked.

Leonid nodded.

"Your team? I thought you two are all there is," Anna said. "And your American boss of course."

"Don't believe everything you hear," Leonid advised her.

Dinara was surprised when Anna stepped forward and embraced Leonid.

"Thank you," she said. "This might just save my neck. I'm sorry I couldn't be of more help."

"You owe me then?" Leonid asked.

"I didn't say that." Anna flashed a smile. "Good luck."

She turned on her heels and started back along the icy boulevard.

"So we've got nothing?" Dinara remarked.

She sensed Leonid wasn't listening, and realized his attention had drifted to three men who were coming west along the boulevard. Dinara looked to her left and saw two others beside the long pavilion, heading south, directly toward her.

"Either Anna is part of this and walked us into a trap, or they were alerted by her inquiries and followed her here," Leonid said urgently.

Dinara's stomach tightened and her legs went weak.

"Dinara," Leonid said, his voice pleading and fearful. "Run!"

CHAPTER 77

DINARA AND LEONID ran south beneath Krymsky Bridge. The traffic thundered overhead, and when she glanced back, Dinara saw the two men by the pavilion break into a sprint.

She and Leonid burst from the shadow of the bridge onto the riverfront plaza that abutted the high gates of Gorky Park. The plaza hadn't been plowed and was buried beneath deep snow.

"This way," she said to Leonid, urging him toward the park, but they stopped dead when they saw two men running through the open gates.

"The stairs!" Leonid pointed toward a set of stone steps that led up to the bridge.

They ran as fast as they could, fighting the draining resistance of the deep powder. Dinara's legs went numb with cold, and her lungs burned with each freezing breath, but she pressed on, fueled by the memory of her abduction by Veles and his men.

Like a specter summoned by thought, the fearsome killer appeared a hundred meters to their left, halfway along the bridge. He was with another man, and both of them started sprinting when they caught sight of Leonid and Dinara running through the snow.

Dinara forced herself toward the steps. She glanced behind her and saw the pair exit Gorky Park and start across the plaza. The other duo emerged from beneath the bridge, their hot breath clouding the air in rapid bursts as they ran across the plaza. One of them drew a pistol, and Dinara reached for her own and opened fire. Her shots went wild, but their pursuers scattered. The gunman and his companion retreated beneath the bridge, and the pair from Gorky Park ran for a concrete structure that protruded from the park's museum.

They didn't stay hidden for long.

"Here!" Leonid yelled as the crack of gunfire rose above the noise of nearby traffic, and bullets snapped through the air around them.

He grabbed Dinara's arm and pulled her in front of him. When she looked back, she saw him falter as he was hit in the back by a bullet. He was hurt and stumbled in the snow, but quickly found his feet.

"I'm OK," he insisted. "I'm wearing my vest."

They made it to the steps and crouched as they ran up them. A stone wall shielded them from the shots, and the air around them filled with dust and debris as bullets chipped at the protective barrier.

Up on the bridge, Veles and his companion were no more than fifty meters from the top of the stairs.

"Come on!" Dinara urged.

She opened fire, and the wild shots had the desired effect, slowing Veles and the other man down. She and Leonid crested the last flight of steps and reached the bridge twenty-five meters ahead of Veles. She was about to turn east, when she saw the trio of men who'd been coming along the boulevard running toward them along the pavement on the other side of the bridge. Further down the street, she saw Anna Bolshova hurrying in their direction. Either she'd been attracted by the commotion, or she was part of the ambush.

Dinara cast around for an escape route, and realized the stairs on the other side of the bridge were their best hope. If they could get down them and run east, they might be able to make it to the Interior Ministry or one of the other nearby government buildings.

"This way," Dinara said, and she pulled Leonid forward.

They leaped the ice-cold steel girder that was the anchor for the bridge's suspension system, and ran across seven lanes which were crowded with rush-hour traffic. Cars screeched to a halt, and cab drivers tooted their horns. They reached the other side, and Dinara vaulted the northern anchor. She sensed movement behind her and turned to see Leonid get tackled by Veles.

The assassin's companion sprinted forward, jumped the girder and came at her. Dinara reacted instinctively and fired a brace of shots that hit him in the gut. The man staggered back a couple of steps and fell to the ground, his face twisted in horror.

Beyond him, Dinara saw the four men who'd chased them across the plaza emerge from the staircase on the other side of the bridge, and the trio to their east were almost upon them. Traffic had stopped now, and drivers were out, watching the unfolding violence.

Dinara's eyes moved to Leonid and Veles, who were slugging it out on the bridge. They traded vicious punches, and Leonid seemed to be holding his own. Dinara searched for a shot, but the men were moving too quickly, and she couldn't be sure she wouldn't hit Leonid.

Then, to her horror, she saw a flash of silver. Leonid swung his right fist and Veles ducked the blow, stepped inside it, and drove a gleaming blade into Leonid's side.

"No!" Dinara screamed.

Leonid looked at her with a mix of shock and disbelief, and Veles pulled out the knife and stabbed her friend twice more, in the collar and throat. Leonid's shock turned to despair, and then there was nothing.

His eyes went blank and the life left him.

Tears filled Dinara's eyes, but she remembered her gun, and pulled the trigger as Leonid's body fell. Veles was quick and sidestepped the shot, which was the last in the magazine. As Dinara tried to reload, the assassin rushed forward. He was almost at the anchor when Dinara heard the roar of an engine, and turned to see a car hurtling along the bridge's emergency lane. Anna Bolshova was driving, and she didn't slow. Veles tried to jump clear, but the car caught him and knocked him down.

There was a screech of brakes, and the passenger door flew open.

"Get in!" Anna yelled.

Dinara could see Veles' accomplices across the bridge, and the trio further down. She leaped the girder, dived into the passenger seat and was thrown around as Anna hit the accelerator.

Bullets thudded into the chassis and smashed the rear window, but soon there was nothing except the roar of the engine as they sped out of range.

Dinara wept, consumed by the thought of Leonid lying dead, his blood freezing on the cold tarmac beneath him.

CHAPTER 78

I WAS IN the library studying the files Justine had sent when I heard a commotion coming from somewhere in the building. There were raised voices, shouts of disbelief and crying. I ran toward the source of the noise, and found a crowd of people in the lobby, all clustered around Dinara. The detective who'd attempted to interrogate me, Anna something, stood next to her.

I pushed my way through the chattering crowd, and even though I couldn't understand a word they said, their meaning was clear. Something terrible had happened. Feo, the big bear of a man, was comforting Dinara, whose eyes were red raw. She broke into fresh tears when she saw me.

"What's the matter?" I asked. "What's happened?"

"It's Leonid," she said between sobs. "He's dead. Veles killed him."

I went to her and she fell against me, weeping. Stunned, I looked at Anna, who nodded somber confirmation.

"How?" Feo asked, and I sensed the mood of the crowd change.

The residents were all former cops, and shock and dismay were being replaced by anger at the death of one of their own. For some, Leonid had been a friend, for others, a benefactor, but he was a former Moscow police officer to them all.

Anna replied to Feo's question in Russian, and I felt Dinara sag with each word, doubtless an account of the horror. I looked down and saw she was teetering on the edge of consciousness.

"Let's go," I said, and, supporting her, I ushered her through the crowd.

No one paid us much mind. They were all listening to Anna. I was desperate to know exactly what had happened, but I couldn't understand a word she was saying, and Dinara's welfare was my priority.

Soon we'd broken free of the crowd and I took Dinara through the building. She seemed delirious and was muttering in Russian. I half carried, half steered her to our accommodation block, and as we started down the corridor, I found my eyes drawn to the very end. The door to Leonid's room. It would never open for him again.

I took Dinara into her room and laid her on the bed. I removed her coat and discovered her trousers were soaked through and freezing cold from her thighs to her ankles.

"Dinara," I said, stroking her arm.

I touched her forehead to check for a fever. She felt a little warm, but not enough to worry me.

"Dinara," I tried again. "I need you to focus."

I was about to go and get help, when she suddenly turned to look at me.

"Jack, I couldn't save him. I couldn't ..." She trailed off.

"It's OK," I said. "There's nothing you could have done."

She was haunted by the ugly memories, and her eyes reflected the horror they'd witnessed.

"He's gone," she said simply.

Her eyes filled with fresh tears.

"He's gone."

CHAPTER 79

THE DINING HALL was full. More than eighty residents sat at the long tables, drinking and talking in somber tones. I couldn't understand a word, but I didn't need to. It was a wake, and like all such occasions it was rich in reflection, memory and sorrow. I sat alone near the windows, looking outside to see the clouds were finally shedding their loads. Large flakes floated down in the bright pools cast by the exterior lights, settling on the frozen ground like the souls of so many dead. Beyond the lights, there was nothing but black night, so impenetrable the rest of the world might have ceased to exist.

I nursed a small glass of vodka, which I'd been given for one of the many toasts that had been raised for Leonid Boykov, but I had no interest in drinking. My mood was already bleak, and alcohol would have tipped me into misery. A good man had lost his life investigating the murder of a fraud and a liar—an investigation I had brought Leonid into.

I was at the very end of one of the long dining tables, surrounded by empty chairs. A few of the ex-cops had gathered at the other end, and there were more spread across the neighboring tables. They didn't pay me much mind as they sank their drinks and talked quietly. None of them knew the details of the investigation into Karl Parker so I doubted they blamed me as much I blamed myself.

Anna Bolshova was with Dinara, who had stayed in her room. She too blamed herself and kept saying she could have saved him. I hadn't been able to get through to her, but perhaps Anna could.

Feo was nowhere to be seen. He and another resident had left the building shortly after I'd come into the dining hall.

I was snapped out of my miserable reflection by my ringing phone, and was relieved to see Justine's name flash on screen.

"Jack," she said, when I answered. "I got your message. I'm so sorry. What happened?"

"Veles, the man who killed . . ." I hesitated. What should I call my former friend? I opted for simplicity, even though it perpetuated a lie. "The man who killed Karl Parker. He murdered Leonid. Dinara witnessed the whole thing."

"Oh no. I'm sorry, Jack. Is she OK?"

"Not really," I replied.

"And you?"

I hesitated. I wasn't sure what I was feeling, but I knew it wasn't good. "I'll be OK," I lied.

Feo entered the dining hall, and I could tell by his demeanor that he had news. He scanned the room, and when he spotted me, he strode over.

"I've got to go, Justine," I said. "I'll call you as soon as I can."

"Please be careful, Jack," she replied.

"I will," I assured her before I hung up.

Feo's face was devoid of the levity I'd grown accustomed to. He looked stern and fearsome, and his size made his dark mood even more palpable.

"I've been to the city," he said, taking the seat opposite. "My old colleagues in the Moscow police have been told to find you."

My shoulders slumped and I exhaled slowly. I knew what was coming. It was the smart move and I should have expected it.

"They say you are the main suspect in the murder of Leonid Boykov," Feo continued. "The story is beginning to leak to the newspapers. By morning, every police officer in Russia will be looking for you. I tried to tell them . . ." He trailed off and held my gaze. "Even if they'd believed me, it wouldn't have made a difference. One or two officers can't overturn this. There's something much bigger behind it."

He paused, clearly building up to something he didn't want to say.

"You're going to be labeled a cop killer," he said. "We don't treat such people well in this country. If you stay in Russia, there's a good chance you will die before you make it to trial."

CHAPTER 80

I STARED ACROSS the table. I was grieving for a man who'd worked for me, but I was also mourning the loss of a friendship that had turned out to be nothing more than an illusion. And now I was being framed for murder. My anger rose, making my skin flush with a crackling heat.

"You must go," Feo said.

"You know I can't do that," I responded flatly. "Not until this killer has been caught."

"I had a feeling you might say that," Feo replied. "You seem an honorable man. A coward runs. He might live, but he lives as a coward, and he can never run from himself. The honorable man might die, but he passes in glory. Just like Leonid Boykov." He glanced around. "Listen to me, talking wisdom like I know about life. I need a drink," he said, getting to his feet.

As he went to a table with bottles and glasses, I saw Anna and Dinara enter. Everyone fell silent, and then a few of the assembled residents rose from their seats and offered Dinara their sympathy as she crossed the room. Her eyes glistened and I could see her fighting back tears. Anna gave her a steadying hand, and I stood as they approached.

"How are you feeling?" I asked.

Dinara replied with a faint smile, but she looked punch-drunk. She took the seat Feo had vacated, and he returned with a drink and sat next to her. Anna pulled up the chair to my left.

Feo spoke to the two women in Russian, and their eyes widened and they both looked at me.

"I was there. I can tell people the truth," Anna offered.

"You've been reported missing," Feo said. "Be very careful. Missing can become dead."

"They wouldn't. I'm a police officer," Anna remarked.

Feo inclined his head and gave her a withering look. "You know the kind of people who are behind this. Police officer means nothing to them."

"I'm sorry," Dinara said. "If I'd been faster ..."

"This wasn't your fault," I assured her. "You did everything you could. The fact you're even here is a miracle."

"That is thanks to Anna," Dinara replied. "She saved my life."

"What do you suggest we do then?" Anna asked. "Sit here and drink?"

"For tonight," Feo replied. "We need to find out who we can trust before we do anything. At the moment, that's no one outside of this building." He filled a glass and passed it to her. "So you might as well drink."

He stood up and raised a brimming shot glass to his fellow residents, "Leonid Boykov, *vechnaya pamyat*," he announced loudly.

Dinara's eyes filled anew and she leaned toward me, her voice straining with emotion: "It means let him be remembered forever."

Everyone in the room stood, and we all raised our glasses. I joined a chorus of voices who all cried out in unison. "Leonid Boykov, *vechnaya pamyat*."

Let him be remembered forever.

CHAPTER 81

GOD WATCHES OVER those who are careful, and death stalks those who are not.

Maxim Yenen thought about his instructor's words as he hurried through the private parking lot beneath his apartment building. He'd bought an entire floor of parking spaces and had filled them with one of Russia's most extensive car collections. His prized pieces included a Bugatti Royale Kellner Coupe, a Jaguar XKSS, and an Alfa Romeo 33 Stradale, but he rarely used anything other than his Bentley Bentayga. His choice was dictated by his security detail. The Bentley SUV and the Range Rovers his bodyguards used had an imposing presence. According to Diak Nesterov, his head of security, the cars were big, heavy and, particularly in the Bentley's case, fast.

God watches over those who are careful.

Yenen had heard about the death of Leonid Boykov, who, like so many before him, had fallen at the hand of Veles, a masterful assassin. The public were being told that Jack Morgan was the suspect, but Yenen and a handful of others knew the truth.

Without warning, Yenen's heart skipped a beat. It happened every now and then, but it had been getting worse recently. Anxiety had been his constant companion ever since he'd metamorphosed from a simple smuggler to a petrochemical oligarch. Of course, in truth he'd never just been a simple smuggler, his life had always been much more complicated. But it had taken on new complexity and risk with every step closer to the Kremlin. The more money he made, the more anxious he became. The more power he acquired, the more trapped he felt.

As they made their way along one of the six aisles that ran between the rows of expensive cars, Yenen looked at the men responsible for keeping him safe. Diak Nesterov, the grim-faced leader of his team, was almost certainly FSB Counterintelligence Service, and Tisha Bobrik, the former weightlifter who'd spoken with Leonid Boykov about past Olympic glories, was likely Military Counterintelligence Directorate. These men weren't just bodyguards, they were jailers, and their watchful eyes saw everything. Nothing Yenen said or did could escape the Kremlin.

Well, he thought, *almost nothing.*

The Bentley and Range Rovers were parked halfway along the row nearest the elevators. Miron Sizy, a gaunt, methodical man who was responsible for vehicle security, was using a telescopic sensor to check the underside of the Bentley. There was a flight case of EMF sensors and counter-surveillance equipment at his feet.

"Anything?" Diak asked.

"It's clear," Miron replied. "They all are."

The cars were swept every day, as was Yenen's apartment, and the elevators. Yenen had no doubt the men were ordered to ignore Kremlin-approved devices, but anyone else who tried to spy on him wouldn't get very far.

Yenen climbed into the back of the Bentley, and his entourage split between the three vehicles. Tisha drove the Bentley, and Diak rode beside him. Yenen settled into the soft cream leather as the engine purred to life. They rolled toward the metal shutter that secured his floor, the very lowest, from the rest of the building. They drove through the five public levels and turned onto a grey, cloud-covered Mosfilmovskaya Street. As they drove past the magnificent forty-story tower that was Yenen's home, one of the Range Rovers overtook the Bentley, which was now sandwiched between the two larger vehicles. Even in the gloom of an overcast day, Yenen's building shone like a monument to success.

It was a twenty-five-minute drive to the Kremlin, where Yenen had been summoned to a meeting with Yevgeny Salko, a director of the SVR, to discuss the threat Private posed. It was a conversation Yenen wasn't looking forward to. He'd hired Private without realizing the attention the firm would bring.

The convoy was heading north along Mosfilmovskaya Street, a broad four-lane boulevard, and Yenen was rehearsing his conversation with Salko. As they crossed the intersection with

Kosygina Street, Yenen became aware of rapid movement to his right. A fourteen-wheel truck careened past a line of traffic waiting at the lights, and smashed into the lead Range Rover.

"Go! Go! Go!" Diak yelled at Tisha.

The former Olympian stepped on the accelerator, and the Bentley shot forward.

Yenen felt sick, and his nausea deepened when he turned to see a large van smash into the trailing Range Rover. The two mangled vehicles crashed into the sidewalk. Both protective vehicles were out of commission, and the Bentley was speeding along Mosfilmovskaya Street alone.

Lines of vehicles dawdled along, their exhausts spewing clouds into the freezing air, but Tisha threaded past them expertly. They weren't far from Krasnoluzhsky Bridge, where they might be able to lose their pursuers in the heavy traffic on the beltway. Yenen could see the arch of the steel railway bridge against the gray morning sky. If they could get there, they might be safe.

They didn't make it.

As they shot past the junction with a side road that ran up from the river, a van surged forward and swiped the Bentley. Another van cut across the median and hit Yenen's SUV from the other side, smashing the Bentley in a sandwich of grinding screeches, awful crunching and shattering glass.

The Bentley came to an abrupt and violent halt, and Yenen's head hit the back of Diak's seat. Airbags burst, Yenen's ears rang and, as the edges of the world were frayed by darkness, he saw a gang of masked men stream from each of the vans.

He heard the crack of gunfire and realized that Diak and Tisha had been shot. Then, as the dark edges grew, he saw the masked men coming for him.

They loomed at the shattered windows like monsters from a childhood nightmare.

God watches over those who are careful, and death stalks those who are not.

His door opened.

He felt hands take him.

Then he blacked out.

CHAPTER 82

THE COLD WOKE him. His feet felt as though they were being dragged over shards of glass, and every inch of his skin burned with cold fire. He opened his eyes, but the world refused to come into focus. All he saw was gray. Then his other senses returned and he realized he was moving, or, more precisely, he was being moved.

He heard the crunch of footsteps on snow, and felt hands beneath his arms. Gloved hands against his bare skin. Where were his clothes? His eyes started to regain focus and he could now see his bare legs and feet trailing through snow, his limbs numb and distant, as though they were someone else's.

He raised his head and saw two men, both in ski masks and dark clothes, one either side, lifting him by his arms.

It was night, and their way was lit by a man at the head of a trailing group. A macabre procession of at least nine people, all of whom were also masked. There might have been more, but Yenen could only count nine before his eyes failed against the darkness.

"He's awake," one of his captors said.

Yenen prepared for the inevitable blow, but none came. He wore nothing but a pair of boxer shorts, and for a man accustomed to comfort and safety, his near nakedness left him feeling vulnerable. But the lack of immediate violence emboldened him, and after a few moments, he plucked up the courage to say something.

"Does Salko know about this?" he asked.

The man to his right, a towering figure twice as wide as the average person, glanced back at the man with the torch.

They said nothing, but kept pulling him on.

Where? Where were they taking him?

Much more time in the open, and he would die.

He peered into the darkness ahead and tried to pick out shapes. He saw black silhouettes against a gunpowder sky, and followed the edges to discern the outlines of some buildings. The curved roof of a warehouse, the flat roof of an office ... *wait ... no ... it couldn't be.*

But part of him knew it was. He hadn't seen this place for years, but it was branded in his memory like an owner's mark. Boltino Army Base. He'd never be free of its legacy. Not unless ... He stopped himself. Now was not the time for dreams. Even if he could escape whatever dark fate this night held, true freedom was an impossibility.

His captors dragged him into the main administration block. They hauled him through the building and, as the flashlight beam fell here and there, Yenen's memory brought the decayed place to life. Colonel Arman Zhuk, the camp commander, a man long since dead, had his office along this corridor. Yevgeny Salko, the young intelligence agent whose zealous mind dreamed up everything they'd done here, had been two doors down. Everywhere he looked, Yenen saw bursts of the past, and he wondered whether the cold had got to him. Was he beginning to hallucinate?

The men dragged him into what had once been a classroom. Now it contained nothing but snow and a broken desk, a relic of what had once been.

His captors tossed him into the snow, and the leader shone the flashlight in his eyes as the group encircled him. There were more than nine. Including the two who'd carried him, there were fifteen people in total. Men and women, all masked, all in dark clothes.

"Please," Yenen pleaded with the leader. "I'll die in this cold."

"It's good you know that." It wasn't the leader who spoke, but the huge man who'd dragged Yenen to this place. "It means you won't delay in giving us the information we need."

Yenen rubbed his hands against his frozen torso, and a wave of painful needles tracked the course of his fingertips. His teeth chattered and he felt as though death already had hold of him.

"What happened here?" the big man asked.

The question cut through the numbing cold, and woke Yenen's deteriorating mind.

Who are these people? How much do they know already?

"You're dying," the big man said. "What happened here?"

"Things designed to change the balance of power," he replied.

"What things?" the big man asked.

Yenen's jaw snapped shut intermittently as automatic functions overrode his conscious mind. His body was rigid with cold, and was doing everything it could to keep him alive. "There was a program called Bright Star. It was designed to give Russia the advantage in the twenty-first century."

The man with the flashlight, the leader of the group, shone the beam in Yenen's eyes.

"I need to know what he's saying," the man remarked in English.

Yenen recognized the voice, but from where? Yenen fought to focus his panicked mind.

Then he realized who his captor was.

CHAPTER 83

POWER IS NOTHING but an illusion. We come into the world helpless and we leave the same way. In between, we might be able to convince ourselves and sometimes others that we are masters of our own destiny, but fate always conspires to give us a stark demonstration of the truth. Maxim Yenen was learning that lesson. We'd taken the billionaire from his life of power, and in a few simple steps had transformed him into a pitiful creature. He crouched in the snow, his skin red in the torchlight, his lips blue, his hands desperately rubbing his torso, trying to generate warmth. I wondered whether he was aware of the injuries he'd sustained in the crash, or if the cold had dulled his senses.

A mottled purple bruise covered his left ribs, he bled from a wound on his forehead and his right ankle was black and swollen; it looked as though it was broken. He needed medical attention, but if he didn't get out of the cold very soon, none of his injuries would trouble him. He would die of exposure.

I didn't like what we had done, but I liked losing a colleague even less. Maxim Yenen was clearly linked to Veles in some way—the trap he walked us into after firing us from the investigation into Yana Petrova's murder had confirmed that—so he had Leonid's blood on his hands.

"Please," he begged. "Please, Mr. Morgan, give me some clothes. Something to protect me. Anything. I'll tell you whatever you want to know. I'll tell you all about Bright Star."

I nodded at Feo, who'd been leading the interrogation, and he signaled one of his men, who tossed him a blanket. Feo handed it to Yenen, and the semi-naked man fumbled as he wrapped it around his shoulders.

"Start talking, or it goes," I said.

The blanket must have given him courage as well as warmth, because he looked at me defiantly. "You're not a killer, Mr. Morgan."

"Don't test me, Mr. Yenen," I replied. "All I have to do is walk away."

His gaze faltered and he looked beyond me at the squad of former police officers Feo had assembled. Our operation had been oversubscribed with almost every resident volunteering to play a part, so Feo had been forced to choose the thirteen men and women who stood behind me.

"Alone," Yenen said. "I'll talk with you alone." His teeth chattered.

"You worried what they'll do to you?" I asked.

"I'm not scared for me," he snapped. "I'm scared for them. What I know brings death. If you want to know it too, that's your concern, but don't inflict this knowledge on others."

I glanced at Feo. Like mine, his face was concealed beneath a ski mask, but his eyes expressed understanding. He said something in Russian to the squad, and they filed out of the room. He followed them out, and, within moments, it was just me, Maxim Yenen and one other masked figure.

"I said alone," Yenen complained.

The figure removed her mask.

"I watched my friend die," Dinara said. "So you will talk to me too."

Yenen nodded. "OK."

He shivered. "I've been leaking Russian intelligence secrets. I was using Yana Petrova to spread this information. I discovered she was Otkrov and made contact. She was more than happy to be the conduit. Someone in the Kremlin, I don't know who, must have discovered her identity and they had her killed, as noisily as possible, probably to serve as a warning to her co-conspirators."

"Why?" I asked. "Why betray your country?"

"The closer I get to the heart of the Kremlin, the more ugliness I see. The world works best when there is balance, Mr. Morgan," Yenen replied. "America checks Russian power. Russia checks American ambition. Neither has free rein." He hesitated. "But that is about to change. The Bright Star program will give Russia geopolitical dominance. It will change the balance of power for a hundred years. What we've done with the Bright Star program will reshape the world."

CHAPTER 84

"WE?" I ASKED.

"I was part of it," Yenen admitted. "I sat in this very classroom as a child. There were dozens of us. Children from all over Russia, some from other countries. Orphans mainly. All taught to be Americans. Your democracies think short term. A four-year presidency? Ha! What can you achieve in four years? In Russia, a president can enact a plan to train children to infiltrate the highest echelons of American power, and he can still be in office when his plan comes to fruition."

"Was Karl Parker one of these Bright Star agents?"

Yenen nodded, and I felt numb as the last tattered threads of my relationship with my former instructor were cut away.

"His real name was John Kubu. He was an orphan from Kenya. He assumed Karl Parker's identity when he was nineteen, just before he joined the Marines."

I shook my head in disgust. The man who'd trained me, my friend and mentor, was a traitor. I bristled with shame.

"Ernest Fisher and Elizabeth Connor—were they Bright Star too?"

Yenen nodded. "Yes."

"Why would the SVR kill its own operatives?" Dinara asked. "Veles is SVR, correct?"

"He is."

"Then why is he killing Russian agents?" Dinara pressed.

"I don't know," Yenen replied, "but we've lost twelve Bright Star operatives this month."

"Twelve?" I said.

"Yes, Mr. Morgan. The ones you know about are the high-profile deaths. People Veles couldn't reach easily. They had to be liquidated in a way that made a lot of noise."

"Which explains the invention of the Ninety-nine," I remarked.

"Exactly. A cover designed to throw people off the scent. But there have been many more quiet deaths. Bright Star agents who didn't climb quite so high in American society."

"Robert Carlyle?" I asked.

"Yes."

"Why aren't you in America?" Dinara asked. "If you were part of the program."

"Not all of us went," Yenen replied. "I was a graduate of the last year. By then, the program's resources had been spread thin. Imagine what it takes to set someone up in a new life in America. To give them help along the way. Connections and money to make sure their business thrives and their life is successful. By the time my class graduated, the well had run dry."

"Do you know how many there are?" I asked.

"The program ran for four years. There were twenty-four children in my class. My contemporaries in the last class didn't get deployed, so my guess would be seventy-two people at most."

"Your guess?" I asked.

"We did not know children from other years. We were kept apart to reduce the risk of exposure. I only know about the man you call Karl Parker because he died and a report was made. The same with Robert Carlyle, Ernest Fisher and Elizabeth Connor. The agents who are still alive are invisible. Their identities a secret only one man knows."

"Who?" I asked.

"Salko," Yenen replied.

"Salko?"

"Yevgeny Salko," Dinara explained. "He's a director of the SVR."

"Can you take me away from here, Mr. Morgan? I've told you everything I know," Yenen said.

I nodded. "Let's get him back to Moscow," I told Dinara. "Hold him until the case is through."

"No," Yenen responded quickly. "This is my chance. My bodyguards work for the Kremlin. They are jailers. This is the first time I've been free of them for years, Mr. Morgan. This is my chance to escape. I want you to take me to the American embassy. I want to defect."

CHAPTER 85

WE MADE OUR way through Moscow in Feo's pickup truck. I was in the front passenger seat, Feo was driving, and Dinara was in the back with Maxim Yenen, who'd slept all the way back from Volkovo. We weren't far from the American embassy, and dawn was breaking over the city. Heavy snow was falling, making driving conditions treacherous and reducing visibility to no more than thirty paces. There were four vehicles in our convoy, one ahead and two tailing, and we all moved slowly through the snowfall.

In a few minutes Maxim Yenen would be handed over to the US authorities, identified as an intelligence asset, debriefed and disappeared. This would probably be my last chance to talk to him, but I couldn't think what else he might be able to give us.

I reached into my jacket pocket and pulled out the old photograph of Karl Parker, Ernie Fisher and Elizabeth Connor in the Novoko Bar. I hadn't shown it to Yenen.

I felt a flash of inspiration as I held the photograph.

"Wake him up," I said to Dinara.

Dinara shook Yenen awake, and he groaned and rubbed his eyes.

"Ernie Fisher, Elizabeth Connor and Karl Parker all knew each other," I said, showing him the photo.

He focused on the photograph and I saw recognition.

"That's the bar in Volkovo," he said. "I went there after I graduated. We heard some of the older kids used to sneak out of the base, but I thought it was just a myth."

"You said the years were kept separate," I remarked.

"Yes. We were kept apart to minimize the risk of identification. If we were ever captured and interrogated, the worst we could do was give up those in our class. The other years would be safe."

His words were like a spark in darkness, and they lit a fuse.

"Karl Parker, Elizabeth Connor and Ernie Fisher knew each other, so must have been in the same class. What if Robert Carlyle and the others were all in that class too? What if they're being killed because they're the only ones other than Salko who can identify each other?"

"That's possible, but why?" Yenen asked.

"To protect someone," I replied. "To protect someone important. The Kremlin knows it has a leak. It doesn't know who or where. Here's this program you say could shift the geopolitical balance. What if one of these Bright Star agents has worked their way into a position of real power? How far would the Kremlin go to protect them?"

CHAPTER 86

FEO FOLLOWED THE lead vehicle and took a right onto Bolshoy Devyatinsky Lane, the street that ran in front of the embassy.

"Karl Parker called me to New York to tell me something," I said.

"That's why Veles didn't kill us when he had the chance," Dinara suggested. "He needs to know what Karl Parker might have told you, and contain any further spread of information."

"We've got trouble," Feo said, and I turned to see chaos materialize through the whiteout.

A Moscow police checkpoint blocked the street fifty yards from the embassy gate. There were a dozen uniformed police officers, along with men in long dark coats who looked far too shady to be cops.

"Those men," Dinara said. "I recognize two of them. They were with Veles when he killed Leonid."

They must have suspected we'd seek asylum at the embassy if things got too hot. They were probably also staking out the Private office, and Dinara's home.

On its own, the roadblock might have been orderly and well organized, but the chaos stemmed from the squad of six Marines led by Master Gunnery Sergeant Marlon West, who was remonstrating with the Moscow police captain. I couldn't hear what he was saying, but I could tell West was objecting to the roadblock outside his embassy.

"Back up!" I told Feo, but I was too late.

One of the police officers noticed our convoy, immediately drew his weapon, and shouted to his comrades. In an instant, the cars were surrounded and commands were being barked in Russian.

"Stand down!" West yelled. "Stand down!"

He and his squad drew their sidearms and aimed them at the cops.

"This is sovereign territory of the United States," West said.

"Not beyond those gates," one of Veles' men countered. "Out here it is Moscow. Our city. Our rules." He turned to the idling vehicles. "Get out! Now! You are all under arrest."

"Drop your weapons!" West yelled, and he and his squad spread out in fire formation.

Half the Moscow police officers turned their weapons on the Marines, while the others held on us.

"If we can just get inside the embassy," I said urgently. "Can we break through?"

Feo shook his head. There were four police cars chicaned across the road, and barricades blocked the sidewalks.

The Marines and cops yelled at each other and the tension rose. It would only take one wrong move to trigger a bloodbath.

The rear passenger door of the lead vehicle in our convoy opened, and Anna Bolshova stepped out. She wasn't wearing her coat, deliberately I suspected, because her Moscow police uniform caught the attention of the officers around her.

"My name is Detective Anna Bolshova of the Criminal Investigations Department, on assignment to the Ministry of the Interior," she said, and the cops and Marines fell silent. "These men"—she pointed to the two guys Dinara had recognized— "were accomplices in the murder of Leonid Boykov, a former officer of the Moscow police. I witnessed his killing and I saw their involvement with my own eyes. You have been lied to, and you are standing with cop killers. Arrest them now!"

She yelled in Russian, barking sharp commands, and half the officers present turned on Veles' men. The other half rushed to their sides and soon the standoff had become an internal struggle, with one faction of Moscow cops yelling at the other.

"Come on! This could be our only chance," I said.

Yenen nodded, and he and Dinara slipped out of the rear passenger door. I followed them into the street.

West noticed instantly.

"Protective formation," he commanded, and his squad formed up around us, firearms facing outwards, bristling in every direction like spines on a sea urchin.

As we ran for the embassy, I saw Veles' men catch sight of us through the snow. They yelled something in Russian, and Anna Bolshova countered their command with one of her own.

They ignored her and pushed past the officers that had rallied to her cause. We were a hundred yards from the embassy gates, and broke into a sprint.

"Back off!" West yelled.

"Those people are under arrest," one of Veles' men shouted. He drew his pistol as he ran toward us. "Stop, or I will shoot."

"It'll be the last thing you do," West responded harshly. "Get those gates open," he ordered, and his point man raced ahead.

Dinara, Yenen and I were bundled along at the heart of the heavily armed squad, but when we were fifty yards from the gate, I saw another roadblock at the other end of the street. Ten police officers and two men in long dark coats turned as we neared the gates, no doubt alerted by radio. They sprinted toward us.

"This is your last warning," one of our pursuers shouted.

He dropped to one knee and raised his weapon. His companion did likewise, and I waited for the inevitable barrage, but none came. Instead, an ogre-like shape burst out of the snow and tackled both men. It was Feo, and the huge bear rained furious blows down on the men. He was quickly joined by the retired cops who'd helped us abduct Maxim Yenen. They were eager to avenge their friend and benefactor Leonid Boykov.

We reached the gates before the officers from the other end of the street, and were hustled inside the compound by more Marines.

The gate was slammed behind us, and as Yenen, Dinara and I were led toward the embassy building, I saw Master Gunnery Sergeant Marlon West stand at the threshold like an impassable sentinel.

"This is the sovereign territory of the United States of America," he told the frustrated men on the other side of the gate. "Any aggression against it will be met with lethal force."

CHAPTER 87

CARRIE UNDERWOOD, THE ambassador's security adviser, was waiting in the embassy lobby. She introduced herself to Dinara.

"Heck of a way to arrive," Carrie exclaimed, gesturing at the Marine guard that had accompanied us into the building. Then: "Mr. Yenen," she said.

"I would like to claim political asylum," Yenen replied. "And will offer in exchange everything I know."

Carrie studied Yenen for a moment. "If you'd like to follow me, we'll put you somewhere safe while we figure out what happens next."

Somewhere safe turned out to be a windowless meeting room on the third floor, at the heart of the embassy. I had little doubt it was one of the hardened communications centers designed to provide staff with a secure working environment in the event Russia turned hostile. The long walnut table seated twenty-eight, and the wall furthest from the three-inch-thick door had been given over to screens, computers and communications equipment, all of which were idle. The door matched the table, but there must have been steel beneath the veneer, and the rubber trim that lined the interior and exterior edges looked as though it could inflate to create an airtight seal. I studied the wood-paneled walls and wondered if there were any weapons concealed somewhere within them.

News of Maxim Yenen's arrival and his role in feeding America information rippled through the building, and a handful of people came to meet the billionaire who'd been leaking Kremlin secrets. After his interrogation at Boltino Army Base, we'd given Yenen some old clothes salvaged from the Residence, and he looked more like a dock worker than an oligarch, but if he felt uncomfortable, he didn't show it. He talked to the FBI legal attaché, the embassy's in-house counsel, and a handful of other men and women who didn't give their job titles, but who could well have been Agency. They came and went, buzzing excitedly, and with good reason. If he defected, Yenen would be the most significant intelligence win for Uncle Sam since Arkady Schevchenko.

After forty minutes, a tall, thin woman with sinewy fingers and a gaunt face entered. Her blond hair was pulled into a bun, and she wore a red trouser suit.

She greeted the three of us, and introduced herself as Erin Sebold, the CIA Head of Section.

"It's good to finally meet you, Mr. Yenen. We'd given you the codename Bishop, and we had six possible candidates for your real identity. I'm sorry to say you weren't on the list of possibles our analysts came up with," she said.

"I'm pleased to hear it," Yenen replied. "It means I covered my tracks well."

"When the communication channel dried up, we thought something had happened," Erin said.

"It had," Yenen remarked. "To my associate. She was murdered."

"The Boston Seafood Grill a few nights back," I remarked.

"Mr. Yenen hired us to find the killer," Dinara added.

"I had hoped to find out who'd discovered Yana's identity without risking my life," Yenen explained. "That's why I engaged Private. When I realized they were also looking into the Bright Star killings, it was too dangerous to be anywhere near them."

"Bright Star?" Erin asked.

"It's one of many things I can share with you once we've agreed the terms of my asylum," Yenen said.

"What do you know about this Bright Star, Mr. Morgan?" Erin asked.

"I know it's something you need to know about," I replied. "I'll leave it to Mr. Yenen to explain."

Carrie Underwood entered the room.

"Erin, you mind if I grab these two?" she asked, indicating Dinara and me. "The ambassador wants to see them."

"Sure," Erin replied.

"What's going on?" I asked.

"You ever been the cause of an international incident?" Carrie asked. "I don't know what you've been up to, but the Russians are mad, and it looks like all hell is about to break loose."

CHAPTER 88

AS AN FSB agent Dinara could never have dreamed of getting inside the American embassy, and yet here she was as a private citizen, not only inside it, but on her way to the ambassador's office. She knew she should have been impressed, but there was no lifting the shroud Leonid's death had placed over the world. She was still numb and his passing was too recent for her to feel much beyond hollow grief.

Dinara followed Carrie Underwood and Jack Morgan through the building. The common areas were deserted, since the embassy was closed to the public on Sundays. When they reached the large, traditionally decorated room on the top floor, Ambassador Thomas Dussler was waiting with Master Gunnery Sergeant West. The Marine was in a somber mood, but the ambassador was genial and upbeat.

"Well, you sure know how to anger the bear, Mr. Morgan," Dussler said. "Have a seat." He gestured at a couch and some chairs.

"This is Dinara Orlova, the head of Private Moscow," Jack said as they all took seats.

"Thomas Dussler. Pleased to meet you," the ambassador replied.

"Thanks for getting us inside," Jack said to West, who responded with a gracious nod.

"The Russians have lodged a formal complaint with State, saying we're harboring a couple of murder suspects," Dussler revealed. "They say you're wanted in connection with the murders of Ernie Fisher and Leonid Boykov."

"We had—" Jack began, but Dussler cut him off.

"West filled me in on what happened to Ernie, God rest his soul. And Carrie gave me an update on Mr. Boykov's tragic death, so we know the Russians are trying to play us. What I'd like to know is why."

"We believe they're trying to protect an espionage operation codenamed Bright Star. They want to know what we know about it. A Russian operative known as Veles, the man who's really behind the murders of Ernest Fisher, Leonid Boykov and others, has already tried to interrogate us."

There was a knock at the door, and the CIA Head of Section, Erin Sebold, entered.

"You've brought us a tremendous gift, Mr. Morgan, Ms. Orlova," she said. "The man we'd codenamed Bishop is downstairs, sir," she told Dussler. "He's agreeing terms with legal." She pulled up a chair.

"That's quite an achievement," Dussler congratulated Dinara and Jack. "The Kremlin keeps all its top people on a tight leash. The question we have now is what we do with you both."

"Ambassador Dussler," Jack said. "Mr. Yenen—Bishop—told us the man running the Bright Star program is SVR Director Yevgeny Salko."

"Salko?" Erin remarked. "He's an old-school hardliner of the worst kind."

"I'd like to see if we can access his files to discover the real name of the man codenamed Veles," Jack said.

"We can also see if we can get intelligence on Bright Star," Dinara added. "Find out who the deep-cover operatives are."

"When you say 'access' . . ." Dussler left the remark hanging.

"We know Salko's calling the shots. We know where he's based. We access his computer and see what we can find," Jack replied.

"Access an SVR director's computer?" Erin scoffed. "Like it's a terminal in a public library?"

"I think my team can do it," Jack replied earnestly.

"I can get us inside," Dinara added.

"My tech can get round his security," Jack said.

"Mr. Morgan," Dussler replied. "If you're seriously planning to hack the computer of a director of the SVR, I'm afraid I have to officially advise you against such a reckless and criminal course of action."

"And there's no way the CIA could condone an operation like that," Erin chimed in somberly. "Of course, if you're successful, we'd appreciate a look at whatever you find," she said with a smile.

"And speaking off the record," Dussler remarked, "if you ignore my official advice and go ahead with the reckless and criminal action, I wish you every ounce of good old-fashioned American luck."

"You realize what happens if you're caught?" Erin asked.

Dinara looked at Jack, and the two of them shared a moment of understanding.

"We're aware of the risks," she said. "But we owe it to Leonid. He saved my life." Her voice started to tremble, but she took a breath and fought for composure. "I couldn't save his, so the least I can do is make sure his killer faces justice."

CHAPTER 89

"HOW'S DINARA HOLDING up?" Justine asked.

"It's hit her pretty hard," I replied. "But she's throwing herself into the case."

"What about you?"

"I'm OK," I told her. "How are things over there?"

"Your story has been picked up by US media," Justine told me. "We're starting to field calls from clients, and we lost our first account. The Wabash investigation out of LA."

The Russians were putting tremendous pressure on the State Department to turn me over. They'd taken their disinformation to the media and I'd scanned countless articles on mainstream news websites that identified me as a murder suspect and possible terrorist working with the Ninety-nine. Thanks to the geopolitical implications of the story, and rumblings of a serious diplomatic incident, I was known as a wanted man around the world, and Private was suffering as a consequence.

"Try and hold the fort," I advised Justine. "If we start losing more clients, I'll have to step down."

"You can't do that, Jack," Justine protested. "You are Private."

"Just until this blows over," I replied. "I've got to do whatever it takes to protect the business."

"I wish I was there to help you through this," Justine said.

"I'm glad you're not," I responded instinctively, and I immediately sensed her hurt. "I'm sorry, I didn't mean it like that. I meant I need you safe and holding things together."

"I know," she replied. "I appreciate it."

It was 3 p.m. in Moscow, and I was in the secure embassy meeting room on the third floor, surrounded by the detritus of a sandwich lunch. Dinara and I had been working on our plan to access Salko's computer since morning, and she was somewhere else in the building with Erin Sebold, who was being very supportive for someone who'd officially disavowed the operation. If nothing else, the CIA was opportunist, and Dinara and I had presented Erin with a plan that offered little downside, but could deliver a motherlode of intelligence.

"Mo-bot's here," Justine said. "I'm putting you on speaker."

I'd been coordinating the technical requirements with Private New York, and had been on the line with Justine while Maureen performed her final checks.

"Jack," Mo-bot said. "Sorry to hear about Leonid. Sounds like you've been through hell."

"I appreciate it," I replied.

"I've modified a cracking program," Mo-bot said. "It's designed to overcome Russian encryption technology, and I can oversee the program in real time. The only downside is you need to access the target machine and install the program via a USB drive. SVR firewalls are too sophisticated for remote penetration."

"We've been working on that assumption," I told her. "Our preparations are well in hand."

"What's the plan?" Justine asked.

"Dinara and I are going in," I replied.

"No. It's too dangerous," Justine objected.

"What other option do we have?"

"You should let the Agency take care of this."

"The Agency can't back us on this. It could start a war."

My remarks were met with silence.

"I know the risks, Justine, but if I don't do this, I stay a wanted man, and I'll never be able to clear my name. If I want my life back, I need to find the real killer and bring him in."

"We can find another way, Jack," Justine said.

"No, we can't," I replied. "Mo, send over the program."

"I'll email it to Dinara," Mo-bot said. "Along with installation instructions. When you get inside, call me so I can monitor what's happening."

"Will do," I replied. "Thanks. I'll contact you the moment we're in," I assured her before hanging up.

I paced the room anxiously. Justine was right. What we were about to do was incredibly dangerous. If we were caught, we'd be turned over to Veles and tortured and killed.

The door opened, and Dinara and Erin entered.

"We've got SVR identification, courtesy of Ms. Sebold," Dinara said.

"Acting in an unofficial capacity," Erin remarked. "If you're ready, we'll give you a ride. Also in an unofficial capacity, of course."

"How do we get out of the embassy without being arrested?" Dinara asked.

Erin gave us both a cryptic look. "How are you guys with confined spaces?"

CHAPTER 90

DINARA'S HEART RACED as she heard the heavy movements of the two police officers searching the vehicle. Pictures of what would happen to her if she was caught invaded her mind, and she fought the urge to cry out. Jack touched her hand, and squeezed it reassuringly.

The two of them were side by side in a cramped compartment concealed beneath the flatbed of an old long-wheelbase Land Rover Defender. Master Gunnery Sergeant West was driving, and he'd explained the compartment walls were filled with countermeasures to defeat X-ray and infrared equipment. Dinara guessed at a lead lining and some sort of cooling system, but West hadn't elaborated other than to say the vehicle was very useful for getting things into and out of the embassy in secret.

The compartment was two meters long, a little over a meter wide and thirty centimeters deep. If she took a deep breath, Dinara could feel cold steel pressing against her chest.

"You know you're breaking every international convention," Dinara heard West say.

The Moscow police were still running checkpoints at both ends of Bolshoy Devyatinsky Lane, and were searching every vehicle entering and exiting the embassy compound, in direct contravention of the privileges accorded to diplomats.

"If you are unhappy with your treatment, your State Department can make a formal objection to the Interior Minister," a Russian voice replied.

The two officers above them banged away at the false flatbed, searching for anomalies. They'd find none. The hinges and catches to open the secret compartment were on the inside.

"It's clear," one of the men directly above them said in Russian.

Dinara heard more movement, and then the sound of the two officers jumping out of the Land Rover, their boots crunching rock salt and grit as they hit the road.

"You can proceed," the Russian voice said, and the Land Rover rumbled forward.

They made a series of turns and a few minutes later, the chunky SUV pulled over.

"Time for coffee," West said, using the pre-agreed phrase that signaled it was safe for them to leave their hiding place.

Dinara sensed Jack feeling for the catches, and heard him snap open three of them in rapid succession. She helped him push the heavy flatbed and squinted as her eyes adjusted to the light.

They clambered out of the tiny compartment, their presence concealed by the Land Rover's privacy glass.

"I bet that feels better," West remarked as they closed the false flatbed and sat on the bench seats that ran along the Land Rover's flanks.

"You OK?" Jack asked.

Dinara nodded. "Let's go," she replied. "We've got a job to do."

CHAPTER 91

MASTER GUNNERY SERGEANT West drove to Konkovo where we were supposed to meet Feo. My heart sank the moment we turned onto Maklaya Street, a quiet side road in a residential neighborhood. I saw a Moscow police patrol car directly ahead of us.

"This could get ugly," West warned as he stepped on the brakes.

The Land Rover came to a rapid halt, and West threw it into reverse as the patrol car doors opened, but I recognized the people who stepped out of the vehicle.

"It's OK," I said. "That's Feo Arapov and Anna Bolshova. They're friends."

West stopped the Land Rover. "You sure?"

I nodded.

West pulled over, and we got out into the bitter chill of late afternoon. The snowstorm had stopped, but dark clouds brooded and swirled overhead, promising more.

"You can't be here," Dinara said to Anna.

"After what happened at the embassy my superiors don't know whether to suspend or promote me. Some of them know the official story stinks. Others are loyalists. You've opened a box of trouble, Mr. Morgan."

"Happy to oblige," I replied.

"Where are we going?" Anna asked.

We hadn't shared our intended destination with Feo, who'd simply been instructed to provide us with a clean vehicle. We could hardly drive into the SVR complex in a US diplomatic car.

"Yasenevo," Dinara replied.

Feo cursed in Russian, and then whistled.

"SVR Headquarters?" Anna asked. "Are you crazy? He's the most wanted man in Russia."

"You still want to help?" Dinara asked.

Anna thought for a moment, and then nodded. "My career will only be safe if I can expose what's been happening. If I don't restore my reputation, I'll end up in records, or taking early retirement, and I can't do that. I have to be where the action is."

"You OK here?" West asked.

"We're good, thanks," I replied.

"Here's your comms unit," West said, reaching into the Land Rover for a small flight case Erin Sebold had given us.

"Thanks," I said, taking it from him.

"I'd better get to the RV," he said.

We'd arranged to meet at a different rendezvous point as a security precaution.

"Good luck." West climbed in the Land Rover, turned the vehicle around and headed back the way we'd come.

"Well, I suppose if you're planning to infiltrate Yasenevo, there are few things less likely to arouse suspicion than a Moscow police patrol car," Anna remarked.

It was hard to disagree.

"Come on, let's go," she said. "If we're going to die today, I'd rather not do it chilled to my soul."

Feo smiled wryly, and Dinara and I followed them to their car.

CHAPTER 92

THIRTY-FIVE MINUTES LATER, we were heading east along the MKAD, a ten-lane beltway that encircled the outer regions of Moscow. Dense, snow-capped forest lay to our right, but there was a sudden break in the treeline, and I saw a white, twenty-four-story tower block rising above the sea of trees like a headstone.

"That's it," Dinara said.

She and I were in the back, dressed in the clothes we'd asked Feo to bring from the Residence. Dinara wore a navy blue dress, and I was in a single-breasted black suit.

A couple of kilometers further on, we left the highway and went south along a winding road that cut through the forest. Only this was no ordinary woodland road. There were camera and sensor towers every hundred meters, and everything about our approach had been logged and tracked before we reached the gatehouse.

A high wire fence marked the perimeter of the huge compound, and beyond it I saw the white tower block, and a shorter but wider building in the shape of two Y's linked together by their stems.

A guard emerged from the gatehouse and checked Feo and Anna's police identification. Dinara handed over the credentials Erin Sebold had provided, and the guard ran them through a handheld scanner. My heart skipped a beat when I realized he was checking them against a central database. I held my breath for what seemed an eternity, but nothing bad happened. The guard returned the IDs to Dinara and waved us through.

The CIA must have had someone inside the SVR or access to the central identification database to have created authentic records. There were long-standing rumors the Russians had a back door into the visa systems of western nations, and it wouldn't be surprising if the Americans had even more sophisticated capabilities to generate false Russian credentials, including intelligence identification. However she'd done it, Erin Sebold had provided us with identities that stood up to official scrutiny.

A little further along the inner access road, another guard in a heavy coat waved us toward a vast parking lot that lay to the east of the sprawling complex.

"This is as far as we go," Anna said after she'd pulled into a parking space. "A police escort inside the building would raise questions."

I opened the flight case West had given me, and distributed the gear. Dinara and I each took a tiny in-ear transceiver, and I gave Anna and Feo handheld relay units they could use to talk to us and link to the phone network.

"When we get inside, connect us to the number stored in preset one," I said, and Anna nodded.

"You ready?" I asked Dinara.

"Let's go," she said.

"Good luck," Feo called after us as we left the police car.

Dinara and I crossed the parking lot, which was almost completely full.

"It's busy for a Sunday," I observed.

"The SVR never sleeps," Dinara replied.

Each car represented at least one person, and I estimated more than 350 vehicles. There were a lot of people in this complex, and every single one of them had to be considered an enemy.

Dinara produced the pistol Feo had given her. She checked the weapon before putting it back inside her purse.

"If anything goes wrong," she said, "you need to know I won't let myself be taken alive."

With my mind playing out the implications of that grim statement, we headed for the imposing white headstone that loomed high above us.

CHAPTER 93

DINARA ORLOVA PINNED a stern, officious expression to her face as they entered SVR headquarters. The tall office block was one of the most secure places in Russia and, no matter how hard her heart pounded and her stomach churned, she was determined to look as though she belonged.

She and Jack passed through a metal detector without incident. They had nothing other than their SVR credentials, some money and the pistol Feo had given her, which was in the purse that was sliding into the X-ray machine. The CIA transceivers were constructed of a composite material that evaded the metal detector and the more thorough wand search performed by a guard. They were then waved on to a second uniformed guard, who conducted a fingertip physical search of them both.

"Your weapon will be stored until you leave," said one of the guards staffing the X-ray machine.

He put the pistol in a nearby locker, and handed Dinara a token.

"Thanks," Dinara replied in Russian, but as they walked away, she shared a look of concern with Jack. They'd lost their only weapon.

Erin Sebold had informed them Salko was located on the executive floor, and as they made their way to the elevators, Dinara chatted to Jack in Russian, and they both made an effort to appear at ease when they passed SVR personnel.

They took one of the cars to the twenty-first floor, and stepped into a quiet corridor. Dinara had been to SVR head-quarters before, but she had never seen the executive floor. According to Erin's information, Salko had a large office in the northwest corner of the building.

They started toward it, and walked past a line of offices, complete with outer cubicles where administrative assistants sat. They attracted a couple of inquiring looks as they passed, but most of the men and women were too busy with their work to pay them much attention.

"Hey!" a voice yelled behind them.

Dinara turned and saw a face she recognized. It was poking out of one of the offices they'd passed. It was Spiridon Fomin, a former colleague from the FSB. He must have transferred to the SVR.

"Dinara Orlova," he said. "I thought that was you."

His tone was not that of a man who knew she was a wanted criminal, and her initial flush of panic subsided.

"What are you doing here?" he asked as he approached. "You're looking great."

Spiro was a tanned, dark-haired former sprinter who exploited his good looks as often as he could. Despite his best efforts, Dinara had never succumbed to his charms.

"You've moved up in the world, Spiro," she said.

He smiled and nodded. "Who's your friend?" he asked.

Jack looked at the man and smiled blankly.

"I didn't know you'd transferred," Dinara said enthusiastically, trying to change the subject. It wouldn't take him long to realize Jack couldn't speak a word of Russian. "It's so good to see you. We have a few minutes. Is there somewhere we can catch up?"

"Sure," Spiro replied. "My office."

He gestured for them to follow, and led Dinara and Jack past his administrative assistant into the large room that lay beyond.

"This is quite some place," Dinara said, trading a conspiratorial glance with Jack. "You must be doing well."

"Can I get you a drink?" Spiro asked, going to a console that took up an entire wall. He opened a cabinet to reveal an extensive liquor collection.

"I'll have a martini," Dinara said, closing the office door.

Spiro turned around to fix her drink. "And your friend?" he asked. "Sorry, I didn't catch his—"

When Spiro had turned to the liquor cabinet, Jack had crossed the room silently, and Dinara watched him wrap his arms around Spiro's neck, cutting him off mid-sentence. Spiro dropped the cocktail shaker onto the thick carpet, and made a rapid succession of choking sounds as he struggled against

Jack's relentless grasp. Finally, the fight left him, and he fell to the floor.

Jack checked his pulse. "He's down, but not dead. Come on, we don't have long."

CHAPTER 94

WE WALKED OUT of the SVR executive's office as though it was just any normal day. Dinara said something in Russian before she shut the door behind us, and the man's assistant glanced up from her work and gave a knowing smile.

I was shocked when Dinara lashed out at the woman, knocking her unconscious with a couple of quick punches.

"Help me get her inside," she said.

I glanced around nervously. Cubicle dividers prevented the other executive assistants from seeing, but if anyone walked along the corridor . . .

I grabbed the woman's shoulders and Dinara took her feet, and we carried her inside her boss's office, and laid her on the floor beside him.

"I told her he was having an afternoon nap, but the first thing she would have done when we set the alarm off would have been to try to wake him up," Dinara explained as we left the room.

"Good work," I whispered as we hurried along the corridor toward the fire stairs Erin had told us were located near Salko's office.

We found the fire escape where we'd expected, and went into the stairwell.

"Ready?" I asked, and Dinara nodded.

I smashed a tiny glass panel, and activated the fire alarm. A klaxon sounded almost immediately, and we ran up two flights of stairs to the upper service level before the first people began streaming through the fire doors below us. We concealed ourselves behind an air-conditioning unit, and the stairwell filled with people chatting as they shuffled downstairs.

When the last of them had left, we hurried down to the twenty-first floor, quickly slipped through the fire door, and sprinted to Salko's office.

"Connect us," I said.

"Connecting," Anna replied via my in-ear transceiver.

Salko's room was locked, but Dinara and I grabbed his assistant's desk, turned it to face the door, and pushed as hard as we could. The heavy desk surged forward and smashed the door open, and we clambered into Salko's grand corner office.

"Go ahead, Jack," Mo-bot said.

"We're in the target's office," I told her as I raced to his huge desk.

"Plug the USB into his computer," Mo-bot replied.

I pulled a tiny plastic USB drive from inside my shoe. Dinara had downloaded Mo-bot's program onto the tiny device. After a brief search, I found Salko's computer in one of the cabinets built into his desk.

"Come on, Jack," Dinara said, watching the doorway nervously.

No amount of fast talking would explain away the wreckage. I thrust the USB drive into one of the ports, and when the computer woke, I was greeted by a password screen.

"I'll take it from here," Mo-bot said, and I saw a series of DOS windows open. "Shouldn't take too long," she remarked, and the password screen vanished and was replaced by a desktop home page full of file icons.

"We're in," Mo-bot said. "I'm going to copy his entire drive."

A status bar filled the screen, displaying a job completion percentage. The klaxon, which had been constant since we'd triggered the alarm, suddenly fell silent.

"They'll have started checking the building," Dinara warned.

I looked at the status bar, which was three-quarters of the way along. Mo-bot's tech was impressive. Copying an entire hard drive in such a short space of time was no mean feat. Even so, we were in a precarious situation.

"Anything I can do to hurry this along?" I asked.

"You can have something done fast, or you can have it done well," Mo-bot replied.

"I just want it done," I told her sharply.

"I know you're under a lot of pressure, Jack Morgan, so I'm going to forgive your tone," she replied. "Almost ... There."

The status bar disappeared.

"You're good to go," Mo-bot confirmed. "Just grab the USB and get the hell out of Dodge."

I didn't wait to be told twice. I pulled the USB drive from the port, and Dinara and I scrambled over the desk, jumped through the doorway and ran along the corridor toward the elevators.

We took a car to the first floor and stepped into a lobby full of people being allowed back into the building.

"They know it was a false alarm," Dinara whispered, translating the muttered conversations around us.

We pushed to the edge of the crowd, and made our way to the exit.

"Salko," Dinara whispered urgently.

I followed her eye-line to see a grizzled man in his late fifties. He wasn't much taller than Dinara, and his wrinkled face looked as though it was set in a permanent scowl. The guy radiated ruthless hostility.

Dinara and I turned away from the man who had ordered the city scoured for us, and hurried out of the building.

My heart raced like a jackhammer as we walked away from the gigantic headstone, and the burning adrenalin didn't subside until we were in the car and on our way to rendezvous with Master Gunnery Sergeant West.

CHAPTER 95

"ARE YOU GOING to be OK?" I asked Anna and Feo.

Anna shivered in the evening chill, and nodded.

"We have our cover story, if we need it," Feo explained. "You took us hostage at gunpoint and forced us to drive you to SVR headquarters."

"Mr. Morgan," West said, "we have to go now."

He stood beside the modified Land Rover, and eyed Veyernaya Street anxiously. There was no one else to be seen, and the surrounding industrial units stood idle.

"Take care," I said, shaking Anna Bolshova's hand. "And thank you for everything you've done."

"Good luck, Mr. Morgan," she replied.

I offered Feo my hand, but he pulled me in for a hug. "We're family now. You let me know if you ever need anything else, American, OK?"

"Thank you, Feo. That means a lot," I said when he released me.

Dinara said her farewells in Russian, and minutes later we were in the Land Rover, watching Moscow roll by as West headed for the embassy. When we were a few blocks from Bolshoy Devyatinsky Lane, Dinara and I returned to the secret compartment, and West smuggled us through the police checkpoint.

An hour later, having been debriefed by Erin Sebold, who was in awe of our audacious, simple plan, we were waiting impatiently in the secure meeting room on the third floor.

"What's taking so long?" Dinara asked. "We should never have handed it over."

"The tools they have in this building will outperform anything else, even the tech we have at Private," I replied.

The door opened and Carrie Underwood entered. "The ambassador would like to see you," she said.

We followed her to Thomas Dussler's office, and found him with Erin Sebold and Master Gunnery Sergeant West. Dussler greeted us warmly, and invited us to take a seat. Erin watched us with a mix of glee and astonishment.

"I don't know how you pulled it off, Mr. Morgan. You must have diamond-hard nerves. You've given us enough intel to keep our analysts busy for years. All of Salko's files. It's a treasure trove," she said. "The downside is that Salko is livid. Surveillance footage clearly identified you. He's accused you of being CIA spies and is demanding we hand you over with the stolen data. We're pleading ignorance, of course."

"You get anything on Veles?" I asked.

"A series of communiqués," Erin replied. "They're coded, but we've been able to decipher the most recent one. It orders Veles back to the United States to protect Minerva. Salko is concerned you might know Minerva's identity."

"Minerva?" I remarked.

"We're going through any records that refer to Bright Star. There aren't many, which suggests Salko keeps any data related to that program somewhere else, but there is a report to the President, saying Minerva is the culmination of the Bright Star program and will redefine Russia's place in the world."

"Nothing else?" I asked.

Erin shook her head. "There might be some other coded material, but that's all we've found so far. Naturally the identification of Minerva has become an Agency priority. We're coordinating with the NSA and FBI to expedite the process."

I knew what was coming. I could sense the shift in the air. The plumbers had fixed the broken pipes and now the owners wanted them out of their house.

"We appreciate everything you've done, Mr. Morgan," Erin said, "but this is now a national security matter. We'll take it from here."

I fought the urge to sneer, and looked at Dinara, who smiled wryly.

"You can't stay in Moscow," Dussler said. "Your continued presence here is likely to spark a serious diplomatic incident. According to our information, Director Salko is willing to tear the world apart to get to you."

"We've arranged transit for you back to the States," Erin revealed. "Wherever you need to go."

"And Dinara?" I asked.

Erin hesitated.

"You think I'm leaving her here after what happened to Leonid Boykov?"

"A second passenger won't be a problem, will it, Ms. Sebold?" Dussler asked.

Erin shook her head. "Of course not, sir. Master Gunnery Sergeant West will take you to the airport. We have a plane waiting, and we'd like to have you airborne within the hour."

"In that case, we should get going," I said, getting to my feet.

Dussler offered me his hand. "Thank you, Mr. Morgan. We can't make any of this public, but we will try to clear your name, and I'll be sharing a full report with the President."

"I understand, Ambassador Dussler," I replied. "And I appreciate whatever you can do. Ready, Master Gunnery Sergeant?"

West nodded. "Let's get you home, Mr. Morgan."

CHAPTER 96

WE LEFT THE embassy in the Land Rover's secret compartment, and were one of three identical vehicles that set out from the compound at the same time, each heading for a different Moscow airport.

West had told us not to come out of the compartment after the initial search at the police checkpoint on Bolshoy Devyatinsky Lane. He was worried Russian intelligence would have picked up the presence of three CIA birds fueled and ready to fly at three different airports, and might have tied them to an escape attempt.

His fears seemed well founded, because the Land Rover was pulled over and searched twice en route to the airport. When we were stopped a second time, Dinara held my hand and squeezed it tight. We were in absolute darkness, so I couldn't see her face, but her clammy palm and rapid, shallow breathing told me everything I needed to know. She was afraid, and, deep down, so was I. It would only take one exceptionally vigilant police office, or a failure of the Land Rover's countermeasures, and our lives would be forfeited.

"You guys know you can't search the diplomatic pouch," West told the unseen officers.

We could hear them rifling through the mail sack above us. The bag was West's official reason for driving to the airport. The police officers ignored his complaint, and after a few minutes we heard a grudging Russian voice.

"You can go."

The engine roared as we gathered speed, and Dinara released my hand.

"Not much longer," West yelled. "We're a few minutes out."

I was thrown against Dinara as the vehicle made a sharp right turn.

"Sorry," I said.

"It's OK," she replied.

The rest of the journey passed in tense silence, and a few minutes later, the Land Rover slowed. We'd arrived at Domodedovo Airport.

"Another checkpoint," West said.

The Land Rover was searched again, and we heard West explain the purpose of his trip a fourth time.

"I'm delivering an urgent diplomatic pouch to a State Department plane."

Every panel was thumped and we could hear the beeps and alerts of sensor equipment, but even after a thorough investigation, our hiding place remained undiscovered. I could sense Dinara bristling with nervous tension, and I longed to be free of our cramped sarcophagus.

"OK," a voice said.

The engine sprang to life, and the Land Rover started moving again.

I took a deep breath, and sensed Dinara relax, but our relief was premature.

"We've got a problem," West said. "Two unmarked cars have followed us onto the airfield."

My heart started racing, and Dinara's breathing picked up again. Soon, I heard the familiar sound of jet turbines idling. We came to a halt and West applied the parking brake.

No one said or did anything for what seemed like an age, and I felt my body charge with pent-up energy. I needed to run or fight.

"Here's the situation," West said. "We're twelve feet from the plane, by the airstairs. The two cars, I'm guessing FSB or SVR, are about twenty feet behind us. They're parked in a 'V', passenger doors side on, so they'll have a good firing line the moment things kick off."

I hadn't thought it possible, but my pulse quickened further.

"We don't have a choice," West said. "We're going to have to wrestle the bear. I want you to come out as slowly and quietly as you can."

I searched for the latches and opened the compartment. Dinara and I climbed out slowly, so we didn't cause the Land Rover to make any telltale movements. Our presence was concealed by the vehicle's privacy glass. West was in the driver's seat, and he kept looking straight ahead as we took our places on the bench seats and closed the secret compartment.

"I'm going to walk to the back," he said above the noise of the jet engines. "When I open the rear door, I want you to climb into the front and make a run for it through the driver's door. I'll cover you."

"You don't have to do this," I said.

"You got a better way?" he asked.

I said nothing.

"OK then," he continued. "On my mark."

He opened his door and climbed out. The cold air that filled the cabin couldn't counter the blaze of nervous energy, and I felt beads of sweat prick my forehead and neck.

I looked at Dinara, who was gripped by fear, but she nodded bravely. West's steps became a solemn countdown as he walked round the vehicle.

He opened the rear door, looked at us both and said, "Go!"

I climbed over the front seat and jumped through the driver's door onto the asphalt. The Gulfstream G650 jet was a few paces away, and a man in a suit stood at the top of the airstairs.

"Come on!" he urged.

I heard a voice shout in Russian as Dinara jumped out of the Land Rover.

"Stop!" another Russian voice yelled in English.

I grabbed Dinara's arm and we started running as the first shots rang out. I glanced over my shoulder to see the silhouette of men ducking for cover behind two unmarked vehicles as

Master Gunnery Sergeant West pinned them down with pistol fire.

Dinara and I raced up the short run of steps, and the suited man bundled us inside and closed the door.

"Go! Go! Go!" he hollered.

The engines roared and the G650 started to move.

"Please have a seat, Mr. Morgan, Miss Orlova," the suited man said. "My name's John Hudson, and I'm here to make sure you get home safely."

I sat port side and looked back to see West raising his hands in surrender. One man confiscated his weapon, two more took him into custody, and a fourth spoke furiously into a radio. But whatever he was saying and whoever he was saying it to couldn't stop the inevitable, and moments later the engines surged, and we took to the sky.

I glanced at Dinara, who smiled with relief as we left Moscow.

CHAPTER 97

DINARA REALIZED SHE was trembling. She never got airsick, but she was feeling a profound nausea that made her toes curl. She knew it was nothing to do with the Gulfstream's steady progress. She'd fled her homeland with nothing more than the clothes on her back. She'd made enemies of some extremely powerful people, and she was going to America as a refugee. She'd lost her friend and colleague, and the life she'd known was gone. Her mind whirled with questions. Could she ever go home? What would she do when they arrived in America? Would she ever be safe?

The man who'd introduced himself as John Hudson emerged from the cockpit. He reminded Dinara of a young Tom Cruise.

"I was just on the horn with Erin Sebold," he said. "She's glad to hear we made it. The pilot says the control tower tried to rescind our flight clearance, but we were already airborne."

Hudson took a seat at the same table as Jack. The two men sat opposite each other, across the aisle from Dinara.

"We've got a couple of MIGs off our flank, trying to force us back," Hudson remarked.

"I saw them," Jack replied.

Dinara's stomach rolled, and she fought the urge to vomit. She leaned over to the window and registered the silhouette and navigation lights of a Russian fighter jet off their starboard side.

"They won't shoot us down," Jack said, giving Dinara a reassuring look. "They want us alive."

"The pilot agrees. He thinks they'll stay with us until their tanks run dry," Hudson said. He had a languid inflection, but Dinara wasn't sufficiently familiar with American accents to place it. Florida perhaps? Maybe Georgia?

"You got any comms on this bird, Agent Hudson?" Jack asked.

"Mr. Hudson," the suited man replied, "'Agent' would involve me confirming or denying my employment by a government agency, and in truth I prefer plain old John. But, to answer your question, we've got whatever you need."

"I think Karl Parker saw someone he recognized—a Bright Star agent," Jack revealed. "You remember what you said to me?" he asked, turning to Dinara. "About never being able to hide who you really are? These kids were brainwashed into thinking they were doing right by Russia, but I think Karl Parker was fundamentally a good man. I think he asked me to New York to tell me the truth."

"Why not go to the FBI or CIA?" Dinara asked.

"Maybe he was worried they'd been infiltrated by Bright Star operatives? Maybe he even knew they were? He knew he could trust me. And Private has resources and connections," Jack replied. "I might not have known the truth about his background, but maybe you're right. Maybe I really did know the man. You can't hide good, and the man I knew as Karl Parker was good. I think that's why he left a trail for me. He was trying to expose this without putting his family in jeopardy. I think he loved them and I have to believe he had grown to love America. I think he was going to give me the identity of Minerva."

"The identification of the Russian agent known as Minerva has become a strategic priority," Hudson remarked.

"Who's overseeing it?" Jack asked. "Whoever it is, how do you know they're not Bright Star?"

Hudson said nothing.

"Karl left a trail only I could follow. He led me to the basement that revealed he was a spy. I've got to believe he wants me to know the truth. If he knew Minerva's identity, he would have left a clue, something I could use, something only I would recognize," Jack said.

"We've got people working on this," Hudson assured him.

"I don't know who they are or who they report to," Jack replied. "But I do know my team and I trust them with my life. I'd like two phones and a couple of computers please. Miss Orlova and I need to get to work."

CHAPTER 98

MAINSTREAM MEDIA OUTLETS all over America had run the story of me fleeing Moscow as a murder suspect. Russian authorities had given interviews portraying themselves as the victims of a coordinated conspiracy, and painting me as the villain. The Russian ambassador to Washington had lodged a formal protest demanding my immediate return to Moscow to face justice. Justine had emailed me the worst articles, so I could gauge the threat to Private, and they were currently open on the laptop John Hudson had given me.

"It's not good, Jack," Justine said over the speakerphone. "We lost TradeBank."

TradeBank was a big client. Jessie Fleming had been leading a team out of Private's New York office, investigating a possible financial fraud by organized criminals making use of the bank's overseas branches.

"They said they can't afford more scandal," Justine revealed.

I sighed. "I'm going to have to quit Private," I said. "At least until—"

"Don't you say another word," Mo-bot cut in.

She and Justine were in the New York office, poring over the huge data dump they'd shared with us. Everything we could pull on Karl Parker.

"You quit and everyone will think you have something to hide," Mo-bot said. "And predators never go easy on a wounded animal."

"I'm gambling everything," I replied. "I'm putting all your livelihoods at risk."

"Do the right thing for the right reasons, Jack Morgan," Mo-bot said. "And we'll back you all the way."

I looked at Dinara, who sat across the aisle, studying files on the laptop Hudson had given her. She glanced up and nodded.

"Don't let them win," she said.

"OK," I responded reluctantly. "But this can't go on much longer."

"Did you check the diary?" Dinara asked.

She turned the computer to reveal one of the crime-scene photos taken of Karl's basement, which had been shared with Private by the NYPD before they'd stopped cooperating. I recalled the blank desk diary that had been lying beside the false passports and stacks of foreign currency.

"Yes," I replied. "It was blank."

I was struck by a thought. What if we weren't supposed to look in the diary? What if the diary itself was a message?

"Have you been through his appointments?" I asked.

"We've checked his schedule for the past three years, and everything going forward," Justine replied. "It's in the folder marked 'Admin.'"

Dinara went through the zip files we'd been sent via the high-speed satellite link and found Karl Parker's digital calendar in the admin folder. She started flicking through the daily planner, and I saw something that made me lean forward suddenly.

"Go back," I said.

"What is it?" Mo-bot asked.

John Hudson stood up and came round the table to peer at the screen.

"What have you seen?" Dinara asked.

I pointed at a diary entry. A midday lunch with Ann Kavanagh, the CEO of a company called Enterprise Web Services. The meal was scheduled to take place tomorrow.

"It's the lunch with Ann Kavanagh," I told Justine and Mo-bot.

"We checked it out. Enterprise Web Services took over the tech platform of Karl Parker's company, Silverlink International, about a month ago," Mo-bot replied.

"So Karl Parker would probably have met Ann Kavanagh only recently," I remarked.

"Ann Kavanagh?" Justine said. "Would the Russians really go to such lengths to protect the CEO of a tech company?"

"That's her," I said. "That's Minerva."

"How can you be sure?" Dinara asked.

"The name of the restaurant where they're supposed to meet, DC Legitum," I replied. "'DC' is a military acronym for 'danger close' and 'legitum' is shorthand for a legitimate military target."

CHAPTER 99

"ENTERPRISE WEB SERVICES is a massive data provider. It competes with Amazon for enterprise-level data management," Mo-bot explained. "Banks, video streamers, the military . . ." She trailed off, and I felt the familiar thrill of a lead.

"Jack, there was no way Ann Kavanagh was ever going to make that lunch date," she revealed. "Tomorrow at midday, the Pentagon will activate its real-time cloud network, linking battlefield operations with live intelligence. It's designed to give America the strategic advantage, but guess which company is providing the tech behind it?"

"Enterprise Web Services," I replied.

"Bingo," Mo-bot said. "It's called the Field Operations Resource and Communications Engine, otherwise known as the FORCE System. The date for the activation ceremony was fixed months ago. Ann Kavanagh will be there. That's what Karl

Parker's calendar entry must signify. I've sent you a link to an article in *Jane's Defence Weekly*."

I checked my email and found Mo-bot's message. When I clicked on the link, a window opened, revealing an in-depth feature about the Pentagon's state-of-the-art battlefield solution, and a profile of Ann Kavanagh, the technical genius behind it.

"If she is Minerva, the Russians will be able to see our every move. Every troop deployment, every base, all our military and intelligence secrets will be open to them," I concluded with a sinking feeling as the scale of the threat became clear. Technology, not politics, not conventional espionage, was going to give the Russians the keys to the republic.

"She fits the profile," Justine advised. "I'm sending you what I've been able to get on her, Jack. Raised in Ryegate, Montana, she was another small-town orphan who became a ward of the foster system. She enlisted in the Navy aged eighteen, and served with distinction. She started Enterprise Web Services after a short career at IBM, using investment funds provided by a syndicate of European banks and financiers."

"This is it," I told Hudson. "You've got to run this up the chain of command. Stop the FORCE System going live."

"I'll radio it in right now," Hudson said, moving toward the cockpit.

"Justine, I want you to call Erin Sebold. Tell her everything," I said, but I could hear commotion at the other end of the line.

"Jack," Justine replied. "We're being raided. It's the FBI."

I heard people tramp into the meeting room where Justine and Mo-bot had set up their operations center.

"Step away from the computers," a man's voice commanded. "We have reason to believe Jack Morgan is a spy for Russian intelligence. This entire organization is under investigation for espionage activities against the United States."

"Don't come home, Jack," Justine whispered. "It isn't safe."

"Who are you talking to?" the intruder asked at the other end of the call. "Move away from that phone," he ordered.

An instant later, the line went dead.

CHAPTER 100

DINARA COULD SEE Jack was stunned by what had just happened. She turned to her computer, opened a fresh browser and went to the Otkrov blog. The top story identified Jack Morgan as a rogue SVR spy, and outed Dinara as his Russian handler. It was a bold move that demonstrated Salko's desperation to discredit them. It made them targets in both countries, and meant it would be almost impossible for them to find safe haven anywhere. It also took Private out of the equation. The entire organization was now tainted.

"Jack," Dinara said, turning the laptop toward him. "They've upped the stakes. This story identifies you as a rogue SVR agent and says I'm your handler," she translated. "They've given us nowhere to go."

"We still have friends," he replied, getting to his feet.

He went to the cockpit door and knocked. "John," he said. "I need to get a message to Erin."

The door opened, and Hudson emerged looking somber. He put his arm on Jack's shoulder, and led him back to his seat.

"I've just heard what's happened," Hudson said. "It's a world-class screw-up. One agency not talking to the other." He slid into the chair opposite Jack. "We'll get this cleared up. You must have really got the Russians pissed. Breaking into Salko's office, assaulting Spiro Fomin and his assistant."

Dinara's stomach lurched, and she looked at Jack, who'd also registered the significance of Hudson's words. They hadn't mentioned Spiro Fomin in their debrief to the CIA; it hadn't seemed relevant. The only other people who knew Spiro Fomin had been assaulted were the Russians. Hudson must have sensed the change in mood and realized his mistake, because his hand whipped beneath the table, and when it came back up, it held a pistol.

"No sudden moves," he told Jack. "Damn. Never volunteer information. That's the key to pulling off a good cover, right?"

"Where's the real CIA jet?" Dinara asked in Russian.

Hudson smiled. "Quarantined in a hangar at the airport," he replied in English.

Jack glared at the Russian operative. "You hurried us onto the plane, so our escort couldn't verify your identity."

"People get sloppy when under pressure," Hudson replied. "We knew the Americans would try to get you home. Three jets, three airports. It wasn't much of a challenge to have substitutes waiting at them all. And we've kept your people in custody, so

Erin Sebold and her fellow plotters at the embassy are in the dark. They don't know whether your escape was successful."

Dinara felt the jet bank into a sharp clockwise turn.

"We now know what you know," Hudson said. "So you will be taken back to Moscow, where you will face justice."

Dinara felt a wave of panic. The Kremlin had learned exactly what she and Jack knew. Hudson had listened to it all, and she had no doubt all their electronic communications on the plane had been processed through a Russian satellite. They'd neutralized Private. No one would believe anything Justine and Mo-bot said, and Dinara had no doubt Russian intelligence would find a way to take them out permanently. She was under no illusions; she and Jack would be taken back to Moscow, where they would be executed.

Jack must have reached the same conclusion, because he sprang forward. Hudson fired, but the bullet zipped past Jack, who moved sideways, and buried itself in the plush headrest of Jack's chair.

Jack swatted Hudson's gun and punched him in the face. Hudson fell out of his seat and, as he tumbled, his hand hit the table and the pistol clattered free. Dinara grabbed Hudson while Jack picked up the pistol. Hudson headbutted her and Dinara lost her grip on him. Hudson sprang toward Jack, who fired, shooting him in the neck. As Hudson fell, choking, the cockpit door opened, revealing the pilot, who held a pistol. Jack shot him twice in the chest, and he fell to the ground.

Dinara and Jack froze, staring at the two men lying dead on the floor. For a moment, the aircraft was still. The only sound was the constant roar of the engines.

Jack snapped out of his daze. "Find out where the FORCE System is located," he said. "It was mentioned in the *Jane's Defence* article. Find out where the activation ceremony is taking place."

"OK," Dinara replied.

Jack headed toward the cockpit. "I'm going to turn this plane around, and we're going to do whatever it takes to stop this thing."

CHAPTER 101

I'D BEEN TRAINED to fly Sea Knights, and I hadn't piloted a fixed wing for a long time, but our high-speed satellite connection put the Internet at my fingertips, and with it the sum of human knowledge. A combination of information gleaned from the aircraft's flight manual and online tutorials enabled me to supplement my general flight skills with a specific understanding of the G650's controls. Once I'd corrected course, and set the autopilot, I dragged Hudson and the pilot to the rear of the aircraft and put their bodies in the small baggage hold in the tail.

I said a quiet prayer for the men as I shut the door to the compartment. I had killed before, when there'd been no other option, but the taking of a life never got any easier. Hudson and the pilot had been a threat, but they'd been turned into my enemies by circumstance. In another world, we might have talked sport over beers. I harbored no ill will toward the fallen men. They'd done what they thought was necessary. Just like me.

"The FORCE System is run out of Naval Air Station Fallon, Nevada," Dinara revealed as I returned to the main cabin.

"Bring your computer," I said, picking up my machine and the satellite phone. "Let's get set up in the cockpit."

Dinara grabbed her laptop and followed me through the cabin.

"Fallon," I remarked as I took the pilot's seat and Dinara slid into the co-pilot's chair. "That's north of Vegas."

I used my laptop to check the nearest civilian airport and discovered Fallon had a municipal field that was rated for the G650. I thought about attempting to land at NAS Fallon, but an unidentified civilian aircraft approaching a military base would almost certainly be shot down.

"We can land at the local airport," I told Dinara, "but we're going to need help."

I picked up the phone and dialed one of many numbers I knew by heart.

"Private Vegas," an operator answered.

"This is Jack Morgan," I said.

"Mr. Morgan—" the operator began, but I cut him off.

"I know. Don't believe everything you hear on the news. Put me through to Hector Lopez, and if anyone asks, you never heard from me."

"Yes, sir," the operator replied.

The line went silent; then there was a ringing tone and the call connected.

"Jack?" Hector Lopez said.

I could hear the disbelief in his tone. He was the new head of Private Vegas, and was a decent, honest man. The rumors and scandal wouldn't have been easy for him.

"No names," I said. "This isn't a secure line. I've been framed by Russian intelligence. Whatever you've heard is a lie."

"I never thought otherwise," Hector replied.

"What's the situation where you are?" I asked.

"Feds are freezing our assets and operations," Hector informed me. "Part of a counter-espionage operation. My read is someone's putting the squeeze on you."

"You read it right," I told Hector, relieved I'd hired this perceptive former FBI agent out of the Vegas field office. "I need you to meet me upstate. Municipal airfield. Name of a late-night talk-show host."

If Salko, Veles or any of their SVR associates were listening in, they'd probably guess where we were heading, but I wasn't going to make it easy on them.

"Got it. What's your ETA?" Hector asked.

I performed a quick calculation. "Flight time of around twelve hours. We should touch down just before eleven."

"I'll be there," Hector said.

"Come prepared," I replied.

"Copy that," he said, before hanging up.

"We're going to be cutting it fine," Dinara observed. "The system goes online at midday."

"We'll make it," I replied, but in truth I wasn't so sure.

CHAPTER 102

INSTEAD OF FLYING over the continental United States, which would have attracted attention, I tracked the Pacific coast over international waters. Dinara managed a few hours' sleep, but I was too amped to rest and was running on adrenalin. I disabled the aircraft transponder, but there was nothing I could do about radar except keep clear of known installations and air corridors. I spent a long time studying everything I could find on Ann Kavanagh. Justine had been right; Kavanagh fit the Bright Star profile. A ward of the state, distinguished service in the military, a successful career, a wealthy recluse. She wasn't often photographed, but the pictures that did exist showed a tall, athletic woman with blond hair, pale, unblemished skin, and wide, flat eyes. There was something ethereal about her, and she looked as though she might have had Scandinavian heritage.

We finally entered American airspace over the Mendocino National Forest, a large stretch of wilderness some 350 miles from Fallon, approximately forty minutes out. My gamble paid off, and we weren't challenged until we were a hundred miles from Fallon and had started our final descent.

"Unidentified aircraft, this is Naval Air Station Fallon. Identify yourself and state your destination," a stern voice said over the radio.

"This is November Six Three Zero Sierra Tango," I replied, giving the tail number of a G650 based in San Francisco. "We've run into electrical problems. All our systems are failing inter- mittently. We're heading for Fallon Municipal, and will put down there until we can get an engineer out."

"Copy that," the NAS Fallon controller said. "Do not deviate from your current course."

"Understood," I replied. "Will stay on heading one-three- two."

Dinara entered the cockpit.

"Better strap yourself in," I said.

She took the co-pilot's chair and buckled up.

I switched to Fallon Municipal Airport tower frequency. "FLX Fallon, FLX Fallon, this is November Six Three Zero Sierra Tango flying from San Francisco to New York. We've encoun- tered an electrical fault and need to land to make repairs."

"Copy that, November Six Three Zero Sierra Tango," a man replied. Calm and measured, he lacked the authoritarian tone of the military air traffic controller. "Are you deadstick?" he asked, using the aviation term for an unresponsive aircraft.

"Negative," I replied. I didn't want the airport crash tenders being deployed. "We think it's a blown fuseboard."

"Copy that," the Fallon Municipal controller replied. "Stay on approach one-three-two. Runway thirteen is clear."

"Copy," I said, making my final preparations. "We'll be on the ground in ten minutes," I told Dinara. "I hope Hector's there, because when they realize our tail number doesn't match the one I've given them, there's going to be trouble."

CHAPTER 103

I NEEDN'T HAVE worried. Hector was there waiting in a gray Jeep Grand Cherokee and drove across the airfield to meet us the moment the airstairs touched the asphalt. Hector Lopez had a high forehead, chiseled cheekbones, and narrow eyes that exuded intelligence. He was an approachable man with a strong sense of honor, and I'd warmed to him the instant he'd arrived for his interview. He stepped out of the jeep, wearing a light blue bomber jacket, a navy shirt and black jeans.

"Good to see you, boss," he said as we hurried over to the SUV. "Wish it was under better circumstances."

After the freezing cold of Moscow and New York, the sweet, cool breeze of a mild Nevada winter seemed almost tropical. I jumped in the passenger seat, and Dinara climbed in the back. The dashboard clock said 10:51 a.m.

"How did you get on the field?" I asked as he started driving toward the small terminal building.

"I flashed my old Bureau ID," Hector explained. "I know, I know, it's a felony to impersonate an FBI agent, but I used to be one, so it's kind of a gray area. At least in my mind. I told the airport manager that no matter what he heard, this plane was Bureau and it was not to be interfered with."

I was impressed with Hector's resourcefulness.

"Hector Lopez, this is Dinara Orlova," I said. "Hector runs Private Vegas. Dinara is head of Private Moscow."

"Good to meet you," Hector said.

"You also," Dinara replied.

"So where are we going?" Hector asked.

"Naval Air Station Fallon," I replied. "We need to get inside."

Hector puffed out his cheeks and exhaled slowly, and a look of disbelief swept across his face. "I don't think my old Bureau ID will work on those fellas."

"Leave it to me," I said. "I'll get us in."

Hector didn't look convinced, but he nodded. He flashed his Bureau ID at the airport gate guard, and moments later we were gathering speed on Rio Vista Drive.

CHAPTER 104

THE MUNICIPAL AIRPORT was located northeast of Fallon, and the Naval Air Station was seven miles directly south, on the other side of town. They traveled through a flat, arid landscape, which was broken only by the occasional single story-home. High mountains wrinkled the distant horizon. No one said anything, and Hector Lopez covered the distance in twelve minutes.

Dinara had felt strange being introduced as the head of Private Moscow. She'd appreciated Jack's gesture, but it had rung hollow. There wasn't really anything to be head of. Leonid was gone, which only left Elena Kabova. Dinara wondered if the office administrator had been pulled in for questioning, or whether she was sitting in the Moscow office, puzzling over what had happened.

Dinara had slept on the plane, and her kaleidoscopic dreams had been dominated by Leonid's death. She kept replaying the awful moment, despairing at her inability to save him. She'd slept but she didn't feel rested, and the flat, desolate, alien landscape made her experience feel even more surreal. She was traveling with one of the world's most wanted men, and they were about to attempt to infiltrate a high-security military installation.

Dinara studied Jack for any clue to his plan, but he was stony-faced. Did he even have a plan? Or was this simply the last gamble of a desperate man?

"Here goes," Hector said as he made a left off Pasture Road onto a private driveway that led to a guardhouse. A wedge barrier blocked the road ahead of the guardhouse; then there were a couple of chicanes and finally a gate. Signs either side of the driveway warned trespassers they would be prosecuted.

"Want to tell me what you've got in mind, boss?" Hector asked.

"Show your ID," Jack replied as the SUV rolled toward the wedge barrier.

A uniformed Marine emerged from the guardhouse. He held an assault rifle in the ready position. Dinara could see him looking at Hector's ID from a distance.

"Just get us to the guardhouse," Jack muttered.

"Then what?" Hector asked, but the question went unanswered.

Dinara's entire body bristled with nervous energy, and her heart felt as though it might burst from her chest. But she sat perfectly still and pretended to be calm.

Up ahead, the Marine finally nodded at someone inside the guardhouse, and the wedge barrier descended into the road.

"Boss?" Hector asked.

"Drive on," Jack replied.

Hector steered around the chicanes slowly, and stopped beside the Marine.

Dinara took a deep breath and held it as Hector lowered his window.

"State your business," the Marine said.

Dinara gasped when Jack Morgan produced Hudson's pistol and pointed it at Hector's head.

"I want to see Colonel Steve Fuller, the base XO. If he's not here in three minutes, I will execute these hostages."

The Marine stepped back and raised his rifle. "Put the gun down!" he yelled.

A klaxon sounded, and more Marines ran from the guard-house and surrounded the vehicle, their weapons trained on Jack.

"Boss," Hector said anxiously.

Dinara was trembling, but when she looked at Jack, she saw nothing but ice in his eyes.

"Two minutes thirty," Jack said.

"Drop it!" another Marine commanded.

"Put the gun down!" the first Marine shouted. "Or I will open fire."

"Jack," Hector said nervously.

Dinara jumped when there was sudden movement, and Jack's passenger door was yanked open and he was pulled roughly from the car. A huge Marine pushed Jack to the ground, and ripped the pistol from his grasp.

Two other Marines pointed their assault rifles at Jack's head.

"Don't move!" one of them commanded.

The look on Jack's face made it clear to Dinara that she'd just witnessed the last gamble of a desperate man.

CHAPTER 105

"YOU'VE GOT TO listen to me, corporal," I said. "I need to see Colonel Steve Fuller right now."

I was in the back of a Marine Corps Police vehicle. The large white Dodge Durango SUV was flashed with the red and blue livery of the Corps, and a gold Marine Police badge dominated both front doors. I'd thought my days of being subject to military justice were long gone, but I was in the charge of a corporal, who sat in the front passenger seat, and a private who was driving. The corporal was in his mid-thirties; he had a weather-beaten face and the calm demeanor of someone with a great deal of experience. He was too old for advancement and too young for retirement. The private couldn't have had more than a couple of years under his belt. Unlike his partner, he'd looked anxious when the fire-watch team at the guardhouse had handed me over.

"The national security of the United States is at stake, corporal," I said, focusing my attention on the older man, hoping his experience would enable him to recognize I was telling the truth.

I saw a flicker of interest, but the private shot the corporal a skeptical glance.

After my arrest, my wrists had been cable-tied and I'd been frogmarched to the Durango. If I couldn't convince the corporal and his sidekick, I had no doubt I was headed for the brig, where I'd be held until they could figure out which particular branch of law enforcement got me first. News of my capture would travel fast, and the vultures would already be circling.

"Come on, corporal. I was a winger, a Corps pilot, in Afghanistan with MAG Forty. I'm a patriot, corporal. I served with honor, and I swear by God and country that I'm telling the truth."

I saw him waver, but the change was momentary, and was quickly replaced by stern detachment.

I hadn't seen what had happened to Dinara and Hector, but they would be safe. I hadn't shared my plan for fear they'd try to talk me out of it. There had been a good chance of me getting shot, but I'd bet my life on the training and discipline of the Marine Corps, and I hadn't been disappointed. I had been about to surrender my weapon when I'd been hauled out of Hector's car. It had always been my plan to get taken into custody; I just hadn't expected to get winded in the process. Becoming a military prisoner seemed the surest way for a wanted fugitive to get on base.

"Come on, corporal," I said. "You're smart. Just give me five minutes with Colonel Fuller and if he doesn't believe me, you can lock me up and throw away the key."

The Durango came to a halt, and the corporal and the private jumped out. I saw a concrete building directly ahead of us. A blue sign hung above a security door and white letters declared this was the "Transient Personnel Unit Pre-Trial Confinement Facility Fallon." The brig. If I was taken inside, all was lost.

"Corporal, what time is it?" I asked as they opened the Durango's back door.

He checked his watch. "Eleven twenty-five."

"We've got thirty-five minutes," I told him. "You have to listen to me."

He considered my pleas. "I will contact Colonel Fuller once you've been processed."

"That will be too late," I protested. "We don't have time."

"Bring him out," the corporal ordered.

The private pulled my arm, and I got to my feet. When I stepped onto the lip of the footwell, I lashed out and kicked the private in the face. He fell onto the corporal, who fumbled for his sidearm as he and the private collapsed in a heap.

I jumped from the Durango and raised my hands high behind me, until it felt as though my shoulders might slip from their sockets. As I hit the asphalt, I brought my wrists down against the small of my back and snapped the cable tie. I rushed the private, who was trying to pick himself up, but before he could react, I punched him, reached down to his waist, flipped his holster open and stole his sidearm. I aimed it at the corporal, who had managed to get hold of his own weapon.

"Drop it," I commanded.

He hesitated.

"Do it now!" I yelled.

The corporal glared at me, but complied and tossed his gun.

"Corporal, if I take you hostage, there's a good chance you and the private here will face disciplinary charges," I said. "And I wouldn't want that."

He backed away as I stepped toward him.

"I'm not going to hurt you," I assured him. "All I ask is that you trust me the way I'm going to trust you."

I took a deep breath and played the biggest gamble of my life.

"*Semper fidelis*," I said as I flipped the pistol and offered it to him. "Always loyal."

CHAPTER 106

"I DON'T KNOW about this, Ryan," the private said to the corporal as we drove across the base.

"Stow it, private," the corporal replied. "It won't cost anything but time to let the man have his say."

Time was my enemy. After I'd surrendered the pistol, the corporal ordered us back into the Durango, and we set out for the command block.

"We're here," the private announced, and the Durango shuddered to a halt.

"Come on," the corporal said, and the three of us jumped out of the vehicle and double-timed into the command building. We ran into the lobby and the corporal swiped us through a security door that led to the administration block.

"This way," he said, and I followed him at a run, with the private trailing behind me.

We raced up the stairs and came to the senior officers' wing. Someone yelled something down the corridor, but we ignored it and ran on.

We came to the executive officer's suite, and a private sat at a desk outside a door marked "Colonel Steven Fuller."

"Hey!" the man at the desk exclaimed as the corporal ran past and burst into Fuller's office.

I followed him inside, and found Steve Fuller seated at his desk. He was in his late thirties, and had close-cut blond hair and bright, intelligent eyes. He exuded the kind of authority no rank could imbue. He reminded me of a hardened frontiersman, whose power to conquer mountains came from deep within.

"Corporal, there had better be one heck of an explanation for this," Fuller said as he got to his feet.

"Colonel Fuller, my name is Jack Morgan," I said. "Somewhere on this base a ceremony is taking place to mark the activation of the FORCE System. We have to stop it."

"Your face is on every news bulletin. I know who you are, Mr. Morgan," Fuller replied, stepping out from behind his desk. "And I know what people are saying about you."

"None of it is true, sir," I responded. "I have evidence that Ann Kavanagh, the woman who will be responsible for running the FORCE System, is a deep-cover Russian operative."

"I assume this man was headed for the brig?" Fuller asked. "Who took the decision to bring him here?"

The private looked sheepish.

"It was my call, sir," Corporal Ryan replied.

"Colonel Fuller, you have to listen to me. We have less than fifteen minutes. If I'm right, the moment the system comes online, the Russians will have access to America's most sensitive security information," I said. "They can start downloading everything and even if we shut it down later, we'll never know what they've seen or taken. Our entire military and intelligence infrastructure will be compromised."

During the flight from Moscow, I'd spent some time researching the officers posted to Naval Air Station Fallon and had chosen to target Fuller for a reason. It was time to play my hand. "Sir, you served with Lieutenant Colonel Edward Frost and Master Gunnery Sergeant Marlon West in Iraq. Lieutenant Colonel Frost is an old friend. He can vouch for me. And Master Gunnery Sergeant West has been involved in breaking this case. Call him. He can confirm what I'm saying."

Fuller studied me intently.

"Corporal," he said. I felt my chest tighten and I held a breath. "Take this man, and wait outside."

"Yes, sir," Corporal Ryan replied.

I gave a silent prayer of thanks and followed the corporal and the private out of Fuller's office.

The corporal closed the door behind us, and we stood by the XO's administrator's desk and waited. Seconds seemed to last hours, and impatience and frustration swelled within me, but it couldn't have been more than two minutes later when Fuller emerged from his office, alive with a sense of urgency.

"Let's move," he said.

He didn't wait for us, but started jogging along the corridor. The private was incredulous, and Corporal Ryan gave me a respectful nod.

"Come on, Mr. Morgan," Fuller shouted back at me, and I started after him. "Master Gunnery Sergeant West vouched for you in the strongest possible terms. It seems the flight crew assigned to bring you home were abducted by the Russians. He was extremely surprised to hear you'd made it back safely."

"I'm glad to hear he's OK," I said. "Last time I saw West, he was in a tight spot."

"He told me," Fuller replied. "Said it was hours before the Russians 'found' his diplomatic credentials and released him."

"Sir, I came on base with two colleagues," I said. "We may need their help."

"Corporal Ryan, I want you and the private to bring Mr. Morgan's team to the FORCE Command Center ASAP," Fuller ordered.

"Yes, sir," Corporal Ryan replied.

"We'll meet you there," Fuller said. "I hope you're ready for this. You're about to goat-rope a lot of brass."

CHAPTER 107

FULLER'S STATEMENT ABOUT upsetting a lot of senior commanders made more sense when I saw the FORCE Command Center, which was a huge, hardened bunker to the east of the air traffic control building. About the size of four football fields, the bunker was constructed in matt black, and the flat roof was covered in sensor arrays, communication equipment and a massive cooling system.

As we approached the building in Fuller's open-topped Humvee, I saw a convoy of more than forty vehicles parked outside the main entrance, and, in addition to Marine guards, there were a number of men and women in suits, wearing the distinctive lapel pins of the US Secret Service.

"What kind of brass are we talking?" I asked as Fuller pulled up outside the building.

"Secretary of Defense, most of the chiefs of staff, Pentagon types," Fuller replied. "This is the Defense Department's show-piece tech for the twenty-first century. It's supposed to redefine warfare."

We jumped out of the Humvee and I swallowed hard as we ran up the steps toward the smoked-glass doors.

Two Secret Service agents moved to intercept us; a tall, mus-cular woman who looked as though she knew her way around a chokehold, and a short, sinewy man who moved with the graceful elegance of a predator.

"Can we help you?" the woman asked.

"We need to see Secretary Carver," Fuller replied, referring to the Secretary of Defense.

"He'd kind of busy right now, sir," the man replied with a self-indulgent smile.

I caught Fuller gesturing behind his back, and glanced over my shoulder to see four Marine guards at the bottom of the steps, drawn by the arrival of the air station's second-in-command. They were watching his hand movements, signals instructing them to make ready. They drifted up the stairs nonchalantly.

"We need to see the secretary right now," Fuller said. "It's a matter of national security."

If the Secret Service agents sensed danger, they gave no hint of it.

"I'm sorry, sir," the woman replied. "Everyone who's meant to be in this building is already inside. No one else gets in."

"Sergeant," Fuller commanded, "take these people into custody."

The four Marines who'd been coming up the steps sprang into action and raised their weapons at the Secret Service agents.

"This is Naval Air Station Fallon, and I am the executive officer," Fuller said. "You are hereby under military arrest."

"Stop!" a voice yelled, and I turned to see two Secret Service agents who'd been standing by the convoy draw their weapons.

"Corporal!" Fuller shouted at the leader of another squad of Marines by the cars. "Hold those men!"

The second squad swarmed the other agents.

"Guns down! Guns down!" the Marines bellowed.

Fuller turned to the sergeant who led the team holding the man and woman at gunpoint. "With us, sergeant. You men hold fast."

I followed Fuller and the sergeant into the building, where we encountered a pair of puzzled Marine privates, who'd seen what was happening outside.

"You men with us," Fuller said, and they fell in behind me.

We ran through a large lobby, and Fuller used his base security pass to get us into the main block. We sprinted down a long corridor, went round a corner and saw two Secret Service agents either side of a blast door.

"Down!" the sergeant yelled, raising his rifle at the startled men.

"Hold them," Fuller commanded the two Marine privates we'd picked up in the lobby. "With me, sergeant."

Fuller used the biometric palm reader and iris scanner to open the blast doors, and we stepped into one of the most secure places on Earth.

CHAPTER 108

LIKE ROWDY PARTY crashers, Fuller, the sergeant and I burst into a huge air-cooled room. More than eighty people were seated theatre-style, facing a podium that had been decked out in the Stars and Stripes. This was a gathering of some of the most senior military commanders in the United States, and there were a lot of uniforms and chest candy—brightly colored ribbons—on display. Marines and Secret Service agents were dotted at key points around the room. Beyond the seating area, two glass walls overlooked a vast server farm that stretched as far as the eye could see. A large clock hung from one of the interior walls, displaying a countdown that had just cycled through three minutes. The audience had been listening to Eli Carver, the Secretary of Defense, who was at the lectern, partway through his speech. He paused and looked at us in bemusement.

"Can we help you gentlemen?" he asked.

The assembled audience turned as one, and two Secret Service agents started toward us.

"Excuse me, sirs," one of the agents said.

"Mr. Secretary, you have to stop the countdown," Fuller responded.

"XO, what the hell do you think you're doing?" a brigadier general asked as he got to his feet. I guessed it was Mark Hawkins, the base commander.

"Stop the countdown?" Secretary Carver asked. "Now why would we want to do that?"

"Because you're about to hand all our military intelligence over to the Russians," I replied.

"And you are?" Carver asked.

"My name isn't important."

"That's Jack Morgan," a woman said.

A murmur of disquiet rippled through the audience, and I scanned the room to find the speaker near the front. It was Ann Kavanagh.

Minerva.

Her words caused sensation among the crowd, who clearly recognized my name from news reports.

"He's wanted as a Russian spy and this is clearly an attempt by a hostile government to stop us deploying technology that will give America significant tactical advantage," Kavanagh lied.

"Take that man into custody," Brigadier General Hawkins said.

"I can't allow that, sir," Fuller replied.

A squad of six Marines formed up and moved toward us, and they were joined by a couple more Secret Service agents.

"What do we do, sir?" the sergeant asked Fuller.

"Hold your ground," Fuller replied.

"What the hell has gotten into you, Fuller?" Brigadier General Hawkins asked.

"You need to listen to this man, sir," Fuller declared, pointing at me.

"He's a spy and a traitor," Ann Kavanagh countered. "He should be in prison."

A four-star US Army general near Kavanagh stood up and barked an order. "Seize those men!"

The Marine guards and Secret Service agents rushed us, and Fuller and the sergeant raised their weapons.

"Back off!" Fuller yelled, forcing a standoff.

Everyone froze, and there was a silent, nerve-racking moment of ice-cold tension.

Only one person moved. Ann Kavanagh leaned over and spoke to a man in a dark suit. He had his back to me, but I recognized him nonetheless. I could tell who he was by the set of his shoulders. He turned to face me, and when our eyes locked, I felt a rush of anger. It was Veles, and he was posing as a member of Kavanagh's entourage.

I couldn't help myself. I rushed forward instinctively, and found myself staring down the barrels of a number of weapons.

"Stand down!" someone roared.

"Drop your weapons," Fuller shouted in reply.

We were outgunned and outnumbered. It didn't take a genius to see what would happen. The Marine squad moved in quickly, and disarmed Fuller and the sergeant, who surrendered their weapons reluctantly. I was manhandled by the Secret Service team, and the three of us were thrown face down onto the concrete floor.

We'd tried to prevent a strategic catastrophe, and we'd failed. It was over.

CHAPTER 109

AS BLEAK AS things looked, I wasn't prepared to give up.

"Mr. Secretary, you've got to stop this!" I yelled. I glanced up at the countdown and saw it pass through one minute. "If my story doesn't check out, you can restart the countdown."

Someone pressed my face into the floor.

"Shut the hell up!" a voice commanded.

It would take more than that to make me shut up. "This is our national security we're talking about. Surely it's worth checking out."

"Can we get these people out of here?" a voice shouted. I was pretty sure it was the four-star general who'd been sitting near Kavanagh. "And let's get this machine online."

I felt strong hands lift me up, and I was frogmarched toward the blast door. Fuller and the sergeant were pushed ahead of me.

"Hold on there," Secretary Carver said. "Someone switch this thing off."

I glanced round and saw him gesture at the countdown.

"The man's right. One last check won't hurt. And if he's wrong, we just start it up again. No harm no foul. It's not like anyone's got anywhere more important to be."

There was a ripple of laughter, and the mood lightened, but I noticed two people who weren't smiling: Ann Kavanagh and Veles.

"Mr. Secretary—" the four-star general began.

"Indulge me, general. Let's hear what this Mr. Morgan has to say," Carver cut him off.

The blast door opened, and Corporal Ryan entered with Hector and Dinara.

"More guests?" Secretary Carver remarked. "Why not? The more the merrier."

Another ripple of laughter ran through the audience, but it stopped when the first gunshots rang out.

Six members of Ann Kavanagh's entourage were on their feet, wielding handguns and shooting at the nearest Marine guards and Secret Service agents. Kavanagh ran behind the podium, while Veles leaped onto it, grabbed Carver and took him hostage.

I watched in horror as the Russian assassin disappeared behind the large swirling Stars and Stripes. He followed Kavanagh, dragging the US Secretary of Defense with him.

CHAPTER 110

THE CROWD SCATTERED as the firefight intensified between members of Kavanagh's entourage and the Marine guards and Secret Service agents. Screams filled the air, punctuated by semi-automatic gunfire. Jack and the two Marines with him were released and the men who'd been holding them captive joined the shootout.

"Fuller!" Jack yelled. "With me!"

He set off with Fuller in pursuit. The other Marine who was with them took a couple of paces, and was shot in the shoulder.

"Help him," Dinara said to Hector, who nodded and rushed to the fallen man's side.

Dinara ducked as she set off after Jack. He and Fuller ran round the seating area, behind the podium and down an access corridor that led away from the auditorium. They were chasing Kavanagh and Veles, who was being slowed by dragging a struggling man at gunpoint. A Secret Service agent was also chasing them. The agent was twenty or thirty paces ahead of Jack and Fuller, and Dinara was twenty paces behind them.

"Stop!" the Secret Service agent yelled.

Veles opened fire in reply, and hit the man in the leg. The agent went down as Kavanagh reached a security door. She opened it with a swipe card, and Veles unleashed a couple of wild shots, forcing Jack, Fuller and Dinara to take cover behind columns that lined the corridor walls.

When Dinara broke cover, Kavanagh, Veles and the hostage were gone, the security door was closed, and Jack and Fuller were beside the fallen Secret Service agent.

"Veles," Dinara observed as she joined them.

Jack nodded. "And Kavanagh. I think they're going for the servers. Can they switch the system on from in there?"

"I don't know," Fuller replied. "We can't wait here to find out, but if someone doesn't stay with this man, he's going to bleed out."

The sound of gunfire crackled along the corridor, rising above a bed of screams and commotion.

"I have to finish this," Jack said.

Fuller studied him for a moment, and then nodded. He handed Jack his sidearm. "Take this."

Jack rose, and Dinara made to follow.

"No," he said.

"What do you mean, no?" Dinara replied haughtily. "You think I'm sitting this out after what they did to Leonid?"

Jack thought for a moment, and quickly relented.

"Here," the wounded Secret Service agent said, and he handed Dinara his pistol.

"You'll need this." Fuller gave Jack his swipe card, and then set about using his belt to tie a tourniquet around the injured agent's leg.

"Come on," Jack said.

He ran down the corridor; Dinara followed. She checked her pistol as they came to the security door.

Jack paused, gave her a confirmatory nod, and she replied in kind. He swiped the key card and the pressure door unlocked with a clunk and a hiss. He pulled it open, and Dinara followed him inside.

CHAPTER 111

WE ENTERED A vast, super-chilled server farm. Rows of inactive servers ran back as far as I could see. They were stacked in floor-to-ceiling racks inside climate-controlled glass cabinets.

The security door closed behind us, and thick mortise locks snapped into place and the pressure seal gasped as it inflated.

None of the computers were on, and the thick door had muted the sound of the gun battle. Veles' team must have used ceramic weapons to circumvent the base's security measures.

I looked at Dinara and could sense her anxiety. I felt it too, and the silence somehow made it worse.

We crept through the huge room. Dinara checked the aisles running away to our left, and I kept my eyes on the ones going right. There was no sign of Veles, Kavanagh or Secretary Carver.

We picked up our pace as we passed one deserted row after another. After another two dozen rows, the narrow alleyway seemed to open up a short distance ahead, and I signaled Dinara to slow. We crept forward, and I saw we'd reached a control station at the heart of the server farm. A thirty-foot-square space was broken only by a ten-foot bank of screens and computer terminals set in an onyx plinth.

Ann Kavanagh stood at a computer in the center of the console, her back to us. I signaled Dinara to stay put, and inched into the control station.

"Don't bother, Mr. Morgan," Kavanagh said without turning. "Veles isn't here. He's with the secretary. An insurance policy in case you try to be disruptive. I needed Secretary Carver's biometrics to override the FORCE System's security controls, but I don't need him anymore, so his life is very much in your hands. Behave yourself and you both might live."

I was startled when every single server suddenly came to life. Thousands of operating lights illuminated, and the machines began to hum as one.

"Step away," I said.

"Shoot me, and the secretary dies. Stop me and the secretary dies," Kavanagh said. "I've worked far too long to let you interfere with what's happening here, Mr. Morgan. In six minutes, the system will link with the Pentagon satellite network and it will go online."

She turned to face me, and I saw triumph writ large. "And you know what that means?"

I didn't dignify her gloating with a response.

"We'll be able to access every single American military and intelligence system. They put everything in here"—she gestured around the huge room—"thinking it would give them real-time strategic advantage. They thought it would make them stronger, but it is their biggest weakness."

"Karl Parker wanted me to stop you," I said. "Doesn't that tell you something?"

"It tells me he was weak," she replied.

"He'd come to love America," I countered.

"He'd forgotten who he was," Kavanagh declared. "I haven't. And I never will."

I cast around, looking for Veles. He had to be nearby. Somewhere he could watch and listen. As I looked around the room, I realized Dinara was gone.

CHAPTER 112

DINARA CREPT AROUND the server racks. She didn't have long, and her options were limited. She couldn't clear her plan with Jack, and in truth it wasn't much of a plan, but pressure had made her desperate.

Once she reached the end of the row, she started jogging swiftly, moving silently between the racks. She kept looking right to see Jack and Kavanagh in a standoff. Passing up the rows made the scene flicker like a movie playing through an old projector, and Jack moved toward Kavanagh in jagged jump cuts. Dinara realized he couldn't possibly see the pistol Kavanagh held behind her back.

When Dinara was to Kavanagh's rear, she ran along the row, flanked by high cabinets on either side. She gathered speed as she reached the last rack, and was sprinting by the time she burst into the open space. Kavanagh looked startled, and tried to bring the pistol up, but she wasn't quick enough, and Dinara tackled her.

They went down, and as Kavanagh tried to rise, Dinara smacked her with the pistol, and the Russian spy hit the floor, dazed.

"Find Veles," Dinara said. "I'll make her deactivate the system."

"Now you've done it," Kavanagh said in Russian. "The Secretary of Defense won't be alive much longer. And neither will you."

"Then there's no point playing nicely," Dinara replied.

She pressed her pistol into Kavanagh's knee and pulled the trigger. The thunderous gunshot resounded around the room, and the older woman screamed. When her cries of agony had subsided, Dinara said, "Tell me how to deactivate the system or I'll kill you by inches."

Dinara glanced at Jack, who had frozen. He seemed shocked and torn.

A feeble cry came from their right.

"Go!" Dinara yelled.

Jack hesitated for a moment, and then started running.

CHAPTER 113

I SPRINTED TOWARD the noise I'd heard—a guttural cry. I came to the end of a row of servers and discovered an access aisle. I ran left and soon reached a service area full of giant power transformers, refrigeration compressors and communications boxes. Eli Carver stood in the center of the space. His hands were bound behind his back, and a length of cord was tied around his neck. The other end of the noose was attached to a hook, which was connected to a winch and gantry system used to move heavy gear around the facility.

"Help," Carver cried as he caught sight of me.

I heard the hum of a motor and the rattle of a chain being wound. The winch coiled, dragging the hook up, and pulling the cord tight around Carver's neck. His legs flailed and he made a horrible choking sound as he was hoisted into the air. He didn't have long, and his eyes locked onto me, pleading.

Every fiber of my being wanted to rush to his aid, but I knew it was a trap. I was meant to go to him, and once I reached his side, I'd be executed and he'd be left to die. I looked around the space, trying to figure out a way to save the man without dying in the process.

Another gunshot echoed around the server farm, and it was swiftly followed by a woman's screams. I prayed Dinara would keep Kavanagh alive until I returned.

Secretary Carver looked at me with utter desperation as his face started to turn purple. I was running out of options and had to move now. I checked my pistol and then scanned my surroundings once more. There were two good vantage points that offered a clear line of fire. One was on top of a transformer unit that rose from the floor and stopped a few feet from the ceiling, and the other was a service gantry that ran behind a row of cooling vents. I could only keep my gun and eyes on one. I opted for the gantry, and stayed locked on it as I ran to the secretary.

I felt a chill scrape its way down my spine, and thought I'd made the wrong choice, until I saw Veles step out from behind one of the vents. I emptied the clip at him, and he managed one reflex trigger pull as he tumbled backwards off the gantry and fell to the floor behind a cooling unit.

I turned and lifted the secretary by his feet to relieve the pressure on his throat. I searched for the remote unit that controlled the winch, but it was probably on the gantry where Veles had been hiding. I didn't think Carver would survive long enough for me to reach it, but I saw a stepladder behind one of the transformers, and ran over to grab it. Carver flailed behind me, and I knew I had to be quick.

I returned with the ladder, propped it open, and raced up the steps. There was a third gunshot in the distance, and more screams, but I ignored them as I climbed to the top of the ladder. I held the muzzle of the pistol against the taut cord that led up from Carver's neck and pulled the trigger.

The bullet ripped through the cord, and the Secretary of Defense tumbled like a sack of stones. I jumped off the ladder and raced to him.

He was clawing at the noose, so I set down my pistol, and together we managed to pull the cord away from his throat.

He gasped a hideous, rasping lungful of air. His eyes widened with terror, and he tried to say something. All that came out was a throaty cry, but I knew it was a warning, and managed to duck and roll just in time to avoid the slash of Veles' blade.

CHAPTER 114

I ROSE TO face the Russian assassin, and saw his suit and shirt had been shredded by bullets to reveal the protective vest he wore next to his skin.

He lunged at me with a ceramic black-handled blade, and I stepped aside and drove a fist into his face.

My heart was racing and my body crackled with adrenalin. This man had killed so many people, including my friend. Karl Parker might have been a spy, but I was convinced he'd been trying to make good. He hadn't deserved to die, and neither had Leonid Boykov, another good man. The memories of these two fallen victims spurred me on, and I stepped forward and kneed Veles in the gut.

He lashed out with the blade, but I moved inside his swing, parried his forearm with my elbow, and hit him with an upper cut. As he staggered back, I delivered a devastating combination of jabs and crosses that sent him reeling. He held the blade in front of him, a defensive move, I thought, until I realized what it really was. I turned just in time, an instant before the blade shot from its handle, and instead of striking me in the neck, where he'd been aiming, Veles hit me in the shoulder.

The ballistic knife, favored by Russian Special Forces, buried itself deep in the fleshy muscle, but I was so amped on adrenalin, I scarcely registered the pain.

Veles reached behind him and produced another knife. He didn't give me a moment to recover, but came at me like lightning. His left fist lashed out, and I ducked the punch, only to be confronted by the second knife darting toward my neck. I lurched back, but momentum carried me too far, and I stumbled. My feet hit each other, and Veles took advantage of my clumsy maneuver and kicked me in the chest. The blow winded me and sent me flying. I landed heavily on my back and didn't even have time to roll before Veles leaped on me.

I thrust my hands up and instinctively grabbed his right wrist to stop him driving the knife into my neck. He punched me in the temple with his left, and I bit back a yelp of pain. My right hand whipped out to block another disorientating blow, and I grabbed him by the wrist. We were locked in a grim stand-off, but I knew it couldn't last. He was strong and full of hate, and had the advantages of a weapon and gravity. I saw the tip of the blade creeping toward my throat, and fought against the inevitable with all my strength. The sinews on his neck strained, and his eyes blazed with murderous hatred. The blade was millimeters away from my skin. I had to do something.

I went slack for a fraction of a second and the sudden lack of resistance threw off his balance, enabling me to direct the knife over instead of into my throat. I felt the blade kiss my Adam's apple, and Veles fell across my body and hit the floor beside me. I rolled to one knee as he picked himself up into a crouch and leaped toward me. In one fluid move, I turned my body to avoid his strike, pulled the ballistic blade from my shoulder and drove it into the startled assassin's neck.

He staggered back, clutching at the mortal wound. He made a terrible, wet choking sound and fell to his knees.

He couldn't believe what had happened, and, for a moment, his expression was one of pure shock, until surprise was re-placed by burning hatred. Then finally his eyes went blank, and he slumped forward, dead.

CHAPTER 115

"YOU'RE GOING TO be OK, Mr. Secretary," I told the terrified, trembling man before setting off at a sprint for the control station.

Servers whizzed by, and moments later, I raced into the space to find Dinara pressing her pistol against Kavanagh's head.

"You've got one last chance," Dinara told her.

Kavanagh had bullet wounds in both knees and her shoulder, and she was whimpering, but offered nothing intelligible.

"Tell me how to deactivate the system, or you die," Dinara said furiously.

"Dinara," I tried gently, but she looked at me with the purest fury in her eyes.

Everything she'd lost, everything she'd been through, it was all focused on Kavanagh in that moment. The pressure to pull the trigger must have been almost irresistible.

"Dinara. Don't," I said.

I ran to the central console, which displayed a countdown. There were less than two minutes until the FORCE System came online.

"It's no good, Dinara," I said. "She's prepared to die for what she believes in. Just like me. Just like you."

Kavanagh eyed me defiantly.

"Give me her phone," I said urgently.

Dinara hesitated, her eyes on her gun.

"Killing her won't bring him back," I told her.

I could feel the struggle within her as she fought the urge to kill Kavanagh, but after a moment that seemed like an age, my words reached her and she lowered the gun. Kavanagh slumped with relief. Dinara searched the Russian spy for her phone. She found it in Kavanagh's jacket, and used the indignant woman's thumb to unlock it.

"Here," Dinara said, tossing me the device.

I was about to try a Hail Mary, but that's where we were: out of options.

I dialed a number, and said a silent prayer as I heard a ring tone.

Come on, answer, I thought.

"Hello?" a familiar voice said.

"Maureen," I responded with relief.

"Jack! What the heck is happening? One minute we're in custody as enemies of the people, the next we're told we can walk," Mo-bot said.

"I don't have time to explain," I said. "I'm in the central control station of the FORCE Command Center and I need to know how to shut down the system before it goes online."

"How long do we have?" Mo-bot asked, her voice coming alive with urgency.

"Ninety seconds," I replied.

"Tell me what you can see," she said.

"There's a countdown on the central console," I replied. "And beside it is a visual display of the satellite link-up. It's showing the communication relays coming into alignment."

"You need to activate a command window," Mo-bot said. "Press *control-alt-T*."

I did as instructed, and a black window appeared with a flashing cursor.

"I'm going to assume you're through any security protocols," Mo-bot said.

"Kavanagh had to get past them to activate the system," I responded.

"Good," Mo-bot remarked. "I want you to type *GREP*, leave a space, then type *period EXE*," she said. "And then hit *return*."

I punched in the command, and a list of programs populated the window. The countdown went through the sixty-second mark.

"What can you see?" Mo-bot asked.

"A list of programs," I replied.

"Those are the programs the network is currently running," Mo-bot revealed. "This won't be elegant, and it's going to cause millions of dollars of damage, but needs must. I want you to type *RM dash ALL.*"

I did what she said, but I sensed sudden movement behind me, and was horrified to see Kavanagh force herself to her feet and wrestle the pistol from Dinara's grasp

The Russian operative brandished the gun menacingly.

"Step away from the machine!"

CHAPTER 116

I HAD NO doubt Kavanagh would shoot me if I moved. The only thing keeping me alive was the possibility I might shut down the system with my dying breath if she took the shot while I was standing by the console. I stayed put as the countdown cycled through thirty seconds.

"Move!" Kavanagh yelled.

Dinara had been caught off guard by the injured woman's speed and agility, but she quickly regrouped and knocked Kavanagh's arm out of the way and moved in to tackle her.

"Jack, you have to stop this thing," I heard Mo-bot say as I put the phone down on the console, but the program wasn't my primary concern anymore. I had to help Dinara.

As the two women struggled for control of the gun, it went off, and a bullet tore through a nearby server rack. I ran toward the scuffle and grabbed hold of Kavanagh. Dinara punched her in the face, dazing her. I yanked the pistol out of Kavanagh's hand and Dinara and I stepped clear of the formidable, vicious Russian agent.

'Stop!' I shouted, but Kavanagh came straight for me, so I pulled the trigger and shot her in the left leg.

She gave a guttural cry of anger as she went down.

"Here," I said, tossing Dinara the pistol. "Keep her covered."

Relentless and desperate, Kavanagh made another lunge for Dinara, and was rewarded with an angry smack across the face. Dinara hit her with the pistol again, and this time I shuddered at the sound of bone cracking. Kavanagh collapsed. She was out cold.

I ran back to the console and saw the countdown cycle through six seconds. I grabbed the phone.

"What do I do?" I asked hurriedly.

"Hit *enter*."

I pressed the button and a prompt immediately appeared, asking if I was sure I wanted to delete all programs. I selected *yes* as the countdown reached three seconds. Nothing happened for a moment, and the countdown flipped to two, and then the console suddenly went blank, and every single machine in the gigantic room stopped working.

"What happened?" Mo-bot asked.

I stared at Dinara wide-eyed.

"We did it," I told Mo-bot. "We did it!"

Mo-bot said something in reply, but I wasn't listening. I suddenly became aware of the wound in my shoulder, as the tide of adrenalin receded. I felt myself sag with fatigue and relief.

Dinara took the phone from my hand and put it on the console. She put her arm around my waist, and supported me as we walked slowly toward the exit.

Neither of us said a word.

We were beyond them.

CHAPTER 117

THERE WAS SO much sadness in the room. Kevin Parker stood by the large window, watching the waves gently lapping the beach. Victoria Parker sat opposite me, but struggled to meet my gaze. I was in the grand library in the Parkers' Long Island home, and had just presented them with two thick folders that contained Private's findings in the investigation of the murder of Karl Parker.

"I know your world's been turned upside down," I said, "but you need to hold on to one thing: Karl was a good man, and he loved you both very much."

My remark was greeted by silence.

"What was his real name?" Kevin asked finally. He didn't look at me.

"We believe he was called John Kubu," I replied. "At least, that's what Russian government records show. It seems the SVR purchased him and the other children from orphanages around the world. According to the files they've released, your father came from Kenya."

Kevin's shoulders slumped, and I suspected he was crying. This wasn't just about Karl Parker's true identity, it also impacted who Kevin thought he was and where he believed he came from. His father's secret had changed Kevin's sense of his place in the world.

The worst of winter was over and, outside, the snow had melted and the garden was starting to show signs of spring. Inside, the house still seemed chilled by grief and trouble.

In the weeks following the showdown at Naval Air Station Fallon, the Russian government had been forced to disavow Yevgeny Salko as a rogue operator who instituted and ran the Bright Star program without proper authorization. He'd been arrested, and certain Bright Star files had been made public, largely to mollify American anger. The Russians had recalled twenty-two US citizens, who, they said, represented all that was left of the cadre of embedded Bright Star operatives. Yenen had told us that there could have been up to seventy-two Bright Star agents. There was no way of verifying whether the twenty-two business leaders, politicians, financiers and journalists were really all that was left of the sophisticated program.

Ann Kavanagh hadn't been so lucky. Instead of being re-called, her attempt to subvert the FORCE System saw her brought up on charges of espionage, and once she'd recovered from her injuries, she faced life in federal prison.

"Thank you for everything you've done, Jack," Victoria said, looking me in the eye for the first time. "You've made huge personal sacrifices and taken unimaginable risks to find justice for our family. We'll never forget it."

"I meant what I said," I replied. "He was a good man. The people who sent him here brainwashed him, but his life, the people he met and loved here, they changed him, and when it came down to it, he couldn't betray the country he'd come to regard as his home. In the end, he did the right thing in a way that guaranteed your safety. He clearly loved you both very much."

Victoria lowered her head and fresh tears sprang to her eyes.

"Our assessment of the timeline leads us to believe that when Enterprise Web Services won the contract to run Silverlink International's IT platform, Karl met Ann Kavanagh for the first time since they'd trained together in Russia. He figured out the FORCE System would be exposed through her, and invited me to New York to tell me the truth. Whether it was Maxim Yenen's leaks or a report from Ann Kavanagh that she'd been recognized by Karl, we don't know, but something triggered Salko to order the execution of every Bright Star operative in Kavanagh's intake. Salko was protecting his most valuable asset. Thankfully, Karl had taken steps to leave me a trail of clues in the event of his death, something he must have known was a possibility when Robert Carlyle died. Your husband couldn't reveal Kavanagh's identity to the CIA or FBI in case they'd been infiltrated, and he couldn't leave the information with you because it would have jeopardized your safety, so he involved me, someone he knew he could trust. What Karl did ultimately prevented a disaster of almost inconceivable proportions."

There was an awkward silence, and Victoria smiled at me wanly. "It's just going to take time for it all to sink in," she said.

"I understand," I replied, getting to my feet. "If there's anything you need, please don't hesitate."

She nodded somberly. "Thanks, Jack."

I showed myself out. Karl's deception had troubled me deeply and it had taken me a while to forgive him. I could only imagine the impact the truth was having on his wife and son. It would take years for them to come to terms with it.

Ermilita, the housekeeper, walked me to the door, and I found Justine waiting beside the Nissan Rogue Private New York staff car.

"Ready?" she asked.

CHAPTER 118

"THEY DON'T HAND those out with fish," Berdy Kotov said, gesturing at the medal on Dinara's desk.

It was a Gold Star, which marked her out as a Hero of the Russian Federation, the highest honor available to a civilian. The President had presented it to her two weeks ago, and she was still bewildered by her sudden change of fortune.

A few weeks previously, she'd been an enemy of the state, hunted by the instruments of government, and facing mortal danger at every turn. Now, she'd received Russia's highest accolade, and she and Private had been exonerated and commended by the government for the role they'd played in exposing a rogue intelligence operation. Dinara wasn't sure how rogue the operation had really been, but the government was certainly going to great lengths to rehabilitate Private, and business was booming as never before.

People like Kotov had flocked to the office with assignments. Kotov was convinced his lawyer was embezzling funds from his book-wholesaling business. Elena Kabova, the office adminis-trator, had been run off her feet, fielding inquiries from business people, suspicious spouses, lawyers, accountants and wealthy Muscovites, and it was starting to feel like the large and varied client list of any other Private office.

"So, do you think you can take my case?" Kotov asked.

"What do you think, Dinara?" Feo remarked. "Can we take Berdy Kotov's assignment?"

Kotov looked nervously at the big man, who'd offered to help out until Dinara could staff the office properly. She'd already hired a number of his associates from the Residence on short-term contracts to cope with the workload.

"We'd be happy to help," Dinara said, rising from her desk.

"Thank you, thank you," Kotov replied, and Dinara ushered him out of the partitioned office she'd installed to give her a little privacy.

"Elena will be in touch with our client-services agreement," Dinara said, and Kotov nodded and headed for the exit.

Elena poked her head around the corner. "Lunch is ready, and there's someone to see you."

Dinara walked through the open-plan office. Almost all the desks were occupied by Feo's people, who were either on the phone, doing paperwork or working on computers. Only one desk was empty: Leonid's. There was a framed photo of the de-tective on the otherwise bare surface, a small tribute to a good man.

Dinara walked round the corner into the reception area and saw containers of solyanka soup lined up on Elena's desk. Another small mark of respect. Each day, they had Leonid's favorite lunch, and it was almost impossible not to think or talk about the man while eating the soup he'd loved.

Dinara was surprised when she looked across reception to see a familiar face in the waiting area.

"Hello, Dinara," Anna Bolshova said. She wore a dark skirt and jacket, and had a green woolen coat slung over her arm.

Her work on the Bright Star case, and in bringing Erik Utkin and his Black Hundreds drugs gang to justice, had earned her a promotion, so Dinara was surprised to see her in civilian clothes on a weekday.

"Hello, Anna," Dinara replied.

"So ..." Anna hesitated. She smiled sheepishly. "I've always been ambitious, and I've always said I want to work where the action is. The politics of the police ... well, let's just say my recent experiences have left me a little jaded toward the official instruments of the state."

Dinara broke into a broad smile, and Anna responded in kind.

"Anyway, to get to the point," Anna said. "I understand you're hiring."

CHAPTER 119

"HOW ARE KEVIN and Victoria holding up?" Justine asked as we started our journey to the airport.

"It's a lot to handle, but hopefully they'll learn to forgive him," I replied.

"What about you?" Justine asked.

"I'm getting there."

"And the shoulder?"

It had taken three hours of surgery, and weeks of special rehabilitation exercises, but I was almost back to full mobility. "I hardly notice it," I replied honestly.

"I . . ." Justine began, but she hesitated. "I don't know what I would have done, Jack."

I could sense her anguish at the thought of losing me, and felt my own emotions rise. "I know," I replied.

I didn't trust myself to say anything else, and our shared fears of what might have been hung over us.

"But we came through it," I said at last, trying to lighten the mood.

"Yeah," Justine agreed with a hesitant smile. "We did."

We spent the journey from the Parkers' Long Island home to John F. Kennedy Airport talking shop. Private had been exonerated and the handful of clients we'd lost had returned. Most offices were seeing an uptick in business thanks to the high-profile success of the Bright Star investigation. But with success came a different set of challenges: mundane issues such as hiring, budget approvals and hundreds of other operational decisions, many of which needed my attention. The distraction of the day-to-day kept us occupied until we reached the perimeter of JFK Airport, but when we turned onto the North Service Road, I sensed a change in mood. Justine was building up to something, and as we approached the perimeter airfield gate, she finally said, "I've been replaying the conversation we had in the bar before you went to Moscow, and I've been wondering whether we need some confusion in our lives. Maybe we'd make the same mistakes all over again, but what if we didn't?"

I thought back to my unfinished highball at the Library bar in the Nomad Hotel and searched for a reply, but was distracted by the scene on the other side of the gate. A Gulfstream G550 waited at a stand, and there were four vehicles parked beside it: three town cars and another Nissan Rogue, this one in red.

"A powerful friend insisted we fly private," Justine revealed.

A crowd of people stood near the airstairs, and I recognized some of the faces. Mo-bot and Sci were there, along with Jessie Fleming, the head of Private New York, and Rafael Lucas, our legal counsel. They were talking to Eli Carver, the Secretary of Defense. His Secret Service detail stood a few paces away, and kept a close eye on him and his surroundings.

The gate guard checked our credentials, and waved us through. When we pulled up by the aircraft, Secretary Carver came over to greet us.

"Jack Morgan," he beamed. "I wanted to thank you in person."

He wore a silk scarf tucked into his shirt collar, no doubt to conceal the scar that encircled his throat.

"I appreciate it, Mr. Secretary," I responded. "But you didn't have to."

"It was the least I could do, and please call me Eli," he said. "I owe you my life. If that doesn't put us on first-name terms, I don't know what will."

"You don't owe me anything, sir," I began, but I registered Carver's raised eyebrow, "Eli, I mean," I continued without skipping a beat, "I did what anyone in my situation would have done."

"Well, let's just agree to disagree about that," Carver said with a smile. "If there's ever anything you need, you call me." He handed me a card. "My cell number and my private line."

"I appreciate it, Eli," I replied.

"Now if you'll excuse me, I have to get back to Washington. We're still dealing with the fallout from this thing," he said, moving toward the convoy of town cars.

"You take care, Mr. Secretary ... Eli," I corrected myself.

I joined Mo-bot, Sci and the others as Secretary Carver and his detail got in their cars and drove away.

"Thanks for everything," I said to Jessie and Rafael.

"Just doing our jobs," the lawyer replied.

"We've got our weekly call next Wednesday," Jessie reminded me.

I smiled, grateful for a return to the mundane. "I look forward to it," I said.

"Have a safe trip," Rafael responded.

He walked toward the red Nissan, and Jessie took the black one Justine and I had arrived in.

"Shall we?" Mo-bot asked, gesturing at the airstairs.

"After you," I said, and she and Sci headed into the aircraft.

I took Justine's arm, and gently pulled her toward me.

"I owe you an answer," I said, when Mo-bot and Sci had climbed aboard. "I'm not a fan of confusion, but I am a fan of forgiveness. If I've treated you badly in the past, I apologize and I hope you'll forgive me."

"Jack," she began, but I hadn't finished.

"I hope we can start fresh."

"I'd like that," she replied.

She hesitated.

"We never got a chance to finish our drink," she said.

"No, we didn't," I remarked as we walked toward the jet. "What are you doing tomorrow night?"

She replied with a smile that brightened my day, and we boarded the aircraft that would take us back to Los Angeles.

We were heading home.

ACKNOWLEDGMENTS

We'd like to thank our editor, John Sugar, and the team at Cornerstone for their wonderful work on this book. We'd also like to thank you, the reader, for coming on this adventure. We hope you'll join us for the next one.

Adam would like to thank his wife, Amy, and children Maya, Elliot and Thomas for their support, and his agent, Hannah Sheppard, for her sound advice.

ABOUT THE AUTHORS

JAMES PATTERSON is one of the best-known and biggest-selling writers of all time. His books have sold in excess of 385 million copies worldwide. He is the author of some of the most popular series of the past two decades – the Alex Cross, Women's Murder Club, Detective Michael Bennett and Private novels – and he has written many other number one bestsellers including romance novels and stand-alone thrillers.

James is passionate about encouraging children to read. Inspired by his own son who was a reluctant reader, he also writes a range of books for young readers including the Middle School, Dog Diaries, Treasure Hunters and Max Einstein series. James has donated millions in grants to independent bookshops and has been the most borrowed author in UK libraries for the past thirteen years in a row. He lives in Florida with his family.

ADAM HAMDY is a British author and screenwriter who works with studios and production companies on both sides of the Atlantic. He is the author of the Pendulum trilogy, an epic series of conspiracy thriller novels. *Pendulum* was a finalist for the Glass Bell Award for contemporary fiction, was selected for BBC Radio 2 Book Club and chosen as book of the month by Goldsboro Books. Adam's most recent novel, *Black 13*, has been described as a scorching contemporary espionage thriller. Keep up to date with his latest books and news at www.adamhamdy.com

Have you read them all?

PRIVATE

(with Maxine Paetro)

Jack Morgan is head of Private, the world's largest investigation company with branches around the globe. When his best friend's wife is murdered, he sets out to track down her killer. But be warned: Jack doesn't play by the rules.

PRIVATE LONDON

(with Mark Pearson)

Hannah Shapiro, a young American student, has fled her country, but can't flee her past. Can Private save Hannah from the terror that has followed her to London?

PRIVATE GAMES

(with Mark Sullivan)

It's July 2012 and excitement is sky high for the Olympic Games in London. But when one of the organisers is found brutally murdered, it soon becomes clear to Private London that everyone involved is under threat.

PRIVATE: NO. 1 SUSPECT

(with Maxine Paetro)

When Jack Morgan's former lover is found murdered in his bed, Jack is instantly the number one suspect, and he quickly realises he is facing his toughest challenge yet.

PRIVATE BERLIN

(with Mark Sullivan)

Mattie Engel, one of Private Berlin's rising stars, is horrified when her former fiancé Chris is murdered. Even more so when she realises that the killer is picking off Chris's friends. Will Mattie be next?

PRIVATE DOWN UNDER
(with Michael White)

Private Sydney's glamorous launch party is cut short by a shocking discovery – the murdered son of one of Australia's richest men. Meanwhile, someone is killing the wealthy wives of the Eastern Suburbs, and the next victim could be someone close to Private.

PRIVATE L.A.
(with Mark Sullivan)

A killer is holding L.A. to ransom. On top of this, Hollywood's golden couple have been kidnapped. Can Private prove themselves once again?

PRIVATE INDIA
(with Ashwin Sanghi)

In Mumbai, someone is murdering seemingly unconnected women in a chilling ritual. As the Private team race to find the killer, an even greater threat emerges . . .

PRIVATE VEGAS
(with Maxine Paetro)

Jack Morgan's client has just confessed to murdering his wife, and his best friend is being held on a trumped-up charge that could see him locked away for a very long time. With Jack pushed to the limit, all bets are off.

PRIVATE SYDNEY
(with Kathryn Fox)

Private Sydney are investigating the disappearance of the CEO of a high-profile research company. He shouldn't be difficult to find, but why has every trace of evidence he ever existed vanished too?